AUTUMN
Blockbuster
2024

| MARIE | KATE | SUSAN | NAIMA |
| FERRARELLA | HARDY | CARLISLE | SIMONE |

MILLS & BOON

AUTUMN BLOCKBUSTER 2024 © 2024 by Harlequin Books S.A.

THE LAWMAN'S ROMANCE LESSON
© 2019 by Marie Rydzynski-Ferrarella
Australian Copyright 2019
New Zealand Copyright 2019

First Published 2019
Second Australian Paperback Edition 2024
ISBN 978 1 038 90596 3

A WILL, A WISH, A WEDDING
© 2020 by Pamela Brooks
Australian Copyright 2020
New Zealand Copyright 2020

First Published 2020
Second Australian Paperback Edition 2024
ISBN 978 1 038 90596 3

FIREFIGHTER'S UNEXPECTED FLING
© 2019 by Susan Carlisle
Australian Copyright 2019
New Zealand Copyright 2019

First Published 2019
Second Australian Paperback Edition 2024
ISBN 978 1 038 90596 3

A KISS TO REMEMBER
© 2021 by Naima Simone
Australian Copyright 2021
New Zealand Copyright 2021

First Published 2021
First Australian Paperback Edition 2024
ISBN 978 1 038 90596 3

MIX
Paper | Supporting
responsible forestry
FSC
www.fsc.org
FSC® C001695

Published by
Mills & Boon
An imprint of Harlequin Enterprises (Australia) Pty Limited
(ABN 47 001 180 918), a subsidiary of HarperCollins
Publishers Australia Pty Limited (ABN 36 009 913 517)
Level 19, 201 Elizabeth Street
SYDNEY NSW 2000
AUSTRALIA

® and ™ (apart from those relating to FSC®) are trademarks of Harlequin Enterprises (Australia) Pty Limited or its corporate affiliates. Trademarks indicated with ® are registered in Australia, New Zealand and in other countries. Contact admin_legal@Harlequin.ca for details.

Printed and bound in Australia by McPherson's Printing Group

CONTENTS

The Lawman's Romance Lesson

Marie Ferrarella

WESTERN

Rugged men looking for love...

Books by Marie Ferrarella

Harlequin Special Edition

Forever, Texas

The Cowboy's Lesson in Love
The Lawman's Romance Lesson

Matchmaking Mamas

Diamond in the Ruff
Her Red-Carpet Romance
Coming Home for Christmas
Dr. Forget-Me-Not
Twice a Hero, Always Her Man
Meant to Be Mine
A Second Chance for the Single Dad
Christmastime Courtship
Engagement for Two
Adding Up to Family

The Fortunes of Texas: The Secret Fortunes

Fortune's Second-Chance Cowboy

Visit the Author Profile page
at millsandboon.com.au for more titles.

Dear Reader,

Welcome back to part two of Wynona and Shania's story. At the end of the last book, Wynona agreed to marry Clint Washburn. When we pick up the story here, Shania is now living alone in the house that she and her cousin rented when they returned to Forever. Shania doesn't do well alone and fills her time by keeping busy teaching math and physics. One of her students is a particular challenge at the outset. Elena is sixteen and has just discovered partying. Elena is also Deputy Daniel Tallchief's younger sister. Daniel is both mother and strict father to the teen, having taken on the roles after their parents were killed in an auto accident several years ago. As it turns out, Daniel didn't just lose his parents, he lost his fiancée, Lana, as well when the latter gave him an ultimatum: it was her or his sister. But now his sister is giving him trouble and he has no idea how to get her to come around.

Fortunately for him, Shania takes on this problem and, by making the girl realize how much potential she has, gets Elena to come around as well as settle down.

Daniel finds himself indebted to the woman. When the irrepressible Miss Joan steps in, one thing leads to another and Daniel's faith in love is renewed. Come and watch the evolution as a good man discovers that there is such a thing as a second chance.

Thank you for taking the time to read my book, and from the bottom of my heart, I wish you someone to love who loves you back.

All the best,

Marie Ferrarella

To
Patience Bloom
And
Gail Chasan
With Gratitude
For Allowing Me
To Live In Forever
A Little
Longer

PROLOGUE

THE EVENINGS WERE the hardest for Shania. Somehow, the darkness outside seemed to intensify the silence and the feeling of being alone within the small house she used to occupy with her cousin.

Before she and Wynona had returned to Forever, Texas, the little town located just outside of the Navajo reservation where they had both been born, noise had been a constant part of their lives.

Joyful noise.

Noise that signified activity.

The kind of noise that could be associated with living in a college dorm. And before that, when they had lived in their great-aunt Naomi's house, there had still been noise, the kind of noise that came from being totally involved with life. Their great-aunt was a skilled surgeon and physician who was completely devoted to her work.

Because Naomi volunteered at a free clinic at least a couple of days a week as well as being associated with one of the local hospitals, patients would turn up on their doorstep at all sorts of hours. When she and Wynona grew older, Aunt Naomi thought nothing of having both of them pitch in and help out with her patients. She wanted them to learn how to provide proper care.

Between the volunteer work and their schooling, there was never any sort of downtime, never any time to sit back, much less be bored.

She and Wynona had welcomed being useful and mentally stimulated because that was such a contrast to the lives they had initially been born into. Born on the Navajo reservation to mothers who were sisters, Shania and Wynona spent their childhoods together. They were closer than actual sisters, especially after Wynona lost her mother. She'd never known her father. Shania's parents took her in to live with them without any hesitation.

Shania herself had been thrilled to share her parents with her cousin, but unfortunately, that situation didn't last very long. Nine months after Wynona had come to live with them, Shania's father was killed in an auto accident. And then less than six months later, her mother died of pneumonia.

At the ages of ten and eleven, Wynona and Shania found themselves both orphaned.

The girls were facing foster care, which ultimately meant being swallowed up by the social services system. Just before they were to be shipped off, their great-aunt Naomi, who had been notified by an anonymous party, suddenly swooped into town. In the blink of an eye, the strong-willed woman managed to cut through all manner of red tape and whisked them back to her home in Houston.

And after that, everything changed.

Shania and her cousin were no longer dealing with an uncertain future. Aunt Naomi gave them a home and she gave them responsibilities as well, never wanting them to take anything for granted. They quickly discovered that their great-aunt was a great believer in helping those in need. Naomi made sure to instill a desire to "pay it forward" within them.

They had found that their great-aunt was a stern woman, but there had never been a question that the woman loved them and would be there for them if they should ever need her.

Shania sighed and pushed aside her plate, leaving the food all but untouched. Having taken leftovers out of the refrigerator, she hadn't bothered to warm them up before she'd brought them over to the table. She could almost hear Aunt Naomi's voice telling her, *If you're going to eat leftovers, do it properly. Warm them up first.*

Shania frowned at the plate. She really wasn't hungry.

What she was hungry for wasn't food but the discussions they used to have around the dinner table when Aunt Naomi, Wynona and she would all talk about their day. Aunt Naomi never made it seem as if hers was more important even though they all knew that she made such a huge difference in the lives she touched. Each person, each life, Aunt Naomi had maintained, was important in its own way.

When she and Wynona had moved back to Forever, armed with their teaching degrees and determined to give back to the community, for the most part those discussions continued. She and her cousin had been excited about the difference they were going to make, especially since both the local elementary school and high school, for practicality purposes, were now comprised of students who came not only from the town but also from the reservation. The aim was to improve the quality of education rendered to all the students.

But there were times, like tonight, when the effects of that excitement slipped into the shadows and allowed the loneliness to rear its head and take over. Part of the reason for that was because she now lived alone here. Wynona had gotten married recently and while Shania was thrilled beyond words for her cousin, she had no one to talk to, no one to carry on any sort of a dialogue with.

At least, not anyone human.

There was, of course, still Belle.

Just as she got up to go into her den to work on tomorrow's lesson plan, Belle seemed to materialize and stepped into her path. The German shepherd looked up at her with her big, soulful brown eyes.

"You miss her too, don't you, Belle?" Shania murmured to the dog that she and Wynona had found foraging through a garbage pail behind the Murphy brothers' saloon the first week they moved back. After determining that the dog had no owner, they immediately rescued the rail-thin shepherd and took her in.

Belle thrived under their care. When Wynona got married, Shania had told her cousin to take the dog with her. But Wynona had declined, saying that she felt better about leaving if Belle stayed with her.

Belle rubbed her head against Shania's thigh now, then stopped for a moment and looked up.

"Message received," Shania told the German shepherd with a smile. "You're right. I'm not alone. You're here. But there are times that I really wish you could talk."

As if on cue, Belle barked, something, as a rule, she rarely did. It was as if Belle didn't like to call attention to herself unless absolutely necessary.

"You're right. I shouldn't be feeling sorry for myself, I should be feeling happy for Wyn." Dropping down beside the German shepherd, Shania ran her hands along the dog's head and back, petting the animal. "You really are brighter than most people, girl," she laughed.

As if in agreement, Belle began licking her face.

And just like that, the loneliness Shania had been wrestling with slipped away.

CHAPTER ONE

DEPUTY DANIEL TALLCHIEF could feel his anger increasing in waves. He told himself he wasn't going to say anything to the girl sitting in the seat next to him until he calmed down. He didn't want to say anything to his sister that he might wind up regretting later, after he'd had a chance to cool off.

Right now, it felt as if that was never going to happen.

And keeping his temper under control wasn't easy. Not when he wanted to shout into Elena's face and demand to know how she could do something not only so stupid, but so incredibly disrespectful to the memory of their parents as well as to him.

So far, Daniel had been silent. Silent the entire drive home, even though he could feel angry words clawing at his throat, all but choking him in their eagerness to be released.

Elena wasn't much help to him in that respect. His sixteen-year-old only sister was sitting in the passenger seat, obviously fuming. Her very body language, not to mention what she was actually saying to him, were goading him to lose his temper.

"I don't know what you're so mad about," Elena retorted, folding her arms in front of her chest just like their mother used to do when she was displaying anger. "You told me I couldn't have parties in our house while you were gone and I didn't have one," she informed him haughtily. "In case you didn't notice, that was Matthew's house you storm trooped into, not ours. His house is a lot nicer," she deliberately pointed out. "Matthew has a right to throw a party if he wants to and I have a perfect right to be there if I want to." She punctuated her statement by tossing her head defiantly, sending her long, shining black hair flying over her shoulder.

The best laid plans of mice and men, Daniel had read somewhere, *often went awry*—or words to that effect. Right now, that described his plans for waiting until he had cooled off to a T.

So rather than driving straight home in silence—at least *his* silence—Daniel pulled his car over to the side of the road and glared at his angry sister, the person who was responsible, at least in part, for his taking a job as a sheriff's deputy rather than finishing college and getting a degree. Not finishing college put an end to his being able to go on to medical school and to eventually achieve his lifelong dream of becoming a doctor.

It had also wound up putting an end to Lana and him.

The hell with cooling off. "Number one," Daniel enumerated, "Matthew doesn't have the right to have a party loud enough to disturb all his neighbors just because his parents were naive enough to leave him home alone for a week. Number two, *you* don't have the right to attend a party where alcohol was being unlawfully served. From what I could see, everyone there was a minor so if I was as hard-nosed as you seem to think I am, I would have arrested them all on the spot instead of giving them a warning that I'd come down hard on them if this happened again."

Daniel took a breath. It was a real struggle to keep his voice down.

Apparently, his self-restraint was wasted on his sister.

She glared at him. "Not much that they can do in the way of partying now that you took away all their liquor."

"I *confiscated* it," Daniel corrected. "And when Matthew's parents get back and ask about what happened to their incredibly large supply of alcohol, I'll hand the bottles over to them."

Elena's frown intensified. "Along with a lecture, no doubt, about how they should make an effort to be better parents." She fumed, looking at him darkly. "You know, not everyone wants to be like you, Daniel."

"Right now," the deputy told Elena, starting up his car again and heading back to town, "*I* don't even want to be me."

Refusing to appear intimidated, Elena raised her chin defiantly. "Well, it's no picnic being your sister, either."

Daniel bit his tongue to keep back the hot words that were hovering there, aching to be released. Saying them to Elena might very well produce momentary gratification, but he knew that he'd wind up paying for that gratification in the long run. Paying for it with the amount of damage that those words could cause to the relationship he had with Elena.

A relationship that already felt as if it was tottering on its last legs.

He and Elena had been close once. Extremely close. He'd helped raise her because both his parents were so busy trying to provide a decent life for his sister and for him. Despite experiencing the typical wants and desires of a teenager, which included hanging out with his friends and all that entailed, Daniel still doted on Elena and found time to be there for her.

But then the world had been turned upside down. His parents had been in a terrible car accident. His mother had died instantly and his father had lingered for a few hours before he died as well. So instead of graduating college and going off to medical school—he had an early acceptance letter he still carried around folded up in his wallet—he had to drop out and find a job in a hurry in order to be able to provide for Elena and take care of both of them.

And, as hard as giving up his education had been, losing Lana had been even harder on him.

The death of their parents had its effects on Elena as well. Always bright and studious, she'd gradually turned her back on all that. Instead, she just focused on living in the moment.

Partying in the moment.

And frustrating Daniel to the point that he was all but incoherent, like now.

"I don't even know you anymore," he told Elena after another ten minutes of silence had passed.

Exasperated, Daniel pulled his car up in front of the small, three-bedroom, single-story house that had once known such happiness but now stood as a lonely reminder of what no longer was.

"That makes two of us," Elena shot back. "I don't know you anymore, and I can't trust you, either."

He bit his tongue again to keep from saying the first thing that popped up in his mind. Instead, he took a breath, tried to collect his thoughts. "I've got to go to the sheriff's office to log this in," he told her, indicating the bottles of alcohol in the back. He looked into his sister's eyes. "I want your word that you won't leave the house until I get back."

"I thought you didn't trust me," she taunted, her tone haughty and arrogant.

"I don't," he answered honestly. "But I'm hoping you'll want to prove me wrong more than you want to run off to find another party that I'll just have to shut down." He let his words sink in before noting, "That can't be making you very popular, being the girl whose brother follows her around, shutting down the parties she attends."

"It doesn't," Elena snapped, glaring at him. She pressed her lips together, as if going over several things in her mind. "All right, you win. I'll stay home," she pouted.

Instead of getting out, Daniel remained seated behind the steering wheel. Eyeing his sister, he asked, "I have your word?"

Elena blew out a long, dramatic breath. "Yeah, yeah, you have my word."

"Good." Daniel nodded, getting out of the vehicle. "Why don't you study while you wait for me to get home?" he suggested. He saw her roll her eyes. It took effort to hold onto his temper. Taking a breath, he told her, "You used to be a great student."

"And then I got smart," Elena responded sarcastically.

Daniel's eyes narrowed as he looked at her. "Not really," he countered.

Elena uttered a frustrated, guttural sound and then stomped all the way to the front door.

Getting there ahead of her, Daniel unlocked the door then opened it and let her in. For his part, he remained standing outside. "I'll get back home just as soon as I can."

"I can't wait," Elena retorted sarcastically.

Rather than say anything, Daniel quickly closed the door the moment she was inside the house and then locked it.

"Oh gee, now I can't get out," Elena called out, raising her voice so that it carried to him through the door.

"No, you can't," he informed her. "Because you gave me your word."

Daniel heard another sound, louder and more guttural this time. He could picture the look on his sister's angry face.

He walked to his car and really hoped that he wasn't being an idiot to believe that, despite everything, Elena was going to live up to her promise.

Daniel got into the vehicle.

"Really wish you guys were still here," he murmured under his breath to the parents who were no longer there to hear him.

He would have missed his parents no matter what, but being left to grapple with trying to raise a headstrong, overly intelligent sixteen-year-old teenage girl made everything three times worse. And it *really* made him miss his mother and father.

When Daniel walked into the sheriff's office fifteen minutes later, he was surprised to see Joe there.

Senior Deputy Sheriff Joe Lone Wolf was the reason he had this job. He'd known the older deputy by sight when they were both growing up on the reservation. But then his parents had moved him and his sister into town and the next time their paths crossed, Joe was a deputy, working for Sheriff Rick Santiago. Joe's influence in the scheme of things increased a great deal when he wound up marrying Ramona, the town's veterinarian. Ramona also happened to be Rick's sister. And when Daniel suddenly found himself in need of a job, Joe was the one who not only vouched for him but took Daniel under his wing, teaching him everything he needed to know. It wasn't the job he had dreamed of having, but it was one he felt he could do justice to.

"I didn't know you had the night shift tonight," Daniel said to the other man.

"I didn't. I traded Rodriguez for it. I had a feeling, when you went to answer that domestic disturbance call coming in from the better part of town, that you might wind up coming back." Craning his neck, Joe looked around behind Daniel. "So where's Elena?"

It was unnerving the way that Joe seemed to know about things before they became public knowledge. "She's home."

Joe's eyes never left his face as he rocked back in his chair. "Let me guess, she promised to be on her best behavior."

"I don't think that girl has any 'best behavior' to fall back on any more," Daniel responded. There was no missing the disgusted note in his voice. "But she gave me her word that she wouldn't leave the house until I got back."

Joe laughed dryly. "Then I guess you'd better hurry back before Elena's tempted to break her word again." And then he looked at Daniel, studying him. "Why did you come back?"

"Well, I wanted to log these in at the station," Daniel answered. The next minute, he was going out the front door.

"*These?*" Joe repeated, following the younger man out.

Daniel paused to reach into the backseat and take out the carton he'd used in order to carry all the liquor bottles out of Matthew McGuire's house.

"These," Daniel repeated as he carried the carton crammed full of bottles back past Joe and into the sheriff's office.

Joe uttered a low whistle as he looked at all the semi-filled and three-quarters-filled bottles stuffed into the carton.

"What was the kid doing? Competing with the Murphy brothers' saloon?"

Daniel glanced down at the bottles in his arms. "I'm guessing these belong to his parents."

"Speaking of his parents, just where are these fine citizens?" Joe asked him.

Daniel thought back, trying to remember. "According to what Elena told me through her clenched teeth and her hostile attitude, I gather that Matthew's parents are away for the week, touring a couple of colleges with his older brother."

Joe smile was grim. "In other words, when the cat's away, the mice'll play."

"And get drunk," Daniel added with a deep, disapproving frown.

"Evidence?" Joe asked, nodding at the liquor bottles and curious as to exactly what Daniel planned to do with all of them.

"My first thought was to get these things out of the kids' reach," Daniel confessed. He put the carton down on his desk. "When Matthew's parents get back into town, they can come by the station and get them."

"My guess is that they're not going to be happy about that," Joe commented.

Joe took a couple of the bottles out of the carton one by one and looked at the labels. He wasn't a connoisseur when it came to alcohol, but he could see that there were some very expensive bottles in the carton.

"I'm counting on it," Daniel told him. "Maybe his parents will think twice before leaving Matthew alone with all this temptation again."

"What did Elena say about you doing this?" Joe asked.

Daniel blew out a breath. "Not anything I feel like repeating right now," he answered.

Opening his desk's middle drawer, he took out a pad and a

pen and began to write down the various names that were on the labels.

"Here, let me do that," Joe told the younger deputy, taking the pad and pen away from Daniel. "You go on back to your sister. Like I said, the sooner you get yourself back home, the less tempted she's going to be to fly the coop again."

This was where Daniel would have wanted to say that since Elena had given him her word she'd stay home, he felt confident that she would be there when he walked in through the door. But the truth was that he wasn't confident she'd be there. Not confident at all.

Joe was right. The sooner he got home, the more likely it was that he'd still find Elena at home. Because if she decided to take off again, this time he wouldn't be able to just shrug it off or let it slide. This time, he was going to have to come down on her.

Hard.

And that would do even more harm to their relationship, causing it to splinter and break apart that much more. Maybe even irreparably, because he was only able to hold on to his temper for so long before it exploded on him.

"Thanks, Joe, I owe you," Daniel said, heading for the door.

"Damn straight you do," Joe called out, his voice following the other deputy as Daniel went outside to his vehicle.

How did it all get so confused and heavy-handed? Daniel couldn't help wondering as he got in behind the wheel of his car again.

How did he and Elena go from being practically best friends to being these people who kept snapping at each other and regarding everything the other person did as being suspect?

He wished he knew. Daniel couldn't even remember how it all had started to unravel. All he knew was that somehow, it had. And not just slowly but with what felt like lightning speed. One day he was Elena's confidant, her shoulder to cry on, the next day, he was her enemy, part of "them," otherwise known as a grown-up. And everyone knew that grown-ups or adults were the ones who stood in the way and impeded anything that even remotely looked like fun.

Elena stopped telling him things, stopped confiding in him, stopped looking at him the way she used to. These days, she wasn't proud of him. She was just leery of him and it showed in everything she did, everything she said to him.

How did he go about changing that back to what it had been?

And just as important, how did he get Elena to realize that getting an education was the only way she would ever get out of Forever?

CHAPTER TWO

SHANIA MADE SURE that she always parked her feelings of doubt and insecurity outside the door before walking into any classroom. It was the one major rule she always abided by. She felt it was her personal mission to inspire her students, to get them to focus on not just their schoolwork, but also on their abilities to surmount any and all obstacles that existed in their daily lives. She did her best to instill a work ethic within them that enabled them to work hard at achieving their personal goals.

On those occasions when things got particularly rough for her, it was then that Shania found herself channeling her great-aunt Naomi.

Early on in their relationship, the gruff, far from soft-spoken woman became her inspiration. To Shania's recollection, there was no problem too big or too taxing to bring Aunt Naomi down or cause her to throw in the towel and give up. No matter what it was, Aunt Naomi had taught them that they could always find a way to deal with it.

Today had been about as taxing a day as she could ever remember enduring.

Usually, on those days when her students turned out to be particularly challenging, she'd go home and then she and Wynona would act as each other's cheering section—or support group—whatever way wound up doing the trick.

But Wynona was no longer here. Right after the wedding had taken place, she and Clint had moved in together at the ranch. For a few minutes after her day had ended, Shania debated picking up the phone and calling Wynona just to unwind for a minute.

She would be *damned* if she was going to call her cousin to complain about today. Wynona didn't need to hear her carping. What her cousin needed was to spend quality time with her husband, not to mention that she was also acclimating to being a mother to Clint's nine-year-old son, Ryan.

No, Shania thought, growing more restless, Wyn had her hands more than full with all that going on, plus teaching. Her cousin definitely had no time to offer her a shoulder to lean on, Shania thought, even though Wynona would if called upon.

She wasn't going to call her. But that didn't mean that she didn't still need at least a willing ear to listen to her, Shania thought as she chewed on her lower lip.

She could only think of one place where she could find that willing ear. An ear that only listened, but didn't feel obligated to give advice.

"No offense, Belle," she said, looking down at the rather diminutive German shepherd that was shadowing her every move and weaving in and out between her legs when she walked, "but tonight I really think that I need a human to talk to."

Belle stopped moving and looked up at her with her big brown eyes. Shania could have sworn that the dog understood what she was saying—and forgave her.

"I won't be long," Shania promised as she grabbed her jacket from the coat rack by the door and shrugged into the garment.

Granted it was only just the end of September, but sometimes the weather took an unexpected turn around seven or eight o'clock, becoming cold. The last thing she wanted to do was to catch a cold. It was bad enough having to deal with low spirits, something she was *not* accustomed to having.

Murphy's, the town's only saloon, has initially been owned by Patrick Murphy, the present owners' uncle. A lifelong bachelor, he had taken in the three orphaned brothers when they were just boys after his younger brother, their widowed father, died. Eventually, since they comprised his only family, Patrick left the establishment that was his pride and joy to them when he passed away.

Although the two younger Murphy brothers occasionally took turns operating it, everyone agreed that the saloon was Brett's baby. The oldest of the Murphy brothers was the force behind its present success and he was the reason that most people in and around Forever would find their way there.

Murphy's had an unspoken agreement with Miss Joan, the woman who owned the town's only diner, which was also its only restaurant. Miss Joan's was where people went for food and, on occasion, for advice. Murphy's was where they went to have a drink amid people they knew. It was also where they went to enjoy some camaraderie and have their spirits lifted.

It was exactly the latter that Shania found herself needing tonight.

The moment she walked into Murphy's, she found herself feeling better. Unlike bars that were located in the larger cities, Murphy's didn't shun ample lighting, opting instead to lean toward atmosphere that was created by a lack of darkness. Because of the bright lighting, there were no shadows to hide in, no dimly lit areas to gravitate toward that would enable the patrons to observe without being observed.

Shania quickly looked around. As usual, she noted, Brett was tending bar. Married to one of the town's two doctors, whenever Alicia worked late at the clinic, Brett was the one who worked late at the bar. In any given emergency, he and his brothers traded off shifts, although Murphy's was doing so well, they could afford to hire a bartender for the nights that none of the brothers could be here.

"Don't usually see you here, pretty lady. I know that my paper's overdue, but I'm still working on it," Brett told her with a wink. Wiping down the bar, he gestured toward a stool directly in front of him.

"I've got a feeling you'll be working on it a long time," she told him, sliding in on the stool.

"You could be right," Brett responded. "So, what'll it be?" he asked, flashing a welcoming smile at her as he retired the cloth he was using. "Or are you just here for some good conversation?"

"I'll have whatever you have on tap," Shania told the man.

"Coming right up," Brett responded. As he spoke, he filled up a mug. There was foam taking up two thirds of the space. Placing the mug down on the bar right in front of her, Brett took a closer look at her expression. "Something wrong?" he asked her gently.

Shania squared her shoulders. "Why does there have to be something wrong?" she asked, drawing the mug closer to her.

"Because it's a school night and you're here, having a beer," Brett pointed out.

"I drink beer," she protested defensively.

"Didn't say you didn't," he answered. "Just not used to seeing you drinking it here."

She couldn't really argue with that. Shrugging off his observation, she told him, "Maybe I just came out to make contact with my fellow man."

The look on Brett's face told her that he knew it had to be more than that, but he wasn't about to challenge her.

"This is the place to do that," Brett agreed. Someone called out to him. Brett glanced over in the patron's direction, then excused himself. "Sorry, Shania, duty calls." He hesitated just for a moment. "You'll be all right?" he asked.

Shania nodded. "I'll be fine. I'm not fragile," she assured him.

"That's good to know," a deep voice behind her told her.

Not so much startled as surprised, Shania turned around to see who the voice belonged to and found herself looking up into the softest brown eyes that she had ever seen. With broad shoulders, a taut, trim waist and standing approximately six one, the rest of the man was even more strikingly impressive.

"Fragile women don't have an easy time of it," the man said.

There was something about the man that looked vaguely familiar, but she was fairly certain that she had never met him.

"And you know this how?" Shana heard herself asking the dark-haired man.

"Years of experience," he answered.

Shania saw the badge he was wearing and she made the logical assumption. The man had to be one of the sheriff's deputies. She also guessed that given the man's high cheekbones, he was also at least part Navajo, which instantly gave them something in common.

But rather than comment on that—it sounded like such a line to her—Shania took another sip of her drink. The beer tasted particularly bitter, but she had gotten it expressly for that very reason. The bitter drink would keep her from having another— if she finished this one at all.

"Are you saving this seat for someone?" Daniel asked her, nodding at the empty stool beside her.

Her hands tightened around the mug she was holding. "No, I'm not saving it." Her voice sounded almost tinny, she thought disparagingly.

"Then you don't mind if I sit down next to you?" Daniel asked, still not making a move to slide onto the stool.

Shania shrugged, doing her best to seem nonchalant. It occurred to her that she had spent so much time looking out for Wynona, she had forgotten how to socialize on her own.

"It's a free country," she replied, taking another sip, a longer one this time.

Daniel slid his long frame onto the stool, setting his drink—a beer—down on the bar in front of him. His eyes skimmed over the woman next to him. The second look was even better than the first. Simply dressed, the dark-haired woman was nothing short of a knockout.

He hadn't come here looking for anything except for people who didn't look at him hostilely the way that Elena had. But, having found someone who definitely captured his attention, he wasn't in a hurry to leave.

"I haven't seen you in here before," Daniel commented.

"There's a reason for that," Shania replied, a smile playing at the corners of her mouth as she faced the long mirror that ran the length of the bar.

Daniel's eyes met hers in the mirror and he said the first thing that occurred to him. "It's your first time here?"

"No." While she didn't frequent the saloon on anything that would have passed as a regular basis, she had been here a few times since her return to Forever. But she'd never seen him during any of those times.

"I'm confused," Daniel admitted.

This time she did look directly at him. And then she smiled. "Happens to the best of us," she told him.

His smile was slow as it spread over his lips—and extremely compelling. She could feel something inside of her responding to it.

"I'm also intrigued," Daniel said.

Finding it disconcerting to make eye contact, she lowered her own. "I can't help that."

"Oh, but you might be able to," Daniel told her. Even though he continued sitting exactly where he was, it felt as if he had somehow drawn closer to her.

Shania had to concentrate in order not to fidget. "Oh? And just how do you propose that I do that?"

"Propose?" he repeated, the smile on his face deepening. He had dimples, she realized. One in each cheek. She found herself growing more intrigued than she wanted to be. "Let's not get ahead of ourselves," Daniel told her. "Although, the evening's still young."

Mention of the time had her looking at her watch. "Actually, it's getting late."

Daniel glanced at his own watch. It was only a few minutes past eight.

"No, it's actually not," he contradicted. "It's still early."

But Shania held her ground and shook her head. "Not really." And then she explained by saying, "It's a school night."

Her response only served to confuse him further. "What's that got to do with it?"

And then he looked down at her hand as a belated explanation for her concern hit him. Was she married and needed to get home? There was no ring on her hand, but in this day and age, that didn't mean that the woman was single.

The shortest distance between two points was a straight line, so instead of beating around the bush, he decided to ask her. "You're not married, are you?"

"No, I'm not," Shania answered. Even as she said that, she felt an atypical pang twisting the pit of her stomach.

What was wrong with her? All these years, she had never once felt that marriage was for her. But ever since Wynona had gotten married, Shania had found herself reevaluating everything, including what she'd thought were her deeply rooted feelings about marriage. Maybe it *was* time to rethink her position on that.

Would it be such an awful thing to get married? Marriage had certainly made Wynona happy.

"The conversation just got more interesting," Daniel said with a smile that unnerved her.

Shania thought of finishing her beer in order to dramatically put the empty mug down on the bar and push it away before she got off the stool. But in order to do that, she'd have to actually drink the brew and she decided that she'd had enough. So she just pushed the mug aside.

"I've got to go," she told him, and started to get up off her stool.

He gave her a long, soulful look. "Was it something I said?"

She needed to avoid looking into his eyes, she silently insisted. He had beautiful, sexy eyes and eye contact had a way of making her thoughts evaporate.

"No, I just have to go," she told him seriously. "I have school tomorrow," she explained.

His eyes narrowed as he studied her more closely, doing his best to see past her beauty even though it wasn't easy.

"No offense, but just how many times have you been left back?" he asked.

"Left back?" she echoed, clearly confused about what he was asking.

"Well, yeah. Because I know for a fact that the Murphys are really strict when it comes to serving alcohol to minors." Then, because she was still staring at him quizzically, he clarified it for her. "They don't, which means that you're not a minor even though you're fresh-faced and pretty enough to pass for one."

"I'm not a minor," she assured him, not sure if she was flattered or insulted by his comment.

"Then why...?" He left the end of his question up in the air, waiting for her to finish it.

"I'm a high school teacher," she told him.

"A high school teacher," he repeated.

He hadn't thought of that. He was slipping, he upbraided himself. But then, he wasn't used to putting moves on a woman. Because Elena had aggravated him, he'd wound up doing something out of character.

"Yes," she confirmed in case there was any doubt. "So you see why I have to go."

But Daniel wasn't quite ready to let this go just yet. Questions popped up in his mind. "What do you teach?"

"Algebra and physics," she answered.

He nodded, impressed. "Ambitious."

"Tiring," she countered.

He thought of what he'd just endured trying to deal with his sister today and he understood exactly what this woman was telling him.

"It's a tough age," he agreed.

"You say that like someone who's been in the trenches," Shania noted. "Were you a teacher?"

"Me?" he asked, surprised that she'd think that. "Hell no." Realizing he might have offended her, he corrected himself. "I mean heck no."

She tried not to laugh and only partially succeeded. "That's okay. I find myself swallowing a few choice words too, especially whenever I'm having a particularly bad day communicating with my students."

Although, she thought, those were happily few and far between.

"Was that what this was all about?" Daniel asked, nodding at her unfinished mug of beer. "A particularly bad day?"

"You might say that," Shania admitted. "There are some times when I really don't think I'm getting through to them."

"If it's only 'some times' then you're doing better than the rest of us," Daniel assured her, thinking of Elena. "Why don't you let me buy you something that you enjoy drinking and we can compare war stories?"

She felt a bit confused again. "But I thought you said you were never a teacher."

"And I wasn't," he answered.

"Then I don't understand. How can you have any war stories?" she asked.

"Because my war stories all involve my younger sister," he answered. "My sixteen-year-old younger sister," he specified, as if that should make everything clear to the woman he was talking to.

"Your parents having trouble handling her?" she guessed.

"My parents aren't there to handle her," he answered, doing

his best to mask his reaction to her question. Thinking of his parents always made him feel sad. Then, before she could ask anything further, he told her, "For better or for worse, it's all me. Mother, father and, according to my sister, thick-headed older brother, all rolled up into one big package."

The way he'd worded his response caused something to click in her head. "You said she was sixteen?" Shania asked him.

He nodded and finished his beer. "Yes."

She *knew* the deputy looked familiar to her, Shania thought. Even if she threw the reservation into the mix, Forever was rather a small town.

"What's her name?" she asked.

He narrowed his eyes again as he studied the woman he'd been flirting with.

"Why are you asking me that?" Daniel asked her suspiciously.

Shania tried to sound off-handed as she answered, "I was just curious to find out if perhaps she's in my class."

Bits and pieces of their conversation began to align themselves in Daniel's head, forming an imperfect whole. A whole he didn't really want to own up to.

He suddenly realized that he might have very well just tried to hit on Elena's teacher and, if that was the case, he was fairly certain that if Elena got wind of this, he was never going to hear the end of it.

CHAPTER THREE

HE DEBATED HIS next move—did he mention Elena's name and hope that there'd been some mix-up and this woman *wasn't* her teacher, or did he just not say anything?

At the apex of his debate, Daniel heard his cell phone ringing.

Pulling his phone out of his pocket, he looked down at the screen. Rather than someone's name or a number, he saw that what was vying for his attention was an app. The second he saw it, all thoughts of possibly embarrassing his sister because he was trying to get to know her teacher instantly vanished.

Shaking his head, Daniel frowned at the screen he was watching.

Shania saw the change. "Something wrong?" she asked him.

"Yeah," the deputy answered, closing his phone and putting it away again. "My sister is attempting to escape."

"Escape?" she repeated uncertainly. "Are you holding your sister prisoner?"

"That just might be the next step," he murmured, more to himself than to the woman sitting beside him at the bar. "No, I put up a basic security monitoring camera by the front door while she was at school." He could see by the woman's expression that he needed to explain this a little more clearly. "I grounded her after the last incident—she went to a party during a school night and there was alcohol flowing like the Mississippi River. She's not supposed to go out on school nights for a month and it looks like she's breaking the rules again."

Shania looked at the deputy thoughtfully. A different take on the situation occurred to her.

"Maybe your sister found out about the security monitor and she decided to try to pay you back," Shania suggested.

Daniel's frown deepened. "You sound like you're on her side."

"No," she answered without hesitation. "I just happen to know how the teenage mind works. How *mine* worked for a little while," she added to convince him. "Until I suddenly realized I was being totally selfish and ungrateful."

Shania vividly remembered the confrontation between her great-aunt and herself. The verbal altercation really straightened her out and left her feeling not only very humbled but utterly grateful to the older woman for putting up with her.

"How long did it take you to realize that?" Daniel asked, wondering just how long he and Elena were going to be at odds over absolutely everything from morning until night, because he was *really* getting tired of butting heads with his sister.

"Longer than it should have," Shania admitted ruefully, since she should have realized immediately that Naomi had been under no obligation to take them in, much less put up with her antics.

Daniel saw something in the woman's face that moved him, something that spoke to him even more than the fact that he found her to be an incredibly beautiful woman.

But right now, he had an emergency with Elena to deal with and that took precedence over everything else.

"Look," he told her, "I'd really like to stay here and talk some more with you, but I'm afraid that I've got to handle this."

Shania flashed a smile at him. "I understand perfectly," she told him. Then, on the off chance that she'd correctly guessed whose brother he was, she called after the deputy, saying, "She's a good girl who's just testing you and her boundaries, and being rebellious."

But Daniel had already crossed the floor and gave her no indication that he'd heard her. Within another minute, he was gone.

Shania stared after him, wondering again if she'd accurately guessed who his sister was. She could have very well just been reading into the situation.

"Another one?" Brett asked, standing on his side of the bar right behind her.

Startled, Shania managed not to gasp. Instead, she turned around to look at the bartender. "You really should wear squeaky shoes so you don't scare your customers when you sneak up behind them."

"I wasn't 'sneaking' and squeaky shoes wouldn't help," he told her. "There's too much noise in here to hear anything as understated as squeaky shoes." Brett nodded toward her mug and repeated, "Another one?" He added, "On the house," no doubt thinking that might sweeten the offer and make it more tempting.

But Shania shook her head. "That's okay. One was enough." Brett looked at her doubtfully. When he went on to tilt the mug she'd pushed aside, emphasizing the fact that there was still some beer in it, Shania added, "More than enough, really."

"I can get you another brand," Brett offered. "Something less bitter," he added.

Shania smiled at the man. Brett Murphy was a decent, down-to-earth man, even more so than his younger brothers, and she appreciated his offer to appeal to her tastes, but that really wasn't the problem.

"Maybe next time," she told him, sliding off her stool. "I really just came in for the company."

Brett nodded. "His name's Daniel Tallchief," he told her, even though Shania hadn't asked. After having been behind the counter for as long as he had, Brett prided himself on being able to read people accurately, at least for the most part.

Tallchief. Shania smiled. She'd guessed right, she thought.

"I thought so," she said aloud, secretly congratulating herself, then quickly added, "I mean, I didn't ask."

Brett's smile deepened. "You didn't have to," he told her.

Rather than become defensive, Shania regarded the man a little more closely, then teased, "You're adding mind reading to your list of talents?"

"I'm not one to brag," he replied, his tone indicating otherwise.

"Okay," she answered gamely. Shania's eyes met his. "What am I thinking right now?"

He studied her for a long moment, then deadpanned, "You deal with impressionable young minds all day long. Should you be using words like that?"

It took her a second to realize that he was teasing her. "It's how I survive."

"Whatever gets you through the day," Brett answered. He gave her an encouraging grin, then made one final offer. "How about some coffee? It'll get the bitter taste of that beer out of your mouth."

She looked at him, surprised. "How did you know I thought it was bitter?"

"I could just say it's all part of being a mind reader," he said, for a moment falling back on the label she'd given him. "But the truth is you have a very expressive face, at least when it comes to some things." He leaned over the bar, pretending to share a confidence with her. "I wouldn't let myself be drawn into any poker games if I were you."

"No danger of that," she told Brett just before she turned to leave his establishment. "Poker games require money and I'm just a teacher."

"There is no 'just' in front of the word 'teacher,'" Brett called after her.

Shania smiled to herself, her good mood restored as she walked out the door.

That was why she'd come here in the first place, to forget about everything that had happened today. Everything that she *hadn't* managed to accomplish. Meeting Elena Tallchief's brother turned out to be an added bonus.

Don't go there, she warned herself. The last thing she needed was to entertain anything that was even remotely like a daydream about one of the students' relatives.

Belle was waiting for her just behind the door when Shania walked in a few minutes later. The second the dog saw her, her tail began to thump against the floor, underscoring the fact that the dog was very happy to see her.

Shania grinned, responding to the welcome. "I missed you, too, Belle," she told the German shepherd. When the dog paused to look up at her, Shania put her own interpretation to that look. "I know, I know, if I missed you so much, why did I go out without you? Number one, they don't allow dogs in saloons—"

Belle seemed to whimper in response.

"Yes, I know. That's not very nice of them but everyone likes to have rules. And number two, sometimes I need to communicate with other humans. Other *adult* humans," she emphasized because there were times when she could swear that Belle thought of herself as being her equal and human as well.

Belle barked loudly once, as if in response to the last sentence.

Shania ran her hands over the dog's head, petting her. "Thank you, you're being very understanding."

Ready to settle in and continue petting her dog, Shania heard the house phone ring. Because cell phone reception could be spotty, usually at the worst possible times—especially when the weather was inclement—she and Wynona had opted to keep the landline that was in the house when they moved in.

Curious as to who could be calling her at this hour, Shania crossed the room and picked up the receiver. "Hello?"

The voice on the other end didn't bother with a polite greeting but got right down to business, asking her, "Where have you been?"

"Wynona?"

Recognizing the voice, concern reared its head instantly. Because Wynona taught all day at the elementary school, evenings were reserved for her husband and stepson. Shania made it a point not to call her cousin except occasionally on the weekend. To have Wynona call her during the week and at this hour, something had to be wrong.

Shania felt her stomach tightening as she asked, "Is something wrong?"

"Well, if there was, you wouldn't have been home to find out," Wynona answered.

Shania felt obligated to explain why she hadn't been home this one time. "I needed some company."

If Wynona had been harboring as much as a drop of annoyance—which she wasn't—all pretense instantly vanished.

"You could have called here, Shania. Or just come over," Wynona told her.

"That's called intruding," Shania pointed out, then explained, "I'm not about to invite myself over to your place, Wyn. You and Clint are still in the honeymoon stage."

She heard her cousin chuckle softly before saying, "Well, that's about to change."

"Change?" Shania repeated. "Why?" She was back to being concerned. Was there a problem between Wynona and her husband? "You do realize that men require a lot of patience. Whatever Clint's done, he didn't mean it so just forgive him and move on from there. I guarantee you'll both be happier."

Rather than agree with her, Shania heard her cousin sigh—or was she stifling a laugh? "I'm afraid it's not that easy."

This wasn't like Wynona. Her cousin didn't give up this easily. She was exceptionally stubborn. Shania searched for a way to convince her cousin to dig in and fight for her marriage.

"Sure it is. You just have to be the bigger person, that's all. In every relationship, there's always someone who loves more and someone who forgives more. Sometimes, that's the same person," Shania added, hoping she was convincing her cousin to find a way to forgive Clint if that was what was necessary here and give their marriage another try.

And then she heard Wynona laugh. Was her cousin just putting her on?

"Have you ever thought of writing these gems down in a 'how to make a marriage work' book?" Wynona asked.

"Too busy," Shania answered, letting go of the breath she'd been holding. "So, is everything okay then?"

"Well, that all depends on your definition of 'okay,'" Wynona answered.

They were going around in circles, Shania thought. Why?

"Are you like this with Clint?" she asked. "Because if you are, I can see why he might lose his temper with you."

"Lose his temper?" Wynona echoed. "That's not what happened."

Shania took a deep breath, trying to hold on to her patience, which was quickly being shredded. When did her cousin get this trying?

"What did happen?" she asked. "And no more beating around the bush. Tell me straight out why you called or I swear I'm going to drive over to your place right now and ask Clint to tell me what's going on with you."

"Well, if you put it that way..." Wynona said, still hedging.

Shania took a deep breath, struggling to keep her temper under control.

Why did it sound as if Wynona was grinning? she suddenly thought.

"Wynona," she cried, a warning note in her voice. When her cousin still paused, not saying anything, concern returned in spades. Maybe her cousin was too afraid to tell her what was wrong. "Wyn, please. You can tell me anything, you know that."

"You promise not to tell?" Wynona asked in a subdued voice.

There went her stomach again. This had to be worse than she thought. With effort, Shania reined in her imagination, which was on the verge of running away with her. Big-time.

"I promise," she told her cousin solemnly.

Then, to her surprise, she heard Wynona suddenly start to laugh. "That's okay, Shania. You can tell anyone you want."

Okay, Wynona's life wasn't in danger and neither was her marriage. Relieved, she was back to being annoyed. She'd had enough.

"What I'm going to tell them," Shania told her cousin, "is why I committed justifiable homicide if you don't stop this and tell me what's going on."

"You're going to feel bad about threatening me once I tell you."

From the sound of her voice, Wynona was still grinning, Shania thought.

"I'll be the judge of that. Now talk!" she ordered, coming perilously close to the end of her patience.

The words seemed to burst out of Wynona's mouth all at once. "I'm pregnant, Shania!"

This was the one thing that hadn't occurred to her. Shania's mouth dropped open. "Excuse me? Did you just say—?"

"I did," Wynona interrupted her. "And I am. I'm pregnant!" she repeated because she liked saying it and liked hearing it even more.

Still stunned at the news, Shania asked, "When? How?" Realizing what she'd just blurted out, she amended her question. "I mean, I know how. But when?"

"You want the exact moment?" Wynona asked her, laughing. "Because there've been a lot of them and I can't really pinpoint when we—"

"No!" Shania cried, stopping her. "That's okay. That was just the surprise talking," she explained. She took a breath, collecting her thoughts so that she could sound like a coherent person instead of an overjoyed babbling idiot. "Have you seen a doctor? Did he tell you how far along you might be?"

"She," Wynona corrected. "I went to see Brett Murphy's wife, Alicia."

Shania was equally torn between being overjoyed and being impatient to have her question answered.

"And what did she tell you? When am I going to be an aunt—again?" she added belatedly, remembering that Ryan was her nephew now that Wynona had married his father.

All of this was so new to her, Shania thought, trying her best to get used to the idea.

"Well, according to what she said, you've got about a seven-month wait," Wynona told her.

Her mind was already going full speed ahead. "Great, that'll give me a chance to amass some baby clothes and toys for you."

"Don't get crazy, Shania," Wynona warned her with a laugh.

"Sorry." She couldn't stop grinning as the thought of Wynona being pregnant took root. "Too late. So what does Clint say?"

"Well, at first he was speechless," Wynona told her. "And then he couldn't stop grinning. Actually, he's still grinning."

"Grinning?" Shania repeated. She tried to picture that and failed. "Are we talking about the same Clint?"

"We're talking about the new Clint," Wynona corrected. "He's absolutely thrilled, Shania. And so am I."

"Well, that makes three of us. Four," she amended, looking at Belle. Responding to the mood the dog was picking up on, Belle's tail was thumping against the floor again. "The dog's very excited for you."

"Probably not as excited as Ryan is," Wynona told her.

"You told Ryan?" Shania asked, surprised. "And he's not jealous?"

"Jealous?" Wynona laughed. "He's already stacking up his

old toys and baseball equipment so he can give it to the baby. He can't wait until he gets here."

"What if it's a girl?" Shania asked. Working with her students had made her anticipate problems.

"It doesn't matter. Ryan'll be happy. Besides, girls play baseball, too."

Pregnant. Wynona was pregnant. Shania couldn't get over the news. "This is really great, you know."

"I think so," Wynona agreed. "Well, enough about me. What about you? How's everything going?"

In the wake of her cousin's news everything else paled in comparison, but since she'd asked, Shania felt obligated to answer.

"Same old, same old," Shania told her. "Mostly I'm too busy to notice much of anything. I've got to drill them to get ready to take their PSATs."

"Are you doing all right?" Wynona asked, more interested in the personal aspect than the scholastic one.

"I wouldn't mind a magic wand that would transform some of my rebellious students into studious ones. Got one of those lying around somewhere?" Shania asked.

Hearing Wynona laugh was really the best medicine Shania could ask for.

CHAPTER FOUR

"ELENA," SHANIA CALLED out the next day as the teenager was just about to shuffle out of her classroom along with the rest of the third period algebra class. When Elena turned around to look at her quizzically, Shania asked, "Could I speak with you for a minute, please?"

Elena remained where she was and regarded her with the excessively bored expression that she had managed to perfect in the past few weeks.

"Do I have to listen?" she asked the teacher.

"That would be the general idea, yes," Shania responded, keeping her voice upbeat and friendly and refusing to rise to the bait.

Elena sighed dramatically, then slowly sauntered over to her teacher. "I'll try to do better on the next test."

"Well, you didn't do all that badly on the last one, but that's good to know since we both know you're capable of doing better," Shania told her. "But this isn't about your test score."

A suspicious look came over Elena's face, subduing her fresh, natural beauty. "Then what is it about?"

Shania gestured toward a desk in the front row, indicating that the girl take a seat. At the same time, she sat down at the desk next to it.

After Elena warily sank down, Shania began to talk to her, continuing to choose her words carefully and with precision.

"I couldn't help but notice that you seemed really upset about something today—even more than usual," she added with a small, encouraging smile. "I was just wondering if there was anything I could do."

Well-shaped eyebrows drew together on Elena's brow. "About what?"

"About whatever it is that's making you scowl so hard," Shania replied. There was no judgment in her voice, just a friendly offer of help.

For a moment, Elena seemed to debate denying that there was anything wrong, that it was all in her teacher's head. "That all depends. Can you turn a narrow-minded, judgmental, know-it-all older brother into a reasonable person?"

"Maybe. What happened?"

Elena waved her hand at her teacher, dismissing the offer. "It really doesn't matter."

But now that Elena had started this, Shania wasn't ready to back off. "Now, there we have a difference of opinion, Elena, because I think that it does."

Elena tossed her head, trying to be the very picture of haughty rebellion.

"Oh? And why would you say something like that?" Elena asked, using her best disinterested, bored voice.

"I've looked at your grades, Elena. Your *past* grades," Shania emphasized before the girl could protest this invasion of her privacy despite the fact that they were talking about something that was listed in her file and was a matter of record. "Until this year, you were on your way to being seriously considered for a scholarship that could pay for all four years of your college education." Her eyes met Elena's. The latter looked away, staring off into the air. Shania wasn't about to drop the matter. "That's not something that you should throw away lightly."

Elena's whole body gave the impression that she was shutting down. There was a defensive expression in her eyes as she lifted her chin, ready for a fight. "Maybe I don't want to go to college."

"Okay," Shania said good-naturedly. "What do you want to do?"

Elena looked even more annoyed as she shrugged. "Why do I have to have a plan?" she demanded.

"Because if you don't," Shania told her patiently, "if you just float along without any kind of a goal, you're really going to regret it someday."

The girl shifted impatiently in her seat. "Yeah, yeah," she said, rolling her eyes. "Can I go now?"

Elena began to rise, but Shania raised her hand, indicating that the teen should remain seated a little longer.

"Not yet," Shania told her.

Elena looked at her watch. "Look, you're making me late. I've got another class."

But Shania knew that was a lie. "No, you don't," she replied simply. When Elena opened her mouth to protest, Shania told the teenager, "I looked up your school schedule."

"You did what?" Elena cried. "Why would you do that? Did my brother put you up to this?" Impotent frustration had the girl suddenly letting loose with a guttural yell. "I can't believe he'd do this."

Shania was quick to set her straight. "Your brother didn't put me up to this. I have no idea who your brother is," she told the girl.

It wasn't absolutely true, but Shania felt that she could be forgiven until she actually confirmed if the man she'd talked to last night was Elena's brother. For now, she felt justified in making the denial.

"Then why would you bother looking up my schedule like that?"

"It's very simple," Shania said. "Because you're really very, very bright and I wanted to talk to you to see if I could help you."

Elena's eyes narrowed again.

"Why?"

"Because I hate to see waste," Shania told her simply. "Because quite honestly you are the brightest student I've ever encountered and, in a way, maybe you kind of remind me of me when I was really mad at the world and almost wound up destroying everything, including the aunt who had gone out of her way to try to save me."

Elena closed herself off as she glared at her teacher. "You're just making all this up," she accused the woman.

Rather than deny the assumption, Shania asked the teen, "Why would I do that?"

Elena threw up her hands. "I don't know. I don't have all the answers!"

The girl appeared ready to bolt. Shania went on talking to her in a calm, even voice, trying to get through to the angry teenager.

"Let's start over," Shania suggested. "What made you so upset? *More* upset," she amended. "You haven't exactly been Miss Sunshine since the beginning of the semester."

"My brother actually set up some kind of a surveillance device so he could watch my every move," Elena cried, seething over what she obviously viewed as an insult.

Rather than act indignant for her, or side with Elena's brother, Shania just asked a simple question. "Why would he do that?"

Elena crossed her arms before her chest, pulling into herself. "Because he doesn't trust me, that's why!"

Shania looked at the girl for a long, probing moment. "Should he?"

"He's my brother," Elena retorted indignantly. "Of course he should trust me."

Now they were getting somewhere. "And you haven't done

anything to undermine that trust?" she asked, her eyes meeting the girl's.

"No," Elena protested. But Shania continued just looking at her and finally the teen shifted uncomfortably. "Okay, maybe."

"And how did you do that?" Shania asked her, giving every indication that there would be no judgment attached to anything that Elena said.

Elena glanced away and shrugged. "I might have gone to Matt McGuire's party a week ago," she murmured. And then she quickly added, "But Daniel told me not to have parties at our house and I didn't. I can't tell someone else not to have one at their house."

"No, you can't," Shania agreed. And then she added the part that Elena didn't want to hear. "But you don't have to attend."

"Matt's my friend," Elena protested. "I can't not go."

Shania couldn't help grinning. "That's a double negative, but we'll talk about that later." She got back to the subject under discussion. "Did you ask your brother if you could go to the party?"

The answer came grudgingly and only after a couple of moments. "No."

"Why not?" Shania asked her. Again, there was no judgment in her voice.

Elena's voice grew louder and more assured. "Because I can make up my own mind if I want to go to a party or not."

The girl had to know that wasn't right, Shania thought.

"Elena, like it or not—and yes," she interjected before Elena could protest, "I know it seems unfair—but you are a minor and your brother is responsible for you. That means that you have to ask him for his permission, or at the very least, tell him where you're going to be before you go."

"Why? So he can say no?" Elena challenged her teacher.

"That is his right," Shania informed her. She knew it didn't win her any points with the girl, but it was also true.

"Who says?"

Shania regarded her quietly for a minute before she answered,

"You are a very intelligent girl, Elena. More intelligent than most. You already know the answer to that."

"You're on his side, aren't you?" Elena accused. "I knew it!" She was on her feet in seconds, ready to bolt out of the room.

But Shania caught her wrist, holding her in place. "No, I'm on yours. And I'll let you in on a secret. The best way to earn your brother's trust is to be trustworthy."

Elena huffed loudly.

"Did you ever stop to think that he's just worried about you?" Shania asked.

"Well, he shouldn't be," Elena retorted. "I can take care of myself!"

"That might very well be true," Shania allowed, "but you're going to have to prove that to him."

"How? My brother's got me under lock and key like a prisoner," Elena complained, seething. "Can't he be arrested for that?"

"Not unless he's got you chained up. Does he?" she asked, looking at the teen's face.

"No," Elena mumbled. "But—"

"Okay," Shania told her, "since your brother doesn't have you chained up, my suggestion is that you start acting like a model prisoner and he'll slowly start to trust you and give you back some of those privileges that you're missing."

Elena's face clouded over as she snapped, "No, he won't. He's stubborn and pig-headed and he'll just go on treating me like I'm this kid—"

"I think he's probably fairer than you think," Shania countered, assuring the teen. She could see by the look on Elena's face that she needed something more. Shania searched her brain to come up with something. "And until then," she told Elena, "why don't you think about everything that your brother gave up for you just so that he could make sure you'd be all right."

Elena looked at her as if she had suddenly lapsed into a

strange language that didn't make any sense to her. "What do you mean what he gave up? He didn't give up anything."

But Shania had done her homework when it came to Elena's background. She'd had a feeling that she was going to need all the help she could get. "Your parents are gone, right?" she asked the teen gently.

Elena's back instantly went up. "That's not my fault."

"I didn't say it was your fault," Shania replied calmly. "But your brother *is* taking care of you, isn't he, Elena?"

Elena kept glaring at her. "So?"

Shania's eyes met Elena's. "He doesn't have to."

"Sure he does," the teenager insisted. "There's no one else to take care of me. Daniel's my brother. He *has* to take care of me."

"Elena," Shania said gently, "people don't always do the right thing, even if they're supposed to. People have been known to just take off when they don't want to face up to their responsibilities. I know a lot of people who would love to be in your place and have an older brother to look out for them, to turn to. You might not think so, but you are very lucky to have someone who cares enough about you to put up with everything you're dishing out and still trying to get you to do the right thing. There are those who, given the circumstances, just might shrug their shoulders and shine you on, letting you do whatever you wanted to."

Elena clearly didn't see that as being a bad thing. "Sounds good to me."

"Maybe," Shania allowed, then pointedly emphasized, "If that person is lazy. Otherwise, it's called not caring."

Elena frowned because her point had somehow gotten away from her. "You just like to twist things around, don't you?"

"No," Shania contradicted, "I like to make things clear. You're smart, you're pretty and you have a great deal of potential. You're luckier than most, Elena. You have it all." She looked into the teen's eyes again, appealing to her common sense. "Don't waste it."

"I'm not wasting it," the girl said stubbornly. "I just want to be able to enjoy it while I still can. While I'm still *young*," she stressed. "I want to have fun, Ms. Stewart. You remember fun, don't you?"

"Yes, I do. I also remember working hard and being proud of myself for doing a good job. There's no other feeling like that, trust me. Don't rob yourself of it. That kind of 'fun' you're talking about lasts maybe a few hours. On the other hand, what you'll accomplish by applying yourself and putting in all that hard work will last you a lifetime."

"Maybe it just *feels* like a lifetime," Elena quipped.

"I tell you what, Elena, why don't you give my way a try for a couple of weeks? If, at the end of that time, you find that you're not feeling better about yourself, then you can just go back to phoning it in for the rest of the semester."

Elena's brow furrowed. "Phoning it in?"

"Yes. It means just barely squeaking by," Shania explained.

"And no more lectures?" Elena asked, watching her for her reaction.

"It won't be easy, but no more lectures," Shania agreed.

"And you'll talk to my brother and get him off my back?" Elena asked.

Shania thought about the tall, dark, handsome stranger she'd encountered at Murphy's last night. He didn't strike her as someone who welcomed unsolicited advice.

"I'll talk to your brother," she agreed, "but I doubt if my suggesting that he 'get off your back' is going to be well-received."

"But you *will* talk to him?" Elena pressed, her dark, expressive eyes pinning her teacher down.

Shania nodded. "I'll talk to him. And you'll apply yourself?"

Elena frowned, then said grudgingly, "For two weeks."

"That's all I ask," Shania told her with a warm smile. Hopefully, she thought, two weeks would be enough to do the trick.

Elena muttered something under her breath as she blew out a long-suffering sigh. Shania decided it was best if she didn't ask her to repeat it. Some things were better left unknown.

CHAPTER FIVE

SHORT IN STATURE, large in reputation, Miss Joan had been part of Forever for as long as any of its present citizens could remember, as had the diner that she both ran and owned.

Gruff and abrupt on the outside, soft and understanding on the inside, Miss Joan was also the person that many of the local people went to for advice and guidance when they had nowhere else to turn. On occasion, she was known to take in people, as well as hire them when they found themselves penniless and desperate with no immediate way to rectify that.

What Miss Joan didn't do was coddle people. Instead, she was just as likely to give someone a well-needed kick in the posterior region to get them moving in the right direction. She didn't hold anyone's hand—she didn't want to add to their sense of helplessness. What she did was steer them in the right direction.

In short, due to a variety of different reasons, everyone thought of Miss Joan as the glue that held the town together.

So, whether it was by design or just subconscious motivation, when Daniel felt that he was utterly confused by his teenage sister's rather mercurial behavior, he found himself stopping by Miss Joan's diner to grab a late breakfast—something he very rarely did.

The thin, titian-haired woman, who could make grown men tremble by merely raising a sharp eyebrow, glanced in Daniel's direction the moment he walked in through the diner's door. Topping off a customer's coffee at the far end of the counter, Miss Joan began to move toward the deputy the moment the door closed behind him.

The thin lips curved minutely in greeting. "Well, if it isn't the strong arm of the law."

Daniel took a seat at the counter. "I hate to correct you, Miss Joan, but I think you meant to say the 'long arm of the law,'" Daniel told the woman politely.

Hazel eyes swept over his face. "For your information, Deputy, I always say what I mean," Miss Joan told him. The hint of a smile was gone. "Have you taken a good look at yourself in the mirror lately, Deputy?" she asked.

Despite the concerns that were weighing on him lately, Daniel asked, "Are you flirting with me, Miss Joan?"

The woman didn't answer his question one way or another. Instead, she said, "At my age, Daniel, I get to do what I want."

"What would Harry say?" he asked, referring to the man Miss Joan had finally agreed to marry six years ago after being courted by Harry Monroe for what seemed like an eternity.

"Nothing, if he knows what's good for him," Miss Joan deadpanned. Filling the cup she'd placed in front of him, she got down to business. "So, what brings you here, Deputy? A sudden desire for a home-cooked meal?" she asked, although one look at her face told him that wasn't what she was really thinking.

He wasn't comfortable admitting that he had sought her out, so he said, "I skipped breakfast and realized that wasn't a smart move."

Sharp eyes took slow measure of him, telling him that the woman was totally unconvinced.

"That doesn't sound like something you'd do, Daniel. What's the real reason you're here?" she asked. Then, seeing him looking at his coffee, Miss Joan asked, "Black, right?"

"Right as always, Miss Joan," he replied.

A spasmodic smile crossed her thin mouth. "Now, we can continue this little stillborn charade and I can get you a plate of scrambled eggs," she said, mentioning the way she knew that he preferred his eggs, gleaned from the few occasions that he had come in for breakfast, "or you can just get down to business and tell me what's causing that deep furrow between those deep, soulful eyes of yours." She looked at him intently. "It wouldn't have something to do with your sister, would it?"

Though he had always been excellent at maintaining a poker face, when Miss Joan's guess was so on target, Daniel couldn't immediately suppress the surprise that flashed across his face.

Belatedly, Daniel managed to recover and murmured, "Yes."

Pleased with herself, although not surprised, Miss Joan nodded. "I thought so."

Daniel paused, looking down at his coffee again, wondering if he'd made a mistake coming here after all. And then he raised his eyes, looking directly into the woman's deep, penetrating hazel orbs.

"You know, someday you're going to have to tell me just how you wound up getting that unnerving sixth sense of yours."

"No mystery, handsome," Miss Joan assured him. "It's just intuition."

"It's a hell of a lot more than that, Miss Joan," he told her.

He had to admit, albeit silently, that he did find it more than a little unnerving at times just how accurate she could be.

Miss Joan waved her hand at his words. She had little time for flattery, even if it was sincerely voiced. "You were going to tell me what's troubling you about your sister."

The word *everything* flashed through Daniel's mind, but he kept that to himself. He'd never had any use for complainers and he wasn't about to start sounding like one himself.

For now, he decided to give the diner owner a little bit of background before getting to the heart of the present problem.

"Elena's been going through this rebellious stage," he began.

Miss Joan looked completely unmoved. "She's sixteen, Deputy. It's to be expected."

But *he* hadn't expected it, Daniel thought. Elena had always behaved herself. Her sense of self-discipline had been inherent.

And then everything changed.

"Until this summer, she was quiet, studious and as close to perfect as anyone could possibly hope for," he told Miss Joan, keeping his voice down so that she was the only one who could hear him. He took a breath and then gave voice to the problem. "And then she changed."

"Because she's sixteen," Miss Joan repeated, stressing her words pointedly.

The look on Daniel's face told Miss Joan that he didn't view what she'd just said as an explanation or an excuse. "The thing is, just as suddenly a couple of days ago, Elena goes back to being the way she was before all this flared up."

Miss Joan waited for him to continue. When he didn't, she posed the logical question to him. "Well, did you ask her about it?"

The memory of that particular exchange was very fresh in his mind and he felt another wave of anger pass over him. "I did, but Elena just rolled her eyes at me and said she didn't have time to talk."

"Let me get something straight," Miss Joan said. "Are you *upset* that she went back to her previous behavior?"

Her question caught him totally off guard. He was surprised that she would ask something like that. "Of course not."

"Then what's the problem?" she asked, not clear why he seemed so out of sorts.

"The problem," he explained as patiently as he could, "is that I want to find out what happened to change Elena's mind and make her go back to her old ways. This way, I'll know what 'buttons' to press to make her revert back to the studious Elena instead of the party girl mode she was in a week ago."

It was all falling into place for her, Miss Joan thought. "My guess is that this all might be the influence of one of her teachers," Miss Joan told him. She let the words sink in and then went on to suggest, "Why don't you try talking to her teachers?"

He knew that made sense, but he had never been the type to seek out a teacher for the sole purpose of having a conference with him or her regarding his sister's progress. Up until now, Elena had been doing just fine and there'd been no need to attempt to "get her on the right path." The extent to which he got involved in her schoolwork was signing her report cards, which had always been stellar.

Maybe he should just let it all just ride, Daniel thought. Maybe Elena would just continue on this path now that she'd gotten back to it.

"That would be butting in," he told Miss Joan, finishing up his coffee.

"Some people would call that taking an interest in Elena's education," Miss Joan corrected. She topped off his cup, then shrugged. "You do what you want, Deputy. But if you really want answers instead of floating along blindly, I'd suggest looking into all the possible influences in Elena's life. If nothing else, that way you could find out if there's any way you could encourage your sister on the home front."

Daniel laughed shortly under his breath, thinking of the recent clashes that had taken place between Elena and himself since school had started this year. Instead of a docile little sister, he'd found himself dealing with a spitfire that challenged everything he said.

"The best way I can encourage Elena to do well," he told Miss Joan, "is to pretend I don't notice she's doing well."

Miss Joan looked at him, something akin to pity entering her eyes. "Trust me, Deputy. Every female wants to be noticed."

"Maybe," Daniel responded, not wanting to contradict the woman outright. "But that rule doesn't apply to sisters."

Miss Joan lowered her head slightly, allowing her eyes to

be level with his. Her gaze held him prisoner. "Is your sister a female?"

Daniel looked at the older woman, thinking he had to have heard her wrong. When Miss Joan continued looking at him, apparently waiting for a response, he finally said, "Of course she is, Miss Joan."

She nodded, a triumphant expression crossing her face as she told him, "Then it applies."

Daniel sighed. Miss Joan had a habit of always being right. He saw no reason to think that this time might be different just because this was about his sister who he'd once thought he knew better than anyone else in the world. It was now obvious to him that he didn't.

Daniel shook his head. "Why are females all so complicated?"

"Because otherwise we'd be boring—and men," Miss Joan answered, softly chuckling to herself. "Now stop wasting time standing here and go call that girl's teachers. When you narrow down which one has been influencing her, ask for a conference. That way you might be able to get some clarity on what's going on with your sister."

It didn't strike him until later that in the space of a few minutes, Miss Joan had taken all of Elena's teachers and zeroed in on just a single one.

As if she knew something he didn't.

But then, he silently admitted, somehow the woman always did.

Right now, however, Daniel was keenly aware that he needed to get going. Just to make sure, he glanced at his watch.

He was right.

It was getting late. He'd wasted enough time trying to get insight into the workings of his sister's mind. If he didn't get going, he was going to be late getting to work.

"Thanks for the help, Miss Joan." Standing up, he dug into

his pocket, simultaneously nodding at the empty coffee cup. "What do I owe you?"

"A lot more than you could ever repay me," the woman answered simply. And then, knowing his sense of honor wouldn't allow him to accept a cup of coffee on the house, she told him, "A dollar'll more than cover it."

He placed a five-dollar bill beside his plate. "Consider it a down payment on that debt," Daniel told the older woman as he headed for the door.

"What was all that about?" Cassandra, one of Miss Joan's newest waitresses, asked. She gestured toward the door in case she was being too vague.

"My guess is that we've just witnessed the awakening of Deputy Daniel Tallchief," Miss Joan said. "Now, why don't you follow in his footsteps and get busy with all those dishes?" she told the waitress, gesturing toward the tables that still needed to be bussed.

Cassandra knew better than to sigh. "Yes, ma'am," she answered as she got to work.

Despite what he had said to Miss Joan about being curious about the actual reason behind his sister's sudden reversal in behavior, Daniel was undecided whether or not to take the woman's advice.

Maybe he shouldn't seek out any of Elena's teachers. Talking to them might just be inviting trouble or, at the very least, rocking the boat.

The old adage about leaving well enough alone flashed through his mind.

That was cowardly, he thought the next moment. And he had never been a coward, not even when he'd been a young boy and had stood up to that bully who had been twice his size.

Besides, he'd been serious when he'd said that if there was anything he could do to encourage Elena's sudden renewed interest in studying, he was more than willing to do it. He just needed to be shown the way.

Studying was far preferable to spending time with that Matt kid. That would be a ticking time bomb waiting to go off.

"You're looking more pensive than usual," Joe Lone Wolf commented after fifteen minutes of silence had gone by. Daniel wasn't known to be talkative, but he usually had a few things to say when he came in. This morning the junior deputy had been as silent as a tomb. "Something wrong?"

Daniel was about to say no, then admitted, "I don't know."

"Want to talk about it?" Rick Santiago asked, picking that moment to walk into the room to get himself a cup of coffee. He paused by the space between the two deputies' desks.

"Not particularly," Daniel answered honestly.

Talking to Miss Joan this morning had been something out of the ordinary for him. He usually kept things to himself and at this point, he felt pretty close to being talked out.

However, it looked as if the sheriff had other ideas on the matter.

"Three heads are better than one, Tallchief," Rick told him. "Even if two of those heads are more stubborn than sin," he added.

Daniel thought it might be better for everyone all around if he kept his own counsel for the time being. "I think this is something that I need to work out on my own."

"Whatever it is that you're working out, is it going to interfere with work?" Rick asked.

Daniel gave his superior a look. "You know me better than that, Sheriff."

But the expression on Rick's face was skeptical. "Trouble is, I'm not sure I really know you at all, Tallchief. I appreciate you being self-sufficient and wanting to handle things on your own," he told his deputy, "but you need to know when to ask for help."

Daniel gave it one last try. "I don't need help...exactly," he amended.

The sheriff moved closer to him. "But?" Rick asked, waiting to hear the rest of the man's sentence.

Daniel paused, thinking. He supposed it wouldn't hurt things if he asked a few general questions—just in case he was being too lax about what was going on with his sister's behavior.

"But my sister's driving me crazy," he finally told the other two men.

Rick laughed in response, something Daniel hadn't expected. "Been there," the man told him.

Joe looked at the sheriff sharply. "No offense, Sheriff, but that's my wife you're commenting on."

Rick grinned. "And she's your problem now. Don't mind telling you that you're having a lot better luck getting along with her than I did," Rick admitted. "Of course, Ramona's done a great deal of growing up in the last ten years."

Daniel listened to the two men he'd come to admire and respect over the course of the past couple of years talk. And as he listened, the wall that he kept around himself and his thoughts began to soften and recede to an extent. So much so that he felt that perhaps it wouldn't be interpreted as a sign of weakness if he did ask some questions.

But just before he was about to, he suddenly remembered the woman he'd run into at Murphy's the other night. She'd said something about butting heads with headstrong students. That was the best description of his sister that he'd come across recently. A headstrong student.

"Either one of you know anything about that physics teacher at the high school?" he asked the other two men.

Both men stopped talking and turned to look at Daniel. One smile seemed to spread across two faces.

"Why?" Joe asked.

"You interested?" Rick asked.

Daniel looked at his superior as if the question was too ludicrous to even consider. Instead, he told the two men, "I think she might be Elena's teacher. I was just wondering if she's the kind of teacher to inspire her students to study hard and change their outlook when it comes to doing well."

"I could ask around," Rick told him.

"Might be better if you asked her that yourself," Joe suggested.

Rick nodded, changing his mind about his initial offer. "What he said," he told Daniel.

Daniel had the eerie feeling that somewhere, Fate had just cast a die.

CHAPTER SIX

MORE THAN TWENTY-FOUR hours later, Daniel was still debating whether or not to drop by Forever's high school and introduce himself to the woman he'd probably already met at Murphy's.

Since no names had been exchanged that evening, Daniel was uneasy that Elena's teacher would naturally jump to the conclusion that he was merely trying to complete the pass he had initiated at their first meeting. Therefore, she might not believe that his real reason for going out of his way to talk to her was because he wanted to know what he could do to help encourage his sister with her studies.

But apparently, he realized as he walked into the office, the decision to make that first step had been taken out of his hands.

He had just come back after breaking up a dispute between two ranchers who weren't seeing eye to eye about where one property line ended and the other began. Two steps into the office he became aware that there was someone talking to the sheriff.

A female someone.

Daniel wasn't generally in the habit of eavesdropping, but the sound of the low, melodic voice caught his attention immediately, even before he could make out any of the woman's words.

Going over a report at his desk, Joe happened to look up,

and he noticed the attentiveness on Daniel's face. He observed Daniel for a moment before making any sort of a comment.

"If I didn't know any better, I'd say that you look like a bird dog that just realized he'd had a quail walk across his path."

Annoyed, Daniel waved his hand at the senior deputy, implying that Joe should be quiet.

Daniel strained to listen more closely.

The next moment, he realized that it wasn't his imagination playing tricks on him. He would have recognized that voice anywhere. Not to mention that shapely figure.

It was the woman from Murphy's saloon, the one he was almost certain was Elena's teacher.

What was she doing talking to the sheriff? Had something gone wrong at the high school?

Had...?

And then there was no time left for any more speculation. Because the sheriff was escorting the woman out, bringing her into the general area where the deputies sat.

"Tallchief, I need a word." The sheriff beckoned him over to where he and the woman were standing.

Concern ricocheted through Daniel with each step he took as he approached them.

"Sheriff?" he asked, finding it less disconcerting to center his attention strictly on his superior instead of on the woman standing next to Santiago.

Maybe he could have pulled it off if the woman had been less compelling. But she wasn't. She was the kind of woman who immediately drew all eyes to her whenever she entered a room, even one that might have been filled with other beautiful women—which was definitely *not* the case this time.

Once his eyes met hers, Daniel nodded a silent greeting, doing his best not to focus on the fact that this woman by her mere presence was causing his stomach to pull into itself and all but tie itself up in a knot.

It had been a long time since he'd felt that way—and that had ended in a disaster, he reminded himself.

He felt barriers going up. Protective barriers.

"Ms. Stewart would like a word with you," Rick told Daniel, his expression giving nothing away, including the fact that the three of them had just discussed this woman a little more than twenty-four hours ago. "Why don't you use my office?"

The suggestion was made not to Daniel but to the woman, who it was becoming apparent had come here to speak to him, not the sheriff.

"That's very generous of you, Sheriff," Shania told him, then asked, "Are you sure it's all right? I can just as easily talk to your deputy outside."

"My office will afford you more privacy," Rick answered. "Go ahead. Go right in."

Because there were now questions burning in his chest—was the offer for privacy because the sheriff had anticipated this would hit him hard?—Daniel made no effort to turn down the offer. Instead, he quickly followed the woman into the sheriff's office and closed the door behind them.

The second the reassuring *click* signifying their separation from the others was heard, Daniel couldn't restrain himself any longer. He had to know. "What's wrong?"

Shania looked at him, surprised by his question. "What makes you think that there's something wrong?"

"Well, for one thing, I can't think of a single reason for a teacher to come into the sheriff's office that doesn't have some sort of a dark explanation attached to it," Daniel told her.

Shania smiled. "I can see that you're not the Neanderthal that Elena claimed you are, but you're certainly not given to having optimistic thoughts, are you?"

For a moment, he thought of asking her if she remembered their brief encounter at Murphy's. But given the situation, it really made no difference right now. Instead, he addressed her comment.

"Elena hasn't given me any reason to harbor any optimistic thoughts," he told her, reacting more defensively than he would have thought he would. He ordinarily just allowed things to unfold before him, but Elena was too important for him to merely passively stand by, waiting for questions to be answered.

"Oh, I wouldn't be so sure about that if I were you. Your sister is a very bright girl who exhibits a great deal of potential—"

Daniel swept away the woman's flattering statement to get down to what he felt was the actual crux of the matter.

"Which my sister seems pretty set on squandering away," he pointed out.

She needed him to see that his sister was really trying hard now. "Elena struck a bargain with me that she was going to give studying another try for a short period of time…"

Daniel looked at the attractive teacher, wondering how well she handled disappointment. As for him, he didn't expect any sort of decent breakthrough to take place. "Emphasis on the word 'short.'" It was more of a statement than a question.

She was beginning to understand why Elena would find her brother's reactions daunting. "I thought that maybe you could encourage her, let her know how proud you are of her for trying so hard."

"You don't know my sister," he told her. "The second I say anything to her that even *remotely* sounds like an opinion about anything, she's going to do the exact opposite."

"Then don't say it," Shania answered simply.

Daniel looked at her as if he thought she was just babbling nonsense.

"How's that again?"

Shania took a breath and did her best to put it in a different way.

"Don't say—do," she told the deputy. But she could see that Daniel still didn't get what she was telling him, so she spelled it out, citing something specific—and positive—he could do.

"Take down that surveillance camera you put up by the front door."

"Elena told you about that?"

"Yes, she did. And, more importantly," Shania told him, "I could see how you putting that up made her feel. Like you didn't trust her."

His first instinct was to deny her assumption, but he knew that wouldn't help accomplish anything. Not to mention that it wasn't true.

"I didn't—I don't," Daniel stressed.

"Elena is only going to behave the way you expect her to behave," Shania told him.

He frowned. "Yeah, well, she's already shown me that she can't be trusted. How am I supposed to build on that?"

"Here's an idea," Shania suggested gamely. "Why don't you trust her and let her live up to *that* image?"

Daniel stared at the teacher as if what she'd just espoused was nothing short of crazy. She *had* to know that, he thought.

"She's a sixteen-year-old girl. Do you have *any* idea what can happen to a sixteen-year-old girl running wild like that?"

The man was allowing his imagination to run away with him.

"I think you might be exaggerating, Deputy Tallchief. Elena wouldn't run wild. Besides, Forever is a decent, quiet little town," she reminded Daniel.

But he shook his head. The woman was obviously missing a very crucial point.

"Teenagers are still teenagers. At sixteen, they all think they're immortal and their hormones run hot."

"Short of putting her in a tower and periodically cutting off her hair, there's not much you can reasonably do." When she saw the deputy's eyebrows draw together over eyes that regarded her in total confusion, she made a guess that her reference had gone right over his handsome head. In his defense, she supposed that the man probably wasn't the type who had ever read any fairy tales when he was growing up.

"Rapunzel?" she told him, but the name, like the reference, meant nothing to him. She tried again. "There's only so much you can do to ensure Elena's safety before she starts to feel like she's in prison. So, instead, why don't you get her to *want* to live up to your standards because it's the right thing to do?"

She could see that he didn't think very much of her idea, but, on the plus side, he wasn't dismissing it out of hand, either. There was hope.

Shania went over her suggestion again. "Take down the camera. Also, tell her you and I had a parent-teacher conference and that you're proud of the progress she's made."

"In other words, you want me to lie to her."

Instead of answering him, Shania took a folder out of her purse. She spread out a number of papers she had placed inside the folder. "Take a look at your sister's latest tests scores."

Daniel did as she suggested and then he raised his eyes to Shania's. He was clearly surprised by what he'd just seen.

"Elena never said anything about doing well on her tests."

"Your sister's not the type to brag," she told Daniel. "Don't you know that about her?" Putting the pages back into the folder, then tucking the folder into her purse, Shania turned her attention back to Elena's brother. "Did you ever even ask her about her test scores?"

Guilt made him react defensively. "How was I supposed to know she took any?"

"Seriously?" Shania asked. "She's in high school, Deputy Tallchief. She's *always* taking tests. That's what students do. And, just so you know, my students are going to be getting ready to take their PSATs next month. I'll be holding practice sessions for anyone who wants to take them after hours and on Saturdays."

That sounded like a lot of extra work for the teacher, Daniel thought. Didn't the woman have a life? Or was she just really, really dedicated?

He took a guess at why the woman had said anything to him

about the sessions. "And you want me to talk her into taking them?"

"No, I just wanted you to know that she won't be out running around. Elena will be staying after hours to take these practice tests," Shania told him. "She's already signed up."

That *did* surprise him. "She is?"

"She is," Shania answered. "As a matter of fact, your sister was the first one to put her name down on the list."

Daniel didn't even pretend that he wasn't impressed by all this. And he gave the credit where it was due. At this woman's feet.

"You got her to do all this?" he marveled.

"I really didn't 'get' her to do anything," Shania corrected him. "I just made suggestions. Elena's the one who took those suggestions to their logical conclusion. You know your sister well enough to know that I couldn't have made her do anything if she didn't want to."

He laughed shortly. Maybe Elena's teacher did understand what he was up against after all. "Yeah, tell me about it."

"What I will tell you," Shania said, picking up on the deputy's phrase, "is to try to spend a little time with Elena—not telling her to do something," she pointed out, "but just doing something *with* her."

These days Elena had made it clear that she didn't want to do *anything* with him. He was busy with work and she was hardly ever home. And when she was home, she was locked up in her room. Now he knew she was obviously studying in there.

Since this woman seemed to have all the answers, he swallowed his pride and asked, "Like what?"

"Like—" Her voice trailed off for a moment as she tried to think. "What did you used to do with her when she was younger?"

One thing came to mind and that in turn made him laugh. Shania looked at him quizzically, so he explained, "Elena's a little too big to give her a pony ride on my back."

"True," Shania agreed. "But she's not too big for the two of you to go out horseback riding."

He had no idea how to even get Elena to agree to that idea. "Just like that?"

"Why not?" Shania asked. "My cousin and I used to go out riding on the weekends. It rejuvenates you and gives the two of you the opportunity to talk. Going out like that clears your head, makes you feel closer to nature. And that's kind of important."

Daniel stopped her right there. "Because we're Navajo?"

No doubt about it. Under all that self-assured manliness, the man definitely had a chip on his shoulder, she thought.

"Because we're people," Shania answered simply.

"I wasn't talking about you," he told her. "I was talking about my sister and me."

"I was thinking about my cousin and myself," she clarified. "And before you ask, Wynona and I are part Navajo. Actually," she amended, "we're three-quarters Navajo."

He shrugged. Maybe he did take offense a little too quickly sometimes. "That's none of my business."

"I didn't say it was," she pointed out. "But it's also nothing I'm ashamed of. I'm proud of where I came from and what I've managed to become." Maybe it would help if she shared a little of her own story with this solemn man. "I'm not sure if I would have been where I am if it hadn't been for my great-aunt helping out, but even if she hadn't been there for me, I knew I wasn't going to wallow in self-pity and do nothing my whole life.

"And now that she's been prodded," Shania continued, "neither will your sister. I just wanted you to be aware of what was going on so you could be in her corner and find a way to encourage her." She looked at him for a long moment. "Elena cares about you a great deal."

He didn't believe that for a second. He would have liked to, but he knew better. "Now you're just making things up."

"No, I'm serious," she insisted. "I can see it in her eyes.

Even when she's calling you a Neanderthal, there is affection in her eyes."

"Uh-huh." Again, he wanted to believe that, he really did. But he didn't want to set himself up to be disappointed. He'd already been through that shocking set of circumstances.

More than once.

Still, this teacher with the animated expression and flashing bright eyes seemed to be convinced about what she was telling him. Nobody was *that* good an actress.

"All right," Daniel agreed, although far from enthusiastically, "I'll take down that surveillance camera I've got up."

Shania smiled, happy that she'd gotten Daniel to come around. "Good. And be sure to let her catch you taking it down."

He wasn't sure what the teacher was telling him. "You mean point it out to her?"

Shania shook her head. "No, just make sure you're taking it down when you know she's around. That way you'll get credit for trusting her without making a big speech about it. Less is more in this case," she told him. "Trust me, being subtle makes for the best good deeds."

"I don't know how to be subtle," he told her.

"Sure you do. Don't underestimate yourself," she told him.

He supposed, if he thought about it, her advice about being subtle made some sort of sense. "If you say so."

Her smile grew broader as she rose from her chair. She'd done what she'd come to do.

"I do," she told him. She put her hand out to him. "It was nice meeting you—again, Mr. Tallchief."

"It's Deputy," he corrected, then added, "Or Daniel, if you prefer."

"Daniel," she repeated, wrapping her tongue around his name.

He didn't know why, but he felt as if he had just been put on notice—and the odd thing was that part of him didn't mind.

CHAPTER SEVEN

ELENA'S HEAD SHOT UP, listening intently. The sound coming from the front of the house had registered immediately. She knew her brother was at the sheriff's office, working the late shift, which meant she was supposed to be alone in the house.

The faint sound told her otherwise.

Elena crept out of her room where she'd been doing her homework. Leery, not sure what she'd find, she picked up the bat she occasionally used when she played softball at school. Her palm felt damp as she clutched the wood.

The bat had been her brother's, but he never played anymore.

The journey from her room, located all the way at the back of the house, to the front door felt as if it was taking her forever.

When she saw her brother standing on a ladder, taking down the camera he'd put up only a week ago, she let go of both her breath and the bat she'd been holding.

The bat made much more noise as it hit the floor.

The clatter immediately got Daniel's attention. Turning, he caught and steadied himself just in time to keep from falling off the ladder.

"I guess you're not as defenseless as I thought," he commented, going back to removing the camera.

Picking up the bat, Elena leaned it against the wall in the corner and moved in as close to the ladder as she dared.

"What are you doing?" she asked him, looking up as he worked.

"I don't have much time before I have to get back, but I thought I could use my dinner break to take down the camera." Taking out the last screw, he tucked the screwdriver into his back pocket and then climbed down the ladder, holding the camera.

Elena took a step back, getting out of her brother's way. "Why?"

Putting the camera down on the small table just inside the door, he glanced in Elena's direction. "Why what?"

"Why are you taking it down?" He'd made such a big deal out of wanting it up so he could spy on her, she was surprised that he'd take it down so soon after having put it up.

Daniel thought about just saying that the camera was malfunctioning and leaving it at that, but he decided telling his sister the truth was the better way to go.

He shrugged casually, as if this was no big deal. "Because I thought it over and decided I was sending you the wrong message with this camera."

She continued looking at him, waiting to hear something that would explain all this to her. He couldn't just have decided to be a good guy and leave it at that. Could he? "Go on."

She was going to make him say it, wasn't she? He suppressed a sigh. "I don't want you to think I don't trust you."

Elena cocked her head. Her arms remained crossed before her chest. She was a portrait of distrust. "You don't."

He sighed, taking the ladder and bringing it into the living room. He rested the ladder on its side for the time being.

"That's not true. It's other guys I don't trust, not you," Daniel explained. "But that's no reason to make you feel like a prisoner. I *do* trust you, Elena." He could see she didn't believe him. "I trust you to make the right decisions. I raised you right, so I've got to trust that you'll do the right thing."

She was still skeptical, but she was coming around a little. Still, she needed to know something. "Where did this sudden change of heart come from?"

He doled out a little more of the truth to her. "I had a parent-teacher conference with Ms. Stewart."

Now it was starting to make sense to her. Elena nodded knowingly. "And she told you to take down the camera."

He didn't want to lie to Elena, but if he told her that she was right, that could in all probability negate any possible headway taking the camera down may have gotten him.

So instead, he left her question unanswered and focused on something else instead.

"She told me that you signed up to study for the PSATs with her and she also showed me some of your test scores. Why didn't you tell me how well you're doing in school?"

Elena shrugged, noting that he hadn't congratulated her or said anything positive about her grades. "You didn't ask."

She sounded annoyed, but he wasn't going to allow himself to get sidetracked and get into an argument with her.

"True," Daniel agreed. He could see that his answer surprised her. "I didn't want you to think I was trying to force you into studying."

Elena sighed and he had a feeling that she wasn't really buying this, but for the time being, he let it ride.

"I've got to be getting back. I've got the late shift this week," he told her even though he knew that she already knew that. "But I was thinking, maybe you'd like to go for a ride this weekend."

The suggestion caught her completely off guard. "Why?" she asked suspiciously.

He ignored the accusatory tone. "Well, we used to do that all the time and I thought it might be something you'd like to do again."

A bored, intolerant look came over her face. "So you're willing to suffer through it, is that it?"

Why did she have to turn everything into a confrontation? He struggled to hold down his temper. "I like riding, too."

"I've got practice tests to take," she told him, then added, "PSATs."

Daniel nodded. "Yes, I know. On Saturday, but not on Sunday."

That surprised her. "We'll see," she finally answered, not wanting to be pinned down.

Well, he supposed that he hadn't expected her to immediately jump at the chance.

"Right. Just let me know." Daniel began to turn away. "I'll see you in a couple of hours."

"Is that your way of asking if I'm staying home?" she challenged her brother.

He stopped in the doorway. "No, that's my way of saying that I'll see you in a couple of hours." She still looked unconvinced, so he explained, "It's a school night. I figure you're not going out because that's what we agreed on."

Elena tossed her head dismissively. "I don't remember there being an agreement. I do remember there being an order," she added haughtily, her attitude indicating that she didn't have to abide by it if she didn't choose to.

He saw it differently. "Yeah, well, there have to be some rules."

"For my own good?" she retorted, mocking the very idea of what she assumed he was thinking.

He could feel the argument coming but he forced himself not to rise to the bait. Instead, he gave her a somewhat neutral answer.

"And for mine," he told her. "See you in a bit, Ellie."

He saw the surprise on her face. He hadn't called her Ellie in years, not since she was a little girl. Daniel left his sister standing in the living room as he withdrew.

"I sure hope you know what you're talking about," he murmured under his breath, addressing the teacher who wasn't there as he left the house and walked over to his car.

Belle alerted her that there was someone at the door even before that person had a chance to knock. Rising, Shania glanced at the time.

It wasn't exactly late—once upon a time, she would have considered eight o'clock early—but she didn't usually get visitors at this time.

Instantly, she thought of Wynona. That got her moving quickly. She crossed to the door without bothering to even put her shoes on.

Belle wasn't a fierce dog, but no one would guess that based on the show the German shepherd put on before the door was opened. Aside from loud barking, there was leaping involved, as if Belle was warning whoever was on the doorstep that if they had any wrongdoing in mind, they were going to pay for it dearly.

"Easy, girl," Shania told the dog.

One hand firmly holding on to Belle's collar, Shania craned her neck to look through the door's peephole. Any lingering apprehension vanished.

The next moment, still holding on to Belle, she opened the door.

"What are you doing here?" she asked, surprised to see the brooding deputy on her doorstep. "Is something wrong with Elena?"

She couldn't think of any other reason that would have brought him here.

Daniel looked down apprehensively at the dog that had, just a second ago, sounded like an entire squadron of attack animals.

"Do you need to lock her up first?" he asked.

Shania smiled and shook her head. "No, Belle's not dangerous."

"That's not the way it sounds from this side of the door," he told her, still eyeing the dog.

"Let her sniff your hand," Shania urged, nodding at his hand.

He didn't look entirely convinced that this was a good idea. "Will I get it back?" Daniel asked gamely.

"Most likely," she answered, struggling to keep a straight face.

Daniel relaxed a little. He assumed that she wouldn't have told him to do something that would result in his getting bitten. He slowly put his hand out toward Belle to have her sniff it.

Shania kept her hold on the dog's collar just in case. Then, to her utter surprise, as she watched she saw Belle lick the deputy's hand.

Shania looked at the deputy, clearly impressed. "She's never done that before. I guess that Belle must *really* like you."

A small smile curved the corners of his mouth as he petted the dog's head. "Feeling's mutual," he told Shania. "I like dogs."

Since order had clearly been restored, Shania opened her door wider.

"Come on in," she said, inviting Daniel into her house.

After closing the door behind him, she turned around to see that the deputy had dropped down to one knee and was petting Belle in earnest. For her part, the dog appeared ecstatic.

Although the dog was generally a very friendly animal, Shania had never seen Belle react to anyone like this before—except for Ryan, her cousin's stepson, and even then, there wasn't this effusion of happiness.

She stood there for a moment, watching the interaction between Daniel and her dog. Smiling, Shania asked the deputy, "Would you like for me to leave the two of you alone?"

Daniel brushed off his knee as he rose to his feet. It was obvious that the dog had brought out a softer side to him.

"I had a dog when I was a kid. Chips," he recalled, a fond note momentarily entering his voice. "Chips was a really old dog," he explained. "I found him one day wandering around, looking for food. He had a wicked temper," he remembered. "It took a while until I could get him to trust me." He looked back at Belle, remembering the other dog. "He was a mutt, but I really loved him."

He cleared his throat, thinking that he had said too much. "Seeing your dog brings back memories," he admitted. Then, realizing that his sister's teacher had to be wondering what he was doing here at her house to begin with, he cleared his throat again. "Look, I know that it's late—"

"Not for some people," Shania pointed out. She wanted to give him some slack in case he was apologizing for being here at this hour.

"Yeah, well, I couldn't come earlier because I just got off my shift," he explained before he could get to the heart of what he was doing here.

"All right," she replied gamely, still waiting for the deputy to actually tell her why he was here. Maybe he talked better once some amenities were in place. "Would you like some coffee?" she asked. "Or some cake? I've got cake in the refrigerator if you're hungry."

"No, that's okay," he demurred. "I don't want to take up your time." He shifted slightly as Belle brushed up against his leg, obviously looking to be petted again. "I just wanted you to know that I took your advice."

She waited for him to be a little more specific. But when he didn't say anything further, she asked, "Which part?"

He wasn't the type to use five words when he felt one would do. But since she wanted details, he obliged. "I took down the camera and I suggested that we go for a ride this Sunday."

Pleased, Shania gestured for him to take a seat on the sofa. When he did, she sat down as well, leaving a little space between them.

Her eyes lively, she asked Daniel, "What did she say?"

He gave her the answer verbatim. "She wanted to know why

I was taking down the camera and why I was asking her to go riding with me."

Shania laughed to herself. Elena wasn't a girl to accept things at face value. "I take it that Elena suspected there was something behind you treating her like a human being."

He carelessly lifted a shoulder, then let it drop again. "Something like that. But she wasn't entirely hostile toward me," he added, sounding as pleased as he could, given the circumstances. "I just wanted to thank you for the push you gave me."

Shania grinned, pleased with the result. "Well, Deputy, anytime you want me to push you, just say the word and then brace yourself. Are you sure I can't offer you some coffee or anything to eat?"

Daniel shook his head. "No, I've already taken up too much of your time. I'd better be going now," he told her.

As he got up off the sofa and turned toward the door to leave, Belle moved in front of him, blocking his path to the front door.

Shania laughed as she watched the dog. "I think that Belle has other ideas about you making a quick escape," she told him. "She has really taken a shine to you. I think you might want to reconsider your beating a hasty retreat."

He petted the dog's head, shifting around her. "No offense, Belle, but I've got a sister who, despite popular opinion to the contrary, still might need a little, um…" He paused, trying to find the right word, then gave up. "'Subtle' babysitting."

Shania looked at him, concerned. "You're afraid she might take off?"

"Something like that," he admitted. "The camera's been taken down and I had to work the late shift. There are no eyes on her," he explained. "That's a very tempting scenario." He dared her to contradict him.

"Aside from her regular homework, Elena took home a couple of the PSAT practice tests today," Shania told him, watching his face as he took the information in. "That should keep her busy."

He didn't look completely sold on the idea. "*If* she does them," he pointed out.

He expected her to be judgmental. Instead, he watched a smile bloom on a face that was already compellingly lovely.

"Deputy, you are going to have to work on your trust issues, but the sooner you get those under control," she predicted, "the happier both you and your sister are going to be."

He had to ask her. "Why are you so confident of that?"

She thought of her great-aunt and their less-than-smooth beginning. It had taken her a while to lower her guard—and she would always be grateful that her great-aunt had waited her out. "Because I am living proof that if someone trusts you—if you *realize* that they trust you—most of the time you will try to live up to that trust."

"*Most* of the time," Daniel stubbornly repeated as if that made his argument for him. "But not always."

Shania wasn't ready to surrender the point just yet. "And which category does your sister fall into? The one that says she'll try to live up to your expectations or the one where she'll do whatever she wants to without any regard for you, or your beliefs?"

"A year ago I would have never hesitated answering that question," he told her.

"But you did take down the camera," Shania reminded him. "If you were so sure she was the kind of person who just took off whenever she wanted to, nothing I would have said would have convinced you to remove it."

"Okay," he admitted rather grudgingly. "So I'm guilty of hoping."

Shania shook her head, discarding his explanation. "You, Deputy, are guilty of knowing your sister. And, deep down inside, you know she can be trusted. Especially if you make a point of letting her know that you trust her. Now, go home to spend some time with your sister—as her brother, not her warden," she stressed, walking him to the front door.

Daniel opened it, then paused to look at her. "And she'll know the difference how?"

She put her hand on his shoulder and gently pushed him over the threshold and out of the house. "Because she knows you," she said, then closed the door.

Belle made a mournful noise, then looked up at her mistress.

"Don't worry, Belle. He'll be all right," she assured her pet.

Belle barked again, as if to indicate that she wasn't all that sure about that.

CHAPTER EIGHT

DANIEL HAD NEVER been an optimist. It was a given. Part of him was always waiting for something to go wrong, even when everything seemed to be going right.

That was why, even though Elena seemed to have settled down and appeared to have gone back to concentrating on getting good grades rather than bad boys, Daniel felt as if he was coexisting with a ticking time bomb that would most likely, at the most unexpected moment, just go off.

Still, the brooding deputy *tried*, at least outwardly, to maintain a positive outlook on things.

When Sunday finally rolled around, he got up early, got ready and then waited for Elena to wake up.

For her part, Elena slept in, taking advantage of her only day off. When she did stumble her way into the kitchen, her eyes half closed, she looked surprised to see her brother sitting there.

Recovering, she took a deep breath as she sank down at the kitchen table and fixed Daniel with a probing look. "What are you doing here?"

He raised his cup in her direction as if in silent tribute. "Waiting for you to get up."

Elena blinked, still trying to clear the sleep out of her eyes and still somewhat foggy brain.

"Why?"

Although things seemed to have been going along well between them these past few days, deep down inside Elena kept waiting for the next lecture, the next inquisition to suddenly materialize. Each day that it didn't, she just grew that much more tense anticipating what she felt was the inevitable.

"It's Sunday," Daniel answered.

Her eyebrows narrowed together as she tried to focus on his face.

"And...?"

Elena continued staring at him, trying to understand where her brother was going with this. Did he think that because it was her day off from school, she was going to take off somewhere? Do something he inherently disapproved of?

"I'm not going anywhere, if that's what you're thinking," she told him.

She'd forgotten, Daniel thought. "I thought we had a date."

Elena blinked. "Wait, what?" She stared at Daniel, confused. "A date? With my brother?" she asked as if what he was suggesting was as ridiculous as could be.

"And a couple of horses," he added, trying to jog her memory. When she didn't say anything, Daniel made the natural assumption. "You don't remember, do you?"

The cloud began to lift from her brain. Bits and pieces came back to her. She stared at Daniel as if she was watching him grow another head.

"You were serious?" she cried.

"Of course I was serious."

She thought for a second, then shrugged. She proceeded to let him off the hook—or so she believed. "You don't have to. I know you've been working all week. This is your only day off and you don't have to spend part of it with me."

"You're right," he agreed, his voice totally unemotional. "I don't *have* to. I *want* to. Don't you?"

Daniel had caught her off guard with his question. She looked as if she was torn for a minute.

She wasn't. She liked the idea, but she didn't want him to think he was doing her a favor. That would put her in his debt and she didn't want that.

"Well, if you really want to, I guess I can get dressed and go riding with you," she said with just the right touch of resignation.

"Good. Because I've been looking forward to it all week."

Elena rolled her eyes before she got up from the table. "No, you haven't," Elena said as she left the room to get dressed.

"Yes, I have," he called after her, half rising in his seat.

As he sat back down in his chair and sipped what was left of his coffee, Daniel smiled to himself. Maybe that cute little physics teacher actually did know what she was talking about, he thought. So far, the woman was two for two.

Jake McReedy owned and operated Forever's only stable, simply named McReedy's. He could always be found there, even when the stable was closed for the night. That was mainly because he slept in a tiny room that was located just at the rear of the building. In general, most people thought he had a far better relationship with the horses that were housed there than he did with the citizens of Forever.

The deeply tanned older man had far more hair on his face than he did on his head. That, at times, made it difficult for anyone to see his expression. In addition, his squinty eyes were partially hidden by his bushy eyebrows.

But Jake clearly looked surprised when Daniel came into the stable that morning with his sister.

"What can I do for you, Deputy? Miss?" Jake asked, nodding at Daniel and then his sister. Leaning the straw broom he'd been using to sweep up the small area in front of his office that wasn't covered with straw against the wall, he crossed toward the duo.

"I'd—*we'd*," Daniel corrected himself, sparing a quick glance at his sister, "like to rent two of your best horses for a couple of hours—or possibly longer," he amended, thinking that if Elena didn't start complaining and asking to go back home, they could easily stay out for more than just two hours.

Jake nodded. "We can settle up once you finish your ride and bring the horses back. Something special going on today I don't know about?"

Daniel didn't understand the question. "What do you mean?"

"Well," the older man said, bringing forward one saddle, then a second, "Sundays aren't usually busy until the afternoon, but you're the second and third people to come by so early today. Thought maybe there was something special going on," Jake explained. He began saddling the first horse, a large palomino stallion.

"I just want to go out for a ride with my sister," Daniel told the stable keeper. "We used to do that all the time when she was younger." He stopped there, seeing that he was making Elena uncomfortable.

Jake nodded. Finished tightening the cinch on the palomino's saddle, he prepared to slip on the stallion's bridle.

"Yeah, you can't beat a horse for companionship," he told Daniel. Belatedly, he seemed to realize that could be taken as an insult. He glanced toward the deputy's sister. "No disrespect intended," he mumbled to the teen, awkwardly touching the brim of his hat with two fingers in what passed as a semi-salute.

"None taken," Elena responded.

Wandering toward another stall, she stopped to look at a pinto. The horse was a little smaller than the other horses found in the stable. Saying a few words to him in a very low voice, Elena dug into her back pocket and took out three small lumps of sugar. She subtly offered them to the horse.

Daniel backed up to see what his sister was doing—and was

surprised to catch a glimpse of the sugar cubes before they disappeared. He was pleased to see how prepared she seemed to be.

"You brought sugar cubes," he noted quietly.

Her expression indicated that he didn't have to be so surprised.

"I want the horse on my side. I'm not an idiot," she informed him with an all-too-familiar toss of her head that sent her hair flying almost into his face.

"Never said you were an idiot," he reminded her. "You're a lot of other things, including, at times, a royal pain in my butt, but you were never an idiot—and you're still not."

Jake had finished saddling the second horse, the pinto that Elena seemed so drawn to, while she had been busy bribing it. Taking the reins, one set in each hand, he turned to face the deputy and his sister.

Jake offered them the reins.

"You two want to take these horses out for a ride or are you just going to stand in here, jawing at each other for the next couple of hours?" Jake asked. "Just so you know, the charge is the same either way."

Daniel glanced at Elena, then told the stable owner, "We'll ride."

Elena took the pinto's reins. After eyeing her mount uncertainly for a moment—it had been a long time since she'd gotten on a horse—Elena grasped the saddle horn, put her left foot into the stirrup and fluidly swung herself into the saddle.

For a fleeting second, she looked pleased with herself.

The look wasn't lost on Daniel. "Came back to you, didn't it?"

She'd had her doubts, but that wasn't anything she was about to willingly admit to her brother.

"It never went away," she informed him.

Daniel merely nodded as he swung himself into his own saddle like a man who had been born on the back of a horse.

"I had a feeling," he said, going along with the scenario Elena was trying to create for his benefit.

Now that they were both on their mounts, Jake stepped off to the side.

"If you're of a mind to catch up with that teacher, she rode north," he told them.

Just about to urge his horse forward, Daniel abruptly held himself in check.

"What teacher?" he asked.

"You mean Ms. Stewart?" Elena asked, immediately making the only connection that she could.

Was it just his imagination, or did Elena's voice sound a little higher than it normally did? Daniel wondered.

"Dunno her last name," Jake admitted. "She paid cash," he explained. "She did say that she'd suddenly gotten the yen for riding after spending all week looking over test papers and lesson plans. I ain't got any kids in school no more, but I figured from what she said, she had to be a teacher." He smiled a little wistfully, as if he was thinking about past opportunities that had slipped away. "Pretty little thing. Eyes that made you stand up and take notice. Makes me wish I was a young man—or at least younger," Jake amended with a deep laugh.

He caught the way both Jake and his sister were looking at him. As if they expected him to ride after the woman. He saw no reason to pretend that he had no interest in going for a ride with the woman. After all, she was Elena's teacher and she was the reason that he and Elena were out riding in the first place.

"We'd better get going if we want to catch up with her," Daniel commented.

The next moment, he kicked his stallion's flanks and horse and rider were off in a gallop.

Elena followed suit, quickly catching up to her brother and riding alongside of him. The second they had left the stable— and the owner—behind, she asked Daniel, surprised, "You want to catch up with Ms. Stewart?"

He had a change of heart about honesty and said, "No, I don't. But I got the feeling that if we didn't get out of there,

Jake was going to go on talking until both our ears fell off in self-defense."

Elena laughed. He caught himself thinking that he'd missed that sound. Again he realized that he was in Shania Stewart's debt.

"I thought he liked keeping to himself instead of talking to people," Elena said.

"Obviously you brought out the talkative side of the man," Daniel said, teasing his sister.

"Anyone could see that he was talking to you, not to me," Elena pointed out.

And then, as the situation hit them—the teasing remarks they were exchanging as well as the banter that was going back and forth—they both laughed this time, their voices blending.

Just the way they used to, years back.

"So," Daniel asked as the laughter died away, "where to?"

Elena glanced at her brother. Despite the exchange that had just taken place, she was surprised. "You're leaving it up to me?"

"Why not?" he asked. "We've got the whole day ahead of us if we want and you're just as capable of picking a direction for us to go in as I am."

An amused expression settled in on Elena's face as she slanted a look in his direction. Daniel thought that his sister looked almost devious as she asked, "How about north?"

Part of her waited for Daniel to negate her choice and pick one of the three other directions. Another part of her hoped that he wouldn't.

"All right," he said with a nod of his head. "North it is."

And then he kicked his heels into the horse's flanks as he pointed the animal northward.

The idyllically quiet morning surrounded her like a familiar old soothing melody. The silence was occasionally interrupted by the chirping sound of birds calling to one another.

If she listened very hard, Shania thought, she could make

out rustling, signifying some small creature that was scurrying to escape possible danger from a predator. Or maybe just foraging for food.

For the most part, though, there was a harmony about the sounds that were around her and she felt at one with the elements and nature.

Though she rarely had the opportunity to do it, Shania liked going out for a ride in the early hours. Liked pretending that she was the only one around for miles.

Not that she had any desire to become a hermit for any true length of time, but a little "alone time" once in a while could be a really nice thing, she thought now with a smile.

She couldn't help thinking that this was a real change from living in Houston. Houston was all movement and chaos while Forever moved at a far slower, more tranquil pace. It was funny how quickly she had acclimated to both ways of life, Shania realized. When she'd lived in Houston, she couldn't imagine going back to live in a little town like Forever. And now that she was here, she caught herself wondering at times how she had managed to survive all the hustle and bustle that existed within Houston.

Shania sighed. *Stop it!*

She was thinking too much. She had come out here to get away not just from all the demands that she had to deal with, but from her own thoughts as well. She needed to empty her head.

She needed to—

Shania slowed her horse down a little as she cocked her head, listening.

Were those hoofbeats in the distance? And not just hoofbeats that belonged to one horse. From the sound of it, she was certain that she made out the sound of two horses.

Was that—? She crossed her fingers and hoped she was right.

Those hoofbeats were definitely growing louder because they were coming in her direction.

She turned her horse toward the sound of the approaching horse beats.

And then, within less than a minute, she smiled as the two riders came into view.

Shania felt validated that Daniel Tallchief had taken her advice.

CHAPTER NINE

BUTTERSCOTCH, THE MARE that Shania had rented from McReedy's stable early this morning, seemed anxious to resume her fast pace. Shania could feel the horse shifting impatiently beneath her, ready to run.

She leaned in closer to the mare, patting Butterscotch's sleek neck.

"What's the matter, girl?" she asked in a low, soothing voice. "Don't you want to have a little company on this ride?"

The mare shifted a little more, as if she understood what was being asked. Shania knew that all she had to do was give the horse her lead and the mare would take off. But she continued to remain still where she was, waiting for the deputy and his sister to come closer.

She told herself it wouldn't be polite just to take off after seeing them approaching, but the truth of it was that Shania didn't mind having a little company herself. And she was curious to find out what, if anything, the deputy would talk about with her. She had been in Daniel's company and she had certainly been in Elena's company, but she had never been exposed to both of the family members at the same time. She was rather intrigued to find out how the two played off one another in a social situation.

Better, she hoped, than she'd initially assumed they did. Especially now that Elena had settled down and started applying herself.

Though she did try to observe both riders as they came closer, if she was really being honest with herself, Shania would have had to admit that her eyes were drawn toward Daniel.

He cut a magnificent figure astride the palomino, moving as if he and the stallion were one. Daniel's slightly unruly straight black hair was flying behind him and he made her think of a warrior on the move. Watching his strong, wide shoulders and his obviously trim body approaching created an electric current that zipped right through her, making every single inch of her feel alive and alert.

Shania did her best to look unaffected, but she wasn't all that sure she succeeded.

"The stallion's nice, too," she whispered to Butterscotch.

As if in response, although still shifting, Butterscotch seemed to be just a little less agitated, but it could have just been her imagination.

"Hi," Shania called out to Daniel and Elena when the two were almost right up to her. "Nice day for a morning ride."

"Yes, it is," Daniel answered. His voice sounded even more formal to her than it usually did.

"I didn't want to come," Elena told her teacher. And then a shy expression emerged on her face. "I wanted to stay in bed, but my brother thought the fresh air would do me some good."

"Smart man, your brother," Shania commented. Deftly, she turned Butterscotch around so that all three horses and riders were facing in the same direction. "So, did you have any particular destination in mind?" she asked the pair, her eyes moving from Elena to the teenager's brother.

Instead of answering, Elena turned in her saddle and looked toward her brother, waiting for him to say something.

Put on the spot, Daniel shrugged. "Wherever you're going is fine with us."

Now that he was up closer to her, he saw that Shania had no makeup on whatsoever. Another woman would have looked plain or washed out, he thought. But Elena's teacher looked positively radiant and glowing. She made him think of one of those flowers that unexpectedly pop up on a cactus, blooming against all odds and ultimately drawing all attention to itself without actually meaning to.

And then, almost as an afterthought, Daniel's eyes were drawn to something else. Shania had a picnic basket tied against her horse's saddle horn.

She was meeting someone, he thought, raising his eyes to hers.

"Won't Elena and I be interrupting something?" he asked her, not even sure he should be saying that.

Shania looked at him, a bemused expression on her face. "Interrupting?" she repeated, waiting for him to explain.

Daniel nodded at the picnic basket. "Looks like you packed for a picnic," he pointed out.

She'd completely forgotten about that. Glancing down at the basket, she realized how that had to look. "Oh, right. I thought eating out in the open instead of huddled over paperwork at my desk might be a nice change," she told the deputy. "But I have a habit of always packing more than I need in case my appetite suddenly gets out of hand because of the invigorating ride—or I run into someone I know," she added with a grin, looking at Elena. "There's more than enough to share if you two get hungry," she promised them.

Daniel glanced at his sister. Judging by Elena's expression, she looked totally open to the idea of joining up and going riding with her teacher. And, he supposed if he was being completely honest about it, the idea of sharing a ride and some lunch with the beautiful teacher was not without its appeal.

"I guess you've twisted my arm," Daniel told Elena's teacher.

"My brother means yes," Elena told Shania. The girl looked really pleased about the whole thing.

"You two up for a brisk canter or would you rather just go slow?" Shania asked them, looking from one to the other.

Daniel's eyes met hers. "I never go slow," he informed her.

He saw amusement curve the corners of her generous mouth. Something within him responded, but he shut it down.

Been there, done that. Won't go there again, Daniel thought.

"A brisk canter it is," Shania agreed.

Then, as her eyes met Elena's, Shania kicked her heels in Butterscotch's flanks. Instantly, horse and rider took off.

Elena made a gleeful sound as she quickly joined her teacher.

Daniel lost no time keeping pace.

"Wow, you really kept up," Elena cried in admiration when all three of them finally reined in their horses to a full stop an hour later.

Winded, the girl slid off her pinto and sank straight down to the ground.

She appeared surprised and pleased when Shania did the same, sitting down right beside her.

"Were you expecting me to fall off?" Shania asked her with a breathless laugh.

"My sister might have had some doubts, but I knew you wouldn't," Daniel told her, his voice rumbling from deep within his muscular chest.

Holding on to his horse's reins, the deputy joined the other two already on the ground, sitting down cross-legged.

Shania regarded the deputy, wondering if he was pulling her leg or if he was being serious with her. For now, she gave him the benefit of the doubt.

"And why were you so sure I wouldn't fall off?" she asked Daniel.

"Your form," the deputy said simply. "You look like you were born riding," he told her, recalling what she'd said when they first came up to her.

"It was my first memory," she admitted. "My dad put me on a horse before I could walk."

"By yourself?" Elena asked her, surprised that a parent would do something so careless.

Shania laughed, but it wasn't a belittling sound. "No, he got on right behind me. My dad didn't let me sit on a horse by myself until I was three, even though I begged him, telling him I could do it and pouting when he didn't trust me.

"And even when he *did* put me on the horse by myself, he walked right next to the horse, holding on to me until he felt confident that I was old enough to do it all by myself." She grinned, remembering. "I was so excited," she confided.

Her eyes were sparkling, Daniel noticed, intrigued and mesmerized by the sight. Again, he forced himself to mentally pull back.

"So, do you come out often, Ms. Stewart?" Elena asked.

Shania smiled. "Whenever I get the chance—which lately winds up being about once a week—if I'm lucky. Usually on Sunday morning," she told the teen. Her smile turned nostalgic as she recalled another time. "I used to go riding with my cousin."

"Why did you stop riding with her?" Daniel asked, curious.

"Wynona got married and now she has other priorities." Her cousin had promised to go riding with her again, but somehow it never worked out and after a while, they stopped making arrangements that wound up falling through. "After a while, horseback riding kind of fell by the wayside."

Sharing something so personal made her feel a little uncomfortable. Looking toward the picnic basket, Shania changed the subject.

"So, is anyone hungry?" she asked Elena and the deputy.

"Yes," Elena said with enthusiasm. Then, self-conscious, she toned it down a little. "I guess." Pausing, the teen asked, "What do you have?"

"Well, why don't we see?" Shania suggested with a grin.

She rose to her feet and began to remove the ropes that held the picnic basket in place against the saddle horn.

"How about you, Deputy?" Shania asked, putting the basket down on the ground. "Are you hungry?"

"I'm fine," he demurred.

Daniel assumed that while whatever Elena's teacher had packed might be enough to split between two people as long as neither was very hungry, he sincerely doubted that she could have packed enough to adequately feed three people.

"Yes," Shania murmured, her eyes meeting his. "I know that. But are you hungry?"

Her unexpected teasing response caught him completely off guard. The next second, Daniel cleared his throat as if that could somehow negate the entire exchange, making it unnecessary for him to address it at all.

When he finally did speak, it was in reference to Shania's inquiry about his appetite. "No, thanks," he answered.

She pretended not to hear him. "I've got a small tablecloth in here," she told Elena. "Want to help me spread it out?"

"Sure!"

Elena was already peering into the basket, ready to take the tablecloth out and spread it on the ground the second that her teacher nodded.

Once the tablecloth was taken out and spread on the ground, Daniel casually glanced inside the basket to see just how much Shania had—or hadn't—brought.

He was surprised to see that the basket was filled to the top with wrapped sandwiches, several cans of root beer and, when those were taken out, what looked like a covered tray of brownies on the bottom. The brownies, judging by the aroma, appeared to have been baked fresh early that morning.

As Shania took out the brownies, he raised a quizzical eyebrow in her direction.

It wasn't all that difficult to guess his unspoken question.

"Yes, I'm a closet baker," she admitted. "It relaxes me."

She didn't bother preparing anything out of the ordinary for herself because she felt her time could be better spent otherwise. But today, she had a hunch, would be different.

"I don't usually get a chance to indulge in my passion, but I decided that there was no reason not to go all out today, so I decided to make my mint chip brownies. You don't have to eat them if you don't want to," she added. "I promise you won't hurt my feelings," she assured them.

"I love mint chip." Elena took a deep breath. "They smell absolutely heavenly," she told her teacher, then asked hopefully, "Can I have the brownies first?"

"You're welcome to the whole tray if you want it," Shania told the teenager. "But I suggest you have one of the sandwiches first."

She noticed that Daniel had quietly reached for one of the sandwiches and was carefully unwrapping it now. Good, she'd won him over. The man was much too rigid. He needed to unwind, not just for Elena's sake, but for his own.

"I think the root beer is probably still cold," she said by way of inviting him to indulge himself.

"It can be warm," Daniel replied. "As long as it's wet, that's my only requirement."

"Then I'd say you're in luck," Shania answered with a warm laugh.

She took a sandwich herself and proceeded to unwrap it.

He waited until the woman had taken a bite of her sandwich before he finally ventured to ask her a question that had occurred to him the moment the tablecloth had been taken out.

"What made you pack so much food in the basket if you were just going to go riding by yourself?" he asked.

Shania regarded him quietly for a moment. He noticed that although she didn't speak, the woman's eyes said volumes.

"Let's just say I had a premonition," she finally admitted.

Still eating, Elena looked at her teacher, clearly surprised. "You *knew* we were coming?"

That sounded a little too pompous and self-assured, Shania thought. "Let's just say that I *hoped* you and your brother were going for a ride this morning."

Finished with his sandwich, Daniel picked up a napkin and wiped his fingers. "What if we didn't come?" he asked.

She glanced at the food that still remained next to the basket. Picking up another sandwich, she quietly pushed it toward Daniel. She was certain that the man had room for more.

"Then I wouldn't have to make dinner," she answered with a smile.

Daniel shook his head. "Got an answer for everything, don't you?"

"I'm a high school teacher," she answered simply. "I'm supposed to have an answer for everything."

There was humor in her eyes as she responded to his statement.

Daniel laughed softly to himself, then let her answer go. Instead, he changed the subject just as she had done earlier.

"So, how do you like being back?" he asked. "You originally came from here, didn't you?" he asked, making sure that he had gotten his facts straight.

"I did and to answer your question, I like it very much," she replied.

"You're going to stay, right?" Elena asked, trying not to appear apprehensive. She'd decided that she had grown to like this unusual teacher, so much so that she didn't want to see her leave.

"Barring something earth-shattering happening," Shania answered whimsically, "I think so."

"Something earth-shattering?" Daniel questioned. What did she mean by that? He felt it was an odd choice of words.

"You can't count on things being written in stone," Shania explained. "Things have a way of changing. I never thought I'd wind up in Houston to begin with. I had a home, parents who loved me and a cousin who lived with us who was more like a sister. Everything was wonderful," she said. "Until it wasn't," she concluded philosophically. "That's when I learned that nothing was forever—no matter what the town was named," she added with an ironic smile.

"Why did you come back?" Daniel asked.

"Trying to get rid of me?" she asked him, amused.

"Trying to understand why you'd leave Houston," he countered. He opened another can of root beer. "There're more opportunities there."

"Agreed. But not the one I was looking for," Shania told him, looking at his sister. "Let's just say that Wynona and I wanted to pay it forward. Brownies?" she asked brightly, holding the tray up to Elena and her brother and once more changing the subject.

CHAPTER TEN

"THIS WAS FUN," Elena announced out of the blue.

Daniel had to admit that he was totally surprised by his sister's reaction. The impatient, hostile teenager he had been living with for the last few months had suddenly receded into the shadows and the sister he loved and would have willingly done absolutely anything for had, at least for the moment, made a reappearance in his life.

"I'm glad to hear that," Daniel told her as they helped finish cleaning up the picnic they'd shared with Elena's teacher and got ready to return to the stable.

Elena cocked her head to get a better view of her brother's expression. "Can we do it again?" she asked.

That question was an even bigger surprise in his estimation.

"Sure." Having packed away the tablecloth, leftover wrappers and cans into Shania's basket, he handed it back to the woman. The latter proceeded to tie the basket to the saddle horn again. Turning toward his sister, Daniel told her, "Next Sunday."

Smiling broadly, Elena barely contained herself as, eyes dancing, she in turn faced her teacher. "Will you come, too?"

Observing this from the sidelines, it was difficult to say which of them was more stunned by Elena's question, her teacher or him.

Probably him, Daniel thought. Now that he took a closer look at the woman, aside from being stunning, Elena's teacher didn't look as if anything could really faze her.

"Don't put Ms. Stewart on the spot, Ellie," he cautioned his sister. Though Shania looked as if everything just rolled off her back, Daniel didn't want to take a chance that Elena's request might cause waves.

Shania put a stop to it before it went too far—the "it" being Daniel's misunderstanding of how she'd react to his sister's question.

It was sweet of the deputy to come to her aid, Shania thought, but it really wasn't necessary.

"She's not putting me on the spot, Deputy," Shania told him. "And if you don't mind my company," she continued, then turned toward Elena to complete what she was saying, "I'd love to come. Riding out here at this time by myself is peaceful, but I have to admit that there's such a thing as *too* peaceful," she confided, lowering her voice as if she was sharing a secret with the girl. And then she really smiled broadly at her student. "I would *love* some company."

"Great!" Elena declared like a proud arbitrator who had just negotiated a new treaty acceptable to all parties involved.

But Shania didn't see this as a done deal—not just yet.

"It *is* all right with you, isn't it?" she asked Daniel in a low voice when Elena doubled back to get her hat before they rode back. "I didn't hear you agree," she explained. Then, because he seemed to hesitate, she came to the conclusion that he was looking for a way out. "I can make up an excuse to beg off. Heaven knows I've got enough work to do to make it sound believable."

For just a single second, Daniel wavered. But by the end of that split second, he realized that he *liked* the idea of going out like this again with Elena and her teacher. It was casual. It was safe. And he got to be around Shania without any accompanying awkwardness—or any expectations on either one of their parts.

"No need to tell her anything," he replied, keeping his voice as low as hers. "Going out for a ride again'll be nice."

"What are you two whispering about?" Elena asked as she rejoined them, her hat firmly planted on her head.

Shania never missed a beat as she replied, "Your brother expressed his doubts about my having made those mint brownies from scratch, so I recited the recipe I used."

It amazed Daniel how quick Shania was on her feet and how easily she came up with a believable lie. He wondered if it was a skill that came from practice and if she did that with any sort of regularity.

There were layers to this woman that bore looking into.

The next moment Daniel reminded himself that he had a lot of responsibilities. The last thing he needed was to take on a new "hobby" that had no future to it and that could only lead him down a path he shouldn't have a reason to follow.

"Daniel's not very trusting," Elena said, referring to Shania's narrative about telling Daniel what ingredients were in the brownies she had made. Elena swung herself into the pinto's saddle.

Responding to what his sister had just said, Daniel couldn't resist saying, "It runs in the family."

Elena's eyes briefly met his. She sniffed. "I don't know what you're talking about," she informed Daniel, then turned her attention back to her teacher. "Home, Ms. Stewart?"

"Home, Ms. Tallchief," Shania responded, doing her best to suppress a grin.

A gleeful laugh escaped her lips as Elena kicked her heels into the Pinto's flanks.

Her horse took off. Shania was right beside her, riding as fast as she could go.

Elena pouted a little because she couldn't seem to pass her teacher by. But on the other hand, she was pleased that the woman had turned out to be so skilled and capable on—and off—a horse. That meant, Elena thought, that her brother had probably met his match.

At least for now, Elena amended.

The three of them got back to the stable all too soon in Daniel's opinion. Reflecting on it, it seemed rather incredible to him that they covered the same amount of distance coming and going and yet it felt as if going had taken far longer than getting back to their starting point.

They caught the stable owner just in time. Jake looked as if he was about to go to the diner to get an early lunch and appeared a little disgruntled that he had to put it off now until he had settled up with the returning customers.

"I see you found each other," he commented, his squinty eyes moving over each of them.

"We did," Shania replied pleasantly. Then, picking up on the man's impatient body language, she got straight to business. "How much do I owe you, Mr. McReedy?"

"Got your bills right here," he told her, nodding at the bulletin board on the far wall.

There were three separate receipts pinned on it and he took off one of them to hand to her.

Daniel was slightly confused. "I thought you wanted to wait until we got back before you did the calculations."

"If you stay out for more than two hours, there's a flat rate," Jake answered. "It encourages return business."

She thought it spoke in the man's favor to offer deals, but it really wasn't that necessary, either. "It's not like you've got a lot of competition," Shania pointed out.

Jake flushed a little, as if he hadn't really thought the matter out that far. The stable owner shrugged awkwardly. "Still no reason to gouge folks. Miss Joan taught me that."

"Miss Joan's been in business longer than you?" Elena asked him in surprise.

Jake laughed, some of his awkwardness abating. "That woman's been in business just a little less longer than God."

"Better not let her hear you say that, Jake," Daniel warned the older man seriously, "or your days'll be numbered—and there's nothing I can do to help you."

"That old woman's not above the law," Jake reminded him nervously.

But the expression on Daniel's face said otherwise, which just made Jake that much more nervous.

"Oh, she's above a lot of things," Daniel told the stable owner. He didn't particularly care to hear any disrespectful remarks aimed at Miss Joan.

Daniel glanced over toward Shania and then reached for the receipt she had in her hand. "Why don't I just take care of that?" he suggested, then looked at Jake. "Is there a discount for three receipts?"

Jake's small dark eyes looked like marbles as they rolled back and forth between Daniel and the high school teacher.

"You two aren't related, now, are you?" Jake asked them.

This time Daniel didn't bother putting the man on. Instead he gave Jake a very firm "No."

"Then no, there's no discount for three receipts," Jake answered.

Shania reached to take back the receipt that the deputy had managed to slip out of her hand.

"I can pay my own way, Deputy Tallchief," she told him.

But Daniel retained possession of the receipt, holding it above his head. Shania wasn't able to reach for it.

"Nobody said you couldn't," he replied. "You shared your lunch with us, the least I can do is pay for your riding time."

It was obvious that Jake clearly didn't care who won the debate as long as he was paid by somebody. As he listened to the debate, his stomach started to rumble in protest.

Jake sighed impatiently. "This going to take much longer?"

Multiplying Shania's receipt by three, Daniel handed the

stable owner the amount owed for all three rides. "Nope, not long at all, Jake," he answered the man.

Money in hand, Jake counted it quickly. He smiled in satisfaction, his grin showing the space between two of his lower teeth before he suddenly remembered it was there. His lips quickly closed over it like a curtain coming down on an unplanned performance.

"Nice doing business with you folks," Jake said, nodding at them. "Come again," he called after the three people as they were leaving his stable.

"See you tomorrow, Ms. Stewart," Elena said, raising her voice as they walked out. They were heading in two different directions.

Shania paused just long enough to look at the girl. Her eyes smiled at Elena as she said, "I look forward to it."

And then she hurried over toward where she had parked her vehicle.

Watching the woman get into her car, Daniel forced himself to start moving. He opened the door on the driver's side of his vehicle, aware that Elena had already opened hers.

"So things are going well between you and Ms. Stewart." It wasn't a question on Daniel's part, but an assumption.

Daniel avoided his sister's eyes as he got into the car. Elena had already climbed in on her side.

He could feel Elena's eyes on him, as if she was debating whether or not to answer his question or just ignore it.

She went with the former, asking a question of her own. "Yeah, why?"

Daniel played along, even though they both knew why he'd ask her the question. "Well, a few weeks ago, you looked like you were ready to spit nails at the woman because she was giving you too much homework and trying to make you dig deep into yourself."

Elena waved dismissively at her brother's explanation. "That's just your imagination."

"Pretty sure it was more than that," he said. "I was just wondering what changed between the two of you."

"Nothing." He heard a defensive note reentering his sister's voice. "I just decided that it's smart to be smart. Anything wrong with that?"

Daniel allowed himself a small smile. He decided that Shania Stewart was nothing short of a miracle worker.

"Not a thing in the world," he replied. He glanced at her, then looked back at the near empty road. "Would I be ruining something in your opinion if I told you that I was proud of you?"

Elena shrugged, doing her best to look indifferent to his words of praise. "You don't have to say you're proud of me."

"I know I don't have to," Daniel answered. "I *want* to," he said, stressing the middle word. "You know me well enough to know I don't do or say things because I 'have' to."

If anything, Elena seemed to grow a little stiffer. The look his sister slanted at him was one he couldn't quite fathom.

And then she finally said by way of a rebuttal to her brother's argument, "I don't know about that. You're taking care of me."

What was at the bottom of all this? he couldn't help wondering. "Again, it's because I *want* to," Daniel told her.

Elena sighed. "Uh-huh."

It was obvious that she was in the mood to discount what he'd just said.

Daniel decided to drop the subject for now and turned to another one. He glanced at her, then said, "Thanks for going riding with me."

Surprised, Elena looked at him. And then the teen suddenly laughed. "I figured if I didn't, you'd probably tie me up and *make* me come with you."

"Well, as it turned out, luckily, that wasn't necessary," he said. "And I think you'll agree that it all turned out for the best—like you getting along better with Ms. Stewart," he couldn't help throwing in again, hoping this time to get his sister to respond the way he hoped she would.

"Yeah, she's all right," Elena answered, adopting a lofty tone. And then she suddenly turned the tables on her brother by telling him, "You sure seemed like you liked her."

Caught off guard, it took Daniel a second to pull his thoughts together. The one thing he knew was that he wasn't about to get pulled into *that* discussion.

Instead, he said, "I like most people."

He didn't expect his sister to hoot at the response. "Yeah, right. What's that fairy tale about that puppet whose nose grew whenever he told a lie?" she asked him innocently.

"Why are you asking me about that?"

She pressed her lips together before she answered his question. "'Cause yours is about to break your truck's windshield."

Unable to maintain a serious expression any longer, Elena grinned from ear to ear, tickled by the image she'd just painted.

She fully expected her brother to vehemently deny her observation. When she heard him laugh instead, she was at first surprised—and then she had to admit that his reaction pleased her a great deal.

They laughed together, something that was thankfully becoming a more common occurrence.

Shania walked into her house and was immediately greeted by an extremely energetic Belle. In her enthusiasm, the German shepherd came perilously close to knocking her down.

"I wasn't gone *that* long, girl," Shania protested, laughing.

But the amount of energy the dog was incorporating into her welcome told Shania that perhaps she'd misjudged the time element—at least as far as Belle was concerned.

"I forgot, you can't tell time very well, can you?" Shania laughed as she rubbed the dog's head. Wynona had once told her that an hour seemed like a day and a day was like an eternity to the dog.

"You know, maybe next time, I'll take you along with me. But you're going to have to do a lot of running to keep up," she warned the dog. Belle barked. "Maybe that'll do you some good," Shania decided. "I know you would have liked who I ran into. Elena, one of my students," she told the dog, then added, "And her brother." She cast a side glance at her pet as she went to refill Belle's water dish and get the dog something to eat.

"You've already met him. It's that deputy you gave a bath to with that big, sloppy tongue of yours," she told Belle.

There was no way in the world the dog could have understood her, Shania reasoned. But Belle seemed to get really enthusiastic when she "heard" Daniel's description.

"You know, Belle, anyone would think that you have a crush on that man," she said with a laugh. "Well, he's all yours, girl."

Belle circled her several times, then plopped down on her back right in front of her.

Shania sank down beside the animal and began petting her. "Rehearsing for when you run into him next time?"

Belle barked.

"I thought so," Shania answered.

CHAPTER ELEVEN

IN SHANIA'S OPINION, as she replayed it, it seemed like an unusual request. But then Miss Joan was an unusual woman by everyone's standards. Still, the owner of the diner had never sent one of her waitresses to ask her to come to the diner after school had let out for the day before.

Until today.

Even so, Shania had demurred at first, citing the fact that she was holding a PSAT class at the high school after hours.

Surprisingly, Violet the waitress seemed prepared for that. She had obviously been coached by Miss Joan for exactly this eventuality. Violet told Shania that Miss Joan wanted her to come whenever she was finished with the class.

Cornered, Shania didn't feel she could really beg off after that. However, she didn't rush through her class, either. Instead, she fielded all the questions that the small group of students in the after-hours class wanted to ask.

Once the last student had left the room, only then did she make her way to the diner. It was a few minutes after five before she was able to show up. The diner was about half full. The dinner crowd hadn't begun to show up in earnest yet.

The minute she walked in, Shania made her way straight to

the counter. Now that her class was over, her curiosity finally got the better of her. Why did the woman want to see her?

Try as she might, she couldn't come up with a single reason.

Standing behind the counter, Miss Joan was just pouring some fresh coffee into a cup when Shania reached her.

Miss Joan certainly didn't act as if anything was wrong, she thought. But then, Miss Joan was known to play poker regularly.

"You wanted to see me?" Shania asked the woman. In her opinion this wasn't the time for small talk and she didn't bother with any.

"I wouldn't have sent Violet to fetch you if I didn't," Miss Joan replied, smoothly moving the cup and saucer closer to her.

"About?" Shania asked, curbing her impatience.

What was going on here? When Violet had sought her out, giving her Miss Joan's message, the waitress had made it sound urgent. Yet Miss Joan looked and acted as if she had all the time in the world.

Instead of answering her question, Miss Joan nodded at the empty stool Shania was standing next to.

"Sit," the older woman told her. "Take a load off. Have some coffee."

Since it was obvious that she wasn't about to get the answer to her question until she complied with Miss Joan's instructions, Shania did as the woman said.

She sat down, loosened her coat and had a sip of coffee. Once she did, Shania looked into the woman's eyes and asked, "*Now* will you tell me what I'm doing here?"

"Sitting and having a cup of coffee," Miss Joan answered as if that should have been very obvious to her.

This *was* a game to the woman, Shania decided. She had no recourse but to go along with whatever this was until it played out. "Violet made it sound urgent," Shania stressed.

"Violet has a tendency to be overly dramatic," Miss Joan answered, waving a thin hand at the idea that this was an urgent meeting.

And then the woman gave her one of her famous long, penetrating looks. The kind Harry, her husband, swore could get a hardened criminal to make a full confession even if he was about to get away with the crime.

It seemed like an eternity later before Miss Joan finally spoke. When she did, she didn't say anything that Shania had been expecting.

"I haven't seen you in a while." The hazel eyes looked at her intently. "Not since Wynona's wedding."

Shania couldn't help thinking that something was definitely up. Miss Joan had never expressed a desire to have her come by before.

At a loss, she made something up. "I've been meaning to drop by the diner, but there never seems to be enough time. I've been kind of busy, what with teaching and holding those extra study classes after hours."

Although everything she was saying was true, Shania couldn't help feeling as if she was coming up with excuses. Excuses that Miss Joan saw right through.

"Uh-huh," the older woman murmured. Probing hazel eyes swept over her again. "How are you holding up?" Miss Joan asked without warning.

"Holding up?" Shania repeated. She had no idea what Miss Joan was really asking her. "Holding up" sounded as if she was referring to some sort of a crisis and there wasn't any.

"Well, Wynona's moved out of the house and she's busy starting a new life while you're going on with your old one," Miss Joan said.

"I'm all right," Shania replied haltingly, her voice sounding rather tinny to her own ear.

"How about the baby?" Miss Joan asked, the woman's eyes still pinning her down. "You must be excited about the little one coming."

For a second, Shania could only stare at the woman. She knew that Wynona had wanted to keep the news under wraps for a few more weeks, which meant that she hadn't told anyone else. That included Miss Joan.

Yet the woman knew.

Shania suppressed a sigh. She wasn't about to waste time asking Miss Joan how she'd found out about Wynona's pregnancy. It was almost a given that Miss Joan *always* knew everything before anyone else did.

In this case, probably before Wynona knew.

She was about to give the woman a vague response when she saw Miss Joan looking around her shoulder toward the door.

It was too much to hope for that someone had come in to divert the woman's attention away from her, Shania thought.

But, even so, Miss Joan definitely looked as if someone had caught her interest.

If whoever had just walked in came over to engage the woman in a conversation, she might even be able to make good her escape. Shania crossed her fingers.

But before she could even attempt to slide off her stool, she heard the person Miss Joan was looking at ask almost the same question she just had when she'd walked in.

"The sheriff said you wanted to see me, Miss Joan. Here I am. What's the problem?" Daniel asked the woman before he realized that he was standing one empty stool over from Shania.

Shania turned and their eyes met. Somewhere, she could have sworn she heard electricity crackle.

"I didn't say there was a problem," Miss Joan informed the deputy matter-of-factly. She shook her head. "You'd think that someone like the sheriff would relay messages correctly."

"What message should he have relayed?" Daniel asked her, playing along.

Miss Joan lifted her thin shoulders and let them drop in a careless shrug.

"Doesn't matter," she informed him crisply. "The problem's been resolved." She filled another cup with coffee and moved that cup and saucer toward the empty stool. The one that was right next to Shania's. "Why don't you have this cup of coffee on the house as payment for your time, Deputy?" Miss Joan suggested.

Daniel looked down at the cup, appearing just the slightest bit amused. "You know I can't accept any kind of a payment for services rendered, Miss Joan."

"But you didn't render any services," Miss Joan pointed out.

He tried again. "Even so—"

"Just sit down and drink the damn coffee, Tallchief," Miss Joan ordered. "Didn't anyone ever teach you not to argue with your elders? Take a page out of her book," she said, jerking a thumb at Shania. Then, because the deputy still continued standing there, she asked Daniel, "You do know how to sit, don't you, Deputy? Just bend your knees and let gravity do the rest." Seemingly satisfied that he would do as he was told, Miss Joan was already moving away. "I'll be back in a few minutes to see if either of you needs a refill."

Shania leaned her head toward him as Daniel took his seat. "I think we were just threatened."

"I don't 'think,'" he responded. "I know. That woman gets stranger every year." He took a long sip of the coffee Miss Joan had ordered him to drink. "Lucky thing she makes good coffee."

"Right, because that's the only thing Miss Joan's got going for her," Shania replied, glancing around the diner with an amused smile.

Tempting aromas were wafting out from the kitchen.

"I didn't mean for it to come out like that," Daniel amended. "The woman's got a good heart." There were tons of examples to back that statement up. "But you can't argue that she is rather unique in her approach to things."

Shania laughed. "'Unique' is putting it rather mildly." Following his example, she took a long sip from her coffee cup, then tentatively set it down. "Why do you think she summoned us?"

It was definitely not a coincidence that the woman had asked both of them here at what turned out to be the same time.

His shrug was noncommittal. "Beats me." And he knew that trying to figure it out without the woman's input was just a complete waste of time. "Nobody knows what's on that woman's mind. I'm just happy she's on our side."

"Our side?" Shania repeated, thinking that was rather an odd way for Daniel to phrase it.

Belatedly, Daniel realized his error. "The side of the good guys," he told Shania. "I didn't mean to make it sound as if you and I were on a side."

Now he really had her wondering. Shania studied the man next to her. "We're *not* on the side of the good guys?" she asked him.

"Yes, we are. We're just not there in the full sense of the word." Daniel sighed. His tongue was getting tangled up—just like his thoughts. "This isn't coming out right, is it?"

"Not even close," Shania told him. She made no effort to suppress her amusement. "Don't worry about it," she counseled. "Miss Joan does have that sort of effect on people. She can literally make you forget how to talk."

"You, too?" Daniel asked, surprised.

Smiling, she inclined her head. "Definitely me, too. Not the best thing for a high school physics and math teacher to admit, but there you have it," Shania told him with a self-depreciating shrug.

He supposed he might as well take advantage of this impromptu meeting. "Well, since we ran into one another—" Daniel began.

"Or so it looks," she couldn't help adding, glancing at the far end of the counter toward Miss Joan.

The woman looked as if she was busy slicing up a fresh apple pie, but Shania was convinced that Miss Joan was watching their every move—and reading lips since they were sitting too far away from her to allow the woman to hear them.

But Daniel wasn't looking at Miss Joan, he was looking at

Shania. Somehow, he'd allowed himself to be distracted and reined himself in.

"What do you mean?" he asked.

But Shania shook her head. Maybe she was just being paranoid.

"Never mind. Go ahead," Shania urged. "You were saying?"

It took him a second to collect his thoughts and remember what he wanted to tell her. "I just wanted to thank you for what you're doing with Elena."

Shania shook her head. "As much as I love being on the receiving end of gratitude," she told him, "I think you're making a mistake. I haven't done anything with Elena."

Was she just being modest, or was there something he was missing? "I don't understand."

Shania smiled. While she liked the fact that he felt grateful to her, she wanted Daniel to give credit where it was due.

"All I did was point Elena toward the books she needed to be reading and the work she needed to do in order to pass my courses. Your sister did all the rest. She showed up and did the work," Shania summarized. "And she's the one who continues to do the work, walking that extra mile with those practice PSAT tests.

"I could talk until I was blue in the face," Shania concluded. "If Elena didn't want to do it, if she didn't want to get those good grades and to get into college, then none of this would be happening. She's the one who deserves all the credit."

He hadn't expected this degree of modesty. Beautiful, smart and modest. Shania Stewart was a hell of a package. If he were inclined to get involved, she would be the kind of woman he'd pick. But getting involved wasn't on his agenda. He had made a vow to himself that that was never going to happen again. Besides, he had a job that took up all of his time and a sister to raise. Those two things filled a thirty-six-hour day and there was no time left over for anything else.

Still, he was not about to allow the teacher to shrug off the credit that he felt was so very obviously due to her.

"We've got a slight difference of opinion here," he informed her. "You're right in everything you just said—except for one thing."

He saw her lips twitch just a little, trying not to smile. "And that is?"

"If you hadn't been there to inspire Elena—and keep on inspiring her—none of this would be happening right now," Daniel told her simply. "Elena can be an extremely headstrong person—"

"Wonder where she gets that from?" Shania speculated. She stopped trying to hold back her smile.

He was losing his battle to ignore the effects of that smile, he thought, no matter how hard he tried.

"And nothing I said to her was getting through to her even though, until about four months ago, we had a pretty decent relationship." He shook his head as he thought back. "I still don't know what happened to change that," he admitted.

"She turned sixteen," Shania told him simply. She couldn't help being impressed by the fact that despite his busy life, Daniel really cared about his sister and the way she reacted to things. "Consider yourself lucky. Most girls rebel long before that. You were living on borrowed time."

He opened his mouth to argue with her, but then he shut it again. He knew Shania was right. And that made him doubly glad that Shania had happened into his sister's life.

"I guess maybe I was," he admitted.

That was the moment that Miss Joan picked to sweep back to them.

"The booth over in the corner just opened up," she announced.

When, instead of getting up, the two people sitting at the counter just looked at her, puzzled, Miss Joan sighed as she shook her head. "That means hustle your butts over there, you two."

Daniel remained where he was. "Why would we want to do that?"

"Because booths are more private than just sitting out in the open—or at the counter," Miss Joan informed them.

"All right," Shania agreed. Her voice trailed off as she waited for the woman to explain why that should mean anything to either of them at this particular time. They weren't talking about anything that was secretive.

Miss Joan fisted her hand at her waist, waiting for them to comply. When they didn't, she gave them an order. "Now, get on over there. Debbie will be there in a minute to take your order." And then, in case there was still any doubt about the matter, she looked pointedly into the deputy's eyes and said, "You're buying your sister's teacher dinner for all the hard work she's done with that girl." She waited a beat for her words to sink in. "No further questions, right?"

"Miss Joan, Daniel's on duty," Shania protested.

"He's on a dinner break," Miss Joan corrected. "I already cleared it with the sheriff, so don't argue with me. Either of you," she added sharply.

Shania turned toward Daniel. The last thing she wanted was to have him feel as if he was being strong-armed into buying her dinner. While she wouldn't mind having dinner with him, this wasn't the way she wanted it to happen.

"Listen, you don't have to—"

But Daniel cut her short. "No, Miss Joan's right—"

"I'm *always* right," the older woman agreed as she continued to observe the pair.

He could see that Shania was about to voice another protest. He tried to quiet her conscience. "You did put in a lot of work with Elena and the least I can do to show my gratitude is to buy you dinner—unless you'd rather I didn't."

Miss Joan sighed. "Do you two need a fire lit under you? You did the work, he's grateful. He wants to show his gratitude by buying you dinner. Enough said," she declared. "Now, go sit down in the booth."

Shania exchanged glances with the deputy. "Yes, ma'am," they both answered Miss Joan almost in unison.

Daniel allowed himself a smile as he walked behind Shania to the booth.

CHAPTER TWELVE

"I KNOW WHAT you're doing."

Unfazed by the knowing tone, Miss Joan casually looked over to her left to see that her step-grandson had entered the diner. Apparently Cash Taylor, one of Forever's two attorneys, had been quietly observing the interaction between her, the deputy and the high school teacher.

"Running the diner, the way I've always been, Cash," Miss Joan answered, turning back to what she was doing. "No big mystery there."

"That might be true," Cash allowed, making himself comfortable on the stool that Shania had just vacated. "But you're also playing cupid."

Miss Joan continued to keep her eyes on the two people she'd just sent off to have lunch in the rear booth.

"I don't know *what* you're talking about, boy," she informed him. Picking up a cloth, she began to clean a spot on the counter—and then continued rubbing it after the spot had disappeared.

Amused, Cash laughed at Miss Joan's denial. "I just put the pieces together. Not that they were so difficult to figure out. You sent for Shania and Daniel to come here, knowing that no one would ever ignore a summons from Miss Joan."

Miss Joan slanted a confident glance at her husband's grandson, a man she had watched turn into a fine human being after some rocky false starts. "Not if they know what's good for them."

"Exactly." Cash paused in case Miss Joan had anything to add. She didn't, so he asked her, "Now tell me *why* you're playing cupid with these two?" They seemed like an unlikely couple to him.

Miss Joan frowned impatiently. She didn't like having to explain herself.

"Because, Counselor," she informed him, "sometimes even smart people are too dumb to see what's right there in front of their noses. Now, instead of butting into my business, why don't you have some of Angel's fine rib-eye steak before you go home to that pretty little wife of yours?" It was more of an order than a suggestion.

Cash inclined his head and said in a pseudo-docile voice, "Yes, Grandma."

Miss Joan looked at him sharply. "You mind your mouth, boy. It might serve you well when you're in court, but I require a more respectful tone from the people who walk through those doors. Even from you."

Amused, Cash pressed his lips together, doing his best to suppress a grin. "Yes, ma'am."

Miss Joan nodded her approval. "That's better," she told him, then stopped wiping the counter.

Any other questions he might have had, Cash kept to himself.

"I think that woman would have made one hell of a fine general," Daniel told Shania once they had sat down at the booth.

"Because she's so good at ordering people around?" Shania guessed.

"There's that," Daniel agreed. "But I was actually thinking of the way Miss Joan seems to enjoy mapping out and implementing strategies."

Shania was about to ask him what he meant, but just then Debbie, their waitress, approached their booth. Debbie Wilcox had just recently graduated from high school and that was all due to Miss Joan. Hearing that the girl was about to take off, Miss Joan had kept after Debbie to stay in school.

When things disintegrated at home and her widowed stepfather had thrown her out, Miss Joan had taken her in. It was Miss Joan who had put a roof over the girl's head as well as hired her to work at the diner in order to put money into her pocket.

The woman made sure that the hours she gave Debbie worked around her school schedule. Although she made no attempt to remedy Debbie's home situation, there were rumors that Miss Joan had given Arthur Wilcox a severe tongue-lashing and the kind of dressing-down that left a permanent impression on a man for years to come.

Given all that, Shania was not about to discuss anything regarding Miss Joan in front of someone the woman had so obviously rescued. Instead of continuing her conversation with Daniel, she placed her order, asking for water and a salad.

"What?" she asked, catching the look on Daniel's face.

"A salad?" he asked her. His tone sounded almost mocking.

Shania raised her chin slightly. "Yes. What's wrong with a salad?"

He had a feeling Shania was ordering a salad because she didn't want to have him pay too much for her meal. "Nothing's wrong with it—if you happen to be a rabbit." He gave her a look that told her he was on to her—and that Miss Joan wasn't going to let her get away with it. "I don't think you're going to be able to get out of here ordering anything less than that steak that's on the menu."

Shania didn't need to look toward the counter to know that Miss Joan was keeping an eye on them. She could *feel* it.

"Fine," she relented. "I'll have the steak and mashed potatoes."

"How would you like your steak?" Debbie asked, making notations on her pad.

"Small," Shania answered. When Debbie looked at her in confusion, she amended, "Medium."

Smiling, Debbie nodded, then looked toward the deputy. "And you, sir?"

Daniel frowned. Being called "sir" by someone so young made him feel old before his time.

"Same thing," he told Debbie. "Except make mine rare— just barely dead."

"Got it," Debbie said, happily making the notation. Then, putting the pad back into her apron pocket, she collected the two menus and withdrew.

"It's healthier for you to eat a medium steak than a rare one," Shania told him.

"Not looking to be healthy," Daniel responded. "Just looking to enjoy what I'm eating."

Shania realized that Daniel probably thought she was lecturing him. Occupational habit. She was spending too much of her time with students, not enough with people her own age.

Taking a breath, Shania changed the subject—or actually brought the conversation back to what they were talking about before the waitress had appeared.

"What did you mean about Miss Joan mapping out a strategy?" Shania asked. "What strategy?"

Daniel looked at her. He'd thought it was obvious, but the woman wasn't playing dumb, Daniel realized. She really didn't see it. She didn't see what Miss Joan was doing.

It had to be wonderful to be that innocent, that unassuming, he couldn't help thinking. Heaven knew he was tired of being so suspicious of everything, and at times so paranoid, always looking for the hidden reasons behind people's actions.

This time, though, there was nothing to be suspicious about in the true sense of the word. He had a feeling that this was just a case of Miss Joan being Miss Joan, overseeing everyone's life in general.

Since Shania was looking at him, apparently still waiting for an answer, he said, "Did Miss Joan ask you to come to see her or did you just drop by?"

"As a matter of fact, she sent Violet as a messenger to ask me to come in. I'd been meaning to come see her," Shania confessed, readily shouldering the blame, "but, well, you know how it is." She shrugged. "Life kept getting in the way."

Daniel merely nodded. "Did she tell you why she asked you to come in?"

"Yes," she answered. "She wanted to know how I was doing on my own, now that Wynona wasn't at the house anymore."

He supposed he might as well follow the groundwork that Miss Joan had set up. It occurred to him that he didn't know all that much about this woman who had become so important in his sister's life.

"And that's it?"

Shania nodded. "That's it."

"Nothing more? She didn't ask anything else?" he prodded.

"If there was more, she didn't get a chance to ask because that was when she spotted you coming into the diner," Shania told him. "Once she saw you, her whole countenance changed."

That just confirmed what he thought. "I don't doubt it," he murmured.

Shania looked at him more closely. There was something in his voice that aroused her interest. "Would you like to let me in on it?"

"Well, Miss Joan called the sheriff and told him that she wanted to see me—same as you," Daniel pointed out. "Then, when I came in, all she said was that whatever reason she'd wanted to see me had taken care of itself. You heard her."

She also heard what the deputy wasn't saying. "You don't believe her."

His eyes met hers and she felt that same warm ripple traveling through her again. "Do you?"

She had a feeling she knew where he was going with this, but she discounted it because it seemed almost silly to think this way.

"It's Miss Joan," she reminded him. "Eccentricity is her middle name."

He laughed then. There was no point in pushing this—and he didn't want to embarrass Shania. If nothing else, the woman was a godsend for his sister.

"I always wondered what it was." Before he could say anything further about Miss Joan's possible middle name, Debbie returned with their dinners.

"My guess is that we'd better not leave anything on our plates unless we want Miss Joan scowling at us," Shania commented to Daniel once Debbie had put their dinners on the table and withdrawn again.

"Not a problem," Daniel assured her. "This smells even better than it usually does. I skipped lunch."

"Dedicated or dieting?" Shania asked. Realizing that it sounded as if she was being critical, she quickly said, "Not that you should. Diet I mean, not be dedicated. You should be that." She stopped herself, pressing her lips together as if to hold back any further torrent of words. She flushed as she raised her eyes toward Daniel. "I don't usually babble like this."

Daniel found the pink hue that had suddenly risen to her cheeks rather sweet. The next second, he realized that he was staring. Daniel forced himself to look away. "I hadn't noticed."

"Yes, you had," Shania contradicted. "But I think that it's very nice of you to pretend that you hadn't." When she heard Daniel laugh softly to himself, she asked him, "What's so funny?" before she could think to stop herself.

"I'm not accustomed to hearing the word 'nice' used to describe me," he admitted.

Didn't the man have any close friends? Someone to bolster him up when he was down on himself? "You're kidding."

The lopsided smile answered her before he did. "Something else I'm not known for."

She pretended that he was a student and she did a quick assessment of the man before her. "You know you're being very hard on yourself."

"Not hard," he contradicted. "Just honest."

She had no intention of letting this slide. If he *had* been one of her students, she would have done what she could to raise his spirits—or maybe it was his self-esteem that needed help.

"Well, *I* think you're nice—and you *do* have a sense of humor."

"If you say so," Daniel replied, not about to dispute the matter. He had a feeling that arguing with Shania would be pointless. "But just so you know, I'm not about to chuck my career and become a stand-up comedian."

She grinned at his words. "See, I told you that you had a sense of humor," she declared happily. The next moment, she looked down at what was left on her plate—just the denuded bone. "I am really glad you talked me into getting this. This steak is really good."

That wasn't his doing. "Angel really knows her way around a kitchen."

"Angel?" she repeated quizzically.

He nodded, then got that she probably didn't know about the woman. A lot of things had happened in the years that she had lived in Houston.

"Miss Joan has her cooking most of the meals. Angel's another one of Miss Joan's secret good deeds. Gabe found her unconscious in a car," he said, mentioning the other deputy who worked for the sheriff. Gabe was also the man who became Angel's husband. "There'd been an accident. When she woke up, she had no memory of who she was or how she got there. Miss Joan took her under that very large wing of hers. When it became obvious that Angel could work miracles in the kitchen, Miss Joan put her to work in the diner."

She appreciated Daniel filling her in on the things that she had missed while she'd been away. "Did Angel ever get her memory back?"

"She did," he recalled. "But she liked being useful and cooking, and she was so grateful to Miss Joan for all her help that she went on working for her at the diner even after she got married. And before you ask," he said, "the guy she married was the one who rescued her out of her car."

"And did her name really turn out to be Angel?" she asked.

"No," he answered, "but that's the name she goes by because, as she told Miss Joan, she was reborn in this town, so having a new name fit right in with the narrative." Finished with his meal, he pushed aside his empty plate. "Anything else you want to know?"

"Not offhand," she admitted. And then she smiled. "But I now know who to go to if something else occurs to me."

"Fair enough." Daniel paused for a moment as he framed the question he wanted to ask in his mind. "Okay, I've got one for you."

"A question?" she asked. When the deputy nodded, Shania braced herself a little bit then said, "Okay, go ahead."

"Why did you come here?" he asked.

She thought they'd already covered that earlier. "I already told you, Daniel. Miss Joan sent Violet to come get me."

He shook his head. She didn't understand what he was asking. "No, I mean why are you in Forever? Why did you *come back* to Forever?" Daniel clarified.

She would have thought that he of all people would have understood. "Wynona and I were both from here. We saw the kind of life that they don't write about in storybooks. Both of us would have wound up in the foster care system by the time we were eleven and twelve. And then, out of nowhere, a miracle happened," she remembered with a smile. "A great-aunt neither one of us even knew about suddenly popped up in our lives and came to Forever to collect us."

He was curious as to how the dots were connected in this case. "If you didn't know about her, how did she wind up suddenly coming to your rescue out of the blue like that?"

She could see the suspicion in his eyes. He either didn't believe her story, or he was suspicious of this woman who materialized just in the nick of time. A woman who took them in, provided for them and, when the time came, sent them off to get their college degrees so that they could have careers. In her own way, her great-aunt was as tough and demanding as Miss Joan. And she'd had an equally soft heart.

Shania was surprised that he hadn't figured it out already. "Same reason that the two of us are sitting right here, talking to one another."

"Are you talking about 'fate'?" he asked her, sounding even more skeptical about this story than before.

"No, Deputy Tallchief," she informed him, "I'm talking about Miss Joan."

He wasn't sure that he followed her. "Come again?"

She gave him the background behind what happened. "Somehow, Miss Joan stumbled across the information that we had a great-aunt—Great-Aunt Naomi, I think she found it in my mother's papers—and Miss Joan got in contact with her. I don't know exactly what she said to the woman, but whatever it was, it did the trick. By the end of the week, Aunt Naomi was here, snatching us out of the clutches of the foster care system and taking us to her home in Houston. There," she concluded with a smile, dropping her napkin on her empty plate. "I think you're officially all caught up."

Looking at Shania, he didn't quite share that opinion, but for now, he kept it to himself.

CHAPTER THIRTEEN

HIS SENSE OF obligation had Daniel glancing at his watch a number of times, wishing there was a way to make time stand still. But there wasn't. There was no putting it off any longer. He had already lingered far too long over dinner, but sitting here opposite Shania had made the time go by so fast.

"Well, I'd better be heading back to the sheriff's office," Daniel said rather reluctantly. Looking around he saw Debbie and signaled to the waitress to have her bring the bill.

"Right. And I've got a lonely dog to get home to," Shania told him.

Twisting in her seat to see if Debbie was coming, she decided she had enough time to say something else since the young woman was still half the length of the diner away.

Shania turned back to face Elena's brother and told him quietly, "This was nice."

"Yes it was, wasn't it?" Because she'd opened up the door, Daniel felt it was safe to ask, "Would you like to do it again sometime?"

She hadn't expected him to ask that. Caught off guard, her response came out before she could think it through and weigh the pros and cons of telling him *yes* so fast.

"Yes." Then, since she probably sounded way too eager to

him, she tried to backtrack and temper her answer. "That is, I mean, I need to check my schedule and see if—"

"Too late," Daniel told her, stopping Shania before she was able to negate her answer. "Sorry, no do-overs allowed."

Staring at him, Shania blinked. This wasn't the response of the serious, semisomber person she had gotten to know. "Excuse me?"

"Your first response was spontaneous," Daniel explained. "In view of this rather..." he hunted for the right word before saying, "*Unusual* first dinner we just had, we could give this another shot, see if this was just a fluke, or if maybe we could guide this into a friendship." He was making this up as he went along. The words that came out weren't really what he wanted to say, but on the other hand, he didn't want to risk scaring Shania away—or himself for that matter. He felt that too much pressure and too many expectations could ruin something before it ever even had the proper chance to evolve.

"A friendship," Shania said, repeating the word he'd used. Daniel wasn't sure if she liked the idea of their having a friendship or if she was annoyed by it.

And then she smiled and he felt as if he had just completed a triathlon and had raced across the finish line to capture first place.

"Sure," she told him. "That sounds good."

Debbie came just then and placed the check facedown in front of Daniel. "I hope you both found everything to your satisfaction," she said, her bright blue eyes sweeping over both of them.

Looking at the bill, he took out a twenty and a ten and placed them on top. He also placed a five on the table as a tip.

"I have no complaints," Daniel told the young woman.

Flattery was definitely not this man's strong suit, Shania thought, amused. It made her reexamine what he'd said to her before Debbie came to their booth. Shania realized that she should be flattered.

Looking at the waitress now, she made a point of saying, "Everything was delicious."

Debbie grinned. "I'll be sure to pass that along to Angel," she said, leaving.

They rose almost in unison. Daniel accompanied Shania to the diner's entrance. He glanced back at Debbie, who waved to them.

"I guess what you said sounded a lot better than what I did," he speculated.

That he even took note of the waitress's reaction in each case meant that there was some hope for the man.

Shania tried to make him feel better about his response. "You're just not an effusive guy," she told him.

Daniel held the door open for her. "I save effusion for the really important things," he deadpanned.

"Got it. Remind me to be there when it finally happens," she told him, walking past him and stepping outside.

They went down the two steps that were in front of the diner, which officially brought them to the diner's parking lot. The temperature had dropped by at least ten degrees since they had walked in. He noticed Shania pulling her coat closer to her. She was cold, he thought.

"Where's your car?" he asked her, looking around the area. He didn't see it.

"In the shop," she told him. A slight sigh accompanied her words. "It decided it didn't feel like running for me. I called Mick and he came by and towed it to his shop." Mick Henley was Forever's exceptionally capable—as well as its only—mechanic. "He told me that it should be all fixed up and running like new in a couple of days. Meanwhile," she concluded, doing her best to focus on the upside of her situation, "walking is good for me."

"Yeah, but freezing isn't," he commented. "C'mon," he urged, "I'll take you home."

She didn't want to be the reason that he got into trouble. "I thought you had to get back to work."

"I do, but it's not exactly like Forever's having any sort of a crime spree," Daniel told her. "In the last week, I had to bring home an inebriated husband who apparently was drinking to forget he was married and I had to break up a fight between two men who couldn't hurt a fly between them if they tried. So," he concluded, "my being twenty minutes late getting back from my dinner break isn't going to make much of a difference. You, however, will definitely feel the difference between walking home from here in this weather or getting a ride home."

The wind was picking up. The weather was definitely on his side. Still, she hesitated just a little. "If you're sure it's okay—"

"Just please get in the car," he told her. His eyes met hers. "Don't make me have to pick you up and deposit you in the backseat," he warned. "Well?" he asked when Shania made no move toward his vehicle.

"I'm thinking about it," she told him with the straightest face she could manage. However, when her mouth began to curve the next moment, Shania gave up her pretense. "Okay, the answer's yes," she told him, then added, "And thank you."

"Just doing my job, keeping the good citizens of Forever safe—and warm," Daniel added as they walked to the extended parking lot that was behind Miss Joan's diner. His car was parked at the very edge.

She looked at him when they stopped next to his vehicle. "I didn't know the 'warm' part was part of your job description."

"My job description envelops everything and anything," Daniel told her, opening the passenger door for Shania.

She slid into the seat and buckled up. Daniel firmly closed her door.

"I appreciate this," she told him once he had rounded the hood of his car and gotten behind the wheel.

Gratitude made him uncomfortable. He never knew how to respond, but this time, at least, he had something to fall back on. "Not nearly as much as I appreciate you going the extra mile with Elena."

"No extra mile," she protested as Daniel started the car. "It's my job."

He had a different view of that. He'd attended the school system in Forever. More specifically, the reservation schools. Anything he had accomplished, he had done on his own. There hadn't been a "Miss Shania" in his life.

"It's your job to show up and to go over the curriculum," he told her, pulling out of the parking space. "According to the manual, finding ways to reach a stubborn sixteen-year-old and get her to buckle down to do her work is not considered to be part of your job."

He'd done his homework, as well, Shania thought. "Okay, let me rephrase that then. It's what I *consider* to be part of my job."

"And that is the reason why I'm grateful," he pointed out.

Still, she didn't want him thanking her, not until the job was completed. "Save that until after Elena takes her test and passes."

"Why?" he asked as he drove. "Are you expecting there to be a problem?"

A smile played on her lips as she thought back to another time in her life. "I learned a long time ago not to count my chickens until they not only hatched, but took their first steps, as well."

Daniel heard the fleeting grim note in her voice. Pulling up in front of Shania's house, he turned off the ignition and then turned to look at her. "I think that you and I had the same lesson. Except that, for the most part, you came out of it being pretty optimistic."

"I work at it," she told him. And at times, it was a challenge not to just throw her hands up in the air. "I also learned that just thinking dark thoughts gets to be really depressing, so I do my best to think happy thoughts when I can. In other words, I prepare for the worst but hope for the best."

He gave the woman credit, he thought. A lot of the people he had grown up with had gone the other route. More than a couple were dead, having given up and abandoned life altogether.

"I supposed that's a good philosophy if you can manage it," he told her.

"I work at it every day," she told him.

And then she pulled back. She hadn't meant for the conversation to get this serious. There was something about the man that seemed to coax her innermost thoughts out.

There was also something about him that spoke to her soul, making her think things and feel things that she realized were normally buried so deeply, she gave them no thought at all.

Until now.

Shania took a deep breath. "Well, I should get out of your car. I'm keeping you from getting back. And, like I said, I don't want you getting in any trouble on my account."

The space within the car felt as if it had somehow grown smaller. Daniel looked at the woman sitting in his passenger seat for a long moment. Unbidden thoughts and feelings were inexplicably ricocheting madly around inside him.

He thought of what she'd just said. "Might be worth it," he murmured more to himself than to her.

Shania had heard anyway. She felt her face growing hot in response to his words, could almost *feel* the pink color creeping up along her cheeks.

You're past this, she silently insisted, impatient with herself and her reaction. She was a grown woman, for heaven sakes, not some prepubescent girl nursing her first crush.

The word *crush* caught her up short.

Why had she just thought that? Where had it even come from? Had it really been *that* long since she'd had even the mildest form of a relationship in her life?

She suddenly realized that even though she was trying to remember just how long ago that actually was, the truth of it was that she couldn't recall *when* she had been in a relationship. It had been *that* long ago.

Feeling unaccountably nervous, Shania cleared her throat. "Belle probably thinks that I must have run away from home."

Daniel surprised himself when he told her, "Can't have that."

"No, we can't," she murmured. One hand on the door latch, she still hesitated. What was she waiting for? she asked herself.

Forcing herself to open the door, she heard Daniel call her name.

Turning around to look at the deputy, Shania asked, "What?"

And then she had the answer to the question she'd asked, even though Daniel didn't say anything in response. Instead he slipped one hand behind her, cupping the back of her head just enough to bring her a shade closer to him.

And then he kissed her.

The very air in her lungs felt as if it had backed up as every single nerve ending within her was instantly alert—and waiting for more.

Shania could feel all sorts of feelings waking up within her. Dormant feelings she hadn't even realized had gone to sleep until this very second.

She laced her arms around his neck, absorbing every nuance of what was happening to her.

She couldn't explain what it was—she was only aware that it was, and that she liked it.

Liked *him*.

And that she didn't want this to just be an isolated incident.

Even as Daniel deepened the kiss, he could feel guilt seeping in.

This wasn't like him. He never lost control of himself, not even for a split second. And he read signs first, made certain that he wasn't presuming things. Before he even kissed a woman, he knew for a fact that she wanted him to kiss her.

He didn't know anything here.

He was like a blind man feeling his way around in a world that was completely hidden from him. He'd kissed Shania because he felt this compelling *need* to kiss her and that was all that seemed to matter.

Daniel drew back from Shania even as he felt his heart going into double time.

"Sorry," he apologized.

By all rights, she could have easily read him the riot act if she wanted to, but she didn't. And because she didn't, his own guilt increased.

"I didn't mean to do that," he told her.

Shania stiffened and just like that, a beautiful moment seemed to just vanish into nothingness as if it had never existed.

"I'm sorry to hear that," she told him formally. "Thank you for the ride."

She got out of the car quickly and made it to her front door while Daniel continued to remain sitting where he was, still struggling to figure out what had just happened.

He felt the need to go after her and apologize again, but Shania had already gone inside the house.

There was something very final sounding about the way she'd closed her door.

Idiot! Daniel upbraided himself.

He'd never behaved like that, even in his teens. What had come over him? He had no doubt that he had just single-handedly ruined whatever slim chance he might have had to see Shania socially.

Well, he couldn't sit here and brood about it, he thought, annoyed with himself. If he wasted any more time like this, he would not only be looking at the ashes of a relationship that never even had a chance to take root, but he'd also be out looking for a new job. Forever being what it was, that wouldn't exactly be a piece of cake, even for a former deputy.

He knew that as a last resort, he could take Elena with him and move to one of the larger cities in Texas, but that would probably involve tying his sister up and dragging her with him. And that didn't even take into consideration the fact that unlike so many other people his age in Forever, he had no desire to pull up his roots and plant them somewhere else.

He *liked* the small-town feel of Forever now that he had found his niche in it.

When had things gotten so complicated? Daniel wondered.

Okay, Tallchief, no more thinking. You need to get to work before the sheriff realizes that he can do without you.

Securing his seat belt again, Daniel turned his key in the ignition and felt the vehicle come back to life. Thinking only of the mechanics of driving and nothing more, he turned his vehicle around to head back to the sheriff's office.

Just before he took his foot off the brake to shift it to the gas pedal again, he looked one last time toward Shania's house.

The lights were all on the lower level, but with the drapes drawn, he wasn't able to make out any silhouettes. Or actually, the one particular silhouette he was looking for.

Just as well. He sure as hell didn't need any more visual aids to set him off again.

What he needed, he told himself, was to get his mind back on work as well as his body back to the job.

End of story.

But was it? he couldn't help wondering. Or was there more to the story, something that he was going to find out before too soon?

He really wished that Miss Joan hadn't suddenly decided to play cupid. He liked his life uncomplicated and it didn't look like it was going to be that way, at least not for a long, long time.

CHAPTER FOURTEEN

GABE RODRIGUEZ, the deputy who had been hired before Daniel, decided after watching Daniel for more than a week that he needed to speak up. To him it was like deciding to come to aid a wounded, slightly feral, animal.

He waited until Daniel went to get a cup of coffee from the small lunch nook, gave him until the count of ten and then came up behind him.

Rather than bother with small talk, Gabe went straight for the heart of the matter.

"You know, I don't make it a habit to stick my nose into someone else's business," Gabe said quietly.

"A very admirable quality," Daniel said, commending the other deputy.

Although he was just about to fill up his cup, Daniel left the coffeepot where it was and turned on his heel, heading back to his desk.

Now that he'd made the decision to say something, Gabe wasn't about to just let it go. Abandoning his own unfilled cup next to Daniel's, he followed the other deputy back to his desk.

"But I've been watching you for over a week now—" Gabe continued as if there hadn't been a notable pause.

Daniel sat down at his desk. It was obvious to him that Gabe

was not about to cease and desist. He didn't need any more unsolicited advice.

"Maybe you should ask the sheriff to give you something to
do that could utilize those special skills of yours," Daniel suggested, hoping Gabe would take the hint and back off.

But Gabe didn't.

"And you've been acting surlier than usual," Gabe told him.
"Something crawl down your throat and die there?"

Daniel looked at him darkly. "No, but thanks for asking."

The cryptic comment was meant to end the exchange, but
much to Daniel's annoyance, Gabe just refused to take the hint.

"Then what is bothering you, Tallchief?" Gabe asked. "Because something *is* definitely bothering you."

Daniel's look just grew darker. "Other than you?" he asked
Gabe.

"Other than me," Gabe replied good-naturedly. The man
had a really thick hide, Daniel thought, because Rodriguez just
wasn't taking the hint. "Maybe I can help."

"I don't need any help," Daniel retorted, then added, "And
nothing's bothering me."

A third party joined the discussion. "That's not what I heard,"
Joe Lone Wolf said.

Because he'd been quiet as usual and oblivious to the conversation, both men had forgotten that Joe was even there. Now
that he had spoken up, Gabe turned to Joe as a potential ally.

Looking delighted that Joe might have something additional
that could be used as ammunition, Gabe slid his chair across
the common area, using his feet to propel his chair over to
Joe's desk.

Gabe's eyes almost gleamed brightly as he asked, "And what
was it that you heard?"

The expression on Joe's face didn't change. For all the emotion there, he might as well have been reading that day's menu
from the diner.

"That Miss Joan got Daniel to break bread with that really

pretty high school teacher, the one who's putting in extra time tutoring his sister," Joe told the other deputy.

Daniel glanced up sharply. "It's not just Elena. There are other students in that class that she's tutoring," he said defensively.

"I'm sure there are," Joe answered mildly, looking back at the report on his desk that he was reviewing. "Shania Stewart's a dedicated educator. Wish we had more like her."

Nodding his head, Gabe turned his attention back to Daniel. "So what's the deal with you two?"

What little patience Daniel had left was quickly evaporating. "There is no 'deal.'"

"Is that the problem?" Gabe asked sympathetically. "There is no deal?"

"If I were you, I'd try to seal one," Joe advised mildly, not looking up this time. "I wouldn't be surprised if a lot of the men in Forever would like to get closer to her, maybe even become teacher's pet," he added.

Daniel didn't welcome having all this attention focused on him, especially given the subject of that focus.

"You two have entirely too much time on your hands," he fairly growled at the other two deputies in disgust. On his feet now, he headed for the door.

"Just looking out for you, that's all," Gabe said, calling after Daniel.

Daniel's parting words just as he crossed the threshold were, "I don't need anyone looking out for me. Clear?"

He thought he heard Joe say, "That's your opinion." But he wasn't about to double back to find out if he was right. Right now, he just wanted to walk off the full head of steam he'd been building up before he wound up saying something they'd all regret.

Daniel chose a path that didn't run through the heart of the town, a path where he could be alone with his thoughts without having to stop to either exchange pleasantries with someone or answer any spur-of-the-moment questions put to him by one of Forever's citizens.

It had been a full week since he'd kissed Shania. A full week since he'd actually seen her, as well. And rather than have things get better—and by better he just wanted it all to fade away—they got worse.

Thoughts of Shania kept invading his mind. The way she'd looked, the way her lips had felt beneath his. The way he had almost felt her body yielding to his.

The only good thing about the incident was that it seemed to have no repercussions, at least not as far as Shania working with Elena was concerned. Shania went on preparing Elena, along with the other students, for her PSATs.

His sister didn't seem to know anything had happened between her teacher and him. If she did, Daniel was certain that Elena would have gone into a full rant about it because of the embarrassment that she'd claim was attached to her brother socially seeing her teacher. That she said nothing proved to him that Shania had not alluded to what had happened between them in his car.

But while he was grateful that she hadn't, it didn't alleviate what he was feeling. If anything, it seemed to make the itch he was experiencing even worse.

Not to mention that it seemed to confuse things even more.

He needed to resolve this. Now, before it ate away at him any further.

Daniel was back at his desk twenty minutes later. Apparently having gotten the message, Joe and Gabe left him alone and to his own devices, each working on the tedious reports that periodically needed to be filed.

He did the same.

Daniel waited until he was fairly sure that the after-school class was over—and then he tacked on an extra fifteen minutes to that just in case there was a straggler or two who was still in Shania's classroom, asking her questions or working on one of the sample tests.

Pulling up in his official vehicle, Daniel waited outside the school building just in case Shania had decided to leave early, but she hadn't.

The woman was most definitely married to her job, he thought, finally entering the building.

Taking the stairs, Daniel quickly went up to the third floor where Shania's classroom was located. At this hour, the school was almost empty. The building was rather quiet. He could hear the echo of his own footsteps as he went down the hall.

All the classroom doors were closed and presumably locked, except for one. That door was open. He came up to it, knocked on it once before walking in.

Shania was sitting at her desk, busy making notes on a yellow pad. If this same scene was taking place in one of the larger cities where funding was not an issue the way it was here, Daniel had no doubts she would have been plugging entries into a laptop instead of using a pencil and paper.

Finished, Shania looked up. He saw a fleeting look of surprise on her face before it disappeared. "If you're looking for Elena in order to walk her home, she already left," she told him primly. "She went out with Jacquelyn," she added, mentioning one of Elena's friends.

Having informed him of his sister's whereabouts, Shania looked back down at the notes she was putting together.

"I'm not looking for Elena," Daniel told her quietly. "I came to see you."

Shania raised her eyes again. He saw that the wariness was back.

"Well, you've seen me," she replied with an air of finality. "Deputy Tallchief, I have a lot of work to prepare for tomorrow, so unless there is something else, I really need to—"

This wasn't easy for him, but it was the right thing to do and he knew he owed it to her. "I came to tell you I'm sorry."

If possible, she sat up a little straighter, her shoulders braced a little more rigidly. Her voice was distant as she told him, "You already made that clear in your car."

He shook his head. He needed to make her understand. "No, I came to tell you that I'm sorry I said I was sorry."

Shania continued looking at him, a trace of confusion replacing the wariness. "Maybe you could stand to take a refresher course in English when you have the time, Deputy."

He inclined his head. "Maybe I'll look into that." And then he tried one more time to make himself clear. "When I told you I was sorry, I didn't mean that I was sorry I kissed you—I was just sorry that I assumed that you'd want me to."

Shania gave up pretending to work while he was standing there. Pushing the pad and pencil aside, she looked at Daniel, trying her best to untangle what he was having such trouble saying.

"But you *did* want to kiss me?" she questioned.

He released a sigh of relief. Finally. "Yes, I did. But I didn't have the right to just—"

That was all she wanted to hear.

Shania pushed her chair back from her desk. Standing up, she crossed to him in less time than it took for Daniel to realize what she was doing.

"Shut up, Tallchief," she told him a second before she wrapped her arms around his neck and brought her mouth up to his.

His surprise melted away in less than a blink of an eye. Lost in the moment, Daniel went with his reflexes and pulled her closer to him.

In an instant, Shania realized that he wasn't just returning her kiss—he was kissing her with enough verve to completely blot out her mind, erasing everything except for him.

The kiss was well on its way to overwhelming her, creating

a tidal wave of feelings and desires that could easily make her forget who she was as well as *where* she was.

Catching herself before that happened, Shania drew her head away.

Looking down into her face, he asked, "Does this mean that you forgive me?"

He could swear that his heart rate had sped up to the point that it was emulating the revved-up engine of a race car. Daniel kept his arms around her as he waited for his heart to slow down enough to allow him to breathe normally.

Shania smiled up at him and he could have sworn that he felt her smile searing right into his heart.

"Let's just say we'll work on it," she told him.

Given that it could have gone a great deal worse, he nodded. "Good enough for me. Can I buy you dinner?"

"I'd like that," she told him, "but I'm going to have to take a rain check for now. I already made plans for dinner tonight." Before he could say anything, or think that she was just brushing him off, Shania explained, "I promised my cousin Wynona I'd come over to have dinner with her and her husband and son." She smiled. "We're officially celebrating the fact that she's pregnant."

And then she paused for a second, debating whether or not to say something. Making her decision, she said, "You're welcome to come if you'd like. You can't pay for anything," she told him, knowing the way he thought. "But you can eat," she teased.

But Daniel shook his head. "No, this is a family occasion. It wouldn't be right to just barge in."

He was surprised to hear her laugh at that. "If you knew Wynona, you'd know that you definitely wouldn't be barging in." Her cousin had been after her to start going out more.

Daniel felt that she was just being nice. "I appreciate the invitation, but, um—"

Shania nodded, reading between the lines. "One step at a time?"

He didn't know if he would have put it that way, but it was as good a description as any. Besides, he felt that they needed to spend a little time alone before they ventured out into the world as anything approximating a couple. Daniel was still extremely leery about taking what to him was a huge step.

"Something like that."

They'd definitely made progress, she thought, and she wasn't about to push.

"Understood," Shania told him. "By the way, Elena is doing great. At the rate she's going, when the PSATs are finally given, she is going to ace them. You should be very proud of her."

Realizing that it was getting late, she gathered her things together, packing everything into her oversize shoulder bag.

"And that's all thanks to you," Daniel told her.

He was giving her way too much credit—and not enough to his sister, Shania thought. "I didn't make her smart."

Daniel followed her out of the classroom. "No, but you made her realize that she didn't have to be ashamed of being smart. And you made her realize that it was okay for her to apply herself so she can go to college instead of just being another example of a rebellious teen who failed to do anything with her life."

Shania paused outside of the classroom and smiled at him. "Okay."

"Okay what?" Daniel asked, not sure exactly what she was saying.

"Okay," she told him, extrapolating, "I'll accept your compliment if you promise to stop making this all about me and realize that it's actually about your sister."

"It's always been about my sister," Daniel assured her solemnly. He waited as Shania locked the classroom door. When she slipped the key into her pocket he asked, "How about tomorrow?"

She fell into place beside him. "I need more of a hint than that."

Daniel flushed, realizing that he'd just jumped ahead. "Dinner." And then he forced himself to be completely clear by using a complete sentence. "How about tomorrow for dinner?"

Shania flashed a smile. "Sounds good."

Daniel had expected it to be harder than this. "Then you can make it?"

"No, but it does sound good," Shania cracked. And then the grin returned. "Of course I can make it," she laughed. "You know, I'm not trying to be difficult, Tallchief."

He looked at her, feigning surprise. "Then it comes naturally to you?"

Shania's grin grew wider. "You made a joke. There really *is* hope for you, Tallchief."

"Do you think you could call me Daniel?" he asked. "When you call me Tallchief it makes me feel like I'm on duty."

She couldn't even summon a serious look at this point, even though she gave it her best shot. "You drive a hard bargain, but I'll give it a try, *Danny*."

"Daniel," he corrected. Only his mother had called him Danny, and hearing himself called that brought back memories he still hadn't learned how to deal with. Memories he kept buried.

"Yes, that, too." And then, because he was looking at her, obviously waiting for her to agree, she obliged and said his name. "*Daniel*."

He nodded his approval.

"Well, now that we've resolved that," Shania said when they reached the ground floor, "and that you're not sorry that you kissed me, what will we have to talk about at dinner tomorrow?"

He knew that she was teasing him and he liked it. The whole situation felt strangely normal even though it had been a very long time since he'd even been in a relationship that was worthy of the label. Since then the women in his life had been few and had left no footprints on his soul.

His main focus once he had laid his parents to rest—and Lana had walked out on him after making it clear that she

144 THE LAWMAN'S ROMANCE LESSON

had no patience for the life he was proposing—was his sister. Providing for Elena and making her feel safe and loved in the aftermath of losing her parents had consumed almost all of his extra time and energy.

Whatever was left over brought nothing memorable or lasting with it.

He had made up his mind that this was what the rest of his life was going to be like.

That was why what he was experiencing now with Shania felt unusual and yet oddly comfortable, as well as exceptionally invigorating.

But he was worried, worried that without realizing it, he was going to do something that would cost him this fledgling relationship before it ever had a chance to take flight.

And he just couldn't go through that again.

CHAPTER FIFTEEN

"So, HOW WAS IT?" Daniel asked as he settled into the booth, taking a seat opposite Shania at Miss Joan's diner.

It was several evenings later and it had taken them this long to finally be able to coordinate their two work schedules in order to carve out some time to share dinner with each other.

Even without any preface on his part, Shania knew Daniel was referring to the dinner at her cousin's house. She wasn't aware of doing it—although Daniel had seen it—but she wrinkled her nose as she recalled the occasion.

"It was a good thing that you didn't come," she told him.

Daniel came to the only conclusion he could. "Then I was right when I said that she'd want it to be a family-only thing."

He couldn't quite read the strange expression on her face. "Not exactly."

Daniel looked at her, confused. "I don't think I understand."

She was trying to find the right way to word this. "You know that old expression about being sick to your stomach?"

"I'm aware of it," he said, still waiting for this to make sense to him.

"Well, now so is Wynona." Shania took a breadstick out of the basket and broke it in half before taking a bite. Parts of that evening were coming vividly back to her. She did her best to block them out. "Everything that went into her mouth came out almost at the same time. I have never seen such a glaring example of morning sickness in my whole life," she told him, feeling very sorry for her cousin. "Except that the poor thing doesn't just have 'morning sickness,' she has 'all day sickness.'" Shania shook her head as she recalled what Wynona had told her. "She even has trouble keeping water down."

Daniel looked concerned. "Shouldn't she be in a hospital then?" he asked Shania. "If she can't keep any food down, she's in danger of starving herself, not to mention possibly harming her baby."

Shania like the fact that Daniel actually seemed concerned rather than just picking up on a few random words so he could make acceptable conversation with her about her cousin's condition.

"Unfortunately, the closest hospital is still over fifty miles away," she reminded him. "But at least some things have changed. They did reopen the medical clinic a few years back and the town has a couple of excellent, up-to-date doctors to turn to."

She knew that Daniel was aware of this, but for her it was still a new occurrence. She knew it made a world of difference to a lot of people who lived here.

"Dr. Davenport ran a few tests on Wynona. He put her on supplements and he did discover that there was one thing Wynona seems to be able to tolerate as long as it's in moderation."

"Which is?" Daniel expected her to say something like chicken soup or boiled chicken, both of which seemed bland enough for a nauseated woman to be able to keep down.

Shania paused, smiled and then said, "Stroganoff."

"What now?" Daniel asked. He was certain that he had to have misheard her.

Shania's grin widened. "I know, I know. It sounds weird since Wyn can't even keep crackers down, but she seems to be able to eat—and keep down—beef Stroganoff served over linguine."

"You're kidding."

Despite the smile on her lips, there wasn't even a hint of a clue to indicate that she was putting him on. "Nope."

Just looking at her was drawing him in, making him want to take her somewhere where they could be alone. Daniel forced himself to just focus on the conversation and not the woman across from him.

He shrugged. "Whatever works."

"Speaking of which," Shania said, picking up on his choice of words, "I know that you have a lot vying for your attention, so you might not know that the PSATs are being given next Saturday."

"No, I didn't know," he admitted, grateful that she'd given him a heads-up. He frowned slightly. "Elena hasn't said anything to me about it."

"I didn't think so." Shania saw the look that came over Daniel's face and guessed what he was thinking. That his sister was reverting back to her old rebellious ways and was shutting him out. "She's just stoic, like her brother. Plus she told me that you've really been busy lately and she didn't want to bother you with, and I quote, 'trivial things.'"

He didn't see how Elena could think that way. "Her education isn't trivial."

"Yes, I know that," she said, "and I told her that *you* don't think that it is, either."

"And?" Daniel asked, convinced that his sister had to have an opinion about that. "What's the verdict?"

"Jury's still out," she told him honestly, "but I have a feeling that when it does come in, the jury'll rule in your favor."

Daniel never counted on anything going his way, but since Shania seemed optimistic about the outcome, he wanted to do something to help it along.

"So, is there anything I'm supposed to do?"

"Just encourage her and wish her well on Saturday morning," she said, finishing off the breadstick. "She's a very intelligent girl. Short of going off on a bender the night before, she should do just fine on the test."

His face darkened slightly. "She'd better not go on a bender."

"I was just kidding," Shania quickly assured him. "I really don't think there's any danger of her doing that—but just remember," Shania cautioned, "she does better with encouragement than being on the receiving end of dark scowls."

"I don't scowl," Daniel protested.

She congratulated herself for not laughing at him. Instead, she merely smiled knowingly. "Not as much as you used to, but yeah, you do."

Daniel sighed, then unexpectedly pulled his lips back in a wide grin. "How's this?"

"Frightening actually," she answered, giving in and laughing. Leaning over the table, she patted his hand and promised, "We'll work on it."

He knew that was just a throwaway line that people said, but deep down inside him, he liked the sound of that. Liked the promise that was implied: that this was something that they would be facing together, no matter how minor it actually was.

Daniel thoroughly enjoyed being with her like this and the total lack of privacy kept him from getting ahead of himself before he was ready, he mused as he raised his hand for the check.

They met a couple more times for dinner. Each time they came in, Miss Joan made sure that they were placed at a booth that was tucked into the back. It was as if she wanted to keep them away from prying eyes—other than hers, of course.

It was very evident to both Daniel and Shania that Miss Joan was playing matchmaker, although neither one of them commented on that fact out loud, just in case the other wasn't aware of what was going on.

And then the dreaded Saturday finally came. All the countless hours of studying and taking sample tests came down to this, the moment of truth, otherwise known as taking the PSAT test in earnest.

As expected, Shania was proctoring the test. She had volunteered. As nervous as any of her students, she had gotten very little sleep the night before. She had arrived at the classroom more than an hour before the test was to officially begin. She made sure that all the proper items the students would need were in place so that once the test began, there would be no need to stop for anything.

As the time for the test drew closer, students began to trickle in. She greeted each of them with a wide, encouraging smile. The more her stomach knotted up, the wider her smile grew. At this point, she was certain that she was more nervous than her students, but she also knew that she couldn't show anything except undying confidence that those same students would all do well—or at least pass.

She was aware that they all looked to her and she was not about to let them down.

And then it was time to begin.

It felt as if the minute hand on the wall clock had been covered in molasses and now moved along accordingly, dragging itself from one number to the next.

When the time to take the exam was finally, mercifully over, no one was more grateful than she was.

"Okay, students, time's up. Pencils down," she declared, then looked around the room at the various faces. Some were drawn, some were relieved, but they all shared one thing.

"You all survived," Shania announced cheerfully. "Now come up to the front of the room single file and hand in your papers, then take a deep, deep breath. The worst is over," she told them, her eyes sweeping over a sea of mostly exhausted-looking teenagers.

"When will we get the results?" one lanky teenage boy asked as he handed in his papers.

"Soon enough," Shania answered, then added, "But not today.

Today you go out and celebrate the fact that the test is over. Go and have some fun," she urged, adding, "Relax your brain and enjoy yourself."

When Elena came up to hand in her paper, Shania smiled at the girl. "How do you think you did?" she asked her.

"I blanked out on half the questions," Elena complained.

"That happens more than you think," Shania assured her. She lowered her voice slightly to ask, "Were you finally able to focus?"

Elena nodded.

"Good, then you probably did a lot better than you think you did," she assured the young teen. "Now do what I said. Go see your friends, have fun," she urged. "You've worked really, really hard these last four weeks," she reminded Elena, giving her credit for all the hours she had put into studying for this.

The doubtful expression on Elena's face receded, replaced by a glimmer of a smile. She nodded in response to what Shania had said. The next moment she was out of the classroom like a shot, ready to do exactly what Shania had recommended.

But the very next minute Elena recrossed the threshold and came back into the classroom.

"Something wrong?" Shania asked the girl.

"No, nothing's wrong," Elena answered. Then, looking almost tongue-tied, she looked at Shania and murmured, "I just wanted to say thank you."

Surprised, it took Shania a moment to collect herself. When she finally did, Shania smiled at her student and said, "It was my pleasure, Ellie. My pleasure."

Elena returned her teacher's smile. And then the next second, the girl bolted again, and this time she kept on going.

Shania stood where she was, savoring the moment.

"You look really pleased with yourself."

Startled—she hadn't thought that there was anyone left in the building—she immediately looked toward the doorway. Daniel had managed to come in without her realizing it.

"You just missed Elena," she told him, assuming that was why he was there.

"I didn't come looking for her," he said. "I just assumed that after all the hours of studying, Ellie would want to go and unwind with her friends."

She looked at him, surprised and impressed. "I thought you didn't approve of that."

"I don't approve of wild partying and underage drinking," Daniel corrected her, clarifying his position, "but I think I made the boundary lines pretty clear to her—thanks to your influence. Besides, I'm not an ogre. I do think she's earned the right to have some fun with her friends and unwind."

"That's very understanding of you," Shania acknowledged. "All right," she said, accepting his explanation. "Then if you didn't come to pick up Elena, why did you come?"

He smiled at her. "Isn't it obvious? I came to see Elena's teacher."

She could feel her pulse speeding up even as she warned herself not to jump to any conclusions. This might go to an entirely different place than she wanted it to. He might just be here to thank her for all the extra practice classes she'd held.

"Oh?" she asked warily.

"Yeah. I thought that Ms. Stewart earned a little unwinding time, too."

Maybe this *was* going where she wanted it to, Shania thought. "You know, for such a stoic man, Deputy Tallchief, you're pretty intuitive."

"I'm not always so stoic," Daniel told her meaningfully.

Her smile went all the way up to her eyes, which seemed as if they were sparkling as she looked up at the deputy.

"Oh, sounds interesting," Shania said, then coaxed, "Tell me more."

"I'd be glad to," he answered, then suggested, "Why don't we continue this conversation over a couple of drinks at Murphy's?"

"What kind of drinks?" she asked him.

He had seen too many of his friends have their lives ruined by alcohol, which was why he had never been tempted to surrender himself to it.

"Mild ones," he told her.

She smiled her approval. "You read my mind."

"Not yet, but I think maybe I'm getting closer," Daniel replied.

She took a breath, trying to get her pulse to go back down to normal. It wasn't working.

"Murphy's sounds good," Shania agreed, "but would you mind if we stopped at the diner first so I could get something to eat? Any alcohol on an empty stomach isn't really a good way to go and I haven't had anything to eat all day. Right now I'm hungry enough to eat half a buffalo."

"I don't think Miss Joan serves buffalo," Daniel deadpanned, "but I'm sure she can come up with something you'll like," he told her as he escorted the teacher out of the classroom. "Tell me, why haven't you eaten anything today?"

Shania flushed a little as she admitted quietly, "Nerves."

He didn't quite understand why Shania would be nervous. "You didn't take the test," Daniel quietly reminded her.

"No, but I watched my students take it and I lived every moment of that agonizing experience with them—through their eyes, so to speak. I remember what it was like," she told him.

Daniel looked at her, impressed, as they came to the stairwell and started walking down to the first floor. Looking back over his own educational experience, most of the teachers he'd had all seemed relatively indifferent. The only time he remembered seeing any of them look eager was when summer vacation approached. He supposed that in that, they were no different than the students they taught.

Shania wasn't like that.

"You really do care about these kids, don't you?" he marveled.

"Of course I do," she said. To her, it was a given. "I couldn't do this job if I didn't."

Walking down behind her, he laughed softly. "I really wish you'd been my teacher back when I was Elena's age."

She didn't want to get too serious right now. That wasn't part of unwinding to her. "If I was, then going out with you like this would be highly inappropriate."

He laughed as they both came to a stop on the second-floor landing.

"Always the clear-eyed one," he said with a touch of admiration.

And then, because they were alone, he gave in to the urge that had been with him since the last time they had kissed.

Pulling Shania to him, Daniel enfolded her in his arms and brought his mouth down to hers. He felt her yielding to him, her lips parting in a spontaneous, unspoken invitation.

But then they both thought that they heard the sound of footsteps coming from just above them. They sprang apart like two guilty teenagers caught in a moment they shouldn't be having.

They heard the door leading to the exit just above them opening and then closing. The sound of footsteps was gone.

Daniel smiled, relieved. Taking her hand in his, he said, "Okay, let's get you fed before we go to Murphy's so we can toast a job well done."

"Well, this is progress," she said, following him down the last staircase.

In Daniel's estimation, he hadn't said anything out of the ordinary. "What do you mean?"

"You're sweet-talking me."

Shania managed to get the line out before she started to laugh. The sound echoed around them as they went down to the last landing, and then opened the door to enter the ground floor of the school.

The rosy feeling tightened around her as she went with him to his car.

CHAPTER SIXTEEN

"You must be happy as hell to have those pesky tests behind you," Miss Joan said to Shania as she personally brought Shania and Daniel's order to them. "Careful, the plates are hot," Miss Joan cautioned even as she transferred those same plates from the tray to their table with her bare hands. Miss Joan had been said to have asbestos fingers. "Now you can concentrate on the really major things—like Halloween and Thanksgiving, which are both just around the corner," she reminded the duo needlessly.

Placing two tall glasses of some sort of misty-looking, fruity drink next to the plates, Miss Joan tucked the empty tray under her arm.

Shania looked at the sparkling, light pink concoction and just had to ask. "Miss Joan, what *is* this?"

"Something I whipped up myself." Miss Joan paused for a beat, then added, "Since Murphy's and I have a deal—they don't serve actual food, other than those peanuts of theirs, and I don't serve any spirits—this little number is what I came up with as a substitute. Enjoy," she told them with a wink, then turned away and went back to the rear of the diner.

Taking the glass in his hand, Daniel studied the contents for a long moment. "Looks harmless enough."

"You could say the same thing about Miss Joan," Shania told him, suppressing a grin.

"Oh, not really," Daniel contradicted with feeling. "There is nothing harmless about that woman. Not if you're paying close attention."

"Well," Shania said, wrapping her fingers around the lower part of the glass and psyching herself up, "I'm game if you are."

Daniel raised his tall glass slightly in the air. "All right, we'll both give this a try on the count of three. One, two, *three*."

Shania and Daniel took tentative sips of their drinks at the same time. They looked at each other in surprise as they had the same reaction.

"Not sure what it is," Daniel pronounced, still trying to place the taste and connect it to something, "but it does taste good."

Shania set her glass down on the table. "It does," she agreed, "but right now my stomach is rumbling. It wants food."

Daniel laughed and gestured toward her plate. "Have at it."

And she did.

Quickly.

Without meaning to, Shania wound up finishing the meal that Miss Joan had placed in front of her in what amounted to record time.

Enjoying his own meal, Daniel watched Shania, surprised as well as amused to see how she managed to polish off the meat loaf and mashed potatoes that Miss Joan had brought out.

"Wow," he finally commented, "you weren't kidding about being hungry."

"I never kid about food," Shania deadpanned. And then she looked at Daniel ruefully and apologized. "I'm sorry, I didn't mean to inhale my food like that. Did I make you uncomfortable?" she asked, embarrassed.

"Uncomfortable?" he questioned. "This is admiration on my face. I don't think I could have consumed anything nearly that fast. You must have set some kind of an eating record just now."

Shania laughed. She supposed she had that coming. "Not

exactly something a woman aspires to be known for." A flush of red climbed up her cheeks.

It took Daniel a moment to draw his eyes away. "Well, you can rest easy, Shania. You're known for a lot of things."

"Do I even want to know what?" Shania asked him uneasily.

Daniel was surprised that the teacher was displaying a streak of insecurity. He would have thought that of the two of them, insecurity would have been *his* domain.

"Don't see why not," he told her. "Off the top of my head, I'd say you're known for your patience, your dedication, your ability and willingness to go the extra mile for your students—or anyone else who needs help." His eyes swept over her, taking in all of her. "Not to mention you do all this while managing to be the most beautiful woman around."

"Just what did Miss Joan put in *your* glass?" Shania asked, shaking her head. Flattery always made her uneasy.

"Same thing she put in yours," he countered. "I'm just experiencing a bit of clarity at the moment, that's all," he told her. "Happens to the best of us even when we're trying to keep our nose to the grindstone and our eyes on the ground."

Shania looked at him, confused. "What are you talking about?"

"Stuff I shouldn't be," he answered. He knew he'd already said way too much. The problem was she had a way of drawing words out of him. "It's just that, being around you, I just can't seem to help myself."

"Is that so bad?" she asked him, her voice low and intimate despite the fact that the diner was crowded this time of the day, or more accurately, this time of the evening.

Time, he realized, had seemed to slip away from him. Not just at this moment, he thought, but for a good deal of the time now.

"Now that you're not starving," Daniel said, deliberately looking at her empty plate, "do you want to go to Murphy's?"

Shania turned the tables on him and asked Daniel, "Do you?"

Since she'd asked, he did her the courtesy of answering truth-fully. "Not really."

She nodded. "Me, neither."

"I've got it. Why don't we just sit here until we finish our drinks, whatever is in these things," Daniel added.

"You talked me into it," she told him.

"So this is what it's like to use my powers of persuasion for good." Unable to get through the line without cracking a smile, Daniel didn't even bother to try.

Shania cocked her head, studying him, doing her best to get beyond the compelling planes and angles of his handsome face.

"What's so funny?" she asked him.

He knew he should say *nothing* and then grow serious, but it felt so good to smile, so good to just be with her like this, talking about absolutely nothing and making it sound like they were uncovering the secrets of the universe.

And maybe, Daniel thought as he looked into Shania's ex-pressive face, in a strange sort of way, they actually were.

Shania felt as if his eyes were penetrating right down into her soul, seeing every thought, every impulse she had ever had, even though she knew that was impossible.

"What?" Daniel had to ask when he just couldn't ignore the fact that she was looking at him intently any longer.

She was staring and she blinked, trying to erase the moment.

"Nothing," she told Daniel, taking a breath and squaring her shoulders as she tried to clear her head. "Do you want to go for a walk?"

He suddenly found himself wanting to do anything Shania wanted to do, including walking to the ends of the earth if that was what pleased her.

"Sure," he agreed. "Just let me settle up."

Daniel looked around for the waitress who had originally brought them to their booth before Miss Joan took their order. He reasoned that Miss Joan was busy and he didn't want to give the woman anything more to do than she had already done for them.

Seeing the waitress, he waved and caught the young woman's attention. He had also managed to catch Miss Joan's attention and, the next moment, it was Miss Joan who was making her way over to their table.

"Something else?" she asked, looking from Shania to the deputy.

"No, nothing else," Daniel answered. "We're both beyond full. I'd just like the check."

Miss Joan's eyes narrowed as they pinned him in his place. "Well, that's too bad, because you're not getting one."

Daniel shook his head, unclear as to why she'd say something like that. "I don't under—"

Miss Joan scowled at him. "Don't make me hit you upside your head, boy. Deputy or not, you can't tell me what to charge someone in my own establishment."

She'd really lost him now. "What?"

"You heard me. Go." She waved a thin hand majestically toward the door. "Both of you. Go while the evening—and you—are both still young."

Shania knew how Daniel felt about getting preferential treatment. He's already made that clear and she was ready to try to back him up.

"But—" Shania began to protest.

"Go!" Miss Joan ordered, every inch the ruler of her small kingdom.

Having known Miss Joan for most of his life, he wasn't about to disobey an order when he heard one.

"You heard her," Daniel said, sliding out from his side and coming around to Shania's. "She gave us a direct order."

Miss Joan smiled at Daniel, nodding in approval. "Well, it took you long enough, son, but you're finally learning."

Satisfied that they were leaving, the diner owner walked away.

"But we can't go without paying," Shania protested to Daniel.

"We can if she tells us to," he reminded her.

Helping Shania with her coat, he took her arm and led her to the door. He opened the door and held it for her as she walked out. And then he quickly crossed the threshold and joined her.

Just like the last time, the temperature had dropped once the sun had gone down. Daniel walked slightly behind her so that the wind was at his back, not hers.

"I'll take you back to the school so you can get your car," he offered.

But Shania shook her head. "That won't be necessary," she told him. When he raised an inquisitive brow, she explained, "My car's back with Mick."

That didn't sound right. Usually, when Mick fixed a vehicle, it stayed fixed. "Is there something else wrong with it?"

She sighed. It felt as if it was always something. But she refused to let that dampen her spirits tonight. She'd had a wonderful time at dinner and she was only going to focus on that.

"The alternator cut out on me," she said, answering his question. "Mick's putting in a new one for me at cost, bless him. Although I am beginning to suspect that my car just wants to have Mick baby her."

Bringing her over to his car, he held open the passenger door for her. "Your car's a her?"

"Aren't they all?" she said, surprised that he was asking the question. Didn't men refer to their cars as *she*? "What do you call your car?"

"Car," Daniel answered simply.

She laughed and the light, sexy sound stirred something within him. Something that, no matter how many times he tried to bury it, just refused to remain quiet. He was beginning to suspect that he was fighting a losing battle.

"Then I'll take you home," he said again because she still hadn't gotten into his car. This time, before she could say anything in protest, he sternly told her, "Don't argue with me."

Shania raised her hands in surrender. "Wouldn't dream of it," she told Daniel and then obligingly got into his vehicle.

Pleased, Daniel nodded his approval. "Good."

After a few minutes, Daniel was bringing his car to a stop right before her house. It might just be his imagination, but it seemed like the drive over here was getting to be shorter and shorter. It sure felt that way.

Shania turned toward him after she'd unbuckled her seat belt.

"Would you like to come in for a little bit?" She realized that she'd made it sound more like coaxing than a request so she quickly added, "Belle will be very glad to see you."

Daniel paused as if he was thinking the matter over—and then he nodded. "Sure. Wouldn't be right to disappoint Belle."

"No, it wouldn't," Shania agreed, feigning solemnity. Getting out, she made her way to her door and unlocked it. Turning the handle, she opened the door and gestured for him to go in first.

The dog almost knocked him down in her enthusiasm the second Shania had opened the door and the German shepherd saw Daniel. Without thinking, Shania reached out in an attempt to keep Daniel upright. The next moment, they both wound up going down.

Circling them and obviously thinking this was a new game they were playing with her, Belle starting licking Daniel's face and then Shania's, alternating between the two of them.

Despite being the object of Belle's friendly assault, Daniel managed to sit up.

"Not shy, is she?" he said, laughing. After scrambling up to his knees, Daniel took Shania's hand to help her up.

"That's one thing she's never been accused of," Shania assured him. "Thank you," she said as he brought her up to her feet.

She automatically began to brush herself off. No matter how many times she vacuumed, there always seemed to be dog hair around.

"Nothing to thank me for," he assured her. "If you weren't trying to keep me upright you wouldn't have wound up on the floor like that."

She shook her head. The man was a born lawyer, always arguing.

"Just take the thank-you," she told him. "And you," she said to Belle, "you start acting like you've had some kind of training."

"Has she?" Daniel asked, curious.

Maybe the word *training* would be going a little too far, implying too much, she thought.

"Well, she's housebroken and we're working out the rest of the kinks as we go along," Shania told him.

The pronoun caught his attention. He'd established that she lived alone, but that didn't mean that her status was "single."

"We?" he asked,

Shania flushed a little as she went toward the kitchen.

"My cousin and me," she explained. "I keep forgetting she's not here anymore. We found Belle together." She smiled at the memory. "Belle became our first student. She was our first project, so to speak."

Daniel found himself smiling again. "And how did that turn out?"

The less said, the better, Shania decided. "Like I said, she's housebroken."

"Well, that's a good start," Daniel answered, humoring her.

"How do you feel about beer?" she asked him as she looked into the refrigerator.

Somehow, looking in, she had hoped for a different result from what she remembered seeing in the refrigerator yesterday. But, sadly, there was no hidden fairy godmother to do the shopping for her expressly based on what she'd bought on previous trips to the grocery store.

Why was there never enough time to get everything done?

Daniel raised his voice so that it would carry to her. "Is that all you have?"

"Other than tap water and a container of milk that's probably seen better days, I'm afraid so," she answered, still holding the refrigerator door open.

"Then beer's fine," he told her.

Opening the last two bottles she had, Shania brought them both over to the coffee table and sat down beside Daniel on the sofa.

Daniel picked up his bottle and lightly clinked its neck against hers.

"To a job well done," he told her. When Shania looked at him quizzically, he explained, "Since we didn't get a drink at Murphy's commemorating the end of studying for the PSATs, I thought I'd toast your accomplishment here with this."

Shania inclined her head slightly, accepting his explanation. And then, whimsically, she reminded him, "There's always the SATs next year."

Daniel groaned, feeling a wave of empathy for his sister. "Let's not focus on that."

"I'm a teacher," Shania told him by way of explaining her mind-set. "I always have to focus on the next test that's coming."

"But you don't have to focus on it at this very moment," Daniel stressed.

"No," she agreed. "Not at this moment."

He liked the way her mouth curved as she smiled. He kept his eyes on her lips as he took a long sip from his bottle. He was still looking at her lips as the beer coursed down his throat, moving through his limbs and filling them with a warmth he could only attribute to anticipation.

CHAPTER SEVENTEEN

DANIEL REALLY WASN'T sure exactly how it had all happened.

One minute, he and Shania were discussing how she had really earned a little free time to kick back, at least until Monday morning when her week began all over again. The next minute, the space between them on the sofa had somehow just evaporated to nothingness.

And then he was kissing her.

The moment his lips touched hers, Daniel felt the hunger, the hunger that he'd been doing his very best to bury, suddenly explode to life, going off within him like fireworks that were lined up end to end. Fireworks that were shooting into the air with a breathtaking intensity.

Desires and emotions sprang up inside him, full-bodied and demanding to be recognized. Demanding to be satisfied.

Holding Shania against him, Daniel deepened their kiss layer by soul-vibrating layer until he felt as if he was all but drowning in her.

The enormity of what was about to happen if they continued on this path suddenly, glaringly occurred to Daniel, seizing his attention.

Stunned and chastising himself, Daniel pulled back, even though he was still holding on to her shoulders.

He saw the surprise in her eyes at the sudden separation.

"Something wrong?" she asked, confused.

Daniel couldn't just walk away from her—even though part of him felt it was the right thing to do. But he couldn't just leave without explaining why.

"I've got an awful lot of baggage, Shania," he told her.

What he didn't say was that he felt it wasn't fair of him to bring that burden into a relationship. Lana had done a number on him, giving him trust issues, and that wasn't fair to Shania.

The simple statement was meant to be an apology as well as an explanation, letting her know why he had stopped kissing her—and why he felt it was best to just leave before things went too far.

But Shania deftly aborted his apology with an equally simple statement. "Everyone does."

Was she telling him that was no reason not to continue? Or was she saying that she understood why he'd stopped?

Or was she telling him that she had her demons too and that those demons—his and hers—shouldn't be allowed to stand in the way of their search for happiness?

He didn't know.

The only thing that he did know was that he wanted Shania, wanted her with a fierce, piercing desire that stunned him and rendered him unable to do anything else or think of anything—except losing himself in her.

Still, Daniel wanted to be totally fair to Shania, to give her the opportunity to change her mind at the last moment and just walk away.

"Are you sure?" he asked her, his eyes searching her face for his answer.

Daniel watched in fascination as the smile blossomed on her face.

"You know," she told him, drawing closer again, "for a man of few words, I think you have just used up your allotment for the rest of the month." She paused, letting the words sink in. "So just stop talking and kiss me before I start to think that maybe you've suddenly thought better of the whole thing."

That really surprised him. Did she actually think he thought that? How?

"There is no 'better' than this," he told her with such sincerity, Shania could feel the corners of her eyes moistening.

"Then get back to it, Deputy Tallchief," she "ordered," opening her arms to him in a blatant invitation.

The last of his good intentions were completely dissolved and he had absolutely no strength to keep her—or his own desires—at bay any longer. Pulling Shania to him, Daniel's lips covered hers and he began kissing Shania with such fervor that there was no time to breathe, to reconsider what was happening or to once more attempt to call a stop to what was now so obviously inevitable.

Her head was spinning as she felt him kiss her over and over, each kiss growing in magnitude and scope, more powerful than the one that had come before it. She could feel that there was a fire in his veins, a fire that not only consumed him, but had managed to melt away any of her own resistance, however minor that resistance was. That resistance was completely wiped out before it even had a chance to take form.

Everywhere he kissed her, on her face, on her neck, on her throat, that part instantly joined the symphony of aroused sensations, responding to Daniel and fueling her growing desire for the ultimate fulfillment.

His lips continued gaining more ground, moving ever onward until Shania felt as if all of her had been conquered. She had surrendered to him without even attempting to offer so much as the smallest iota of resistance.

Why would she? Shania now knew that this was where it had all been going since the first moment that they had met one another.

When Daniel suddenly stopped again, her head felt as if it

was swirling. That made it difficult for Shania to pull herself together in order to form a coherent thought.

Breathing heavily, she blinked and did her best to focus on him, waiting for Daniel to explain why he had stopped this time.

"We've got an audience," he told her in a low voice, nodding toward Belle.

Turning her head, Shania saw the soft brown eyes that was watching their every move. At any moment, Belle might just push her way between them and easily ruin everything.

Straightening up, Shania said, "Belle, sit," in an authoritative voice.

Daniel was impressed to see that the German shepherd complied, plopping her rear down on the floor, and then she went on to spread her body out like a bearskin rug.

The next moment, Daniel felt Shania get up. His heart sank as he thought that the interlude was over. But then she was taking his hand.

"Come with me," she whispered.

It never occurred to him to ask where—he just went with her, following wherever she was leading.

Shania led him to her bedroom.

As he continued to watch, Shania closed the door behind them, saying, "So Belle doesn't decide to come and investigate."

His smile was warm as he murmured, "Works for me." Taking her back into his arms, he asked, "Now, where were we?"

Shania rose on her toes, her lips inches from his. "I think if you look very closely, you might just see where you left your place marker."

Daniel grinned just before his lips covered hers again, saying, "You're right. There it is."

And then there was no more need for words, nor room for any because he was kissing her again, picking up just where he had left off. He did so with the same amount of fire and verve he'd built up to just before the feel of small, intense eyes watching him had caused him to stop.

It felt as if any restraints, any of the barriers that might have been there, had all disappeared. There were no more obstacles, no more impedance to get in their way.

When Daniel began kissing her again, it felt as if this was what he knew had been waiting for him all along. He tasted not just surrender in Shania's kiss, but destiny, as well.

His destiny.

Because this wasn't about conquest—it was about finally finding his other half, the woman he had been meant to be with all along.

Don't get ahead of yourself, the voice in his head whispered.

The specter of fear hovered over him in the distance, a ghostly reminder that this wasn't the first time that he had felt that he'd found the right woman, found the one he was meant to be with.

But he'd been a naive kid then. Since that time, he had seen disappointment up close and personal, knew firsthand what heartbreak felt like. Had seen it in the face of the woman he'd believed loved him.

It could happen again, that specter haunting him now whispered. *This one could desert you just the way Lana did.*

Daniel shut out the voice, refusing to allow it back in his head.

He felt as if he was completely drunk on desire. He could practically feel it pulsing in his veins, urging him to continue, to make love with this woman and take what she was offering. And if disappointment was waiting for him in the wings, he'd face it later. Right now, this need he had consumed him.

Daniel began to undress her, drawing away Shania's clothes from her body. He held the urgency that throbbed in his veins in check to the best of his ability so that he could prolong the process, making it last.

Making them both just that much more excited about the end of the journey that waited for them.

As he went on undressing her, Daniel felt her hands on his

body, opening up buttons on his shirt, pulling the material off his shoulders. He caught his breath as she pressed her lips against the skin that was revealed beneath.

Slowly she wove a tapestry of warm kisses along the space that was uncovered, branding him.

His breath caught in his throat, then began to come faster until he felt his heart hammering in his chest so much, it almost made him dizzy.

Each movement she made, he matched it, then made one of his own which she in turn mirrored. The game continued like this until there was nothing left to remove, no place left to anoint. They were on her queen-size bed now, free of their clothing, free of any sort of restraints and inhibitions. And they were both on fire.

Daniel worked his way slowly along her body one last time. He began at her throat and moved by small increments along her body as if he was attempting to commit it to memory by touch and by taste. As he skimmed his tongue along her belly, he could feel it quivering beneath him, the invitation crystal clear.

Traveling back up slowly along her damp, palpitating body, he progressed closer by just fractions of an inch until he was almost directly above her.

Daniel looked into her eyes, holding them captive with his own.

Every breath she took he could feel along his own torso. It only fueled his own hunger.

Holding Shania's arms above her head, Daniel slowly threaded his fingers through hers, joining them together before he moved his body the last few increments of an inch closer to hers.

Unable to hold himself in check any longer, Daniel moved his knee between her legs, parting them.

And then he entered her, not quickly but with slow, deliberate determination.

He heard her draw in her breath, felt her heart beating harder a second before he began to move within her.

The dance began slowly, gently, as if he was afraid of disturbing the rhythm that they had just discovered. But when Shania began to echo his movements, then increase them on her own, he joined her, moving with enthusiasm and going faster and faster until they were both racing toward the end that they knew was waiting for them.

Daniel felt her digging her fingertips into his shoulders, felt Shania arching her back as she emulated him thrust for thrust. He could feel the heat coming from her body as they were now racing toward the top of the summit.

Reaching it together, they clung to one another as they felt the wave of fulfillment sweep over both of them, tossing their bodies down the steep incline.

They held on to one another until the very end. And longer.

The sound of labored breathing filled the room that was otherwise nestled in darkness. And they held on to each other, their arms wrapped around one another, until the feeling of ethereal well-being slowly began to recede and fade.

When Daniel was finally able to gather himself together, he turned toward the woman whose body he'd just enjoyed and worshipped and quietly asked, "I didn't hurt you, did I?"

He felt her smile against his shoulder and could feel a longing begin to bud within him again, even though he'd honestly felt that it wouldn't be possible. By all rights, he should have been too exhausted to breathe, much less go another round with her that even remotely approximated what they had just done.

And yet there it was. Desire. Struggling to grow and take over.

"I believe the expression is I'm feeling no pain," she told him with a smile that made her eyes sparkle.

"That usually refers to someone being drunk," he told her.

"Maybe I am," she allowed. "Drunk on a feeling," she added.

"So I didn't hurt you?" Daniel asked. He was worried now

that maybe he'd gotten too carried away, been too focused on his own pleasure and not enough on what he was doing to her.

She turned her face toward him. "No, you didn't hurt me. You were miles away from hurting me, Daniel," she assured him. Then, suppressing the smile that was trying so hard to surface, she asked, "Did I hurt you?"

The dark hid her face from him and he didn't see the smile that was there, so he addressed her question as if she'd actually asked him the question seriously.

"No, you didn't."

And then, when he heard the soft laugh, he knew she was putting him on. Daniel responded by pushing her onto her back and looming over her.

"You're slender. You couldn't have hurt me unless you had an anvil strapped to your waist."

"That would have made what we just did almost impossible," she told him. "Picture it," she urged, amused.

The glimmer of moonlight pushing its way into her room allowed him to see the wide grin on her face.

"I have a feeling that we would have managed somehow," he told her.

She didn't even try to hide her laugh this time. "I think we would have, too." She threaded her arms around Daniel's neck, arching her back so that her body was once again close to being sealed to his. "Interested in an encore?"

His mouth curved as he looked at her. "You're giving me a lot of credit."

"I don't think you're giving yourself enough," she countered.

Daniel could feel himself wanting her all over again with an urgency that was impossible to ignore. "I guess we'll just have to see who's right."

She smiled up into his face. "I guess so."

And then the words between them faded away as the dance that they had already shared once now began all over again.

CHAPTER EIGHTEEN

"So where were you?"

Daniel whirled around, startled to hear his sister's voice as he passed through the living room. He had let himself into the house quietly even though he had expected Elena to be in her bed, asleep at this hour. The one thing he hadn't expected was to be the subject of scrutiny as he entered his own house.

Elena had apparently been waiting for him on the sofa. Closing the TV monitor, she was on her feet and circling him like an old-fashioned version of an interrogator closing in on her subject.

"You were off work today and as far as I know, Forever isn't in the middle of some crime wave, which means that the sheriff wouldn't have suddenly pressed you into service. And that, in turn," his sister concluded, "means you should have been home by now. You weren't." Elena now looked up at her brother's face and repeated her question. "So where were you?"

He didn't care to have the tables turned on him this way. "Out."

"Out," Elena echoed, enjoying herself as she took on the role that her brother normally played with her. "Out where?"

Daniel waved away her question. "That doesn't matter. I

thought you'd be home, asleep—or taking advantage of the occasion and celebrating with your friends."

"I was celebrating," she confirmed, never taking her eyes off Daniel.

"And you're back this soon?" he questioned.

The Elena he remembered from not that long ago would still be out there. That she wasn't was something to be grateful for—and he was, but at the same time he wasn't all that happy about her delving into his life like this.

"It's late," Elena said matter-of-factly. "And besides, someone once told me that I shouldn't get carried away celebrating too hard." Concluding her story, she pulled her lips back in a patient smile and, inclining her head, told him, "Your turn."

Daniel frowned at her. "I am not accountable to you, Elena. I'm the adult here, remember?"

But his sister was not about to back off. "Someone once told me that age had nothing to do with it. Family is always accountable to family."

She was right, but that didn't help his frustration level at the moment. "Why is it that you remember these things when it's to your advantage to remember?"

Amused, Elena's grin grew wider. "I'm a fast learner," she told him. And then she looked at him with a knowing expression and asked, "Were you out with Ms. Stewart?"

Her unexpected question caught Daniel completely off guard. Only his years of keeping his thoughts and emotions hidden saved him from giving everything away.

"Why would you even ask that?" he asked.

"Oh, *please*," Elena cried, rolling her eyes. At least *that* was something he was familiar with, Daniel thought. But definitely not happy about. "Everyone knows you two are a couple waiting to happen."

"You sound like Miss Joan's grooming you to be her understudy," he commented, completely bypassing his sister's question.

And then Elena said the second thing that night that completely threw him for a loop.

"Would that be so bad?" she asked him. "I mean, everyone looks up to Miss Joan and she seems to have her finger on the pulse of just about everyone and everything in and around Forever." Because Daniel appeared so stunned, she pounced on her initial question. "Okay, stop stalling, Deputy Sheriff Big Brother. Where were you?"

His eyes met hers. "I'd rather talk about you."

Elena didn't give an inch. "And I want to know where you were." Enjoying this game, she couldn't help but laugh.

He took that as an indication that she was backing off. Daniel softened, sitting down for a moment and nodding at the spot next to him. Elena took the hint and sat down.

"How was the test?"

Elena shrugged and then made herself more comfortable on the sofa. "It was okay—thanks to Ms. Stewart." And then she doubled back to her first question. "So, am I right?"

Daniel could only look at her, blindsided by her sudden about-face. "What?"

Elena sighed dramatically as if he was using up her dwindling supply of patience. Slowly enunciating each word, she asked, "Were you out with Ms. Stewart?"

He had just about had it with her questions. This wasn't a topic he was prepared to discuss yet, especially not with his little sister. Certainly not until he knew how Shania felt about their future, or if they even *had* a future.

"Elena—"

"'Cause it's all right with me if you were," Elena assured him brightly.

That managed to momentarily stop Daniel in his tracks. He hadn't expected her to say that. "Oh?"

Elena's smile went from ear to ear. She was convinced that her teacher was good for Daniel, that Ms. Stewart could make him be a happier person. "Yes."

"And why's that?" Daniel asked, turning to face his sister on the sofa. He couldn't remember talking like this with Elena or being this at ease with her, not for a long, long time.

Too long.

Elena didn't even have to pause to think. "Well, for one thing, because she's made you into a nicer person. You're not as grumpy as you've been—at least until just now," she amended.

"Grumpy?" Daniel questioned, then protested, "I haven't been grumpy."

"Yes, you have," Elena insisted, amazed that he could actually deny it. "You've been acting like you had the weight of the world on your shoulders." Until just a little while ago, that would have made her feel guilty. But not anymore. "I know it can't just be me," she told him, "because I don't weigh that much, so it's got to be something else, too. And Ms. Stewart's shown you how to juggle that weight and be a nice guy about it. Like you used to be," she emphasized.

"I could say the same thing about you," Daniel told his sister pointedly.

He watched for her reaction, half expecting Elena's back to go up. But instead, his sister nodded her head, a small smile playing on her lips.

"Yeah, I guess you could at that," she agreed. "That's Ms. Stewart's doing, too," she admitted. "She worked with me, showed me that I didn't have to turn my back on everything I'd been before in order to be able to grow as a person."

"Is that what you've been doing?" he questioned, trying not to look as if her take on her own previous actions amused him. "Growing?"

"Yes, that's what I've been doing," she concluded with quiet pride and a self-assurance that he hadn't heard before.

Something inside Daniel softened as he realized that she was right. And why she was right. Because the same woman who had touched his life had touched Elena's life, too.

"Yes, you have," he agreed.

Elena raised her chin. "So what are you going to do about it?"

His dark brows drew together in confusion. "All right, you just lost me."

Elena was quick to jump in while her brother was still pliable. "Well, we've just both agreed that we've become the better versions of ourselves that we've always wanted to be. The one thing that's changed in our lives is that we've both spent time with Ms. Stewart, being shown the error of our old ways."

She took a breath, her eyes never leaving his face. "So what are you going to do about keeping Ms. Stewart in our lives? In *your* life?" Elena deliberately specified, watching her brother intently.

"Are you telling me to keep seeing her?" Daniel asked.

Elena sighed deeply and once again rolled her eyes. "I'm telling you to do more than that. I'm telling you not to miss the boat. I'm telling you to get the molasses out of your veins, Big Brother."

"And...?" he asked, still certain that his sister couldn't possibly be saying what he thought she was saying.

Exasperated, she asked him, "Do you really need cue cards?"

He made his mind up to deny the existence of anything between himself and Shania. The disappointment if this fell through would be too devastating for both of them. He'd lived through it once. He didn't want Elena going through it with him if this didn't work out.

"I do when it comes to understanding what you're trying to tell me."

In truth, Daniel was afraid to jump to the conclusion that he *wanted* to jump to because once he did... What if the conclusion he wanted with all his heart turned out to be the wrong one? Continuing the fledgling relationship with Shania would definitely be difficult and challenging.

Moreover, if Elena thought he had romance on his mind with the end result being asking Shania to marry him, and his sister *didn't* want him to, he'd find himself facing a huge dilemma.

Elena's next words were prefaced by another very deep sigh.

"Ask the woman to marry you before one of the other unattached men around here beats you to the punch," she told her brother in no uncertain terms.

Just what did it take to light a fire under him? she silently wondered.

Daniel could only stare at his sister. "You're serious."

"Yes, I am," she willingly admitted. "Aren't you?"

All Daniel could tell Elena was that, "It's complicated."

"Complicated is what people say when they get cold feet or don't have the courage to face up to something they should," she told him.

His eyes darkened. "Stand down, Ellie."

She ignored what was obviously an order. "Do you love her?"

The last of his patience evaporated. "Okay, Ellie, game time is over," he told her, getting up. "It's late. Go to bed."

"It's a simple question," she told her brother. "Do you love her or don't you?"

He wasn't up to this right now. "If you won't go to bed, I will," he announced, striding toward the rear of the house.

Elena was on her feet, moving quickly and getting directly in front of him.

"Is that a yes?" she pressed.

He looked down into Elena's face, trying to fathom what was going on behind those expressive eyes of hers. "*Why* do you need to know so badly?"

"Because I do," she answered flatly. "Because things are finally coming together in my life and Ms. Stewart's the underlying reason behind it all—for both of us. Now, do you?" she asked, coming back to her question. Her eyes dared her brother to say no.

He debated not saying anything, or lying, and found that he couldn't. Not to his sister.

"Yes," he finally said. "And it's going no further than right here, understand?" he demanded, putting his sister on notice.

He could have sworn that her eyes were gleaming. But her voice was unusually solemn as she repeated, "Understand."

He knew she didn't really understand. Taking hold of Ellie's shoulders, he held her in place.

"Listen to me, Ellie. I don't want you doing anything, saying anything, *thinking* anything that will make Ms. Stewart suddenly come to her senses and run for her life. *Do I make myself clear?*" he asked, again enunciating each word.

Instead of saying what he wanted to hear, she began to protest. "But—"

He put his hand up to silence her. She stopped talking. "Not a word, Ellie," he warned seriously. "I want you to give me your word."

His sister tried again. "But—"

"Not a word," he repeated, emphasizing each word. "I'm glad you like her and that she's had such a positive influence in your life, but I want to handle this in my own way, at my own pace. In my own time."

She knew that she couldn't change his mind, not when his cadence was this slow, this deliberate. But she still had to tell him what was on her mind.

"I think you're making a mistake," she told him.

"You're entitled to think anything you want," Daniel said. "As long as you remember to keep it to yourself. Understood?" he emphasized again. "Because if you don't, if you decide that you're going to try to butt in like some kind of misguided teenaged Cupid, I swear I'll ground you until you're one hundred and three. Understand?"

Ellie sighed again, frustrated. "I understand."

"Good," he pronounced. "Now I'm going to bed," he told her, once again heading toward the back of the house. "It's been a long day."

Elena was not about to dispute that. "I'll bet it has."

He could hear the grin in his sister's voice even without looking at her.

He just kept going.

"You really are growing up way too fast," Daniel murmured to himself.

He hadn't meant for Elena to overhear, but she had. "Nothing you can do about that, Big Brother," she responded with an even bigger grin.

"You are my last hope, Miss Joan," Elena said with sincerity.

It was Monday. Though she had wanted to talk to the woman at the crack of dawn, she'd forced herself to wait until school was over. The moment it was, she had made a beeline for the diner, bringing her problem to the only person she knew who could find a way to work through the obstacle that was her brother.

Elena crossed to Miss Joan, asking the woman for a private audience, so to speak. Miss Joan compromised by moving her to the far end of the counter, away from the other customers.

She listened to Elena's story, taking it all in without comment. Until now.

"What makes you think I can do anything about that stubborn brother of yours?" Miss Joan asked. "If his mind's made up, I can't make it change."

Elena didn't believe that for a second. "Miss Joan, you could make it rain in the middle of a record dry spell in the desert if you wanted to."

Miss Joan's expression remained unchanged. Only her sharp eyes narrowed. "You think flattery's going to turn my head, young lady?"

"No, ma'am," Elena replied solemnly. "I'm just telling you what I believe is true." She took a breath and then forged on. "Everybody knows that you can do anything you put your mind to."

"I can't hog-tie them and make them sit across from each other until your brother proposes," Miss Joan said, sensing that was where this whole plan of Elena's was going.

"You wouldn't need to hog-tie them," Elena promised. "They just need a little push, that's all." She leaned over the counter, her voice lowering as she said, "I can't say anything to Ms. Stewart because Danny made me promise not to."

Miss Joan knew what was coming. "But you didn't promise that I wouldn't."

Elena smiled, happy that Miss Joan understood. "No, I didn't."

"Don't give me that innocent look, young lady," Miss Joan said sharply. "I can see right through you."

Her tone didn't intimidate Elena. "I know. That's why I'm here."

Miss Joan laughed. It was a sound that wasn't heard very frequently. Elena smiled in response, knowing that she had gotten to the woman and that everything was going to be resolved just the way she hoped. Perhaps it would take a while. She knew Miss Joan couldn't be rushed. But she also knew that Miss Joan got results the way that no one else around Forever ever could. And that was good enough for her.

"Go home, little girl. I've got to think about this," Miss Joan told her.

"Yes, ma'am." Elena slid off the stool she was sitting on. "And thank you."

Miss Joan scowled. "There's nothing to thank me for yet."

Elena just smiled back. "But there will be," she replied. "I know that there will be."

Miss Joan said nothing. She had already turned away and was topping off a customer's coffee.

And thinking.

CHAPTER NINETEEN

WHEN HE WAS younger and dealing with something that weighed heavily on his mind, Daniel would take his horse, ride out as far as he could and just lose himself in his surroundings. He'd ride until whatever was bothering him wasn't there anymore. Until all those oppressive thoughts just evaporated.

But he couldn't do that anymore. He had responsibilities. There was his sister, who still depended on him for all the essentials, and his job, which required him to show up every day. Taking off at the spur of the moment just was not an option. Facing up to whatever was out there with his name stamped on it was now what was called for.

So when he discovered that Elena was hell-bent on butting into his life and that his sister had been seen going in to talk to Miss Joan when she should have been on her way home from school, Daniel got the distinct feeling in his gut that he had to get ahead of whatever disaster might result from all this interference and be waiting to take him down.

This was ultimately the reason why, after having kept his distance from Shania for several days, he gathered up his courage and sought her out.

He went to see her late in the day after his shift was over.

Working on next week's lesson plan, Shania didn't hear the

doorbell when it first rang. It was Belle, her furry bodyguard, that alerted her to someone being at her door.

Taking hold of the German shepherd's collar, she held on to it as she went to the door and opened it a crack.

When she saw Daniel standing on her doorstep, her first reaction was a flash of happiness. Her next reaction was an equal flash of annoyance, the latter because he had stayed away from her for several days without so much as a word of acknowledgment about their time together.

Torn, she decided to opt for neither and fell back on acting blasé and indifferent.

Belle was pulling, eager to express her joyful reaction over seeing Daniel, but Shania held fast.

"Can I come in?" Daniel asked, still standing on the other side of the threshold.

Shania shrugged, then opened the front door all the way, allowing him to come in.

"Deputy Tallchief, what can I do for you?" she asked him formally.

Daniel heard the touch of iciness in her voice and instantly felt guilty about his part in putting that iciness there.

"How are you doing?" he asked, feeling incredibly awkward.

If possible, her voice grew even cooler. "Well, and you?"

They might as well have been two total strangers who knew one another by sight but nothing more.

Belle was doing her part in attempting to breach that gap by jumping up at Daniel. He petted the dog, but his attention was on Shania.

"I'm all right," he finally answered. The next moment, he shook his head. "No, that's a lie. I'm not."

Shania held herself in check, refusing to let her feelings get the better of her. "I'm sorry to hear that. Maybe you should drop by the medical clinic. I'm sure they'd make room in their schedule to see you, seeing as how you're part of the sheriff's department."

But he shook his head. "It's not that kind of 'not right,'" Daniel answered, sensing that she had to already know that.

Shania abruptly turned on her heel and walked into her living room, and then turned around to look at him. "Oh? Then what kind of 'not right' is it?"

Daniel indicated the sofa, nodding toward it. "Can I sit?"

Shania shrugged again, the picture of indifference. "You can do whatever you want."

Daniel still felt like he was the target of frostbite. He took a stab at explaining what was behind his behavior, even though that sort of thing wasn't his long suit. He was far better at keeping silent than talking.

"Shania, you have to understand that I didn't want you thinking that I was moving too fast," he said.

"Too fast?" she repeated, and for the first time he saw just a flicker of amusement on her lips. "Tallchief, there were schools of *snails* that left you in the dust."

He tried again, rephrasing what he'd just said. "I didn't want to crowd you. I wanted to give you room to breathe."

"You left enough room for an entire major city to breathe," she said, the flicker of amusement gone again. Her hurt feelings ran deeper than she'd realized. "Did you ever stop to think that by giving me this much 'room,' you made me think that you were regretting—deeply regretting—what happened between us?"

"Regretting it?" he repeated, saying the words as if he had absolutely no understanding of what they meant.

"Yes, regretting it," Shania emphasized. "As in trying to pretend it never happened, or at least wishing it hadn't," she concluded, feeling more hurt with each syllable she uttered.

Daniel stared at her in disbelief, momentarily speechless. "That would have made me pretty stupid," he told Shania flatly.

She laughed shortly. "Well, if you're waiting for me to argue with you about that, I'm afraid you're out of luck. Whatever you might feel about that night, I don't regret any of it." She could feel tears forming and she blinked hard to keep them from falling. "I just regret how you feel."

"How I feel?" Daniel questioned, lost again.

"Yes, how you feel." She said the words with seething emphasis, struggling to keep back her hurt and her anger. "Embarrassed, ashamed, I don't know—"

"How about grateful," he interjected, raising his voice so she could hear him.

The thoughts forming in her head came to a dead stop at that single word. "How's that again?" she asked in confusion.

"Grateful," he repeated, his voice low but all the more compelling. "I feel grateful that it happened. Very grateful."

She didn't believe him. He was just trying to snow her. "Well, if that's supposedly true, why did you go into hiding?"

He told her part of the reason, hoping that was enough. "Because I didn't want you to feel that I was pressuring you into something. Elena gave me the third degree when I got home that night, acting more like an interrogator than I ever did when she got home late.

"And then a couple of days later, someone happened to mention that she was seen talking to Miss Joan. Miss Joan, who'd been the one who'd tried to play matchmaker with us to begin with," he pointed out. He searched Shania's face, trying to see if she understood what he was telling her. "I didn't want either one of them making you feel as if you were outnumbered and being forced to, well, be *receptive* to the idea of 'us.'"

"But I *am* receptive," Shania insisted. She put her hands on her hips. "Did you ever stop to think that maybe you should just come here and talk to me—the way you are right now?"

"In my mind that would have just been part of crowding you," he explained.

"Or making me feel as if you were interested in continuing what you'd started," she said with feeling. "Instead of regretting it with every breath you took."

"I never not regretted anything more," Daniel protested.

Shania winced despite herself. "I'm a physics teacher and I teach math on occasion. I'm not an English teacher, but you've *got* to know that sentence is so poorly worded it hurts." She paused for a moment before saying, "But I'll take it." A grin curved her mouth.

And then she looked at Daniel's face and saw something more. Something he wasn't telling her. Something that was most likely at the bottom of all this.

"What else?" Shania asked.

His eyebrows drew together as he looked at her. "I don't know what you—"

Shania didn't give him a chance to finish or make denials. "The other night, when you said you had 'baggage' and I said everyone does, it's about that, isn't it?" she asked him. "About your 'baggage.'"

When he made no comment, she knew she had guessed right. Now all she needed was for him to trust her enough to tell her just what that baggage he was carrying around was.

"Why don't you unpack it so we can get it out of the way?" Shania told him, watching Daniel intently, looking for a sign that she was getting through to him. "Unless you don't want to talk about it."

He didn't. But again, that wasn't an option here, not now.

Daniel looked at the woman he had made love with for a long moment and knew that if he kept this to himself, he'd lose her. That exactly what he was afraid of happening *would* happen—and that he would be instrumental in doing it himself.

Taking a deep breath, he began to talk.

"You are not the first woman that I've been in love with."

Shania stared at him. He hadn't realized what he'd just said. For him, this was just part of the story. To her, it *was* the story.

But she kept silent because she knew that this—whatever *this* was—had to come out and if she stopped him now, it might just abort itself before it had a chance to see the light of day.

"Go on," she urged quietly.

"There was this girl, Lana." His face softened as he said the woman's name. "She meant everything to me. We were going to get married and move out West to start a brand-new life together. We had everything all figured out." There was a cold cynicism in his voice that she had never heard before, as if he was mocking himself and the idealist kid he had once been. "And then my parents died and I had to leave school to take care of Elena."

He shrugged. "That didn't fit in with the plan that Lana had for us. She put up with the situation for a little while, then told me that I had to choose. It was either her and our new life, or my kid sister and life in Forever. I was angry that she was doing this to me at a time when I was still reeling from my parents' death and I picked Elena."

He looked at her and she could read what was in his eyes. "I thought she'd change her mind, you know, reconsider. But she packed up her things and was gone before I even knew what was happening. It was like my whole world collapsed twice. I swore I'd never put myself in that kind of a position again."

"And then you fell in love with me," Shania said. When he looked at her sharply, she held her hands up. "Hey, you're the one who said I wasn't the first one you ever fell in love with—which means that you *did* fall in love with me. Or was that just something you said to move the story along?"

He frowned, annoyed with himself for not monitoring his words more carefully. "No," he admitted quietly, "I meant it."

She read between the lines—and things began to fall together.

"And now you're afraid I'll become another Lana and just walk out on you whenever you're facing another crisis." She peered into his face. "Did I get it right, Daniel?"

"Yeah," he agreed reluctantly.

She squared her shoulders just a little. "You do realize that's really insulting, don't you?"

He looked at her in surprise. "I—"

"Because it is," she informed him. "All women are not alike and I'd like to think that something inside of you knows that." Her voice grew very still as she informed him, "I'm not accustomed to sleeping with my students' parents or guardians, nor do I have a passing acquaintance with one-night stands. Never had one, never will," she declared with finality. "The only all-nighter I ever pulled was studying for this one Quantum Physics final."

He wanted to apologize for insulting her. "Shania—"

"I'm not finished," she told him. "Now, if you're trying to put up barriers because you don't want to be stuck with me, just say so and you can consider yourself unstuck. Otherwise—"

Taking advantage of the fact that she paused to take in a breath, he asked Shania, "Do you always talk this much?"

She flushed. "Only when I'm very afraid that something that means a great deal to me is about to be forever lost the second I stop talking," she told him.

"I guess then I'll risk getting into this relationship with you," Daniel said.

She looked at him as if she was scrutinizing him. "Haven't you been listening? There is no risk, Deputy Tallchief," she said. "There's only me, forever and always."

Daniel smiled as he took her into his arms. Heaven help him, he believed her. "I can handle that."

"Good answer," she told him, smiling. "And for the record, Deputy, I do love you. More than I ever thought possible."

But he wasn't finished asking questions yet. "How about Elena?" he asked. "We're a package deal."

If he thought that was a deal-breaker, he was wrong, Shania thought with a smile. "Even better."

"Yes, it is," he agreed just before he brought his mouth down to hers and picked up where they had left off the other night.

EPILOGUE

"YOU KNOW WHAT would make it feel more like Christmas?" Shania asked out of the blue.

She had taken a rare Saturday off from working on her lesson plans and had devoted the entirety of it to getting some heavy-duty Christmas decorating done with Daniel and his sister.

Daniel thought back to that morning, when he and Shania, along with a number of other people in Forever, had gotten involved in Miss Joan's annual tradition of scouting for and bringing back the town Christmas tree. Putting up the thirty-foot tree in the town square took a good part of the day. Decorating it was usually a three-day affair.

"You mean more than helping bring in that giant tree for Miss Joan, starting to decorate that humongous thing and then letting you talk me into hauling another oversize specimen into my own house?" He looked accusingly at the tree. "The one we're presently decorating?" Daniel asked.

The hour was getting late now and she could see that Daniel was just about decorated out.

"This is not an oversize specimen," Shania protested. She was on a ladder, doing her best to hang decorations on the uppermost branches.

"It's a lot bigger than the trees I usually bring in for the occasion," Daniel countered.

Shania gave him a look. "What you were proposing to bring in wasn't a tree, it was a malnourished twig and it certainly didn't deserve to be called a Christmas tree." She hung up another multicolored ball that caught the light and flashed it around the room. "And if you remember, Elena agreed with me."

That didn't carry any weight in his opinion. "You brainwashed her into agreeing with you."

She wasn't about to concede. "I did not. Your sister has free will. She could have disagreed." Stretching, she hung up another decoration.

"Not likely," Daniel contradicted. "You're her hero. She would have been far more apt to disagree with my choice than yours."

"That's because my choice was better," Shania informed him with what he viewed as a triumphant nod of her head.

Daniel pretended to sigh. "Have it your way."

Her eyes smiled first before the rest of her caught up. "Thanks, I will."

He laughed softly and shook his head. "I never doubted it," he said. Daniel scanned the room, as if suddenly aware that they were alone. "Looks like we lost our helper."

"You just noticed?" Shania marveled, amazed as she went up another step, holding on to the ladder with one hand as she reached up for a higher branch with the other. "I think she ducked out on us and went to bed about forty-five minutes ago." Shania smiled at him fondly. "Not very observant, are you?"

He shrugged, picking up a couple more decorations himself and hanging them on the lower branches. "I save that for work."

She was focusing on hooking a decoration on a branch that was almost out of reach. "I see."

Daniel paused to look up at her. The small box in his back pocket felt as if it was pressing against his skin. "And you."

Shania stopped hanging decorations and looked down at him, replaying his last words. "Why me?"

He knew he had to answer her, but his tongue suddenly felt leaden. "I'm just trying to gauge where we are," he finally said.

"For the record, we're in your living room, creating a proper-looking Christmas tree," she answered, turning her attention back to what she was doing.

It was time, he told himself. "That's not what I meant."

"What did you mean?" Shania asked casually as she hung up the last of the decorations she'd brought up with her. Needing another handful, she climbed down again and went to the worn box that Daniel used to house the tree decorations.

"Where *we* are," he repeated, his eyes on hers as he tried to get his point across without having to spell it out for her.

She looked at Daniel over her shoulder, scrutinizing him. Was something up, or was she reading too much into his words?

"Why is that so important?" she asked.

He put his hand on her arm, stopping her as she started climbing back up on the ladder with a fresh supply of decorations.

"Could you hold still for a minute?" he asked her.

"Daniel, I'd like to get this tree all decorated before next Christmas, so now isn't the time for me to take a break. Besides—" she nodded at the tree "—I'm almost done."

"Shania, Christmas isn't for another three weeks," he pointed out. "What's the hurry?"

"So you and Elena can enjoy the fruits of all this labor longer," she answered matter-of-factly.

He looked at her as if her words had caused him to have a sudden revelation.

"So, doing something sooner allows you to enjoy something longer?" he asked, as if trying to get something straight in his mind.

"In most cases. Certainly in this case." She noticed he was still holding on to her arm. "So could you let go of my arm and let me get back to finishing up the tree?"

Instead of letting her arm go, he continued holding it. "In a minute," he answered. "If I don't do this now, I just might lose my nerve."

She had no idea what he was talking about and why he was still holding on to her. Was he anticipating that she was going to bolt for some reason?

"Lose your nerve about what?" she asked him. "I think it's only fair to warn you that I'm fading fast here and if I don't finish this tree in the next few minutes, it's going to have to wait until tomorrow."

"Would that be such a bad thing?"

Maybe he still had a ways to go before understanding her, Shania thought.

"Perhaps not for someone else," Shania allowed. "But I don't like to leave something only half done."

"Neither do I," Daniel agreed.

"Then you understand how I feel," she said, never taking her eyes off his face. He looked uneasy, she thought. Why?

"I hope so," he told her.

His uneasiness seemed to spread to her. "Are we talking about the same thing, Tallchief?"

"Probably not." Before she could ask him anything else, he reached into his back pocket, closed his hand around the small box and pulled it out. "I'm talking about this."

Shania stared at the box, totally speechless and afraid to allow herself to even *think* that it might be what it looked like.

Daniel used his thumb to flip the lid back, exposing a small, perfect-looking pear-shaped diamond engagement ring. He'd used nearly half the money he had managed to save in the past couple of years to buy it.

"I'm dying here," Daniel finally said, unable to take her silence. "*Say* something."

She was mesmerized by the way the diamond gleamed, creating rainbows and flashing them on the wall. "It's beautiful."

That wasn't exactly what he was hoping to hear. "Say something else."

She raised her eyes to his. "Is that for me?"

"Getting warmer," he told her. Taking the ring out of its box, he slipped it onto her ring finger. "It fits," he said, happy that he had managed to correctly guess her size.

She could have gone on watching the way the light played off the ring for hours, but she raised her head to look up at Daniel.

"I think you're supposed to ask me something really important now," she told Daniel.

And then, amid the nerves that were dancing through him and his fear of possible rejection, Daniel realized that he had forgotten to ask Shania the one question that had been on his mind for the past three months.

Taking her hand in his, he asked, "Shania Stewart, will you marry me?"

She let go of the breath she had been holding this entire time. Her heart slammed against her rib cage as she cried "Yes!" just before she threw her arms around his neck and kissed him.

Daniel's heart emulated hers, hammering just as wildly in his chest as he felt hers was pounding in hers.

He drew back his head just for a moment and asked, "You're sure?"

"Yes, I'm sure!" she cried breathlessly. "Of course I'm sure!"

"That's all I wanted to hear," Daniel replied just before he lowered his lips to hers.

He went on kissing her for a very long time.

The Christmas tree was not finished being decorated that night.

* * * * *

A Will, A Wish, A Wedding
Kate Hardy

Forever

Glamorous and heartfelt love stories.

Kate Hardy has been a bookworm since she was a toddler. When she isn't writing, Kate enjoys reading, theater, live music, ballet and the gym. She lives with her husband, student children and their spaniel in Norwich, England. You can contact her via her website: katehardy.com.

Books by Kate Hardy

Harlequin Forever

A Crown by Christmas

Soldier Prince's Secret Baby Gift

Summer at Villa Rosa

The Runaway Bride and the Billionaire

Christmas Bride for the Boss
Reunited at the Altar
A Diamond in the Snow
Finding Mr. Right in Florence
One Night to Remember

Harlequin Medical

Changing Shifts

Fling with Her Hot-Shot Consultant

A Nurse and a Pup to Heal Him
Mistletoe Proposal on the Children's Ward

Visit the Author Profile page
at millsandboon.com.au for more titles.

Dear Reader,

I'm thrilled that this is my ninetieth book for Harlequin!

I wanted to do something a little different and play with one of the tropes I remember reading avidly when I was in my teens: the will with a Very Big Condition. Hugo and Alice are perfect for each other, but both refuse to date. Rosemary uses her will to get them together. And, although they loathe each other on first sight, they discover that they are perfect to help the other move on from the past.

With Alice being a butterfly specialist and Hugo being an architect, I thoroughly enjoyed researching for this book—visiting gorgeous glass domes (especially the Reichstag in Berlin), butterfly houses (London, with my best friend) and sites of special scientific interest (I took my husband to the hill fort where Hugo and Alice see the blue butterflies, and the look of wonder on his face when he realized I hadn't been teasing...that was definitely a romantic moment!).

I hope you enjoy their journey.

With love,

Kate Hardy

To Gerard, Chris and Chloe, who've supported me
all the way through ninety books, with all my love.

Praise for
Kate Hardy

"Ms. Hardy has written a very sweet novel about
forgiveness and breaking the molds we place
ourselves in... A good heartstring novel that will
have you embracing happiness in your heart."

—*Harlequin Junkie* on *Christmas Bride for the Boss*

CHAPTER ONE

YOU DON'T BELONG HERE, oik, a posh voice sneered in Alice's head.

Barney and his cronies would've laughed themselves sick if they could've seen her standing at the foot of a set of white marble steps. What business did the girl from the council estate have here, in the poshest bit of Chelsea?

She lifted her chin to tell the voice she wasn't listening. Ten years ago, she'd been so naive that she hadn't realised that Barney—the most gorgeous man at the Oxford college where they were both studying—was only dating her for a bet. She'd found out the truth at the college ball where she'd thought he was going to propose, while he'd been planning to collect his winnings after proving he'd turned the oik into a posh girl. He hadn't loved her for herself or even wanted her; instead, it had been a warped kind of Eliza Doolittle thing. He and his friends had been laughing at her all along, and she'd been so hurt and ashamed.

Now Dr Alice Walters was a respected lepidopterist. She was comfortable with who she was professionally and was happy to give keynote speeches at high-powered conferences; but socially she always had to silence the voice in her head telling her that she wasn't good enough—especially if her surroundings were posh.

Why *had* Rosemary Grey's solicitor asked to see her? Maybe Rosemary had left some specimens to the university. Or maybe this was about the project they'd worked on together: editing the journals and writing the biography of the butterfly collector Viola Ferrers, Rosemary's great-grandmother. Alice had visited her elderly friend in hospital several times after her stroke and, although Rosemary's sentences had been jumbled, her anxiety had been clear. Alice had promised Rosemary that she'd see the project through. Hopefully, whoever had inherited the journals would give her access to them, but she needed to be in full professional mode in case there were any doubts. Now really wasn't the time for imposter syndrome to resurface and point out that she looked a bit awkward in the business suit and heels she hardly ever wore, there was a bit of hair she hadn't straightened properly, and her make-up wasn't sophisticated enough.

The one thing Barney's callousness had taught her all those years ago was that image *mattered*—even though she thought people should judge her by what was in her head and her heart, not by what she looked like. For now she'd go with the superficial and let them judge the butterfly by its chrysalis.

'This is for you and Viola, Rosemary,' Alice said softly. She walked up the steps to the intimidatingly wide front door with its highly polished brass fittings and pushed it open.

'May I help you?' the receptionist asked.

Alice gave her a very professional smile. 'Thank you. I'm Dr Alice Walters. I have an appointment with Mr Hemingford at two-thirty.'

The receptionist checked the screen and nodded. 'I'll let him know you're here, Dr Walters. The waiting area's just through there. Can I offer you a cup of coffee while you're waiting?'

Alice would have loved some coffee, but she didn't want to risk spilling it all over her suit—and right now she was feeling nervous enough to be clumsy. 'Thank you for the offer, but I'm fine,' she said politely, and headed for the waiting area.

There were a couple of others sitting there: a middle-aged woman who kept glancing at her watch and frowning, as if her appointment was running a bit late, and a man with floppy dark hair and the most amazing cobalt-blue eyes who was staring out of the window, looking completely lost.

For one crazy moment, she thought about going over to him and asking if he was all right. She knew from working with her students that if someone was having a rough day, human contact and a bit of kindness could make all the difference.

But the man was a stranger, this was a solicitor's office, and whatever was wrong was none of her business. Besides, she needed to make sure she was prepared for anything, given the infuriating vagueness of the solicitor's letter. So she sat down in a quiet corner, took her phone from her bag, and re-read the notes she'd made about the butterfly project.

Hugo Grey still couldn't quite believe that his eccentric great-aunt was dead. He'd thought that Rosemary would live for ever. She'd been the only one of his family he could bear to be around when his life had imploded nearly three years ago. Unlike just about everyone else in his life, she hadn't insisted over and over that he shouldn't blame himself for Emma's death, or tried to make him talk about his feelings; she'd simply asked him to come and help her with an errand that almost always didn't materialise, made him endless cups of tea and given him space to breathe. And there, in that little corner of Notting Hill, he'd started to heal and learn to face the world again.

He'd spent the first three months of this year in Scotland, so he hadn't been able to visit Rosemary as much as he would've liked, but he'd still called her twice a week and organised a cleaner and a weekly grocery delivery for her. Once he was back in London, he'd popped in on Monday and Thursday evenings, and she'd been fine—until the stroke. He'd visited her in hospital every other day, but it had been clear she wouldn't recover.

And now he was to be her executor.

Just as he'd been for Emma. Hugo knew exactly how to register a death, organise a funeral, plan a wake, write a good eulogy and execute a will, because he'd already done it all for his wife.

He clenched his fists. He'd let Emma down—attending an architectural conference thousands of miles away in America instead of being at her side when she'd had that fatal asthma attack. If he'd been home, in London, he could've got medical help to her in time to save her. He couldn't change the past, but he could learn from it; he wasn't going to let his great-aunt down. She'd trusted him to be her executor, so he'd do it—and he'd do it *properly*.

He glanced round the waiting room. There were two others sitting on the leather chairs: a middle-aged woman who was clearly impatient at being kept waiting, and a woman of around his own age who looked terrifyingly polished.

It was nearly half-past two. Thankfully Philip Hemingford was usually punctual. Hugo could hand over the death certificate, and then start working through whatever Rosemary wanted him to do. He knew from the copy of the will she'd given him that she'd left nearly everything to his father and there were some smaller bequests; he'd make sure everything was carried out properly, because he'd loved his eccentric great-aunt dearly.

A door opened and Hugo's family solicitor appeared. 'Mr Grey, Dr Walters?'

Dr Walters?

Hugo had been pretty sure this appointment was for him alone; he was representing his father, who wasn't well. Who on earth was Dr Walters?

The terrifyingly polished woman stood up, surprising him. She didn't look like the sort of person who'd pop in to see Rosemary for a cup of tea and a chat. Hugo knew all Rosemary's neighbours, and his great-aunt hadn't mentioned anyone moving into the street recently. This didn't feel quite right.

'Please, have a seat,' Philip Hemingford said, gesturing to the two chairs in front of his desk as he closed the door behind them. 'Now, can I assume you already know each other?'

'No,' Hugo said. And she looked as mystified as he felt.

'Then I'll introduce you. Dr Walters, this is Hugo Grey, Rosemary's great-nephew. Mr Grey, this is Alice Walters, Rosemary's business associate.'

Since when had his great-aunt had business arrangements? As far as Hugo knew, she'd been living on the income from family investments, most of which ended with her death. 'What business associate?'

The solicitor neatly sidestepped the question by saying, 'My condolences on your loss. Now, Mr Grey—before we begin, we need to follow procedure. I believe you have Miss Grey's death certificate?'

'Yes.' Hugo handed over the brown manila envelope.

'Thank you.' The solicitor extracted the document and read through it swiftly. Clearly satisfied that all was in order, he said, 'We're here today to read the last will and testament of Miss Rosemary Grey.'

Hugo didn't understand why this woman was here. Her name wasn't on the list of people who'd been left bequests. Hugo had assumed that today's appointment was mainly to start the ball rolling with his duties as Rosemary's executor, so he could sort out the funeral.

Philip Hemingford handed them both a document. 'I witnessed the will myself, three months ago,' he said.

The will Hugo knew about dated from five years ago, when his great-aunt had first asked him to be her executor. Why had she changed it—and why hadn't she told anyone in the family?

'Dr Walters, Miss Grey has left you the house.'

What? Rosemary had left her house to a *stranger*?

Wondering if he'd misheard, Hugo scanned the document in front of him.

It was clearly printed.

Last will and testament...
...of sound mind...
To Dr Alice Walters, I leave my house...

A house in Notting Hill was worth quite a lot of money, even if it needed work—work that Hugo had tried to persuade his great-aunt to have done so that she'd keep safe and warm, but she'd always brushed his concerns aside. And Hugo had a really nasty feeling about this. He'd been here before, with something valuable belonging to his aunt and a stranger persuading her to hand it over.

'Just to clarify, Mr Hemingford,' Hugo said, giving Alice a steely look. 'My great-aunt left her house to someone that nobody else in my family has ever heard of before, and she changed her will three months ago?'

At least the woman had the grace to blush. As well she should, because he'd just stated the facts and they all very clearly added up to the conclusion that this woman had taken advantage of Rosemary's kindness. It wasn't the first time someone had taken advantage of his great-aunt. The last time had been Chantelle, the potter who'd befriended Rosemary and told her all kinds of sob stories. Rosemary had given Chantelle her William Moorcroft tea service; Chantelle had sold it to a dealer for a very large sum of money and—worse, in Hugo's eyes—stopped visiting Rosemary. Hugo had quietly bought the tea service back with his own money, returned it to his aunt, and kept a closer eye on people who visited his aunt since then.

Except for the mysterious Dr Walters, who'd slid very quietly under his radar.

Unless... Was this the woman his aunt had mentioned visiting, the one she'd said she wanted him to meet? Hugo, fearing this was yet another attempt by his family to get him to move on after Emma's death, had made excuses not to meet the woman. Fortunately this friend had never been available on Mondays or Thursdays, when Hugo visited, so he hadn't had to deal with the awkwardness of explaining to his aunt that he really didn't want to meet any 'suitable' young women.

Now, he wished he hadn't been so selfish. He should've been polite and met her. He should've thought about his aunt and her vulnerability instead of being wrapped up in his own grief and his determination not to get involved with anyone again.

'Miss Grey changed her will three months ago,' the solicitor confirmed, 'and she was of sound mind when she made her will.'

You could still be inveigled into doing something when you were of sound mind, Hugo thought. And Rosemary liked to make people happy. What kind of sob story had this woman spun to make his great-aunt give her the house?

'There are conditions to the bequest,' the solicitor continued. 'Dr Walters, you must undertake to finish the butterfly project, turn the house into an education centre—of which she would like you to assume the position of director, should you choose—and re-wild the garden.'

The garden re-wilding, Hugo could understand, because he knew how important his great-aunt's garden had been to her. And maybe the education centre; he'd always thought that Rosemary would've made a brilliant teacher. But, if Rosemary had left the house to his father, as her previous will had instructed, surely she knew that her family would've made absolutely sure her wishes were carried out? Why had his great-aunt left everything to a stranger instead? And he didn't understand the first condition. 'What project?'

'I'm editing the journals and co-writing the biography of Viola Ferrers,' Dr Walters said.

It was the first time he'd heard her speak. Her voice was quiet, and there was a bit of an accent that he couldn't quite

place, except it was definitely Northern; and there was a lot of
a challenge in her grey eyes.

Did she really think he didn't know who Viola Ferrers was?

'My great-great-great-grandmother,' he said crisply.

Her eyes widened, so he knew the barb had gone home. This
was *his* family and *his* heritage. What right did this stranger
have to muscle in on it?

'Miss Grey also specified that a butterfly house should be
built,' the solicitor continued.

Rosemary had talked about that, three years ago; but Hugo
had assumed that it was her way of distracting him, giving him
something to think about other than the gaping hole Emma's
death had left in his life. They'd never taken it further than an
idea and a sketch or two.

'And said butterfly house,' the solicitor said, 'must be designed and built by you, Mr Grey.'

Rosemary had left him a loophole, then. As an architect,
Hugo knew what happened if there was a breach of building
and planning regulations, or a breach of conditions in a con-
tract. 'So the bequest is conditional. What happens if the conditions of my great-aunt's will are breached?' he asked, trying
to sound more casual than he felt.

'Then the house must be sold and the money given to a dementia charity,' the solicitor explained.

Meaning that any scheming done by this Dr Walters would
fall flat, and something good would happen with the money.
Which was fine by Hugo. It wasn't the money he was bothered about, even though he knew the house would raise a lot of
money at auction; it was the fact that this woman appeared to
have taken advantage of his great-aunt's kindness, and in his
view that was very far from being OK. 'I see,' Hugo said. It
looked as if this was going to be easy, after all. 'Then I'm afraid
I won't be designing or building a butterfly house.'

'But you have to,' Dr Walters said. 'It's what she wanted.'

Or what Rosemary had been *persuaded* that she wanted,

which was a very different thing. Hugo shrugged. 'We don't always get what we want.'

'Rosemary wanted the book finished and the house turned into a proper memorial to Viola,' Dr Walters said, folding her arms and narrowing her gaze at him.

Was that meant to intimidate him? He'd already survived the very worst life could throw at him. He had nothing left to lose, and he wasn't playing her game.

Philip Hemingford looked uncomfortable. 'This is meant to be a simple reading of Miss Grey's will, not a discussion.'

'That's fine by me,' Hugo said. 'I have nothing to add.' He wasn't letting this woman get away with scamming his great-aunt. And it was going to be very easy to defeat her; all he had to do was refuse to build the butterfly house.

'You can't let Rosemary down,' Dr Walters said, glaring at him.

Oh, was she trying to pretend that she cared? 'Perhaps you'd like to explain, Dr Walters, what your business association was with my great-aunt?'

'As I said earlier, I was working with her on Viola's journals,' she said. 'I'm a lepidopterist.'

The only people Hugo knew who were interested in butterflies were his great-aunt and some of her friends who were from the same generation, all of whom had been slightly eccentric and who hadn't cared about whether their clothes matched or even if they'd brushed their hair that morning. This smart, sleek woman didn't look anything like that kind of person. She looked brittle and fake and completely untrustworthy—much like he remembered Chantelle the potter. 'Indeed,' he drawled, putting as much sarcasm into his voice as he could.

'I lecture on lepidoptera at Roxburgh College at the University of London,' she said. 'Your great-aunt contacted my department and asked if I could help with her project. We've been working on it together part-time for the last six months.'

'She never mentioned the project to me,' he said.

She raised an eyebrow. 'Maybe you didn't talk to her enough.'

Playing that game, was she? His eyes narrowed. 'I was working in Scotland for six months from last October, so I admit I phoned rather than visiting—but I've seen her twice a week since I've been back in London.' Not that it was any of her business.

'Maybe she thought you wouldn't approve of her plans, so she didn't discuss them with you.'

If he'd known of Rosemary's plan to leave her house to a stranger, he would definitely have asked questions. Why hadn't his aunt trusted him? Had this woman coerced her?

'I really don't think this is a helpful discussion,' Philip Hemingford said, looking awkward.

For pity's sake. Why were lawyers so mealy-mouthed? If Hemingford wasn't going to stand up for his great-aunt, then Hugo would. 'Oh, I think it is,' Hugo said. 'I'm sure that professionally you'd want to make quite sure that your client hadn't been cozened into making a bequest. There are laws to prevent such things, I'm sure.'

'As you're such an expert in the law, Mr Grey,' Dr Walters said crisply, before the solicitor could reply, 'I'm sure you'll also be aware of the laws of defamation. I had no idea your great-aunt was going to leave me the house and I certainly didn't ask her to do so.'

'As I wasn't privy to the discussions, I wouldn't know,' he pointed out.

'Exactly,' she said. 'You weren't there.'

Hugo stared at her, outraged. Was she trying to claim that he'd neglected Rosemary? The gloves were coming off, now. 'So if the project goes ahead,' he asked, 'what exactly do you get out of it? Let me see.' He ticked them off on his fingers. '*You'll* be the one to bring any of Viola Ferrers's discoveries to light. *Your* name will appear on any papers written. *Your* name will appear on the cover of the journals as the editor, *your* name will be on the cover of the biography, and *your* name will appear as the director of the education centre. You appear to be doing rather well out of my great-aunt, Dr Walters.' The way he saw it, this woman was using Rosemary to further her career—to further it rather a lot.

'I can assure you, Mr Grey, that Rosemary's name will be on the biography and the journals as co-editor,' Dr Walters corrected, 'and I'll give her full credit on any papers. And, if the education centre goes ahead—which I very much hope it does, because it's clearly what she wanted—then *her* name will be prominent because it was her bequest.' She stared at him. 'And it'll be *your* name on record as the designer and builder of the butterfly house.'

'Ah, but it won't,' he said, 'because I'm not building it. Which means the conditions of the will are breached, so the house will have to be sold and the money given to charity.'

Smug, self-satisfied, *odious* man.

And to think that she'd felt sorry for him in the waiting room—that she'd actually considered going over to ask if he was all right. This man wasn't the sweet nephew Rosemary had mentioned to Alice a couple of times—a man who'd been very busy and struggled to see her. Instead, he was just like Barney and his cronies: posh, entitled and living on a different planet from the rest of the population. This was all just some kind of game to him, and he clearly thought he'd won.

Well, he could think again.

The barely veiled accusation that she was a gold-digger had made Alice angry enough to absorb the shock of the bequest and decide that yes, she'd do this and carry out her friend's dream. Hugo Grey wasn't going to get his own way. At all. He might be able to sell the house, under the terms of Rosemary's will, but he certainly couldn't dictate who bought it.

Alice didn't have the money to buy the property, let alone turn it into Rosemary's vision. But she could apply to the university for a grant to buy the house, and apply to plenty of other places for grants to do the work to convert it into an education centre and build a butterfly house. If she couldn't get enough money through grants, then she'd crowdfund it. *Help save Rosemary's butterflies.*

This man wouldn't know a butterfly if it came flapping past and settled on his arm. Rosemary did, and Alice wasn't going to let her friend down. The solicitor might have referred to her as a 'business associate', but the elderly lady was more than that; Rosemary had become a good friend over the last six months, and she deserved better than this arrogant, self-centred great-nephew slinging his weight around. A man Rosemary had obviously seen through rose-tinted glasses.

'As you wish,' she said.

He looked surprised.

Did he *really* think she was some kind of gold-digger?

She wasn't sure whether anger or pity came uppermost: anger at the insult, or pity for a man who clearly lived in a world full of suspicion and unkindness. It was a confused mixture of both, but anger had the upper hand. Hugo Grey might be gorgeous to look at, with that floppy dark hair and those cobalt-blue eyes, but he was as much of a snake as Barney.

Let him think that the world would go his way. Too late, he'd find out that it didn't. Not in this case.

'Do you have a key to the house?' he asked.

And, damn, her face was obviously very easy to read, because he nodded in satisfaction. 'I thought so. You need to hand it over to Philip Hemingford.'

No way. Not until she'd managed to rescue the last few journals so she could finish her work. 'As Rosemary left the house to me, I think not.'

'The conditions of your bequest have been breached, so technically the house belongs to the dementia charity she named in the will,' he pointed out coolly.

'I'm not the one who breached the conditions.'

'Really, really,' the solicitor interjected, squirming and looking awkward. 'This isn't...'

'What Rosemary wanted. I agree, Mr Hemingford,' Alice finished. 'And I don't have the key with me.' That wasn't actually true, but she was working on moral rights. Rosemary would've approved of the white lie, she was sure.

'Then I suggest,' Hugo Grey said, with that irritating drawl, 'that you bring the key here to Philip Hemingford by ten o'clock tomorrow morning.'

'Provided,' she said, 'that you do the same. Because the house doesn't belong to you, either.'

He looked shocked at that. 'It's my great-aunt's house and I'm her executor. I'm responsible for it.'

And *she* was responsible for the butterfly project. 'I'll hand my key over when you hand yours over,' she said.

'That,' the solicitor said hastily, 'sounds like a good solution for now. Perhaps you could both bring your sets of keys to me—say, tomorrow at ten?'

'I'm in a lecture at ten, but I can make it at twelve if that works for you.'

'Twelve's fine.'

'Thank you for your time, Mr Hemingford,' she said, giving him a brief nod of acknowledgement. Then she gave the younger man a glance of pure disdain. '*Mr* Grey.' And she hoped he interpreted 'Mr' as 'Entitled piece of pond-life', because that was exactly what she meant by the word.

And she walked out, leaving both men open-mouthed.

Normally, Alice didn't take taxis, but she needed to get to Rosemary's house before Hugo Grey did, to make sure she could still access the journals. So she whistled the first black cab that passed her—to her shock, it actually stopped for her—and took a taxi to the house in Notting Hill.

It felt weird, letting herself into the empty house. Right now the only moving things here were herself and the dust motes dancing in the sunlight.

It was weirder still, not seeing her elderly friend pottering around in the garden, or sitting at the kitchen table with her cup of tea and a welcoming smile.

Tears prickled against Alice's eyelids. Rosemary Grey was special. Kind, eccentric and with a lively mind. In a lot of ways, Rosemary reminded Alice of her grandfather, and she was sure they would've enjoyed each other's company—despite the fact that socially they were worlds apart.

'I'm not going to let him win,' she said fiercely. 'You deserve better than that entitled, spoiled buffoon. I'm going to finish our book. And your name is going on the cover before mine. I'm not going to let you down, Rosemary, I promise. And I keep my promises.'

She went into the study and found the last volumes of the journals. No doubt Hugo would figure out very quickly that she'd taken them and demand them back, so today she'd need to photograph every page and make sure she backed up the images in three places for safety's sake. Hugo Grey and his pomposity were absolutely not going to get in the way of Rosemary's plans.

'We're going to win,' she whispered to the empty house, and locked up behind her again.

Hugo had half-expected Alice Walters to be there, stripping out whatever she could, when he got to his great-aunt's house; but it was empty. Nothing but dust-motes and echoes. His great-aunt's vitality had gone from the place.

He let himself into the garden and wandered through it. The shrubs were overgrown and needed cutting back, but he could smell the sweet scent of the roses and the honeyed tones of the buddleia, and for a moment it made him feel as if his great-aunt were walking right beside him.

The butterfly house.

He could see exactly where Rosemary wanted it. They'd talked about it three years ago, when he'd been so broken after Emma's death and desperately needed distracting. Rosemary had suggested using the rickety old wall at the back of the garden for one wall of it; they'd talked about a house of glass, filled with plants that were the perfect habitat for butterflies.

Rosemary had loved glasshouses. So had he. She'd taken him to see stately homes with amazing conservatories and domes when he was small, as well as the glasshouses at Kew and the Chelsea Physic Garden. They'd had a road trip to the Eden Project, too, when he was in his teens. They'd both been fascinated by the biomes—Rosemary for their contents, and himself for the structure. And Rosemary had been the one who'd championed him when he'd decided to become an architect, specialising in glass.

Had he been so cocooned in his grief that he'd not paid enough attention? He hadn't thought that she'd really meant it about the butterfly house; he'd assumed it was her way of distracting him. Particularly when she'd talked about using the wall of Viola's old conservatory; he'd checked it out and it would've needed completely rebuilding before it could be used to support a structure. He'd assumed that she'd realised the idea was impractical. Had he been wrong?

Standing with his hands in his pockets, he stared at the space in front of him. A lawn that had been cut but not cared for, so it was straggly and patchy, with weeds taking over completely in places. Overgrown flower beds with shrubs drooping, their dead flower heads unpruned. Right at that moment, it was a mess. But, with careful planning and a bit of hard work, he could just imagine the garden transformed and showcasing a butterfly house. A modern twist on a Victorian palm house, perhaps, marrying the past and the present. Something that looked like the past but had modern technology underpinning it; something that would last for the future.

Back in the kitchen, he made himself a black coffee in one of Rosemary's butterfly-painted mugs and sat at the kitchen table.

'What did you really want, Rosemary?' he asked the empty air. 'If the butterfly house was your dream, then I'll back it all the way and I'll build it for you. But if it's this woman trying to use your name and tread on you so she can get to the top, then it's no deal.'

How did he find out which one it was? He knew nothing about Dr Alice Walters. Rosemary had mentioned her friend but Hugo hadn't really paid attention. He'd been caught up in work and brooding—because, without Emma's warmth in his life, he'd been going through the motions. Existing, not living. It had been hard enough to get from the beginning of the day to the end.

Something about this just didn't sit right. It felt as if Alice Walters had taken advantage of Rosemary in the same way as Chantelle had, using a shared interest as a way to befriend her and then cheat her.

He flicked into his phone and looked up the website for Roxburgh College.

And there she was, listed in the staff of the biology department.

Dr Alice Walters.

He clicked on the link. Her photograph made her look much softer than she had in the solicitor's office. Her light brown hair had a natural curl rather than being ironed into the sophisticated smoothness he'd seen. She wasn't wearing make-up, either; her natural beauty shone through and her grey eyes were huge and stunning.

He pushed the thought away. This wasn't about being attracted to a woman who might or might not be a gold-digger. This was about making sure the woman hadn't taken advantage of his great-aunt.

According to her biography on the university's website, Alice had taken her first degree in biology at Oxford, and studied for her Masters and her PhD at London. She was a Fellow of the Royal Entomological Society. Her research interests were in biodiversity, conservation ecology and the impact of land use—all of which fitted with what Rosemary had asked her to do. She'd written an impressive list of papers, including some on re-wilding; she'd been a keynote speaker at several conferences; and she was supervising half a dozen doctoral students.

The academic side of it stacked up.

But were the ideas in the will Rosemary's, or had Alice influenced her? Was Alice Walters involved in this project because she'd liked Rosemary and wanted to help her make a difference, or because she wanted to make a name for herself and had no scruples about taking advantage of others to get there? Had she lied when she'd claimed to have no idea that Rosemary intended to leave her the house?

Until Hugo knew the truth, he wasn't budging.

CHAPTER TWO

Two weeks later, Alice slid into a pew at the back of the church. She didn't want any animosity with Rosemary's family, but she did want to pay her respects to her friend at the funeral. It mattered to her. She'd leave quietly after the service, so the Greys wouldn't even know she was here.

There were lots of people in the congregation; she recognised some as Rosemary's neighbours, and a few of them smiled at her or lifted a hand in acknowledgement. And she definitely recognised Hugo Grey; he was sitting in a pew at the very front of the church, comforting an older couple she guessed were his parents.

The service itself was lovely, with the organist playing Chopin's Nocturne in E flat major as the pallbearers brought in the coffin. 'Morning Has Broken' was the first hymn—if Rosemary hadn't suggested it herself, whoever had chosen it had clearly known Rosemary's spirit well.

When it was time for the eulogy, Hugo stood up and went into the pulpit.

For a moment, Alice caught his eye and it felt like an electric shock.

No, absolutely *no*. It was totally inappropriate to feel that tug of attraction towards someone at a funeral, and it was even more inappropriate because she and Hugo were on opposite sides. During the last couple of weeks, he'd continued to refuse to change his position about building the butterfly house, so Rosemary's house was going up for sale. Alice had responded by putting together a business plan for the university, asking them for a grant towards buying the house and building the butterfly house; she'd also set up a crowdfunding page and a campaign to save the house. Finally, she'd applied for outline planning permission for changing the use of the house and building the butterfly house in the garden.

Everything was going at a speed she wasn't entirely comfortable with, but she had no other choice; she needed to be ready in case Hugo decided to put the house up for immediate auction rather than selling it through an estate agency. Without the money—or at least the promise of it—behind her, she couldn't buy the house and she couldn't fulfil Rosemary's dreams.

She looked away, and Hugo began speaking. Unlike the other day, his voice wasn't full of coldness and sneering; it was full of warmth and affection and sadness. And Alice was utterly captivated.

'I feel as if I should be reading Ophelia's speech up here about flowers, suggesting rosemary for remembrance, because we'll always remember Great-Aunt Rosemary. When I was a child, I spent a lot of time in her garden, and she'd tell me all about the butterflies and the birds and the flowers. So I'm choosing to read something by her favourite poet, Thomas Hardy; Rosemary noticed things, and I remember her reading this to me when I was a child and telling me that the first verse was about butterflies.'

This was personal, Alice thought. Heartfelt.

And the way he delivered it was full of love and meaning. His voice was clear and beautifully modulated; although it didn't wobble in the slightest, because he was clearly determined to do well by his great-aunt, she could see the glitter in his eyes to show that tears weren't far away.

'"When the Present has latched its postern behind my tremulous stay, And the May month flaps its glad green leaves like wings, Delicate-filmed as new-spun silk, will the neighbours say, 'He was a man who used to notice such things'?"'

It was the perfect poem to choose. Just as Hugo had suggested, it was full of butterflies, and it reminded her of Rosemary. Rosemary Grey had definitely noticed things—not just the environment, but also people. Alice had found herself able to open up to the older woman.

A woman who used to notice things.

A woman who was kind and passionate and inspirational.

And Alice was really going to miss her.

Hugo could see Alice Walters sitting at the back of the church. Today, she wasn't the polished, sophisticated woman who'd sat in the solicitor's office and argued with him. She was wearing plain black trousers and a silky black top, and her hair had the slight natural curl he'd noticed in her official university photograph.

Was she here to pay her respects to Rosemary, or to keep an eye on her own interests?

Hugo knew about her crowdfunding bid to buy the house, and Alice Walters exasperated him thoroughly; yet, at the same time, there was something about her that intrigued him.

How ironic that the first woman he'd really noticed since his wife's death was on the opposite side to him. And this was his great-aunt's funeral. He needed to finish his eulogy and give Rosemary the send-off she deserved, not start mooning about a woman he didn't really know and whom he strongly suspected of being an ambitious gold-digger.

So he shared his memories, making sure that every single person in the congregation—except possibly the woman sitting in the last pew—had something to share, too. Rosemary would want to be remembered with love and with smiles, and he was going to make that happen.

Though he had to hold his mother's hand through 'Abide With Me' and clasp his father's shoulder; the verse about death's sting and the grave's victory caused both of them to stop singing, choked by emotion.

He followed his parents behind the coffin as they left the church; again, he couldn't help glancing at Alice. Her face coloured faintly as she caught his gaze, and he was horrified to feel awareness pulse through him again. Not here, not now, and—actually, no, he didn't want this *at all*. He was done with feeling. It had broken him nearly three years ago, and he never wanted to repeat it.

He'd expected her to be gone by the time the committal had finished, but instead she was talking to some of Rosemary's neighbours in the churchyard. From the way they were chatting so easily to her, he was pretty sure they knew her. Liked her, too, because they were smiling rather than giving her suspicious looks, the way half of them had looked at Chantelle.

Had he judged Alice unfairly?

In which case, he'd really let his aunt down. Then again, if Alice was as ambitious as he suspected, he didn't want her to get away with using Rosemary. He needed to get to the bottom of this.

Guilt had the upper hand at that moment, so he walked over to her and gave her a nod of acknowledgement. 'Dr Walters.'

'Mr Grey,' she replied, her tone equally formal.

'Perhaps you'd like to join us for the wake?'

Her eyes widened. 'Seriously? I didn't think I'd be welcome.'

Today, her manners were as blunt as the hint of her accent. He rather liked that. It suggested that she was straightforward. Or was that a double bluff from an accomplished and ambitious woman?

'I don't want to cause any upset to your family,' she continued. 'Today's about Rosemary and your memories of her, and I don't want to do anything that takes away from that.'

A gold-digger would've said yes to the invitation without hesitating and would've been charming rather than blunt. Maybe he really had misjudged her. Even though she'd set up that crowd-funding site to buy the house.

This wasn't about Rosemary's house. It was about Rosemary. About saying goodbye. And he needed to do the right thing. The kind thing, as Rosemary would've wanted.

'You'll be welcome,' he said. 'It's in the hotel across the road, if you'd like to join us. I'll leave it to you to decide.' He gave her a nod of acknowledgement, then went to join his parents.

Hugo Grey had actually asked her to the wake. Alice couldn't quite get her head round this. They were on opposite sides. He didn't have to be nice to her. Yet today he'd chosen to be kind.

So she followed the straggle of mourners across the road, accepted an offer to sit with Rosemary's neighbours, drank tea from a pretty floral china cup and ate a scone with jam and cream. Rosemary, she thought, would've enjoyed this.

But all the while she was very aware of Hugo Grey.

The way he read poetry.

The sensual curve of his mouth.

And this had to stop. Even if they weren't on opposing sides, she was absolutely hopeless when it came to relationships. After Barney, she hadn't dated for a couple of years, not trusting her judgement in men, but then she'd met Robin, who'd seemed so nice at first—and the opposite of Barney. Down-to-earth. Except Robin had wanted her to change, too; she hadn't been girly enough for him. After Robin, there had been Ed, who hadn't minded how she dressed—but he'd wanted her to be less of a nerdy scientist, so she'd fit in with his artsy crowd. Then there had been Henry, who'd broken up with her because he'd wanted someone whose career would be less stellar than his.

Everyone she'd dated seemed to want to change her. It didn't matter whether they'd met through work, through a friend of a friend, or a dating app that should've screened them so they were the perfect match.

Maybe she was the one at fault, for picking men who couldn't compromise. And every break-up had knocked her confidence a little bit more.

Not that it mattered, because nothing was going to happen between herself and Hugo. He might already be involved with someone else. All she really knew about him was that he was Rosemary's great-nephew and he was an architect. One who'd won a couple of awards, according to the Internet, and was a rising star in the industry; but she hadn't looked up his private life because it was none of her business.

Even as she thought it, he walked over to her, carrying a cup of tea. 'Dr Walters. May I join you?'

Short of being rude, there was only one thing she could say. 'Of course, Mr Grey.'

'Can I get you some more tea, or something to eat?'

'I'm fine, thanks,' Alice said, suddenly feeling gauche and tongue-tied.

And he clearly wasn't going to make it easy for her, with small talk. He simply sat down beside her and waited.

Given that he reminded her so much of Barney and his entitled friends with their over-elaborate code of manners, was he waiting for her to make a mistake? Not hold her cup properly, or use the wrong bit of cutlery, or...

No. She was being unfair to him, especially as he'd been kind earlier. They were strangers, and this was his great-aunt's funeral. She'd try to meet him on common ground. 'Your eulogy was very good.'

He inclined his head. 'Thank you.'

Wasn't it his turn to make a comment, now, to keep the conversation going?

When he didn't, she added, 'I liked the poem.'

'My great-aunt loved poetry,' he said. 'Hardy was her favourite poet, but she loved Keats as well. And Christina Rossetti—whenever I hear leaves rustling in the trees, I think of Rosemary reading me that poem, or when I see the moon in a cloudy sky.'

Hugo Grey liked poetry? Now that she hadn't expected. But she knew the poems he'd mentioned. '"The moon was a ghostly galleon tossed upon cloudy seas."'

He looked surprised. 'You know that one, too?'

She nodded. 'My grandmother loved that one. She read it to me a lot when I was a child.' And she could hear it in her head, in her grandmother's broad Yorkshire accent.

Just for a moment, the crowded room was forgotten: it felt as if it were just the two of them, the poem echoing down the years to them and joining them together.

'"Watch for me by moonlight. I'll come to thee by moonlight,"' he whispered.

And she could imagine Hugo as the highwayman of the poem, with his breeches and his velvet claret coat, lace at his chin and a French tricorn hat on his hair.

Her mouth went dry as she thought of Bess loosening her black hair in the window, and her highwayman lover kissing the dark waves. What would it be like if Hugo kissed her hair, her cheek, the corner of her mouth?

It made her feel hot all over—and ashamed, because this really wasn't the time or place to be thinking like that. Though, given the sharp slash of colour across his cheeks, she had a feeling that he was thinking something very similar indeed.

And she couldn't make a single word leave her mouth. They were all stuck in her throat.

This was terrifying. She hadn't been this aware of anyone since Barney. But she knew her judgement in men was hopeless and she'd given up trying to find Mr Right. Burying herself in her work had been much safer. Looking at butterfly pheromones and ignoring human ones.

Quoting poetry. How stupid Hugo had been to think that was safe: Hardy, Keats, Rossetti and their images of nature.

But of all things he'd chosen to quote 'The Highwayman'. And it wasn't about the moon as a galleon, the road over the purple moors. It was about Bess the landlord's daughter and the highwayman, the woman plaiting her hair and the man kissing it, promising to be back for her. The jealous ostler with his hair like mouldy hay, betraying the highwayman to the redcoats. Bess saving him temporarily with her own death. Love and passion and death.

Alice Walters's eyes were grey, not dark. Her hair was light brown, almost a nondescript colour, rather than the exotic long, black curls of Bess. She didn't have a red ribbon tied through her hair in a love knot.

And yet remembering the line of the poem made Hugo want to bury his face in Alice's hair.

Would she smell of roses, vanilla or honey?

Oh, for pity's sake.

He hadn't so much as noticed another woman in the last three years. He hadn't wanted to. Emma was the love of his life, and after her death he hadn't wanted anyone else.

So what was it about Dr Alice Walters that drew him, made him actually notice her and react to her like this?

Rosemary would no doubt have said this was a good thing. That Hugo would never forget Emma but it was past time that he started thinking about moving on, finding someone to share his life with rather than spending decades and decades alone. He'd half-suspected that was why she'd tried to get him to meet her friend Ally, and it was why he'd made himself unavailable. He didn't want anyone else.

Maybe he did need to move on. But his first choice definitely wouldn't be an ambitious lepidopterist, a woman whose motives he hadn't yet worked out. He didn't even *like* Alice Walters.

Though he had to acknowledge that he was attracted to her. Not to the glossy, brittle woman from the solicitor's office, but to *this* woman, a woman whose lips had parted ever so slightly and he was incredibly aware of the shape of her mouth. It made him want to lay the palm of his hand against her cheek and rub the pad of his thumb against her lower lip.

And he was at his great-aunt's funeral.

This really wasn't the time or place to be thinking about touching someone, kissing them.

Time seemed to have slowed to treacle. It felt as if he were hearing things from underneath an ocean, slow and haunting like a whale song rather than the trill of birds.

Say something.

He needed to say something.

But moving his lips made him think about *her* lips. How soft they might be against his own. Pliant and warm and—

'Hugo? I'm so sorry about your aunt.'

He looked up. Saved by Millie Kennedy, Rosemary's neighbour.

'Thank you, Millie.' He accepted the elderly woman's hug. 'Have you met Dr Walters?'

'Our Ally? Of course I have. Lots of times. She's been working on Rosemary's book.' Millie hugged Alice, too. 'Good to see you again, love. I'm glad you could make it. Our Rosemary deserved the best send-off.'

Millie was nice to everyone, Hugo knew. But she seemed to know Alice quite well, accepting her as one of her own. And surely a gold-digger wouldn't want to get too close to anyone other than her target, in case she was caught out? So maybe Alice wasn't one of the bad guys. Maybe he'd just become a miserable cynic since Emma's death, seeing the worst in the world.

'I really ought to get back to my students,' Alice said. 'But I wanted to pay my respects to Rosemary.' She stood up, and Hugo realised that without her high heels Alice was a good six inches shorter than he was. Petite. *Cute.*

And it set alarm bells ringing in his head. This woman could be very dangerous to his peace of mind.

'Thank you for inviting me to the wake, Mr Grey,' she said politely, and held out her hand to shake his.

It would be churlish not to shake her hand, he thought. But he regretted the impulse when the touch of her fingers against his made him feel as if an electric shock had zapped through him.

'Thank you for coming to Rosemary's funeral,' he said, equally politely. There were other things he wanted to say, but absolutely not in front of Millie. 'I'm sure we'll be in touch.'

Touch. What a stupid word. His libido seized on it and threw up all kinds of images of her touching him, and he could feel the heat rising in his face.

What was it about this woman that made him feel like a gauche teenager?

And what was he going to do about it?

Alice surreptitiously checked her hand when she left the hotel. Shouldn't there be scorch marks on her skin from where Hugo Grey had touched her? Because it had felt as if lightning had coursed through her when he'd shaken her hand.

This was crazy.

She didn't react to men like this.

Maybe she was going down with some peculiar virus.

She was very glad to get back to the safety of her office and a tutorial with her students. And she was not going to spend her time mooning over Hugo Grey. She had things to do. Students to teach, Viola's journals to finish editing, a crowdfunding campaign to run...

But it was hard to concentrate. She kept drifting off and thinking about him. Which really wasn't her; she never let anything get in the way of her professionalism. Why was she letting Hugo Grey affect her like this?

'Alice Walters, get a grip,' she told herself out loud. 'He was just being polite when he said he'd be in touch. You're probably never going to see him again. He's going to sell the house, you're going to buy it, and that's that.'

Though she revised her views, the following Monday, when she had the letter from the planning officials rejecting outline permission for the butterfly house.

She'd given them solid reasons for the change of use to the building and the construction of the butterfly house. The fact the planning office had turned her down made her think that someone had pulled strings—someone who clearly had contacts within the department.

And she had a pretty fair idea of who that someone had to be.

Hugo Grey.

Anger simmered in her heart all morning, through all her tutorials, to the point where she had to ask her students to repeat their answers. Her afternoon was scheduled for working on a paper, but she decided to catch up with that later. Right now she had something much more important to do: pin Hugo Grey down and make him fix the mess he'd made.

A quick phone call to his office in Docklands established that yes, he was in, but he was in a meeting until one o'clock.

So far, so good; if she left the university now, she'd reach his office at just about the same time that his meeting finished and she could tackle him face to face.

His office was in part of an old wharf that had been converted; the yellow bricks had been cleaned until they sparkled and the arched windows were huge. Inside, the lobby was light and airy, and the reception area for Hugo's architectural practice was gorgeous, filled with plants and overlooking the river.

'Can I help you?' the receptionist asked.

'I'd like to see Hugo Grey,' Alice said.

'I'm afraid he's in a meeting,' the receptionist said. 'Can anyone else help?'

'Thank you, but I'm afraid it needs to be Hugo himself,' Alice said. 'I'm aware that his meeting's scheduled to finish at one. That's why I'm here now.'

The receptionist looked surprised that the scruffy woman in front of her appeared to possess organisational skills. Alice wished she'd worn her favourite T-shirt, the one with the slogan 'Don't judge a butterfly by its chrysalis'.

'If his meeting overruns, I'll wait,' she said.

'He might not be av—'

'Oh, he'll be available to see me,' Alice cut in, very quietly. 'Unless he'd prefer me to stand in the middle of this waiting area and explain to everyone within earshot why Hugo Grey is completely untrustworthy and they might be better off taking their business to a different practice of architects.'

The receptionist looked alarmed. 'Please don't do that. I'll talk to his PA and see when he'll be available. Would you mind waiting in the reception area?'

'Thank you. I'm Dr Alice Walters and it's about the butterfly house. And,' she added, 'it's quite urgent.'

Three minutes after the receptionist had made the phone call, Hugo came downstairs, frowning.

'Dr Walters? Why are you here?'

'I think you know why.' She folded her arms and glared at him.

'I'm afraid I have no idea what you're talking about,' he drawled.

'So you're a liar as well as a snake?' She gave a humourless laugh. 'I'm sure your clients will be interested to hear this.'

He narrowed his eyes at her. 'We're not going to discuss this here. Come up to my office.' He looked over to the receptionist. 'Thank you, Anjula. I'm sorry you've got tangled up in this.'

Guilt prickled its way across Alice's skin. It wasn't the receptionist's fault that Hugo had behaved this way; and Alice hadn't exactly been very nice to her. 'I'm sorry, too,' she said.

She followed Hugo up the stairs to his office, allowed him to usher her inside and close the door, and took the chair he offered her.

He sat down opposite her and folded his arms. 'So what is all this about, Dr Walters?'

'It's about you pulling strings with your mates at the planning office, Mr Grey.'

'I have no idea what you're talking about.'

She took the letter from her bag and slapped it down on his

desk. 'Just what you wanted to happen, I believe. I'm sure you'll be delighted to learn that the council turned down the outline planning permission for the butterfly house—if you don't know that already.'

'That has nothing to do with me.'

She scoffed. 'You seriously expect me to believe that?'

'If a new building or a change of use doesn't fall within the local planning authority's development plan, then a project will be rejected,' he informed her. 'It has nothing to do with any objections that people might raise about the building or the change of use.'

Alice shook her head. 'Rosemary would be so disappointed in you. She really wanted the butterfly house built and the house turned into an education centre, and you're doing your very best to block it. And, just so you know, I'm not a gold-digger. I don't care about money—what I care about is butterflies.'

The woman sitting in front of him wasn't the sophisticated, brittle woman he'd met at the solicitor's office, nor even the quiet, slightly shy woman from the funeral, Hugo thought. This woman glowed. Right from the top of her very messy hair down to her well-worn hiking boots.

For the first time since he'd known her, Alice Walters actually looked like a lepidopterist—like one of Rosemary's hippy friends he remembered from his childhood. Mixed with a bit of Roman goddess. A pocket-sized one, with freckles on her snub nose.

She was still speaking. 'Did you know that three-quarters of British butterflies are in decline, and the number of moths has gone down by a third in the last forty years?'

He didn't.

'They're not just silly little flappy things that we don't need to worry our pretty little heads about. Butterflies are important as pollinators—they don't have the fur of a bee for the pollen to stick to, but they cover more ground than bees and that means greater diversity in the gene pool. They're important in the food chain, both as prey and predator, and they're important indicators of the health of the ecosystem. Butterflies and moths are fragile, so they react quickly to change, and if they vanish it's an early indicator of problems in an area.'

This was way outside his area of expertise. But she was clearly both knowledgeable and passionate about her subject, and that passion drew him like a magnet. No way was he going to stop her speaking—even if she did have a few of her facts wrong about the planning application.

'They're important in teaching children about the natural world,' she continued, 'and the transformation during their life-cycle from egg to caterpillar to pupa to butterfly.' She ticked the points off on her fingers. 'And if nothing else they're beautiful. Just look at the delight on a child's face when they see butterflies in the garden or the park or the forest. We need all the beauty we can get in this world.'

He remembered being delighted by the butterflies in Rosemary's garden, as a child. And, now he thought about it, there didn't seem to be as many of them around as there had been when he was young.

But this woman was also accusing him of something he hadn't done, and that wasn't acceptable. 'So you think it's OK to march into my office and be rude to my team, without having a shred of evidence of what you're accusing me of?'

'In the solicitor's office, you said you refused to build the butterfly house, meaning that the conditions of the will aren't met and Rosemary's house will have to be sold,' she said. 'And you're an award-winning architect, so it's obvious that any planner will take notice of what you have to say. If you put in an objection, it'll carry more weight than a normal person's.'

'That isn't how planning works,' he said. 'Did you take advice before you submitted the outline application?'

She folded her arms. 'I might have an accent, but that doesn't mean I'm stupid.'

Interesting. She was chippy about her background? Then again, she'd been to Oxford. Having the wrong accent might've made things harder for her there.

'So you took advice.' He tried to make it sound like a statement rather than a question.

'Yes.'

'May I?' He gestured to the envelope she'd slapped down on his desk.

'Help yourself.'

The angry colour on her cheeks was subsiding, now. But she was still slightly pink and flustered, and Hugo had to stop himself wondering what she'd look like if she'd just been kissed. Would she be equally pink and flustered? Would her eyes glow with that same passion?

He forced himself to concentrate on reading the letter. Then he looked at her. 'Judging by their objections, whoever you went to for advice on your application obviously didn't explain what you wanted clearly enough. Did you submit plans? Sketches? Anything to scale?'

'It was an *outline* planning application. I was told it didn't need anything like that.'

'Sketches and plans would have helped. And a proper explanation.' He looked at her. 'You could talk to someone at the planning department and ask them if modifying your application would change their decision.'

She narrowed her eyes at him. 'Are you offering to help me, now?'

'I...' He raked a hand through his hair. Yes and no. He *could* help her; he just wasn't sure if he wanted to. 'My great-aunt was lovely. She was kind, she was generous, and people took advantage of her.'

Her mouth opened in seeming outrage. 'I wasn't taking advantage of Rosemary. I'd never do that. Apart from the fact that I'm not the gold-digger you seem to think I am, she was my *friend*.'

'Philip Hemingford introduced you to me as her business associate.'

'I was her friend, too. I liked her. She was straightforward. She judged people on who they were.'

That chimed with him. But Alice also flustered him—and she made him angry when she added, 'Rosemary mentioned her high-powered nephew. But you never seemed to be around.'

'I had a six-month project in the wilds of Scotland. It's not exactly easy to pop in to Notting Hill from several hundred miles away.'

'What about after your project ended?'

'I visited twice a week—obviously on days you weren't there. But you're welcome to check with her neighbours, if you want proof. Mondays and Thursdays, to be precise.' He stared at her, challenging her to call his bluff. He'd enjoy seeing her back down and apologise, confronted with the proof.

She met his gaze head on, to make the point that he didn't intimidate her.

It felt as if there should be a military drummer in the room, rat-tat-tatting a challenge.

Just when the tension reached screaming point, she inclined her head. 'Your eulogy convinced me that you loved her.'

The quiet words took all the combat out of it. She was acknowledging that, even though she knew nothing about him, she could tell he'd loved his great-aunt.

Maybe it was his turn to make a concession. 'And her neighbours knew you. Millie liked you; she didn't have any time for Chantelle.'

She frowned. 'Who was Chantelle?'

'Someone who befriended Rosemary a few years ago, told her massive sob stories, and as a potter she fell in love with Rosemary's William Moorcroft tea service—so my great-aunt gave it to her.'

'What's William Moorcroft?' Alice looked mystified.

'It's Art Deco china. Pretty—and also worth a great deal of

money.' He took his phone from his pocket, did a quick search and then showed her a photograph.

She bit her lip. 'Oh, no. I broke the handle off one of those cups, a couple of months ago. I glued it back on, but...' Her eyes widened as she obviously noticed the auction price guide. 'Oh, my God. I thought it was just a pretty cup and it was one of Rosemary's favourites, so I mended it. I had no idea it was worth that sort of money. It should've been done by a proper specialist. I'm so sorry.' She blew out a breath. 'I'll pay for a proper repair.'

And right at that moment Hugo knew that Alice Walters was absolutely genuine and he'd misjudged her. This wasn't a woman who'd tried to inveigle his aunt into leaving the house to her so she could make lots of money. This was a woman who shared Rosemary's love of butterflies and wanted to help her reach her dream. A woman who'd mended a cup she'd thought was worth only a couple of pounds rather than throwing it away, because it was his great-aunt's favourite; and now she knew it was valuable she was offering to pay for a specialist repair.

'Don't worry about it,' he said. 'But Chantelle wasn't the only one who took advantage of my great-aunt over the years, simply the last of them. There were a few others.'

'I'm sorry. That's a horrible thing to do. Betraying someone's trust is just vile.'

There was something heartfelt about her words, and he wondered who'd betrayed her.

'I had absolutely no idea about her will,' Alice said. 'When I got the solicitor's letter, I thought maybe she might have left me some of Viola's specimens for the university collection. I didn't know she'd planned this. And, even though I love the idea of setting up a proper education centre and a butterfly house in Rosemary's name, I do understand that you wouldn't want all her estate going to a stranger.'

'Technically, it goes to charity,' he pointed out.

'Whatever.' She spread her hands. 'What *does* matter, though, are Viola's journals.'

'The ones you took from the house,' he said. He'd discovered that when he'd looked in the office.

'I returned them to the solicitor, the next day, along with my key. And he gave me a receipt for them, if you'd like to see it.' She paused. 'You obviously know that Rosemary was having trouble with her hip.'

No, he hadn't. His great-aunt was of the generation that just got on with things and didn't make a fuss. She hadn't mentioned a word about a problem with her hip.

'That's why she gave me a key—so she wouldn't have to get up and limp to the front door to let me in every time I visited.'

And now he felt bad. Why hadn't he known? Why hadn't he *noticed* that Rosemary actually let him do things for her instead of being her usual fiercely independent self? He'd been so busy trying to keep himself looking like a functioning human being that he'd had tunnel vision, and it made him feel ashamed. Had the trouble with Rosemary's hip had anything to do with her having a stroke?

'I loved working on the journals with her,' Alice continued softly. 'You've no idea how amazing it is, seeing words that are nearly a couple of centuries old, and hardly anyone else has seen since they were written. Sketches and watercolours that are still as fresh as the day they were painted. And, best of all, to hear about the person who created those journals from someone who actually knew her when she was still alive.'

'Actually, I do,' he said.

She blinked. 'You've seen the journals?'

'When I was younger. I just liked the pictures of butterflies. I was too little at the time to try and work out what the handwriting said. But when I was a student I saw the original plans for the Kew Gardens palm houses and it made all the hairs stand up on my arms—so I'm guessing that's how you felt about the journals.'

'It is,' she confirmed. 'Viola Ferrers deserves her place in lepidopterist history. And Rosemary, too. She was a custodian. She kept Viola's work safe, and the butterfly collection intact. Something that I think is worth sharing with the nation, the way Rosemary wanted it—starting with having Viola's study restored to how it was, because it's important for social history as well as scientific history.'

This wasn't a gold-digger talking. At all.

Hugo saw this with clarity, now. Alice didn't want the house for herself. She wanted it for the butterflies. She wanted it to make a *difference*.

'I have a site meeting this afternoon,' he said, 'and I think this is a discussion that needs a bit longer than a lunch break.'

Hope bloomed on her face. 'Are you saying you're going to work with me instead of against me?'

He wasn't promising anything. Not until he'd looked at everything properly. 'I'm saying,' he said, 'that we should talk further. Are you available this evening?'

'Yes.'

He liked the fact that she hadn't tried to make him feel as if she was doing him a favour, claiming she'd have to shuffle things round to accommodate him. Clearly this project was important to her, and as far as she was concerned anything else could be moved. That was a good sign.

'We should meet on neutral territory,' he said.

'The obvious place,' she said, 'would be Rosemary's house. Except neither of us has a key any more.'

Because he'd backed them both into a corner at the solicitor's office, and he knew it. 'OK. I'll get one of the keys back. For today,' he said. 'Until we've talked. What time can you meet me there?'

'Any time. I'm working on a paper this afternoon, so I can be flexible.'

'Five-thirty, then?' he suggested.

'That works for me.'

He held out his hand to shake hers.

Big mistake.

Just like the last time he'd shaken her hand, every nerve-end in his skin felt electrified.

Given that she suddenly looked pink and flustered, did it affect her the same way? Though he couldn't allow himself to think about that. This was about his great-aunt and the butterflies. Nothing else.

'I'll see you out,' he said, and ushered her down to the reception area.

And why was it that he found himself watching her walk away? Why was it that he was starting to feel things he'd thought were damped down for ever?

This was a potential complication that neither of them needed. By the time he met her at his great-aunt's house, he'd better have his head and his emotions completely back under control.

CHAPTER THREE

As HUGO HAD agreed to meet her at Rosemary's house, Alice hoped there might be a chance he was going to listen to her and have a proper discussion about the butterfly house instead of being the bull-headed, irritating man who'd judged her without examining the evidence properly. Which in turn meant that he might actually help her to fulfil her promise to Rosemary. If he agreed, then the money she'd raised so far in crowdfunding could be used for renovations, repairs and building the butter-fly house, rather than the whole lot having to be used to buy the house itself.

Hugo Grey was a businessman first, so she needed to show him the plans she'd made for grant applications. Plans that showed potential footfall and revenue, so he could see that the project would be self-supporting. And then she'd show him the things that really made a difference: Viola's journals, her but-terfly collection and the garden itself. She knew he'd probably seen them all before—but she was also willing to bet that he'd never seen them from her particular point of view.

Armed with her laptop, Alice took the Tube to Notting Hill and walked to Rosemary's house. Hugo was already there wait-ing for her, leaning against the gate. She'd expected him to let himself inside to stake his claim to the house; the fact that instead he'd waited for her outside made her feel a lot more relaxed about the situation. Though, at the same time, her heart skipped a beat as she drew nearer to him. His cobalt-blue eyes really were stunning. He'd changed into jeans instead of the sharp business suit he'd worn in the office and taken off his tie; it was odd how such tiny differences could make him look so much more approachable.

'Thanks for meeting me here,' she said.

'You're welcome.'

Was she? Was that mere politeness, or did he actually mean it? She'd never been able to tell with Barney's set. She'd taken them at face value—and then she'd learned that they'd been laughing at her all along, mocking the working-class girl who'd been stupid enough to think that the privileged classes would ever accept her for who she was.

'Shall we?' He gestured to the front door; once he'd unlocked it, he stood aside for her to enter.

She caught her breath as she walked into the kitchen. 'It doesn't feel right, being here without Rosemary.'

'That's how I feel, too,' he admitted.

'I'd always put the kettle on and make us some tea before we started work on the journals.'

'Proper loose-leaf tea, and make sure you warm the pot first,' he added.

She could almost hear Rosemary saying that; clearly it had been the same for him when he'd visited. She looked at the teapot on the dresser. 'Given what I know now about the tea service, I don't think I'd dare use that teapot ever again. I'd be too scared of dropping it. I can't believe she let me think it was just ordinary.'

'I can,' he said wryly. 'She once told me not to save things for best. She said you need to use things *now* and enjoy them, rather than save them for a special occasion that might never come.'

'She was full of wise words.' Alice felt her voice thicken in her throat. 'I miss her.' But getting emotional wasn't going to help anything. She needed to keep this businesslike. Professional. She looked at him. 'But that's not why we're here.' She set her laptop on the kitchen table. 'What do you want to start with, the journals or the butterfly house?'

'The journals,' he said. 'I assume you had copies made when you borrowed them.'

'Yes. I photographed them myself.' She looked him straight in the eye. 'And, before you ask, the reason I took them was in case you refused me access. I promised Rosemary I'd finish writing Viola's biography and editing her journals, and I think it's important to keep promises.' Especially as she knew how it felt when someone broke a promise to you. 'Just so I don't waste time running through stuff you already know, what do you know about Viola Ferrers?'

'She was born in 1858 into a fairly wealthy family, and she followed the fashion of Victorian women collecting butterflies,' he said promptly. 'Her husband bought this house when they married, and it's stayed in the family since then.'

'OK. First off, Viola was a proper entomologist, so please don't dismiss her as an amateur collector with a "little hobby",' Alice said, making quote marks with her fingers and giving him a hard stare. 'She was much more than that. She studied butterflies scientifically. She wrote papers, though because she was a woman she never got to hear her papers read at the Linnean Society—just like Beatrix Potter.'

He blinked. 'That was a reason for them not to read her papers? Because she was a woman?'

'Oh, they *read* the papers, all right,' Alice said. 'But Viola wasn't allowed to hear them being read. At the time, women weren't allowed to be members of the society. She couldn't even go along to meetings as a guest. But she didn't let any of that nonsense stop her studying butterflies. Let me show you.'

Again, Hugo noticed how vital and animated Alice was when she talked about the project; he really, really liked that. He followed her into Rosemary's study, and she took one of the narrow leather-bound books from the shelf.

'I know you've already seen them, but I want to put them in an academic context for you. Viola kept these journals from the age of sixteen,' she said. 'She used them as a sketchbook as well. She travelled around the country to see botanical gardens; she wrote down the details of the butterflies she saw there and sketched them, too.' She opened the book, flicked through a couple of pages and held the book out to him. 'See?'

Viola's handwriting was very neat and regular, and Hugo noticed that all the diagrams were labelled. 'She's called the butterflies by their Latin names,' he said, surprised; that hadn't registered when he'd been young. There was a water colour of a copper and black butterfly on the page Alice showed him. *'Boloria euphrosyne.'*

'The Pearl-bordered Fritillary. It used to be widespread throughout the country, and now it's mainly found in parts of Scotland, Cumbria, Devon and Cornwall,' Alice said, looking sad. 'They're one of the early spring butterflies; their caterpillars feed on violets.'

'I'm not sure I remember ever seeing any of these in real life,' he said thoughtfully.

'There are some specimens in Viola's collection.' Alice went over to the large display cabinet, opened one of the drawers and slid out one of the frames. 'Here.'

It was a long, long time since Hugo had seen the frames of butterflies. And it still amazed him that these specimens were more than a hundred and fifty years old, yet the colours were still fresh. 'That's beautiful. And also really sad, because— well, shouldn't butterflies be flying, not pinned to a board?'

'I'm glad you said that,' Alice said. 'I agree. Though at the same time we do need to curate the collectors' frames we still have. So many of these haven't been kept properly and the butterflies have just crumbled into dust over the years.'

'I remember Rosemary showing me the big blue butterflies when I was very young,' he said. 'They fascinated me.'

'Those would've been tropical ones from South America,' she said. 'I'm guessing that was *Morpho didius*. That's one of my favourites, too.' She put the frame back carefully and fished out another. 'Here.'

'That's what I remember,' he agreed. 'The colour. Though obviously I've never seen a live one.'

'You wouldn't, in England, unless you've been to a butterfly house. Though there are some blue British butterflies,' she said. She tipped her head very slightly to one side, as if thinking about something, and then said, 'I could show you.'

'In London?'

She nodded. 'Or a bit further afield.'

She was asking him to go on a butterfly expedition with her?

Right then, she looked exactly like what she was: a butterfly specialist. Scruffy, not caring about fashion in the slightest, and totally in love with her subject.

'All right,' he said. Because going further afield with her wasn't the same as going on a date, was it? Alice was proposing a scientific expedition to back up her argument on the butterfly house project, and as he was on the opposite side it made sense for him to accompany her so they were both in full possession of all the facts.

But what if it was a date?

He checked himself. Of course it wasn't. Though, if he was honest with himself, Alice Walters intrigued him. And he was definitely attracted to the scientist, the woman who glowed with passion when she spoke about her subject. That snub nose. The freckles. The light in her grey eyes.

Reining in his thoughts, he brought the subject back to the butterflies. 'The specimens in these frames: are they butterflies that Viola collected herself?'

Alice nodded. 'She went on expeditions abroad. In Victorian times, you didn't actually need a passport to travel, so we don't have exact dates of when she went. But she wrote up her expeditions in her journal. Some of her specimens are in the British Museum.'

Hugo hadn't known that, either. 'And that's important?'

'It means the specimens are of really, really high quality. Lots of collectors in those times offered specimens to the British Museum and were rejected.'

'And hers were accepted? That's pretty special,' Hugo said.

'Exactly. You should be proud of her,' Alice said. 'And she didn't get the specimens solely from expeditions; she used to breed butterflies here in this garden, working out what food plants and habitats helped to produce the best specimens.'

Now he was beginning to understand why Alice thought the journal project was so important. 'And that was rare for a woman in her time?'

'Probably not,' Alice said. 'A lot of women did academic work that their husbands took the credit for—which isn't me having a feminist rant at you, it's just stating how things were back then. Women couldn't even study at university until a decade after Viola was born. Even when they were allowed to attend university, at first they couldn't graduate; they were given a certificate of completion for their exams rather than a proper degree.'

'I had no idea,' he said.

'The University of London was the first one to allow women students and the first one to confer degrees on women. Viola studied there—at my college, which is why Rosemary contacted me in the first place—and she fell in love with one of her fellow students. Luckily for her, he was pretty enlightened and he encouraged her to keep up her scientific work, even after they got married. She bred her butterflies, did her experiments and wrote papers for entomology magazines.' Alice folded her arms and gave him a level stare. 'And I think her name should be a lot better known.'

'Did my great-aunt do something similar?' he asked. What

Rosemary actually did had always been a bit of a mystery to him.

'Yes. But she took photographs of butterflies, rather than going out with a net and a killing jar. That's how I do things, too. I want to conserve butterflies, not preserve them.' Alice put the frame back in the cabinet. 'Which leads me to the butterfly house. Shall we go into the garden?'

'Sure.' He went to the back door; after he'd unlocked it, he stood aside so she could lead him into the garden.

He noticed there were several butterflies resting on the buddleia, soaking up the sunshine.

'Peacocks,' she said, seeing his gaze. 'The blue eye-spots make it obvious why they get their common name—but I bet you didn't know they hiss.'

He stared at her. 'Really? Butterflies *hiss*?'

'Well—it's not *actual* hissing,' she amended. 'It's their third line of defence against predators. The first one is the underside of their wings looking like a leaf; if a bird works out that it's potential food and not a leaf, then the butterfly will open its wings to flash those eye-spots—it's called a startle display. If that doesn't make the bird back off, then the butterfly rubs its wings together and it sounds like hissing.'

'That's amazing.' Hugo could see now why Rosemary had wanted Alice to set up the educational centre. This was the sort of fact that would hold a child spellbound. The way Alice talked held *him* spellbound, too.

'Butterflies are amazing,' she said. 'That buddleia needs a bit of work so it'll have better growth next year. But you already know from Rosemary's will that she wanted the garden properly re-wilded and filled with plants that attract butterflies and bees.'

'And a winding path through it, so you don't see the butterfly house itself until the very last minute.'

She stared at him. 'That wasn't stated in her will, but it's something she said to me a couple of times. So did she discuss it with you?'

'Years ago, but...' He didn't want to tell Alice why he'd needed distracting. He didn't want her to start pitying him. 'There was a lot going on in my life at the time. I guess I didn't pay enough attention to what she was telling me. She hadn't said anything to me about it for quite a while, so I thought she'd shelved the idea.'

'And now?'

'I don't know.' He looked at her. 'You're not like you were at the solicitor's.'

'Not wearing a suit and make-up and high heels, you mean?' She rolled her eyes. 'I'm a scientist, not a fashion plate.'

'So that's what you normally wear for work?' He gestured to her faded jeans and ancient khaki T-shirt.

'Yes.' She shrugged. 'If you're doing fieldwork, wearing strappy sandals is the quickest way to give yourself a sprained ankle, wearing a dress with bare legs instead of trousers tucked into boots will make you vulnerable to ticks, and little strappy tops are no protection at all against sunburn. So I dress sensibly.'

'I don't think I've ever met anyone who wears hiking boots,' he said.

She frowned. 'Surely you have to wear boots and a hard hat on building sites?'

'If it's a working site, like the one I went to this afternoon, yes. Otherwise, ordinary shoes will do.'

She looked at his feet and raised an eyebrow. 'Handmade Italian shoes are *ordinary*?'

Why did that make him feel so defensive? 'They're comfortable.'

'They're the male equivalent of Louboutins.'

Although her tone was slightly acidic, there was a little glint of amusement in her eye. She was teasing him—and, now he thought about it, he was enjoying being teased.

He hadn't felt like this in a long, long time. It was the sort of comment Emma would've made to him.

Emma.

Loneliness washed over him. Would he ever stop missing his wife? Would he ever stop wishing he could turn back time and turn down the invitation to that conference, so he would've been there when Emma had that fatal asthma attack and he could've saved her?

He didn't want to dwell on his feelings, so he switched the topic back to something safe. 'So how do you see the butterfly house working?'

'Rosemary had photographs of the orangery that used to be here—the one Viola used when she bred her caterpillars. There might even still be traces of it on the wall.'

'And you think it should be recreated?' he asked.

'No, because we'll be using the building for a different purpose. We'll need a mix of butterflies, and that includes tropical ones,' she said. 'And I need the kind of tech that means we get the right intensity of light and humidity, as well as the right temperature; the plants can't do all the work. And we need a good design.' She paused. 'Which is where you come in.'

Two choices: he could design the butterfly house, or he could block everything.

He thought about it again. A butterfly house. A confection of glass. A house of dreams.

He loved working with glass, and he was so tempted to build it. 'What sort of thing are you thinking about? A biome, like the ones at the Eden Project?'

'It could be anything you like. The butterfly house at London Zoo is shaped like a caterpillar, and the one in Vienna is a gorgeous Art Nouveau building. The way I see it, you're the glass and architecture specialist. Your imagination is the limit. Well, and the site itself,' she amended. 'Obviously the shape of the garden and the way the sunlight falls will affect what you build.'

He liked the fact that she'd realised that.

A glass building. Complete freedom with the design. Fulfilling his great-aunt's dream. This was the perfect commission. 'The Palm House at Kew,' he said. 'That was the first glass building I fell in love with. And glass domes. Like the one at the Reichstag in Berlin with its double staircase.'

'A dome filled with butterflies free to fly wherever they like. Kind of like a snow globe, except summery,' she said thoughtfully.

Alice Walters actually got it, Hugo thought. She understood the kind of stuff that filled his head. Knowing that made his skin prickle with excitement.

'There isn't really room to build a dome in the garden here. And I'm not making any promises,' he said, 'but maybe we could look at the possibilities.'

'That would be good.' She smiled at him—the first genuine smile she'd ever given him—and it made him catch his breath. It felt as if the world had just flashed into technicolour for a moment before fading back to its usual monochrome.

For pity's sake. He had to get a grip. This wasn't about him. Or her. It was about his great-aunt's dreams and whether they could make it work.

Her stomach rumbled audibly, and she winced. 'Sorry. I kind of forgot about lunch today.'

She'd turned up at his office at lunchtime, he remembered, and thrown that hissy fit on him. 'Because you were too angry with me to eat?'

'Something like that,' she admitted, wrinkling her nose. 'And then I was busy.'

He forced himself not to think about how cute she looked. 'We could get a pizza delivered.' Just to make sure she didn't think he was coming on to her, he added, 'Seeing as we still have a lot to discuss about Rosemary's project, we might as well refuel while we work.'

'Pizza's fine by me,' she said. 'We'll go halves.'

He liked that, too. She hadn't assumed that he was going to pay, just because it had been his suggestion.

Sharing.

Could they share? Was this their chance to start compromising? 'There could be a topping issue,' he said. 'Pineapple or no pineapple?'

'I don't object hugely to pineapple,' she said. Then she tipped her head on one side. 'But olives are essential.'

It sounded as if she was thinking the same thing: they needed to find common ground so they could start negotiating properly. Negotiation by pizza… He'd started it, and she seemed to be running with it. He might as well see where it took them. 'OK. Ham?'

She gave a deep, dramatic sigh. 'Oh, *please*. Prosciutto cotto at the very least.'

He couldn't help grinning. 'You're a pizza snob—and you were lying about the pineapple, weren't you?'

'Yes. I was trying to be conciliatory. I'm prepared to agree to your demands for pineapple,' she said. 'But if you want deep pan or stuffed crust, the deal's off. Proper pizza comes in thin crust only.'

He wasn't quite sure whether she was teasing him or whether she was serious. She was a bit more difficult to read than he'd expected. 'Did you ever eat pizza with Rosemary?'

'Generally I use fresh basil on pizza,' she said, her expression deadpan and her voice dry.

That was a definite tease. Nobody in his life teased him any more.

And then it hit him.

Obviously Alice didn't know about Emma, because she wasn't treading on eggshells round him the way everyone else in his life did; she was reacting to him as if he was a normal human being. And he really, really liked that feeling. It was refreshing enough for him to want to spend more time in her company. 'All right. Thin crust, olives, pineapple, prosciutto cotto. Anything else?'

'No. That all works for me.'

'It's a deal.' Once he'd called the local pizzeria and arranged delivery, they headed back to the kitchen. 'So how would the education centre work?' he asked.

'We might need to remodel the inside of the house. For a start, we need an exhibition room,' she said. 'And a space where children can learn how to help butterflies and wildlife by doing practical things—planning their own butterfly gardens with food plants for both caterpillars and for butterflies, how to build a bug hotel, that sort of thing. I'd like a screen where they can see things like a time-lapse film of a butterfly going through its life stages.' She tapped into her laptop. 'Like this. It's only a couple of minutes long, but it always wows my first-years and I think you might enjoy it.'

He watched the film in silence, marvelling at the photographer's skills. 'That's amazing. I had no idea it was that complicated.'

'And that's only on my laptop. Imagine seeing that on a really big screen, then following the trail through the garden, seeing those exact plants growing, seeing butterfly eggs on leaves and caterpillars munching their way through plants, seeing pupa suspended from canes or even hatching, and then seeing butterflies flying round in the butterfly house. How cool is that?'

Very. But he needed to be businesslike about it. This couldn't be a decision based on emotions. 'Rosemary's investment income died with her. There isn't any money to fund the running costs of an education centre.'

'Which is why we need grants,' she said. 'We can do some crowdfunding, to cover the set-up costs, and then the grants will help keep us going. We'll also charge admission fees—reasonable prices, though, because we want schools to visit in term time and families to visit out of term time. And we also want to attract anyone who's vaguely interested in butterflies or conservation or re-wilding, or just wants a nice morning out with friends. So we'd have a pop-up café on the patio, serving drinks and healthy food. Probably a shop, for books and postcards and butterfly-related goods. I've put together a business

plan with some projected footfalls, for my grant applications.'
She opened another file and let him look at it. 'I can email this
across to you, to give you time for a proper read.'

'That would be helpful,' he said, and gave her his business
card with all his contact details so she could send the file across
to him.

'Do you think you could pause the house going on the market, just until you've seen what the possibilities are and had
time to make an informed decision?' she asked.

She wasn't asking him to stop the sale completely, he noticed.
She was giving him the choice of continuing their discussions,
but without making assumptions that he'd fall in with her plans.

'And what I've put together so far isn't set in stone,' she
said. 'It's simply a start. A working document for discussion,
if you like.'

'So my family could have input.'

She inclined her head. 'Including the butterfly house design,
which Rosemary wanted to be yours. Though maybe I should
take you to visit a few, so you can see what sort of things are
possible.'

He remembered what she'd said earlier about site visits to
see blue butterflies. 'So you're suggesting we should visit butterfly houses and botanical gardens.'

'Butterfly houses,' she said, 'and sites of scientific interest.
I suppose we could include formal botanical gardens, but as
we're looking at re-wilding the garden I think it would make
more sense to look at nature reserves, so you can see the kind
of habitat we can try to create.'

This was treading a very fine line indeed between a date and
a business proposition.

He wasn't sure if the fluttering in his stomach was terror or
excitement. Probably both.

'I appreciate,' she said, 'that you have demands on your time
from work—as do I. But maybe we can look at our diaries and

find a few windows for field trips: some local, some a bit further afield.'

Now Hugo could see that Alice Walters wasn't the ambitious gold-digger he'd first thought she was, he was more inclined to listen to her.

'All right,' he said. 'I'll tell Philip Hemingford to put the sale of the house on hold for a couple of weeks and we'll do some field trips.'

'Thank you.'

He looked at her. 'What about your crowdfunding?'

'That stays,' she said. 'If you decide to put the house on the market after all, the trust will need all the money we can get. If you don't sell the house, then the money will pay for remodelling and building the butterfly house.'

'Trust?' He narrowed his eyes at her. 'What trust?'

'I was thinking, it should be called the Ferrers-Grey Butterfly Education Trust,' she said. 'Honouring both Viola and Rosemary. Oh, and that reminds me: we should have a garden centre section of the shop with butterfly-friendly plants and seeds, obviously including violas and rosemary.'

Acknowledging his great-great-great-grandmother and his great-aunt with plants as well as with the name of the building? He liked that. But that still left him with questions. 'What about you?'

She frowned. 'What do you mean?'

'Don't you want your name on the project?'

'I told you before,' she said quietly, 'it isn't about me. It's about the butterflies. And I'm disappointed that you still think I'm doing this because I'm some power-crazed, ambitious bitch. Clearly you mix with the wrong sort of women.'

He felt the flush of embarrassment and awkwardness creep under his skin. 'I'm sorry. I didn't mean it quite like that.'

'No?' Her eyes narrowed a fraction.

The pizza arrived, at that moment; when he came back from

answering the door, he gave her a wry smile. 'Can we agree to a truce over dinner?'

'I guess. How much do I owe you?'

'This one's on me,' he said, cutting the pizza into slices. 'Next meeting, you buy the pizza or whatever.'

Without further comment, Alice fetched plates from the cupboard and cutlery from the drawer and found two glasses. 'Water?'

'Thank you.'

It was weird, sharing a pizza with a near-stranger, one who'd been pretty much hostile up until now. And Alice found herself feeling unexpectedly shy with him.

Oh, for pity's sake. Just because he was posh, it didn't mean that he was superior—or even that he had a superiority complex. She really had to stop letting what had happened with Barney get in the way of how she handled things. She was older, wiser and much more able to hold her own.

And she needed to be practical about this. 'I could do a field trip on Saturday,' she said. 'Would that fit in with you, or do you need to check with your partner?'

For a second, it was as if someone had closed a shutter over his expression. And his voice was very cool when he said, 'No partner.'

Uh-oh. Did he think she was coming on to him? Maybe she ought to invent a boyfriend. Then again, her love life was a complete disaster zone. Better, perhaps, to suggest something else. 'If you want anyone else from your family to come along, that's fine. Where I have in mind can be rough ground, though, and it's also prime tick season, so I'd recommend whoever joins us wears strong shoes and trousers that can be tucked into socks.'

'That's fine,' he said. 'It'll be just me.' He looked at her. 'Is your partner going to be OK with it?'

'I,' she said, 'am married to my butterflies.' Just so it would be clear to him that she saw this purely as work.

Her fingers accidentally brushed his as they reached for a slice of pizza at the same time, and again she felt that weird flicker of electricity along her skin.

Even if she admitted to being attracted to Hugo Grey, she wasn't going to act on it. Her relationships never worked out, and she wouldn't let anything jeopardise the butterfly project. 'OK,' she said, cross with herself when her voice went slightly breathless. She made an effort to sound professional. 'Do you mind an early start? It'll take us about three hours to get to the first site, maybe more if we get stuck in traffic.'

'How early?' he asked.

'Given that the butterflies I have in mind are usually more active in the morning, six o'clock?'

He looked wary; maybe he wasn't a morning person. 'OK. I'll pick you up.'

'I'll pick *you* up,' she corrected. 'Let me know your address.'

For a moment, she thought he was going to argue, but then he nodded and gave her his address. 'Do you need anything from Rosemary's study, while we're here?' he asked when they'd finished eating.

'No. I've already got copies of the photographs she had of Viola.'

'OK. I'll clear up here, then, and I'll see you on Saturday.'

'All right. I'll email over the files I promised you.' She paused. 'Thank you. I appreciate you listening to what I had to say.'

He inclined his head. 'And I apologise for my earlier prejudice.'

She appreciated that apology; and it was her turn to compromise, now. 'I can understand it, now you've told me about the people who took advantage of her. In your shoes, I think I would've felt the same. Maybe we both started off on the wrong foot.'

'Maybe,' he agreed.

'Can I help with the washing up?' she asked, glancing at the crockery on the table.

'No, it's fine. See you Saturday.'

'Saturday, six a.m. sharp,' she echoed, closed her laptop and left the house.

This field trip absolutely wasn't a date: it was part of a business proposition. So why were all her senses humming?

Probably, she thought, because Hugo Grey was the first man who'd attracted her like this in several years.

But nothing was going to happen between them. She needed to be sensible about this. Her relationships always ended in disaster; and she and Hugo were pretty much complete opposites. Well-worn hiking boots versus handmade, highly polished Italian shoes. It simply wouldn't work, so it was pointless letting anything start.

Even if he did have the most gorgeous eyes...

CHAPTER FOUR

DURING THE REST of the week, Hugo found himself thinking about the butterfly project whenever he had a spare moment. The doodles on his desk blotter were all of potential butterfly house designs—except for the sketches that started to creep in on Friday morning. Little line-drawings of a woman with untamed hair, a snub nose and freckles.

Sketches of Alice Walters.

Not good.

He didn't want to start thinking about Alice, or about anyone else. Emma's death had broken him; although on the surface it looked as if he'd managed to put himself back together, deep down he wasn't so sure he had. Without her, there was a huge hollow in the middle of his life and he didn't know how to fill it. His family and friends had encouraged him to date again, saying he needed someone in his life to stop him being lonely. But Emma wasn't replaceable. And anyway he didn't want to risk loving and losing again. It was easier just to avoid social situations and use work as an excuse. The only person he really saw much of nowadays was his best friend, and—since an incident where Kit and his wife had tried to set him up with a suitable woman, and Hugo had backed off for a couple of weeks—Hugo's non-existent love life was a topic firmly off limits.

Saturday's butterfly expedition with Alice was a field trip, not a date. Hadn't she told him herself that she wasn't interested? You didn't tell someone that you were married to your job if you were even vaguely interested in dating them. This was business.

He dragged himself out of bed on Saturday morning at what he considered an unearthly hour, showered and dressed, ate a banana for breakfast, and was considering whether he had enough time to make himself a coffee to wake himself up properly when his doorbell rang.

Six o'clock precisely.

At least Alice was punctual. He would've been seriously annoyed if he'd dragged himself out of bed and then she'd made him wait around for ages.

She was wearing bright red canvas shoes instead of hiking boots today, he noticed when he opened the door to her. Her faded jeans emphasised her curves, and the slogan on her equally faded T-shirt was very pointed: 'Don't judge a butterfly by its chrysalis.'

She wore absolutely no make-up, and her light brown hair was tied back with a brightly coloured silk scarf, though little tendrils had already escaped at the front. Next to the women he was used to at the office in their sharp business suits, she should've looked a scruffy mess: but actually she looked incredibly cute, completely natural and guileless. When she smiled at him, his pulse actually leapt.

Oh, help.

He didn't want to be attracted to anyone. Particularly to someone whose life had almost nothing in common with his.

He needed to get a grip.

He also needed more sleep.

Why on earth had he agreed to this ridiculous field trip at this even more ridiculous time of day?

'Good morning. Ready to go?' she asked.

How could she possibly be this chirpy at six o'clock? 'You're a morning person, then,' he muttered.

Her smile broadened. 'Of course. It's the best part of the day. You've already missed the sunrise.' She raised an eyebrow. 'Owl, are we?' And then, just to make it worse, she gave a soft, mocking 'Tu-whit, tu-whoo.'

He glared at her, his synapses not firing quite quickly enough to let him make a suitably sarcastic retort.

She just laughed. 'You can always nap in the car, because it's going to take us about three hours to get there, if we're lucky with traffic. Or, if you need coffee, I've a flask and a spare re-usable cup in my backpack.'

Of *course* she'd have reusable cups. 'Thanks.' Though he was aware of how ungracious and grumpy he sounded, and winced inwardly.

She glanced at his feet. 'I'm glad you're not wearing your posh shoes. I forgot to warn you that it can be a bit boggy underfoot in the wetlands.'

'Wetlands? I thought we were looking at butterflies?'

'We are. But one of the sites we're visiting is in the Norfolk Broads.' She spread her hands. 'By definition, it can be a bit wet.'

'Oh.' He looked at her feet again. 'No hiking boots for you, today?'

'They're in the car. I don't drive in them,' she said.

'I'm a bit surprised someone with your green credentials has a car,' he said.

She smiled. 'I don't. But if I can't get somewhere any other way, I hire one.'

'Oh.' And then he felt stupid.

'Feel free to change the temperature or the music,' she said when he'd climbed into the passenger seat.

She was being nice, and he was being impolite and grouchy. 'This is fine,' he said. 'And sorry. I don't mean to sound grumpy.'

She patted his forearm, and his skin tingled where her fingertips touched him. 'Poor little owl. I promise what we're going to see will be worth the early start. Well, as long as the weather holds.'

'Butterflies don't like rain?'

'Or wind. They like calm, bright weather,' she said. 'Or just calm will do. Overcast is all right, if there isn't a wind. I have something with me in case I need to cheat a bit, though.'

'Cheat?' He was mystified.

'Later.' She started the car. 'Go back to sleep, if you want to.'

Hugo had no intention of doing that, though he was glad that she didn't want to chatter inanely. However, lulled by the warmth of the sunlight through the windows and the soft piano music she was playing in the car, he did actually doze off; when he opened his eyes again, they were in the middle of nowhere. The road before them wasn't even a proper road; it appeared to be a dirt track.

'Where are we?' he asked.

'Milk Parsley Fen—named after one of the plants that grows here.' She drove through a gap in the hedge into what seemed to be a field, though there were a couple of other cars parked underneath the trees. 'Do you want some coffee before we go for a walk?'

He wasn't going to cut off his nose to spite his face. 'Yes, please.'

'It's black, no sugar,' she warned. 'I never quite got out of my student habits.'

'That's fine. Coffee's coffee,' he said.

She took a backpack from the back seat, removed a metal flask and two cups, and poured them both a coffee.

'Thanks. Butterflies on your cups?' he asked as she fitted a silicone lid to a cup and handed it to him.

'Of course.' She changed into her hiking boots, put the backpack on her shoulder and slung a camera round her neck. 'Ready?'

'Ready.' The coffee was already making him feel more

human. He followed her down a narrow path; the ground felt a bit spongy to walk on, and there were fronded grasses everywhere he looked. But what he'd expected to see was absent.

'There aren't any butterflies,' he said, knowing he sounded accusatory and a bit like a spoiled child denied a promised treat, but not being able to stop himself.

'They're probably skulking around in the reeds,' she said. 'Wait until we get further in. The reserve managers have cut some paths through the fen so we'll get a decent view of the milk parsley, but at the same time the really vulnerable plants aren't in danger of being trampled on.'

He could follow that line of thinking. 'So paths need to be cut in a re-wilded garden?'

'Absolutely. These are wetlands, so they're not quite what Rosemary had in mind—but there's a specific butterfly I want you to see here,' she said.

There was a stream running alongside them, he noticed, and a small bridge; as they drew closer, a large swan waddled out of the reeds and sat in the middle of the bridge, staring at them.

'Looks as if we're going to have to wait for a bit,' she said.

'We can't just walk past the swan?'

She shook her head. 'My guess is his mate and his cygnets are somewhere nearby. He's likely to be a bit protective. Let's give him some space,' she said. 'Look—there's a Painted Lady and a Peacock.' She gestured to the purple flowers lining the route, and he could see butterflies resting on the plant with their wings outstretched.

And then, all of a sudden, he could hear a kind of peeping noise.

'Cue the cygnets,' she said with a smile.

The swan stood up and started to walk over the bridge, his movements slow and deliberate.

'Let's follow him,' she suggested.

The peeping noise grew stronger; the swan veered off to the side, shaking his tail as he stepped towards a large pool. And then he glided majestically across the water towards another swan and a bevy of cygnets, whose peeping noises grew even louder.

'I love this.' Alice took Hugo's free hand and squeezed it. 'You can just hear them yelling, "Hurry up, Dad, we're going exploring!", can't you?'

He would never have thought of that if he'd been on his own; but now she'd said it he could almost hear it. 'Yes. And I don't think I've ever seen anything like this before.' And now she was holding his hand it felt as if she was leading him into an enchanted landscape. Part of him was skittish—he hadn't expected to hold hands with anyone again—but part of him felt as if he was being drawn back to life. Step by step. Noticing tiny details he'd blanked out before.

He stared at the swans and their cygnets, entranced as they glided to the other side of the pool and then filed out of the water again, the adults walking at each end of the line with the cygnets protected between them. 'That's *such* a privilege.'

'Isn't it just?' Then her eyes widened as she clearly realised that she was still holding his hand. 'Sorry. I tend to get a bit carried away when I see things like this.'

'It's fine.' But how crazy was it that he actually missed her holding his hand when she took her fingers away from his?

They carried on through the marshes, with Alice pointing out various butterflies. It was a long time since Hugo had seen that many butterflies in a single place, and it amazed him. The birds were singing; the sun was bright and warm; and, even though there had been other cars in the field where she'd parked, they hadn't seen another human since they'd arrived. It felt a bit as if they were wandering through some kind of magical oasis.

'I think I'm going to have to cheat a tiny bit,' she said, 'because there's one particular butterfly I really, really want you to see. We're right at the start of first brood, and the weather's almost perfect, but I'm not taking any chances. I don't want you to miss this.' She took the backpack from her shoulder and removed a bunch of sweet williams, which she placed carefully on the ground.

He looked at her, surprised. 'Are butterflies super-attracted to these flowers, then?'

'Yup,' she said, coming over to stand next to him. 'The caterpillars only eat milk parsley—which is why the fenland in this part of the country is the main habitat for them—but the butterflies just love them. It's a combination of the scent and the nectar.' She smiled. 'And now, we wait. I probably should've warned you that there's a bit of waiting around on field trips.'

Hugo, who absolutely loathed wasting time, was a little surprised to discover that he didn't actually mind waiting around with Alice. Time didn't seem to be important when he was with her. It felt as if he was in a different place, somewhere much more carefree than his usual regimented life.

And then he saw it flying gracefully over the reeds before it landed on the bunch of flowers: a butterfly the size of his palm, creamy yellow and black, with a dark blue line and two red spots on the lower pair of wings, which curved down like a swallow's tail.

'That's incredible,' he whispered.

'An English Swallowtail,' she whispered back. '*Papilio machaon.* You only find them here in England in the Norfolk Broads.'

She'd brought him here to see a rare butterfly. The biggest butterfly he'd ever seen flying. And all of a sudden he got why she loved the creatures so much. He was spellbound by it.

Spellbound by her.

Not that he was going to let himself think too much about that. He didn't feel ready for this.

She'd taken the camera out of its case and was taking photographs of the butterfly; Hugo's attention was caught between them both, the concentration and the joy on Alice's face and the sheer beauty of the butterfly.

Once the butterfly had taken its fill of the nectar from the sweet williams, it flew off again.

'That,' he said, 'was stunning. I know you said you only find them around here, but is it possible to get them to breed in London?'

'Not native ones. They'd have to be imported,' she said, 'and they'd need to live in a butterfly house.'

She didn't say anything more. Hugo realised she was letting the butterflies make the case for her.

'And look there,' she said.

He followed where she was pointing, to the gorgeous turquoise insects darting about. 'Dragonflies?'

'Damselflies,' she said with a smile. 'If we're lucky, we'll get to see some rare dragonflies as well.'

He was entranced by the whole thing. She was right: it was definitely worth the early start. And, best of all, on the way back to the car they saw some more Swallowtails flying across the fen and landing on a patch of yellow flag irises.

'That,' he said, 'was amazing.'

'I'm glad you enjoyed it. The first time you see a Swallowtail is a bit special.' She smiled at him. 'And now we're going north. Not wetlands, this time—I want you to see the kind of wildflower meadow that I think would work with Rosemary's plans.'

'Bring it on,' he said.

That smile gave Alice hope that the butterflies were convincing Hugo to give the project a chance.

Yet, at the same time, his smile worried her because it made her heart feel as if it had done a backflip. Nearly all the men she'd fallen for in the past had hurt her—letting her think they wanted her for who she was, yet then they'd wanted to change her. She wasn't posh enough, wasn't girly enough, was too nerdy...

What you looked like shouldn't matter. But, in Hugo's world, it did. And Hugo himself was a fashion plate, with his designer shoes and sharp suits; it was so obvious that she'd be setting herself up for yet another crack in her heart, if she let herself fall for him. She didn't want to take that risk. It would be much more sensible to keep things strictly business between them and avoid the heartache in the first place. As for the way he made her stomach feel as if it swooped, the way her skin prickled with awareness whenever he accidentally brushed against her—she'd just have to ignore it.

It was an hour's drive to their next site and she kept the conversation light on the way. As she drove into the nearest village, Hugo's stomach rumbled audibly.

'Is that a hint you want to stop for lunch?' she asked.

He winced. 'Sorry. We had an early start. I only had time for a banana for breakfast.'

'If you'd said,' she told him, 'we could've stopped on the way for a bacon sandwich.'

'Your butterflies distracted me.'

'They'll do that,' she agreed with a smile. 'Look, there's a pub just up here. Let's stop and grab some lunch.'

She insisted on paying for their paninis and coffee, on the grounds that he'd bought the pizza earlier in the week, then drove them out of the village.

'So this is somewhere else in the middle of nowhere?' he asked wryly.

'That's why it's called a field trip.' Though then Alice made the mistake of looking at him, and the expression in his eyes caused her pulse to jolt again. Worse still, she noticed the curve of his mouth. How easy it would be to reach out and run a fingertip along his lower lip...

She pulled herself together with an effort, parked the car on the verge of a narrow country road, then led him down a track between two high hedges.

'It's as if that little brown butterfly's leading us,' he said.

'It's a Ringlet—*Aphantopus hyperantus*,' she said.

'Named after the little circles on its wings?'

She smiled. 'Absolutely.'

At the end of the track, they reached a stile with an information board next to it.

'This place is an Iron Age fort?' he asked, sounding surprised.

'It's the best-preserved Iron Age fort in East Anglia,' she said, 'and it's home to a lot of butterflies. This place always blows my students' minds, so I hoped you'd like it.'

'Are we actually allowed to walk among this?'

'We are indeed.' She indicated the people walking along the top of the massive circular earthwork; others were halfway down the steep slopes with cameras, bending down and clearly taking photographs of butterflies. 'Come and take a look.'

They made their way to the top of the outer circle. 'The wind's got up a bit, so the butterflies will be looking for sheltered spots,' she said. 'We might see more on the slopes than we do up here.'

'So all the flowers on the slopes and down in the middle of the rings are wildflowers?' he asked.

'And grasses,' she said. 'There are some rare orchids here, but you'll find the common flowers here as well—red clover, oxeye daisies, that sort of thing. And this is pretty much how I'd see Rosemary's re-wilded garden looking.'

'All different colours,' he said, 'like a kind of kaleidoscope. I can see that working.' He frowned. 'What's the shimmery stuff?'

'Butterflies,' she said. 'Stand still for a moment and watch.' Though she found herself looking at Hugo rather than at the butterflies; she enjoyed seeing the expression on his face change as he realised that there were lots of butterflies on the wing, just above ground level. She loved the way he'd clearly just realised how magical their surroundings were, the way his eyes lit up with pleasure as he worked out exactly what he was seeing.

'Blue butterflies,' he said. 'Just what you promised me.'

'Not quite as spectacular as the Morphos in Viola's collection,' she said, 'but I adore the Chalk Hill Blues. The females are actually more brown than blue, but they both have all these pretty circles on their underwings.'

'To make them look more like leaves if a bird happens to be passing?' he asked.

So he'd actually been paying attention to what she'd told him, and remembered it? Funny how that made her feel warm inside. 'Yes.'

To stop herself doing anything stupid—like holding his hand again—she took her camera out of its case and snapped a few pictures of the butterflies. They wandered round the hill fort, walking on the slopes as well as the top, and every so often Hugo stopped to watch the butterflies, looking entranced.

'I can't remember the last time I saw a blue butterfly,' he said. 'Or quite as many butterflies in one place. They're beautiful. Thank you for bringing me here.'

'My pleasure,' she said, meaning it. 'I can take you to some reserves nearer London, next time. I just wanted to show you these two places today.'

'I'm glad you did. It's been a while since...' He stopped.

She said nothing, giving him the space to talk, and eventually he said, 'Since I've been anywhere that made me feel this light of heart.'

The butterflies, the landscape—or sharing it with her? Though she didn't quite dare ask him, because she didn't want him to turn back into the grouchy, suspicious man she'd first met.

'So what made you choose to study butterflies?' he asked.

'My grandad used to take me to the park on a Sunday afternoon and show me all the butterflies on the plants there, whether they were the cultivated lavender in the posh bit or the wildflowers by the hedges,' she said. 'He died when I was ten. I was torn between studying botany and lepidoptery, but I think he would've been pleased about my career choice.' She glanced at him. 'What about you? Why architecture?'

'I guess, like a lot of kids, I liked building things with toy bricks. I spent hours and hours creating things. And then I noticed the way things were built, whenever I went out. I loved the Natural History Museum—but it wasn't just because of the dinosaurs or the big blue whale. I liked the shape of the building and the windows, and the colours of the bricks.' He smiled. 'Rosemary took me to Kew when I was about ten, and I fell in love with the Palm House. It's all the light. That's why I like working with glass.'

Alice really didn't understand what made Hugo Grey tick. But maybe this was her chance to get to know him better. 'What's your favourite thing you've designed?' she asked.

'The project I've been working on in Scotland for the last year,' he said. 'It's a country house on the buildings at risk register.'

'So you like restoring old buildings rather than designing new ones?'

'A mixture of the two,' he said. 'But this one was a bit special. There's a glass dome in the centre of the main hall—sadly, there were only a few fragments of the original glass left, but at least we had some photographs to work with. And there's an amazing spiral staircase beneath the dome.'

The tone of his voice made Alice feel sure that Hugo felt the same way about staircases and glass domes as she did about butterflies. So maybe they weren't quite as far apart as she'd thought.

'So that's what you specialise in? Domes and staircases?'

'Glass and staircases,' he said. 'Some historic, some modern.'

He was surprisingly easy to talk to, now she'd got him onto his favourite subject. She really enjoyed the drive home, to the point where she didn't want the day to end. When she finally parked in his road, it shocked her that she actually felt a lurch of sheer disappointment that their trip was over.

Maybe he felt the same, because he said, 'Would you like to come in for a coffee?'

She did—and, at the same time, she didn't. Getting close to

him made her feel twitchy. She opened her mouth to make a polite excuse, and was surprised to find herself saying, 'That'd be nice.'

From the outside, his house was a Victorian redbrick terrace, with large windows and a front door with a very fancy arch of glass above it. Inside, the house was startlingly modern and minimalist, with the walls painted a soft dove-grey and the flooring pale wood. The hallway had a flight of stairs leading off it; and a door to the left led to an enormous living room with an old-fashioned fireplace, a sofa and a desk with a drawing table. Though there was no artwork of any description on the walls, she noticed, just a very workmanlike clock. No bookshelves, either; or maybe all his shelves were hidden in a clever architectural way.

He shepherded her into a kitchen with white marble worktops, dark grey wooden cupboards and rectangular white tiles on the walls; the lighting was very modern, almost industrial. At the far end of the room there was a dining table and chairs; but what caught her eye was the entire wall of glass looking out onto the garden.

'That's spectacular,' she said. 'Was it like this when you bought it?'

'No. I opened it up,' he said. 'The glass doors fold inwards, so in summer you can open up the whole wall and step straight from the house to the garden.'

She loved the idea of it; though the garden was as minimal as the house, with a stone patio containing a bistro table and a couple of chairs, a square lawn mown very short indeed, and that was it. No shrubs. No herbaceous border. Not even a pot containing a plant of some kind. There wasn't a flower in sight.

'It's lovely,' she said, meaning that it *could* be lovely if he put a bit of effort in. Though maybe, as an architect, he saw the building rather than its surroundings. Given how minimalist the house was, the garden matched it. Though in her view that garden was all wrong. If it were hers, she'd fill it with roses.

There would be herbs and shrubs to attract butterflies and bees. And there would most definitely be a wild patch at the end, with cornflowers and poppies and clover and vetch. Maybe a tiny pond. It would be glorious.

'Espresso?' he asked, breaking into her thoughts.

'Thanks. That'd be nice,' she said politely.

'Feel free to grab a seat.' He indicated the dining table by the glass wall.

And of course he had a posh coffee machine—a proper bean-to-cup machine that ground the beans and made coffee with the perfect *crema* on top, which he brought over to her in a double-walled glass cup.

Posh.

So very different from her world.

Hugo belonged in Barney's world—and she never had. Even though she knew Hugo was trying to make her welcome, she couldn't help remembering the way Barney's set had reacted to her, scoffing that the girl from the council estate really thought she could step into a world of privilege.

You don't belong here, the voice said in her head.

But Hugo had asked her here without a hidden agenda. Feeling wary was ridiculous and stupid, and she needed to stop it. Right now.

To shut the voice up, she asked, 'So do you have any photographs of the house you were working on?'

'Yes.' He took his laptop from a drawer, tapped a few keys, then slid it across the table to her. 'All the photographs are in the same album. Help yourself.'

'Thanks.' She scrolled through them. 'Wow. I can see why you fell in love with it. That's an incredible staircase. And that glass dome...'

'It's pretty special,' he said. 'It's as near a reproduction to the original as I could get. And we managed to save all the original glass that was left in the external windows.'

'That's impressive,' she said, handing the laptop back to him.

* * *

Again, when her fingers brushed against his, it made Hugo's skin tingle.

What was it about this woman that drew him?

He was seriously tempted to ask her to stay for dinner, but he knew it would probably be wise to put a little distance between them, so he could get his head back in the right place.

So he kept the conversation light until she'd finished her coffee. 'Thank you for today,' he said. 'The butterflies were amazing.' And then his mouth ran away with him and spoiled his good intentions. 'Are you busy tomorrow?'

'Do you want to do another field trip?' she asked.

'I was thinking we could take a look at some glass,' he said. 'The British Museum, perhaps, and then Kew.'

'All right,' she said. 'I'll meet you at the British Museum. It opens at ten—is that too early for you?'

'It's a lot later than today,' he said wryly, 'so it's fine.'

'Ten o'clock on the steps,' she said.

He nearly—nearly—kissed her cheek, but managed to hold himself back.

And he intended to spend the rest of the evening working with figures and formulae, until he'd got himself back under his usual control. He was absolutely not going to kiss Alice Walters.

'See you tomorrow,' he said, shepherding her out to the door.

And when he closed the door behind her, he realised that he was regretting not kissing her.

Utterly ridiculous. He'd get a grip before tomorrow. For both their sakes.

CHAPTER FIVE

HUGO FELT LIKE a teenager about to go on his first date with a new girlfriend. Given that he was meeting a lepidopterist, how ironic it was that he had butterflies in his stomach.

Today was supposed to be about his great-aunt's legacy. But his heart still felt as if it had done a somersault when he walked through Bloomsbury and peered through the railings around the British Museum to see Alice standing on the steps beneath the famous pediment, waiting for him. As she'd done the previous day, she was wearing faded skinny jeans; when he drew nearer, he saw that today's T-shirt bore the slogan 'Butterflies do it with pheromones'.

'Nice T-shirt,' he said.

She grinned. 'Here's your fun fact for the day: a male butterfly can sense female butterfly pheromones from ten miles away.'

'Ten miles?' Was she teasing him?

His confusion must've shown on his face, because she smiled. 'Really. I'm full of facts like that.'

'They must have amazing noses.'

'Butterflies don't actually have noses, the way we do,' she said. 'They smell with their antennae and taste with their feet. If you'd said you wanted an anatomy lesson, Mr Grey, I would've brought one of my presentations with me.'

Anatomy lesson. Why did that suddenly make him feel hot all over? For pity's sake. The last woman Hugo had dated was his late wife. He'd closed down his emotions and his libido since Emma's death—at least, he'd thought he had. But, since he'd met Alice, that part of him seemed to have woken up again. She'd shown him things on their field trip that had enchanted him, and now the woman herself was enchanting him. Everything from that sassy slogan on her T-shirt, to the sparkle in her grey eyes and the way she smiled when she'd spotted something that interested her.

'I don't need an anatomy lesson, Dr Walters,' he said—a little more brusquely than he'd intended, because she really flustered him. 'Besides, today is about glass.'

'Indeed. Time to strut your stuff, Mr Glass Expert.'

But there was no mockery in her eyes. She actually looked interested.

Interested in glass, or—his heart skipped another beat—interested in him? He wasn't sure whether the idea scared him or thrilled him more.

Keep it professional, he reminded himself, and ushered her into the Great Court. 'This,' he said, 'is one of my favourite buildings in London.' That was it. Talk about his passion for architecture. Don't think about emotions. Keep it focused on the abstract. Something *safe*. 'I love the way the shadows of the steel beams change as you walk round.'

Hugo's gorgeous blue eyes were suddenly all lit up as he talked about the roof, and he'd lost that slight grouchiness. Clearly he felt the same way about glass as she did about butterflies, Alice thought. And seeing him in love with his subject made him so much easier to deal with.

Though, at the same time, it made him dangerous. Mesmerising.

She needed to get a grip; she'd been burned too often by men she'd been attracted to and then it had all gone wrong. That wasn't going to happen again. 'Tell me about the glass,' she said.

'There are three thousand, two hundred and twelve panes in that roof,' he said. 'And no two are identical.'

'Seriously?' She couldn't understand how you'd build a roof from what seemed to be a jigsaw puzzle. Besides, to her most of the panes looked identical.

'Seriously. It's because the roof undulates,' he said. He took his phone from his pocket, flicked into the Internet and brought up a photograph. 'This is it from above.'

It was nothing like she'd expected. 'It looks like a turquoise cushion, with an ancient brooch in the centre—but, from down here, the glass seems clear. And what's that in the centre?'

'It's the dome of the old Reading Room,' he said. 'And, actually, it's not very much smaller than the dome of the Pantheon in Rome.'

She stared at him, as amazed by the statistic as he'd seemed when she'd explained about butterfly pheromones. 'Seriously? But it looks tiny! I've been to Rome, with my best friend, and the Pantheon's enormous.'

'Which shows you just how huge this courtyard is—it's the biggest covered square in Europe,' he said. 'I would've loved to work on something like this, merging the old and the new.'

Just as he had with the Scottish country house and its dome, she thought. Could he be tempted to build something new—the butterfly house—that would fit into the garden of Rosemary's old house?

Together, they walked around the Great Court; just as Hugo had said, the light and the pattern of shadows changed as they moved round the area.

'This is pretty stunning,' she said. 'Though I'm not sure we could make a design like this work for a butterfly house.'

'It wouldn't.' He smiled. 'You wanted to show me an amazing butterfly yesterday, before you showed me the wildflower site. I wanted to show you my favourite bit of new architectural glass before we go and see the other stuff.'

'It's spectacular,' she said. 'Obviously I've been here before, but I never really noticed it. You've shown it to me in a very different way.'

'Like your Iron Age hill fort yesterday,' he said. 'I know this is going to make me sound a complete heathen, given the treasures within these walls, but I'd really like to skip the rest of the building now and go to the second bit of our field trip.'

Field trip. Of course that was what it was. They were going to Kew together because of the butterfly house project, not because he wanted to spend time with her, she reminded herself. Part of her wanted it to be a date; but at the same time part of her was scared she'd be sucked into trusting someone again and end up being let down. Pushing away the mingled disappointment and wariness, she said brightly, 'Sure.'

At Kew, they grabbed a quick coffee and a sandwich, then wandered through some of the formal gardens; Alice laid her palm against Hugo's upper arm to direct his attention to some butterflies, and instantly regretted the impulse when her fingertips started tingling where she touched him.

'Butterfly,' she said, knowing how stupid she sounded. For pity's sake, she should be speaking to him in full sentences, not mumbling single words at him. What was wrong with her? Why was she being so inarticulate?

'What is it?'

Focus on the science, she told herself. Take your hand off his arm. Stop being flustered. *Focus.* 'It's a *Polygonia c-album*—more commonly known as a Comma.'

'Because of the shape of its wing-edges?' he asked.

She liked the fact he'd tried to be logical. 'No, because of the white mark on its underwing.'

'I love the colour. Especially the contrast with the purple flowers.'

'It's not necessarily purple to a butterfly,' she said.

His eyes widened. 'It's not?'

'They don't see colour and resolution in the way that humans do—even though they have eyes in the back of their head and near three-hundred-and-sixty-degree vision, they can't see the fine detail,' she explained. 'And they can see the ultraviolet patterns on flower petals that we can't.'

'What ultraviolet patterns?' he asked.

'The nectar guides.' She gestured to one of the plants in the lawn. 'To a butterfly, this yellow dandelion looks white at the edges, but red at the centre where the nectar is. And a horse-chestnut flower is yellow to them when it's producing nectar, and red when it's not.'

'That's amazing,' he said, smiling. And that smile made her heart feel as if it had done a backflip. He actually listened to what she said. So far, he hadn't tried to change her.

Could she take a risk?

Or should she be sensible, and find a way of putting some distance between them?

Yet she couldn't. As they walked through the gardens together, their hands brushed against each other. Once. Twice. And then their fingers interlocked, just one at first, and then another, and another, until they were actually holding hands.

She could barely breathe.

This wasn't supposed to be happening.

They were absolutely *not* a couple.

Yet here they were, holding hands, as if they were on a proper date. It was thrilling and terrifying, all at the same time.

'This is what I wanted to show you. The Palm House,' he said. 'Victorian glass and iron.'

Was it her imagination, or did his voice sound a bit funny? As if he was just as flustered by this thing happening between them as she was, and he was trying really hard to keep it busi-nesslike...and failing, the same way she was.

'It's like an upside-down ship,' she said.

'Well spotted. It was the first glasshouse built on this scale,' he said, 'so they used techniques from shipbuilding. And here you see sixteen thousand panes of glass.'

He let her hand go when he opened the door for her—but within moments they were back to holding hands. Neither of them said a word about it or even looked at their hands to draw attention to what was happening. But it was there. A fact. They liked each other enough to hold hands. And Alice wondered if Hugo, too, was feeling the little fizzy bubbles of pleasure that seemed to be filling her own veins.

The fact that Hugo really seemed to be considering building the butterfly house made her heart feel light with hope.

She had no idea how long they spent wandering through Kew, exploring the glasshouses and the gardens, with Hugo pointing out his favourite bits of various buildings and herself pointing out the butterflies flitting over the plants. All she could really concentrate on was the warmth of his fingers curled round hers, and how good it made her feel.

Time blurred, seeming to go in the blink of an eye and yet stretch for a week at the same time. But finally the gardens were closing and all the tourists appeared to be heading for the exits.

'Time to leave, I guess,' Hugo said, sounding regretful.

'I guess,' she said.

They walked back to the Tube station together. Alice knew they'd be taking completely different trains—Hugo to Battersea and herself to Shadwell. He'd sounded wistful earlier; would he want to prolong the time with her and maybe suggest dinner? Should she suggest it, maybe? Or were they back in the real world again, now they'd left the glasshouse behind? Would he want to put some distance between them?

'Thank you for a nice day,' Hugo said, which pretty much sealed it for her.

Distance it was.

Separate trains and separate lives.

She could ask him if he'd like to have dinner with her; but perhaps it would be better to spare them both the embarrassment of him refusing. Instead, she smiled. 'I enjoyed it, too. Thank you for showing me the glass.'

He looked awkward, as if debating something in his head; and then he bent forward and kissed her swiftly on the cheek.

Warmth spread through her, along with some courage. 'Maybe we can go to see a butterfly house, next.' She took a deep breath. 'Wednesday afternoons are usually free for me.'

He took his phone from his pocket and checked something. 'I can do Wednesday, this week.'

They were talking as if this was a business appointment, but it felt like a date. And she was shocked to realise how much she wanted it to be a date.

Forcing herself to sound calm, she said, 'We could meet at Canary Wharf station at, say, one o'clock?'

'I'll put it in my diary,' he said. 'See you then.'

'See you then.' She held her breath, just in case he decided to lean forward and kiss her other cheek—or, even, her mouth.

But he didn't.

He just smiled at her and walked away.

Was she about to make a colossal fool of herself? Should she back off?

But all the same Alice found herself touching her cheek when she sat down on the train, remembering how his lips had felt against her skin.

Would he kiss her again, the next time they met?

Would it be a proper kiss?

And, if so, what was she going to do about it?

Butterfly fact of the day: a butterfly's body temperature needs to be thirty degrees C before it can fly.

Alice regretted the impulse, the second she'd sent the email. Supposing Hugo thought she was trying to flirt with him?

Well, she *was* trying to flirt with him. Even though her head knew it was dangerous and reckless and a very bad idea, that flare of attraction was strong enough to make her ignore her common sense. She couldn't stop thinking about the way he'd held her hand all afternoon, and that kiss on the cheek, and wondering just how his mouth would feel against hers.

He didn't reply. Which served her right, and she forced herself to concentrate on her students and stop mooning over him. But, at the end of the day, there was an email waiting in her inbox.

Glass fact of the day: when glass breaks, the cracks move at three thousand miles an hour.

Flirting by nerdiness?

It was delicious. And addictive. She sent him a nerdy fact by text on Tuesday morning; he replied in kind, later in the day. By Wednesday lunchtime, Alice was practically effervescent with excitement. She couldn't wait to see him.

Just as they'd arranged, Hugo was waiting for her at Canary Wharf station. He was wearing his sharp suit and posh shoes, and she wished she'd thought to dress up a bit, too, instead of being her usual scruffy scientist self.

'Hi,' she said, suddenly shy now she was with him.

'Hi.' And now he looked equally ill-at-ease.

What now? They weren't *officially* dating, so she could hardly greet him with a kiss. But this wasn't just business any more, either. There was definitely something personal.

'Shall we, um...?' She gestured to the platform, where the train was waiting.

He didn't hold her hand on the train. He didn't hold her hand on the way to the butterfly house, either. And he didn't look that impressed as they walked up to the very ordinary glasshouse. Well, he was an architect who specialised in glass. Of course a square building with a gable roof would be dull and functional, in his view.

Then again, this was the man who'd built a removable glass

wall between his house and his garden, and yet his garden was the dullest and most minimalist in the universe. So, the way she saw it, he really didn't have the right to be picky about this place.

'Don't judge it from the outside,' she said.

'Uh-huh.' His expression and the tone of his voice were both firmly neutral.

She'd just have to hope that the inside of the building would work the same magic on him as it did on her. Without comment, she opened the first set of doors and ushered him inside, before closing the doors behind them. And then she opened the inner doors.

She'd timed it deliberately: this was the afternoon lull, when the younger children had gone home for a nap and the older children were still at school, so she and Hugo had the whole building to themselves. The glasshouse was filled with large ferns and tropical plants; dozens of butterflies flitted through the air, a mix of sizes and shapes and glorious colours.

She stopped by one of the feeding stations, primed with slices of banana and pineapple and melon; huge owl butterflies had settled on the fruit and were feeding on the sugar.

'That's impressive,' he said.

Yes, but it wasn't the bit she hoped would really attract him. 'Come this way,' she said, taking his hand.

They passed several Zebra Longwing butterflies that were settled on the greenery, idly flapping their long, black-and-white-striped wings.

'I didn't realise that butterflies could be that shape,' he said. 'They're more like a dragonfly than a butterfly.'

'They're the *Heliconius* type,' she said. 'You'll see other butterflies in here that are the same shape, but with splashes of red on their wings; they're the Postman.'

'Postman because they're red, like a post box?' he guessed.

'No, because they do a daily "round" of their flowers—like a postman delivering letters.'

His eyes lit up. 'That's brilliant. And that one over there's really vivid. I had no idea that butterflies could be lime green.'

'That's a Malachite,' she said. *'Siproeta stelenes.'*

She knew she was babbling, just naming things for him, but it was the only way she could cope. Hugo Grey made her head feel all mixed up.

She took a video on her phone of one of the butterflies hovering above a flower, switching the recording to slow motion mode so she could show him something later that she hoped would amaze him, then continued to walk through the butterfly house with him.

His fingers suddenly tightened round hers. 'The big blue butterflies I remember Rosemary showing me: there's one flying over there in the corner.'

'A Morpho.' The thing she thought—*hoped*—might make the difference. 'Stand still,' she said, 'because they're really curious and they'll come over to have a closer look at you.'

'Seriously?'

'Seriously.'

He did as she suggested, and she watched his expression as one of the butterflies flapped lazily over to them, its wings bright iridescent blue, then landed on his arm. His eyes were full of wonder; all the cynicism had gone from his face. At that moment, it felt as if he lit up the whole butterfly house for her. It was the sweetest, sweetest feeling. As if they were sharing something special. Something private. Their own little world.

'You can breathe, you know,' she said softly. 'You won't hurt it.'

'That's just...' He shook his head, clearly lost for words.

She couldn't resist standing on tiptoe and brushing her mouth against his.

He froze for a moment; and then, as the Morpho flew away again, he wrapped his arms around her waist, returning the kiss. She slid her arms round his shoulders, drawing him closer. And then he really kissed her, teasing her lips with his until she leaned against him and opened her mouth, letting him deepen the kiss. All around them, butterflies flapped their iridescent wings, and she closed her eyes, letting all her senses focus on the feel of Hugo's mouth against hers.

When he finally broke the kiss, she opened her eyes, startled.

'Sorry,' he said. 'I shouldn't have done that.'

'Sorry,' she said. 'Blame it on the butterflies—the excitement of seeing the blue Morpho.'

'Absolutely,' he said.

She was lying; and she was pretty sure he knew it. She was pretty sure he was lying, too. But she had no idea what they were going to do about this. She hadn't felt this attracted to someone for years; but at the same time she didn't want to put the butterfly house project in jeopardy. How did she deal with this, without making a huge mess of things?

'Come and see the pupae,' she said, and slid her hand through the crook of his elbow—just to steer him towards the right place in the butterfly house. It had absolutely nothing to do with wanting to touch him. Though, when he drew her a tiny bit closer, it made tingles run down her spine.

'They're in a box?' He stared at the wooden box with its lines of horizontal canes.

'It's a puparium—the safest place for them to hatch.'

'And they're stuck to the canes?'

She nodded. 'So, once they've wiggled out of the chrysalis, they can hang freely to let their wings dry and fill with blood, ready for flying. In a set-up like this, they might hatch overnight and they'll be let out in the mornings when they're ready to fly. Then they look for a mate and start the courtship ritual...'

Just as she and Hugo were doing. Of sorts. Holding hands. Kissing. Making eye contact, and shying away again, because both of them were so unsure about this whole thing. She felt the colour seep through her cheeks and she couldn't quite look him in the eye. 'The females lay the eggs, and the cycle starts all over again: egg, caterpillar, pupa, butterfly.'

He looked thoughtful. 'It's hotter than I expected in here.'

Did he mean literally or figuratively? It felt hot in here for her, too. Especially when he kissed her. She pulled herself together. Literally, she reminded herself. 'It's the right temperature and humidity for the plants and the butterflies.'

'And it's noisier than I expected, too.'

'That's the air heating,' she explained.

'Maybe we could look at different ways of heating,' he suggested.

Which sounded as if he was thinking seriously about the possibilities of building the butterfly house. Maybe she hadn't ruined everything with that kiss, after all.

'This place is magical. It's a bit like walking through a summery snow globe crossed with a rain forest,' he said.

Did he have a picture of that in his head? Something perhaps that he could do with her project? 'I know a dome wouldn't work, but have you any other thoughts?'

He shook his head. 'Maybe we could have a domed roof. A cylindrical building, with arched windows.'

'Like the ones in the Palm House?'

'That could work.'

If she put the butterfly house first, maybe afterwards she and Hugo could explore what was happening between them.

What was it about this place? Hugo wondered. He'd mused earlier that it was like walking through a summery snow globe. But it wasn't just the brightly coloured butterflies that made it feel so magical; it was Alice, too. There was something special about her. The way she made him feel—with her, for the first time in so very long, it felt as if there was a point to life. As if he was doing more than just existing and trudging from minute to minute. As if her warmth and sweetness had melted the permafrost where he'd buried his heart.

He'd been the one to break the kiss and call a halt. She'd backed off too, blaming it on the butterflies. But it wasn't the real butterflies that had caused that kiss: it was the metaphorical ones in his stomach. The way she made him feel, that swooping excitement of attraction and desire.

What would happen if he kissed her again? Would she back away, skittish as one of her butterflies?

Then he realised that she was speaking.

'Sorry. Wool-gathering,' he said. 'You were saying?'

She was all pink and flustered, and he wanted to draw her into his arms.

'If you're not busy, I could cook dinner tonight. Show you some more butterfly things.'

Was this Alice's way of acknowledging this thing between them and admitting that she'd like to get closer, but was wary at the same time?

That was exactly how he was feeling, too. Wanting to get closer, but scared.

Baby steps.

Starting with dinner.

'I'd like that,' he said.

The pink-and-flusteredness went up a notch. Good. Because she made him feel that way, too.

The Tube was too crowded for them to talk on the way back to her place. Then she went quiet on him during the walk from the station to her flat in Shadwell, which turned out to be in a modern development overlooking a quayside.

'It's a fair bit smaller than your place,' she said, 'but it's home.' She gave him a wry smile. 'Though I do envy you your garden. The nearest I have is a window box of herbs.'

'But you get a view of the water,' he pointed out.

'I guess.'

He realised that her assessment was right when she opened the front door and ushered him inside; her flat really *was* compact. 'The bathroom's there if you need it,' she said, indicating a door off the hallway, then led him into the living room.

There was a bay window with space for her desk and a small

filing cabinet; the rest of the room was taken up by a small sofa, a bistro-style table and two chairs, and a floor-to-ceiling bookcase stuffed with books. The walls were all painted cream, but there were strategically placed framed artworks; some were old-fashioned botanical prints of butterflies, and others were small jewel-like modern pieces. And how very different it was from his own stark and monochromatic home; her flat was full of colour and beauty.

'Is that Van Gogh?' he asked, gesturing to a framed poster.

She nodded. 'It's his *Butterflies and Poppies.* They're Clouded Yellows. I saw the original with my best friend— she's an art historian, and she wanted to go to the Van Gogh museum in Amsterdam to see their collection because he's her favourite painter.' She smiled. 'Ruth also took me to the gardens at Giverny, because she's a huge Monet fan. She was waxing lyrical over the bridge and the lily pond, and there I was on the hunt for butterflies. I guess we're as nerdy as each other.'

'My best friend's nerdy, too. He's got this passion for Regency doors, and whenever we go anywhere he's always darting off to take a photograph. His Instagram's full of shots of fanlights and door knockers.' Kit was one of the few people Hugo saw regularly—but a couple of months back Kit and Jenny had invited one of her single friends over to dinner to make up a foursome, and it had annoyed Hugo to the point where he'd pleaded a headache and left early. Things had been a bit strained between them since then; he knew Kit meant well, but he really didn't want to be set up with a suitable woman.

Yes, he was lonely and miserable. Stuck. Things weren't getting better; the more time passed, the lonelier he felt, and the more aware he was of things he and Emma hadn't had the time to do together. All that stuff about time being a great healer was utter rubbish. He was just *stuck*.

Emma would be furious with him.

He was furious with himself.

But he didn't know how to get unstuck again.

Alice was the first person in a long time who'd made him feel connected with someone. He'd probably spent as much time in her company during the last week or so as he'd spent with anyone else outside the office in the previous six months, apart from his parents and Rosemary. But he couldn't expect her to help push him out of his rut. That was too much to ask from someone who'd known him for less than a month—especially as he'd been at odds with her for more than half that time.

'Can I help with dinner?' he asked instead.

'No, you're fine,' she said with a smile. 'My kitchen's a bit on the small side.'

He could see that for himself from the doorway. It was practically a galley kitchen, with just enough room for a cooker, fridge, and washing machine. He noticed that there was a large cork board on the wall with photographs and postcards pinned to it; it was perfectly neat and tidy, but the personal touches made her flat feel like a home rather than just a place to live, as his own house was.

'Let me grab you a glass of wine,' she said. 'Red or white?'

'I ought to provide the wine, as you're making dinner,' he said. And then he was cross with himself. Why hadn't he thought of that earlier?

She flapped a dismissive hand. 'It's fine. Red or white?'

'What goes better with dinner?'

She tipped her head on one side as she considered it; yet again, he was struck by how cute she was. 'White,' she said. 'Though, before I start cooking, do you have any food allergies or are there any particular things you hate?'

'No allergies and I eat most things,' he confirmed.

The kitchen was definitely too small for two people to work in, because she accidentally brushed against him when she took the wine out of the fridge. He almost wrapped his arms round her and kissed her again, but he held himself back. Just.

'Can I do anything? Lay the table?' he asked instead.

She took cutlery from a drawer. 'You can lay the table and

then come back for the salad, if you like. Then feel free to amuse yourself with the TV or whatever.'

He laid the bistro table; when he came back to collect the bowl of salad and his glass of wine, she was busy chopping mushrooms and boiling water in a pan. He could smell something delicious; funny, it had been so long since he'd noticed food. He'd seen it as nothing more than fuel ever since Emma had died.

Rather than bothering with the television, he glanced through the books on Alice's shelves; there were some very academic tomes on ecology and butterflies, and a few glossy coffee-table-type books with gorgeous shots of butterflies, mixed in with a smattering of crime novels. There were also photographs on the shelves; the young child was recognisable as her, with an elderly couple he assumed were her grandparents. The graduation photos of Alice were at Oxford and London, with a couple who were obviously her parents. There was another picture of her wearing a bridesmaid's dress, with her arm wrapped around the bride: obviously a close friend, maybe the one she'd mentioned going with to Rome and Amsterdam and France.

And how very different this was from his own house; he didn't have any photographs on display at all. They were tucked away for safekeeping, along with his memories. Where they didn't hurt.

A few minutes later, Alice came in carrying two bowls of pasta. 'Fettuccine Alfredo,' she said. 'I hope that's OK with you.'

He joined her at the table. 'This is lovely,' he said after his first taste.

She inclined her head in acknowledgement of the compliment. 'Thank you, but it's just a very simple pasta dish, not something I've slaved over for hours and hours.'

'It's still lovely,' he said.

Strangely, given that they were in her flat, her space, she'd gone all quiet and shy on him. Hugo had the feeling that, even

though Alice had fought like a tigress for Rosemary's butterfly house and she teased him, there was also something about
her that was as fragile as the butterflies she studied. A vulnerability that she kept hidden.

'Who are the people in the photographs?' he asked, hoping
to draw her out a bit more.

'The one of me when I'm small is with my grandparents,
the graduation photos are with my parents, and the wedding is
when my best friend Ruth got married last year,' she said, con-
firming his guesses.

'Nice pictures,' he said.

'Thank you.' She looked at him. 'You didn't have any art or
photos in your house. Have you only just finished the renovations?'

'No. I've been there for just over two years,' he admitted.
'I finished the renovations last summer.' He just couldn't face
putting up photographs which underscored the hole in his life,
or the pictures Emma had chosen, because just looking at them
made him miss her.

To his relief, she didn't push him to explain; she merely
topped up his glass of wine and then turned the conversation
to something much lighter.

And how good it was to spend time with someone else. It
made him realise he should've made more of an effort with
the people around him instead of trying to hide away from the
world and lick his wounds in silence.

After dinner, she let him help with the washing up, then offered him a coffee. 'Though I don't have a fancy machine or
fancy glass cups like yours,' she said. 'The best I can do is a
cafetière and a mug.'

'A mug with butterflies on it, I presume,' he said, trying for
lightness.

'Of course,' she said, and proceeded to make a cafetière of
coffee. 'Oh, and I meant to show you the film I took earlier.'

She put the mugs on the table, found the film on her phone, and handed it to him.

A black and red butterfly was flapping its wings frantically; and then suddenly it went into slow motion. The two upper wings flapped completely separately from the bottom pair of wings, he realised. 'It looks like a swimmer.'

'Doing the butterfly stroke,' she said. 'Isn't it incredible?'

'When it's at normal speed, you just see the mad flapping. But this—it's really amazing.'

She looked pleased. 'I thought you'd enjoy it.'

And there it was: the warmth and sweetness that had been missing from his life for so long. He wanted more of this in his life, but he was so out of practice at dating. He wasn't sure how to reach out to her. Then again, even if he did reach out to her, and even if Alice responded—could he take the risk of falling in love again, and losing her? Intellectually, he knew that the chances of losing her in the same way he'd lost Emma were tiny; but emotionally the fear of going through all the pain and loss again thudded through him, making him want to back away and keep what was left of his heart safe.

He drained his coffee and said, 'I'd better let you get on with your evening.'

'Of course,' she said, all calm and professional; but Hugo had seen the hurt in her eyes before she'd masked it, and felt guilty.

He didn't mean to make her feel bad. But he couldn't explain, either, not without things getting a whole lot more awkward.

'Thank you for dinner,' he said. 'I'll, um, catch you later.'

'Sure,' she said. 'Thanks for coming to the butterfly house.'

And all the way home Hugo kicked himself. Why hadn't he just opened up to her, admitted that he liked her and wanted to see her but he was scared about things going wrong? Why hadn't he been honest about Emma? Alice had made him feel amazing, that afternoon. And the moment when he'd kissed her and she'd kissed him back...

He was an idiot for not kissing her again. For not asking her out properly. For not taking the risk. Life was too short to spend all your time hiding.

He'd call her tomorrow, he decided. Apologise for being rude. Explain.

And he'd just have to hope that she'd listen.

Alice scrubbed the coffee pot clean. And then she scrubbed it again, because it gave her something to do.

What a fool she was. Why on earth had she thought it was a good idea to cook dinner for Hugo? Just because he'd kissed her in the butterfly house and made her feel amazing?

Then again, maybe it was better that he'd realised this early on that she didn't fit into his world. He'd seen her for who she was: and she simply didn't measure up. Further proof that Barney and his cronies had been right all along and it was what you looked like, what you sounded like, that was most important.

She'd just have to hope that she hadn't jeopardised the butterfly house project with her stupidity.

CHAPTER SIX

ALICE SENT HUGO a text with a butterfly fact on Thursday morning, hoping that she could find some way back to the working relationship they'd established, but there was no reply.

Until her phone pinged almost at the end of the day.

Sorry. Tied up in meetings all day. Fact for you: glass isn't a solid.

It wasn't a liquid or a gas, either. And that statement was definitely an opening. She could ignore it; or she could give in to temptation and reply.

So what is it?

Amorphous solid—molecules can still move inside it, but too slowly for us to see.

He was still playing the nerdy facts game with her, then; but it didn't feel quite as reassuring as she would've liked. Especially as he'd left her house so abruptly, the previous day.

OK, so he'd made it clear that he didn't want to take their relationship further. But that didn't necessarily mean he was giving up on the butterfly house project. She just needed to try and keep things light and easy between them.

Friday was Emma's birthday and Hugo woke with a ball of misery in his stomach. He headed for his office early, but keeping busy didn't help. If he was honest with himself, he wasn't keeping busy, either; he was just staring out of the window at the river. Stuck. Miserable as hell.

Life moved on, so why couldn't he?

Then his phone chimed to signal an incoming text. He knew before he looked at the screen who it would be from: Alice.

Your butterfly fun fact of the day: butterfly wings are transparent because they're made of chitin, the same protein as an insect's exoskeleton.

Funny, she was the one person he felt he could handle communicating with today. Probably because she didn't know what had happened, so she wasn't going to tread carefully round him and make things worse. And her text was a really welcome distraction.

She was telling him that butterflies were transparent, but the ones she'd shown him were all different colours. He called her on it.

So how come they look different colours?

Scales. As they get older, the scales fall off and leave transparent spots on their wings. Except for a Glasswing, which is transparent to start with.

He could just hear her saying that. And then she'd find a picture on the Internet to illustrate her point, and maybe she'd test him to see if he knew what the butterfly was and whether this was a male or female of the species. He really liked her nerdy streak; it intrigued him and delighted him in equal measure, and it made him feel as if the world was opening up around him again, as if he was stepping away from the oppression of his heartbreak. Just being with her made him want to smile.

Right at that moment he really, really wanted to see her. The only time he felt vaguely normal nowadays was when he was with her. How crazy was that? Before he could overanalyse things and talk himself out of it, he sent her a text.

Are you busy at lunchtime or do you want to come and see a staircase?

To his relief, she didn't make him wait for a reply. Alice wasn't a game-player. What you saw was what you got.

Staircase at lunchtime is doable. I need to be back for a seminar at three.

Meet at St Paul's? When's a good time?

Half-twelve?

OK. See you by the main entrance at half-twelve.

And how weird it was that, for the first time that day, Hugo felt as if he could actually breathe—that there wasn't a huge weight on his chest, making every breath a shallow effort.

At half-past twelve, he was standing on the cathedral steps, looking out for Alice; it was easy to spot her in the crowd. He lifted a hand in acknowledgement, and his heart gave a little skip when she waved back.

'Thanks for coming,' he said when she reached him.

'I'm looking forward to seeing this staircase,' she said. 'And I know it's not glass, but I assume you're going to tell me about that, too.' She gestured up to Wren's enormous dome.

What he really wanted to do was wrap his arms round her, feel her warmth melting the permafrost around his heart. But that would involve explanations he didn't want to give right now, so he duly smiled and escorted her into the cathedral. 'We've actually got a slightly different tour. Maybe we'll come back another day and I'll show you the dome. Today we're focusing on a staircase.'

'I owe you for my ticket,' she said.

He shook his head. 'My idea, my bill.'

'Then I'm buying coffees and sandwiches after,' she said firmly. 'No arguments.'

They were just in time to join the tour, and when they got to the end of it—the bit he'd really been waiting for—Hugo watched Alice's face, pleased to see how amazed she was by the Dean's Stair.

'It's a spiral staircase, but it doesn't have a column in the middle,' she marvelled. 'I don't get how it just floats in the air like that, without falling over.'

'It's cantilevered,' he said. 'Each step is shaped so it can bear the weight of the next. And it's not going to fall over—it's been there for more than three hundred years.'

He held her hand all the way to the top, pleased that she seemed to enjoy the elegant stonework and wrought-iron railings as much as he did.

'What a view,' she said at the top, looking down at the elegant spiral with the eight-pointed star at its centre. 'I need to take a picture of this for Ruth.'

'The art historian,' he remembered.

She nodded, and snapped the picture on her phone.

And then he heard the cathedral organist start to play. Something he knew well. Bach. A piece Emma had loved and had used to play on the piano he'd given back to her parents, knowing they'd find it comforting. The piece the organist had played at her funeral. And suddenly the weight was right back in the centre of his chest, along with sapping misery.

* * *

Something was wrong. Alice didn't know what, but Hugo looked terrible. There were lines of pain etched round his mouth and smudges beneath his eyes. Once the guide had led them back out into the main part of the cathedral, she said gently, 'I think we need coffee and a sandwich. And somewhere nice to eat it.'

'Sure.'

His voice was flat, worrying her further. She quickly bought coffee, muffins and sandwiches at a shop nearby, then shepherded him to a quiet garden not far from St Paul's.

'I had no idea this place even existed,' he said as they sat down. 'Where are we?'

'Christchurch Greyfriars garden,' she said. 'The church was pretty much lost to the Blitz, apart from the tower, but the authorities have kept the land as a garden. The pergolas are full of bird boxes for sparrows and finches. I love this place because it's full of the most gorgeous blue, purple and white flowers.'

'And butterflies.'

Even now, one was skimming past them. She inclined her head. 'Indeed, because a lot of the plants here are nectar-rich.'

'I'm guessing you know a lot of hidden gardens in London?'

She smiled. 'It kind of goes with my job. I need to know where I can take my students on a field trip semi-locally at different times of the year. Here. Have your lunch.' She handed him a cup of coffee and a sandwich.

'Thank you.'

They ate in silence; it wasn't completely awkward, but Alice could see that he was wrestling with something in his head. She had a feeling that talking about whatever was wrong didn't come easily to him. So, when they'd both finished their sandwich and he was staring into his coffee, she reached out to take his free hand. 'I'm probably speaking out of turn here,' she said softly, 'but you look like you did the very first day I met you—lost.'

'It's how I feel,' he admitted. He looked at her and his eyes were full of misery. 'It's selfish of me, but I wanted to see you today because you don't tread on eggshells round me. You stomp about and you tease me and you teach me things and you...' He shook his head. 'You make me see things in a different way.'

Which was an incredible compliment, but it wasn't what had snagged her attention. 'Why do people tread on eggshells round you?'

He took a deep breath. 'Emma—my wife. It's her birthday today.'

He was married?

But, before she had a chance to absorb that, he continued, 'She died nearly three years ago.'

Widowed, then. And she was pretty sure he wasn't that much older than she was. Her heart broke for him. 'That's rough, losing her so young.'

He nodded. 'She had asthma. After she died, I found out there's something called Peak Week—it's a week in September when allergies and asthma just spike because there's a big rise in pollen and mould, plus the kids have just gone back to school so there are loads of germs and what have you that compromise people's breathing. Emma was a middle school teacher. I was in America giving a paper at a conference when she had a severe asthma attack.'

Obviously in that week in September, Alice realised.

'She called the ambulance and they came straight away, but she collapsed before she even had a chance to unlock the front door. She had a cardiac arrest and she never regained consciousness.' His expression grew bleaker. 'I never got a chance to say goodbye to her.'

No wonder he'd looked so lost, that day at the solicitor's. The meeting had been about his great-aunt's estate, and it must have brought back all the memories of his wife's death. She put her arms round him and just held him. 'That,' she said softly, 'is so sad. I've never lost anyone near my own age—the only person I've lost is Grandad, and although he went a bit before his time it still felt in the natural order of things. Your wife was so young. It must've felt like the end of the world.'

'It did. And then in the cathedral just now...the organ music. It was something she played on the piano at home. A piece—' his breath caught '—played at her funeral.'

Music that had brought back everything he'd lost. 'I didn't know Emma,' she said, 'but she mattered to you, so she must've been special.'

'Very.'

'Do you have a photo of her?'

For a moment, Alice thought she'd gone too far; but eventually Hugo nodded and took out his phone. He skimmed through the photos, then handed the phone to her.

It was clearly their wedding photograph, with Hugo in a tail-coat and Emma in a frothy dress with her veil thrown back; they were both laughing, radiant with happiness, while confetti fluttered down around them. Emma was utterly beautiful.

'She looks lovely, really warm and kind,' Alice said.

'She was,' Hugo said. And, although Alice was a very different woman, she had that same warmth and kindness about her. The thing that had been missing from the centre of his life. The thing he'd tried so hard to live without. But he'd just been existing, not living. Putting one foot in front of the other, taking it step by step. It was all he could do, without Emma. On his own, nothing made sense.

'Remember the love, not the loss,' Alice said gently. 'I know it's hard when you're missing someone and want them beside you, when you want to share things with them and you can't— but you can still share things in spirit. When I see the first butterfly of spring, I think of Grandad and I kind of send him a mental phone call. I sit down wherever I am and I talk to him about it, remember times we'd seen that same species together, and it makes things not hurt quite so much. Maybe you need to give Emma a mental phone call. Talk to her. Tell her about your staircases and your glass.'

Hugo's throat felt as if it were full of sand. He couldn't speak, so he just nodded.

'And you can still celebrate her birthday with cake, because that's how birthdays should be celebrated.' She produced two muffins from a bag. 'It's white chocolate and raspberry. I hope that's OK. I'm sorry I don't have a candle to put in it and light, but we can pretend we have candles and wish Emma happy birthday.'

Hugo's eyes stung. He and Alice had kissed. They'd started to get close, taken the first tentative steps towards a relationship. Yet she still had a big enough heart to make room for his late wife and celebrate Emma's birthday instead of putting herself first.

'I'll spare you the singing,' she said. 'But happy birthday, Emma.' She raised her muffin in a toast.

'Happy birthday, Emma,' he said, his voice thick with unshed tears.

And how odd that eating cake and wishing his late wife happy birthday made him feel so much better, taking the weight of the misery off his heart. He really hadn't expected this to work.

'Emma used to make amazing cakes,' he said. It was why he rarely ate cake nowadays; the memories were too much for him.

'Then,' she said, 'if the butterfly house project goes ahead, maybe we can call the cafe after her. Emma's Kitchen. And then she'll be part of it, too, along with Viola and Rosemary.'

How on earth had he ever thought Alice was an ambitious gold-digger who didn't care who she trampled on her path to the top? She was nothing of the sort. She was inclusive. Kind. Thoughtful. This was so much more than he deserved, given the way he'd misunderstood her.

And she still wasn't taking for granted that the butterfly house would go ahead. She wasn't seeing his feelings as a weakness and using them to pressure him into getting her own way. She was being *kind*.

It made him feel too emotional to speak again. He just took her hand and raised it to his mouth, pressing a kiss into her palm and folding her fingers over it. He hoped she understood what he was trying to say. How much he appreciated her being there. How he wanted things to be different.

She rested her palm against his cheek. 'I have half a dozen students expecting me this afternoon, but I can call them now and reschedule our seminar.'

He shook his head. 'That's not fair.'

'It's not fair of me to leave you right now,' she said.

'I have meetings, in any case.' Meetings that he'd force himself to get through, and he'd do his job well, the way he always did. He had his professional pride. He took a deep breath. 'You've made me feel so much better today. Thank you.'

Her grey eyes were unsure. 'Do you want me to walk you back to your office?'

'No. But I'll walk you back to the Tube.'

'All right.'

She didn't push him to speak on the way back to the station; she just let him be. No wrapping him in platitudes and pity, and he was grateful for that. How often did you find someone who'd just let you be you, with no pressure?

'I'll call you later,' he said.

'OK.' She stood on tiptoe and kissed his cheek. Just once. 'Give that mental phone call a try. It always makes me feel better.'

And then the train pulled up at the station and she'd gone.

Hugo was thoughtful all afternoon, between meetings.

A mental phone call.

Better than that, he'd visit. Just as he always did on Emma's birthday, his own birthday, their wedding anniversary and the anniversary of her death.

He took stocks, her favourite flowers, to the churchyard, and rinsed out the vase on her grave, filling it with fresh water before adding the new flowers.

'Happy birthday, my love,' he said, sitting down next to the grave. 'I can't believe it's nearly three years, now. I miss you so much, still.' He swallowed hard. 'And I know you'd be furious with me for moping. I know I need to move on—to live life to its fullest, the way you used to do. But it's just so hard without you, Em.'

He wrapped his arms round his knees. 'I miss you. And this is incredibly crass of me to say this on your birthday—it's wrong on so many, many levels—but I've been so lost and lonely without you. And I've met someone. She would've liked you, and I think you would've liked her.'

He sighed. 'I'd like to ask her out. I think we could make each other happy. And she's not replacing you—I'll always love you, and I'll always keep your memory alive. She doesn't want to push you out of my life, either; she thinks we ought to call the cafe at the butterfly house after you. This whole thing makes me feel so mixed up. I want to move on, but I feel as if I'm letting you down all over again. If I hadn't gone to that conference...' Would Emma still have been here? Would he have managed to get help to her in time? Or would she still have collapsed and had that heart attack, and the medics still wouldn't have been able to save her and he would still have felt guilty? He blew out a breath. 'Is it selfish of me to want to find happiness again?'

A moment later, a white butterfly landed on the stocks and basked in the sunlight as it fed on the flowers.

Hugo stared at the butterfly. This felt like a sign. As if Emma was giving him her blessing to ask Alice out—and telling him to build the butterfly house.

Emma's Kitchen it was, then.

'I love you, Em,' he said as the butterfly flittered away again. And now he knew what to do.

* * *

'You really do make the best Buddha bowl in the universe,' Alice said, smiling at her best friend as she laid her fork down on the empty bowl. 'Spicy chicken, wild rice and extra avocado. It doesn't get better than that.'

Ruth laughed. 'Indeed.'

And then Alice's phone pinged. Normally she would've ignored a text during dinner, but she noticed Hugo's name on the notification.

'From the look on your face,' Ruth said, 'I'm guessing that's something you need to deal with.'

'I've come to have dinner with you, not be glued to my phone,' Alice said.

'I know, but I'm going to get the ice cream. I think you can be forgiven for reading a text while I've left the table.'

'Thanks.' Alice opened the message, and frowned.

Can I take you to dinner tomorrow night?

Did this mean that Hugo wanted to talk about the butterfly house?

Then her phone pinged again.

That's a social invitation, not a butterfly/glass discussion. Keeping things separate.

Alice stared at the phone, not sure whether she was more thrilled or terrified.

Unless she was being very dense, Hugo Grey had just asked her on a date.

'Everything OK?' Ruth said, coming back with two dishes, a bowl of raspberries and a tub of caramel ice cream.

'Yes. No.' Alice dragged a hand through her hair. 'I don't know.'

'Spill,' Ruth said.

'It's Hugo.'

'Rosemary's great-nephew, the man you wanted to throttle?' Ruth asked.

'We've moved on a bit, since then,' Alice said. 'We've been talking about the project and having field trips.'

'Field trips,' Ruth said, with a knowing look.

'Not dates,' Alice corrected.

'But?'

Alice squirmed. Trust her best friend to notice the invisible 'but'. 'There appears to have been some hand-holding.' When Ruth didn't say anything, just looked levelly at her, Alice caved further. 'And some kissing.'

'That, honey, doesn't sound remotely like what a field trip should be. It sounds as if you're dating.'

Which was what Hugo was proposing now. Something Alice wanted to say yes to—but she was scared that it would all go wrong.

'It's complicated,' Alice said. 'I send him nerdy facts about butterflies. He sends me nerdy facts about glass.'

'Flirting by nerdiness. That sounds good,' Ruth said. 'It means he gets you. So do I take it that he's just asked you out officially?'

Alice nodded.

'Then say yes.'

'You know how rubbish I am at relationships. I always pick someone who wants to change me. Robin, Ed, Henry —and Barney.' She grimaced. 'Hugo's from the same kind of background as Barney, one where I don't fit in.'

'Maybe it'll be different, this time,' Ruth suggested.

'Maybe it won't.' Alice sighed. 'He's a widower.'

Ruth raised her eyebrows. 'He's a lot older than you, then?'

'No. His wife died tragically young—an asthma episode caused a heart attack.' She swallowed hard. 'I think I'm the first woman he's asked out since she died. Nearly three years ago.'

'And you haven't dated in a year. It sounds to me as if you might be good for each other,' Ruth said.

'What if I get it wrong?'

'Then you get it wrong. But if he's as nerdy as you, in his own way, that's a good thing. You'll understand each other.'

'I just don't want to get it wrong,' Alice repeated.

'What if you get it right?' Ruth asked. 'Then, if you say no, you'll miss out. I know Barney really hurt you, but you're an amazing woman and I'm proud to call you my friend. If you back off from the chance of a relationship, you're letting Barney win—and you're worth more than that.' Ruth squeezed her hand. 'The only way you'll find out is to date him. What have you got to lose?'

Alice bit her lip. 'The whole of the butterfly house project. I can't risk that.'

'What did he say?'

Alice handed her phone over.

Ruth read the texts swiftly. 'He's pretty clear about wanting to keep things separate. He's asking you out for dinner. As a date. Nothing to do with the butterfly house. I think you should say yes.'

Alice looked at her in an agony of indecision.

Ruth tapped in a reply. 'OK. Done.'

'What? Ruth! No! What did you say?' Alice asked, horrified.

Ruth handed the phone back.

'"I'd love to. Let me know where and when,"' Alice read aloud, and groaned. 'Oh, no.'

'Ally, you've admitted that you've kissed him and you've held hands and you've been flirting by text. This is the next step, that's all.' Ruth leaned across the table and hugged her. 'I just want you to be as happy as I am with Andy. I know you don't need a partner to be a valid person, but I worry that you're lonely.'

'I've got good family and good friends—the best, when they

don't commandeer my phone and send texts under my name,'
Alice said pointedly, 'and good colleagues.'

'Which is not the same as sharing your life with someone.'

Alice's phone pinged with another text.

Pick you up at seven tomorrow.

So it was a definite date. 'Oh, help. What do I do now?'

Ruth had known her for long enough to be able to guess what
the issue was. 'Ask him where you're going,' Ruth said, 'and
I'll tell you what to wear.'

Alice duly texted Hugo.

Surprise was the answer.

'That doesn't help at all.' Alice bit her lip. 'What if I wear
completely the wrong thing?' Just as she had in Oxford, and
Barney's set had all mocked her for it. 'We're talking about a
man who wears handmade Italian shoes.'

Ruth smiled. 'It sounds to me like a good excuse to go and
buy a new dress.'

'I hardly ever wear dresses.'

'I wish,' Ruth said, 'you'd get over how Barney made you
feel. What you wear isn't as important as feeling comfortable
in it.'

'And I don't feel comfortable in a dress.'

'Because you can't hide behind a T-shirt slogan, hiking boots
and a camera?' Ruth asked, raising one eyebrow.

'The first time I met Hugo, I was wearing a business suit,
and I...didn't come across well.'

'Neither did he, from what you told me. It's got nothing to
do with what you look like.' Ruth frowned. 'Ask him if a little
black dress is appropriate or if he can suggest a dress code.'

'I don't have a little black dress.'

'I do,' Ruth said, 'and you're the same size as me, so there
are no excuses. Text him.'

Alice knew if she didn't, Ruth would simply steal her phone

and do it for her, so she gave in and texted him. When her phone pinged, she read the text. 'He says wear whatever I like, but a little black dress would be just fine.'

'It's you he's dating, not your clothes,' Ruth said. 'I like the sound of that. It's a good thing. Make that leap of faith, Ally. He's not Barney.'

'But I already told you, he's from the same kind of background as Barney,' Alice pointed out. 'The kind of people who judge me and find me wanting.'

'You're a woman who has three degrees and a heart as big as the world: in what *possible* way can you be found wanting?' Ruth asked.

The answer to that was burned into Alice's heart. She'd learned that from Barney and his friends and their mocking laughter. 'The wrong background. The wrong clothes. The wrong manners.'

'Anyone who's that shallow isn't worth your time,' Ruth said. 'And not everyone from that background is like Barney. You've just always chosen Mr Wrong.'

'So what makes Hugo any different?'

'That,' Ruth said, 'is for you to answer. And the only way you're going to find the answer is to date him.'

Alice couldn't really reply to that.

'Now stop fussing and eat your ice cream,' Ruth said, 'because we have a dress to sort out.'

Working on Viola's journals, her current favourite part of her job, didn't manage to calm Alice's nerves, the next day.

Would dating Hugo Grey turn out to be a huge mistake?

Even if he didn't hold her background against her or want to change her, there was the fact that he'd lost his wife in such tragic circumstances. How could she ever measure up to the love of his life?

With her borrowed dress, the shoes she'd worn the first time she'd met Hugo, and the butterfly necklace her parents had given her for her thirtieth birthday, she felt polished enough to cope with wherever he was taking her. Though, when the doorbell rang, she had butterflies in her stomach. Stampeding ones. A whole forestful of Monarchs in the middle of a long-distance migration.

'Hi. You look lovely,' he said.

'Thank you. So do you.' And her voice *would* have to go all squeaky, wouldn't it?

Hugo looked gorgeous in a dark suit that she would just bet was custom-made, teamed with a crisp white shirt and an under-stated silk tie…and yet another pair of handmade Italian shoes. The man was a walking fashion-plate. And, although it would normally have made her worry that she wasn't stylish enough, the way he looked at her—the heat in his eyes, the way he was smiling just for her—made her feel special. The fact that a man as gorgeous and talented as Hugo had called her 'lovely' made her feel as if she were walking on air.

'For you,' he said, handing her a bouquet of delicate flowers in shades of blue and cream—cornflowers, cream-and-pink-swirled Californian poppies, honeysuckle and columbines.

'Thank you. They're beautiful,' she said.

'I asked the florist for something different, because I didn't think you'd enjoy hothouse blooms. And you said you liked blue flowers.'

'I do.' And she loved the fact he'd made such an effort, in-stead of grabbing the first bouquet he saw. There was real thought behind this. Substance, not just style. She breathed in the scent of the honeysuckle. 'These are so lovely. I ought to put them in water before we go. Have we got time?'

'Sure.'

'Come in.'

The cornflowers were almost the same shade of blue as his eyes, and it made her smile. She put the flowers in water and stood the vase on the kitchen windowsill. 'They're perfect. Thank you.'

'Pleasure.' He smiled at her. 'Are you OK to walk in those shoes?'

'I didn't think my hiking boots would quite go with this dress,' she said, aiming for lightness.

'Perhaps not. I thought we'd get the Tube to the restaurant, then maybe have a walk along the river and get a taxi back, if that's OK with you?'

'That'd be nice,' she said, wondering just how flashy the restaurant was going to be and how out of her depth she was going to feel.

But, when they arrived at the restaurant, it was nothing like she was expecting. The waitress led them to the rooftop where there were several glass pods, all containing pots of enormous ferns decked with fairy lights as well as tables and chairs. Most of the pods were already full but there was one clearly waiting for them.

'We're eating in one of these glass pods?' she checked.

'I thought it might be nice to have a view of the sunset over the river,' he said. 'Is this OK with you?'

'It's more than OK,' she said. A glass dome—his favourite thing—plus beautiful plants and a view of the sunset. It was the perfect first date.

Once they'd ordered and the waitress had brought them a bottle of wine, he said, 'When I asked you to dinner, last night, I wasn't sure if you'd say yes.'

'I wasn't sure, either,' she admitted. 'You're still grieving for Emma.'

'But I need to move on. And you're the first woman I've really noticed since she died.' He took a deep breath. 'I took your advice.'

'The mental phone call?'

He nodded. 'I went to her grave. I talked to her about you, and about how I'd like to ask you to dinner. And I'd just finished talking when this white butterfly settled on the flowers I'd taken with me. It felt like a sign. So I texted you when I got home.'

'I was at my best friend's,' Alice said. 'Actually, this is her dress. I, um, don't often wear dresses.'

'Because of the ticks?'

So he remembered what she'd said. That made her feel a lot more confident. 'Something like that. So what does an architect do in his spare time?'

'Work,' he said. 'Make calculations.'

Which sounded very lonely, to her.

'What does a lepidopterist do in her spare time?' he asked.

'Have dinner with friends, go to the cinema, and visit art exhibitions with my best friend—on condition she visits an SSSI with me.'

'A Site of Special Scientific Interest?' he asked.

She nodded. 'When I'm planning a field trip for my students, I scope it out first. So Ruth and I have a girly road trip.'

'Like our field trips?'

'Something like.' She looked at him. 'This is odd. Being here together, not talking about the butterfly house project.' The thing that scared her. 'Actually on a date.'

'On a date.' He met her gaze head-on. 'You know why I haven't dated since Emma died. You told me you're married to your job. Why don't you date?'

Oh, help.

She didn't want to tell Hugo about Barney. About how pathetic and worthless she'd felt when she'd learned the truth about why Barney was really dating her. How pathetic and worthless she still felt, thanks to the men she'd dated since. 'Let's just say I'm not great at picking Mr Right.'

But he didn't let her weasel out of answering his question.

'What normally makes them Mr Wrong?' he asked.

She'd soon find out if he was another of them, so she might as well be honest. 'They want to change me,' she said simply.

He frowned. 'You're supposed to date someone because you like them and you want to get to know them better, not because you want to make them into someone else.'

That was reassuring. 'How do you get to know someone better?' she asked.

'Search me. I'm out of practice,' he said. 'Emma and I met at university, in our last year. Friend of a friend at a party sort of thing. We just clicked, and I never looked at anyone else after that.'

She blinked. 'Are you telling me this is your first "first date" since you were twenty-one?' She wasn't sure whether that made her feel special—or scared that she wouldn't live up to his expectations.

'Yes. So I'm a bit out of practice.' He grimaced. 'I apologise if I'm making a mess of it.'

So was he feeling as nervous as she was? Wanting to reassure him, she said, 'You're not. Whereas I have a PhD in making a mess of first dates. The wrong clothes, the wrong conversation...' She shrugged. 'The wrong everything.'

'Maybe,' he said, 'we shouldn't call this our first date.'

Because he'd already seen enough of her to change his mind? Because she'd crashed and burned yet again?

Her thoughts must've shown in her expression, because he added quietly, 'To take the pressure off both of us. This is dinner between people who might become friends—and who might become something else.'

'So it's a getting-to-know-you sort of thing.' Which was a lot less scary. At his nod, she said, 'As a scientist, I get to know things by asking questions.'

'Go for it,' he said.

She'd start with an easy one. Something that didn't have any real emotional investment. 'What's your favourite food?'

'Cheese. Really salty, crumbly, strong Cheddar, with oatcakes and a glass of good red wine. You?'

'Parkin, like my gran makes,' she said promptly, 'with a cup of proper Yorkshire tea. Strong.'

'So *that's* your accent,' he said. 'I wasn't sure.'

She tried not to flinch. 'Just so you know, I'm proud of being from South Yorkshire.' Even though Barney's crowd had sneered at her heritage. *The lass from t'pit. The oik.*

'And so you should be. Yorkshire's given us Yorkshire pudding, the Brontës and Wensleydale cheese. Kit—my best friend—is from York,' he said.

'My best friend's a Cockney,' she said. 'We have fights about whether London or Yorkshire is better. Our last fight was traditional dishes—jellied eels versus parkin.' She spread her hands. 'I won that one. No contest.'

'Jellied eels are definitely not my thing. Though I couldn't judge fairly, because I've never eaten parkin,' he said.

'Even though your best friend is from Yorkshire?' At his nod, she said, 'Then I'm taking that as a challenge.'

'Good,' he said, 'because tonight might not be our first date—but as far as I'm concerned I don't want it to be our last.'

She was glad of their food arriving, because she didn't have a clue what to say next. The possibilities of where they went from here had completely flustered her.

'OK. So you like the sweet stuff and I'm more savoury,' he said. 'Music?'

'Whatever's on the radio. Though at Christmas I like proper carols, like they sing at home.'

'Kit made me go to a folk festival with him in Yorkshire, when we were students.' He grinned. 'Beforehand, I was planning to tease him about brass bands and Morris dancers—except I absolutely loved the music. And the beer was really good.'

'So you like live music?'

'Pretty much anything,' he said. 'Not super-heavy classical, though I've been to a few proms with Em.'

'Ruth and Andy had an amazing group at their wedding. Quartus. A string quartet which played a mix of popular classical music and pop—it was really romantic,' she said.

'You like dancing?'

She had—until the ball where she'd learned the truth about Barney. That had put her off. Though telling Hugo the whole truth made her feel too ashamed. 'I'm not very good at it,' she said instead. 'You?'

'I have two left feet. I can't do much more than sway, and even then I might not do it to the right beat,' he admitted.

So far, they seemed compatible. 'What kind of thing do you read?' she asked.

'Background reports on architectural projects,' he said. 'Strictly non-fiction.'

'Which explains why you don't have any bookshelves.'

He shrugged. 'Em was the reader, not me,' he said.

And books reminded him of her, so he didn't keep them in his house? she wondered. Before she could find the right words to ask him, he said, 'I already know you read scientific stuff about Lepidoptera, have gorgeous photographic books of butterflies, and you read crime novels.'

'Not gory ones,' she said. 'I like the clever ones where you solve a puzzle.'

'So from a scientist's point of view,' he said.

'I guess.' She smiled. 'I don't like gory films, either. The ones I see with Ruth tend to be arthouse movies or costume dramas.'

'Em loved costume dramas. Anything Jane Austen.' He looked at Alice. 'Do you mind me talking about her?'

'Of course not. She was a big part of your life and you loved her. Not talking about her would be weird.'

'You're so easy to talk to,' he said. 'Yet, the first day I met you, you were terrifyingly polished and unapproachable.'

'That was the idea,' she said. 'To look professional, in case the meeting was about Viola's journals and you were on the side that could cancel the project.'

'But that wasn't who you are,' he said.

She went very still. 'Meaning?'

'You're not a suit. You're a scientist. You're about seeing the world in a different way,' he said.

She felt the colour flood into her face. 'That might be the nicest compliment anyone's ever given me.' She could tell he meant it. He saw her for who she was and, although she found it hard to believe this was real, he actually seemed to like her for who she was. 'Thank you.'

'It wasn't meant to be schmoozy—more trying to say that the real you is a lot more approachable,' he said. 'When I found out who you were... I didn't think you looked like a butterfly expert. Not in that suit. That's why I didn't think you were genuine.'

'Remember what my favourite T-shirt says: "Don't judge a butterfly by its chrysalis".'

'I like that.' He paused. 'I'm glad I'm getting to know you.'

'Me, too.' Even though part of her still worried. Hugo's world was like Barney's. When he got to know her better, would he realise that she wouldn't fit in? Would he change his mind about dating her? Or, worse—despite what he'd said about not wanting to turn someone into something else—once he got to know her better, would he want her to change, the way almost all her past boyfriends had?

The waitress arrived with the food, which was excellent. And thankfully Hugo turned the conversation to food and all the dangerous moments were averted. They watched the sun set over the Thames, the sky looking almost airbrushed and reflecting on the river; after coffee, they walked along the river, holding hands.

'If I was any good at dancing,' he said as they passed a group of people dancing in a fairy-lit square on the South Bank, 'I'd suggest we stop here and join them.'

'Better not. Your posh shoes would be in severe danger,' she said with a smile.

He stopped and drew her close to him. 'But, on the plus side, if I was dancing with you I'd have an excuse to do this.' He brushed his mouth very lightly against hers.

Heat bloomed through her, and she slid one hand round the nape of his neck. 'There are fairy lights. That's all the excuse you need.'

'I'll remember that,' he said, and kissed her again.

Alice had no idea how far they walked, after that; all she was aware of was the floaty feeling being with him gave her, and the warmth of his fingers twined with hers.

He hailed a taxi to take them back to her flat, and walked her to the front door.

'Would you like to come in?' she asked.

'Not tonight,' he said, and kissed her again on her doorstep. 'But if you're not busy tomorrow, maybe we can have a field trip.'

The heat in his eyes made her ask, 'A field trip or a date?'

'A bit of both,' he said.

'What's the dress code?' she asked.

'Whatever you're comfortable in,' he said, and frowned. 'Why do you worry so much about what to wear?'

Explaining that would open up a can of worms she'd rather leave closed. 'Thinking about ticks,' she said lightly. 'Urban or countryside?'

'Both,' he said. 'Your hiking boots are fine. And maybe I can cook us dinner tomorrow night.'

So he wanted to spend the whole day with her? 'That would be lovely,' she said. 'Where do you want to meet, and what time?'

'Chelsea Physic Garden at half-past eleven,' he said.

She grinned. 'I notice you've gone for an owl-type hour.'

'It means we can have brunch,' he said. 'See you tomorrow.' He kissed her lightly.

'Thank you for tonight,' she said. 'It was amazing.'

'Good. And tomorrow's mainly a date, by the way,' he said.

She kissed the corner of his mouth. 'I'll look forward to it.'

CHAPTER SEVEN

THE NEXT DAY, Alice was already waiting by the entrance to the gardens when Hugo got there, and his heart skipped a beat when he saw her.

'Hi.' He'd said goodbye to her with a kiss, yesterday. Could he say hello with a kiss, too? He was so out of touch with dating, and he didn't want to get this wrong. It was ridiculous to feel this nervous and awkward; he was thirty-two, not fifteen. But he had a feeling that Alice could really matter to him, and he didn't want to make a mistake that could take all the possibilities away.

She blushed. 'Hi.'

Her voice was slightly breathy and shy, and that decided him. He kissed her cheek. 'Thank you for coming.'

'I really thought we'd be heading to see a dome or a staircase,' she said, and he loved the slightly cheeky, teasing look in her eyes.

He smiled and took her hand. 'The staircase I want to show you next isn't open at weekends. Maybe Wednesday lunchtime?'

'That works for me,' she said. 'So why did you pick here?'

'I used to come here with Rosemary when I was small. I haven't been for a few years,' he said, 'but I wanted to take a look at the glasshouses.'

'Is that what you meant by *mainly* a date?' she asked. 'Are you in the running to restore the glasshouses or something and you wanted to check them out?'

'Possibly, but that's not what I had in mind,' he said. 'Let's go for a wander.'

She handed him a ticket, pre-empting any arguments over who was going to pay for their admission. 'Seeing as I got here before you,' she said, 'and you took me to dinner last night, our admission's on me.'

'It's my idea, so it's my bill,' he protested.

'No. We're sharing,' she said firmly.

He sighed. 'Alice, I've apologised for ever thinking you were a gold-digger. I know you're not like that.'

'Good. But let's not fight,' she said, and tucked her arm into the crook of his.

Strolling round the gardens with her was a delight. She pointed out her favourite flowers, and several different species of butterflies; but, more than that, Hugo just liked being with her. He didn't have to pretend, with her; he could just be himself. She knew about Emma, and she hadn't judged him or told him what he should be doing. Not having to fake being a normal, functioning human being was so refreshing; and, in a weird way, taking that pressure off meant that he could actually function normally and focus on things he usually didn't have the energy to notice because he was too busy trying to get through the day.

When they stopped at the cafe for brunch of coffee and a bacon sandwich, he said, 'I want to run something by you.'

'Is this the non-date part?' she asked.

'Yes.' He paused. 'I've been looking at your figures for the butterfly house.'

She went very still. 'Uh-huh.'

'Tomorrow I'll instruct Philip Hemingford to fulfil my great-aunt's will.' He smiled. 'Though you've probably already guessed that.'

'I hoped you would,' she said. 'But you hadn't actually said you'd build the butterfly house—just that you'd think about it. I'm so glad.'

'Good. We need to revise our planning application,' he said. 'And I can't guarantee they'll say yes.'

'But it's more likely they'll say yes if you've had a hand in it.'

'Not because of who I am,' he reminded her. 'Just that I'd word it in a different way—I know the guidelines of most planning departments and the words that work for them.'

Her eyes filled with tears. 'I'm so glad you're going to do it. But, just to be clear, that isn't why I agreed to date you.'

'Good. I was hoping it was because you wanted to see me for *me*.'

She nodded. 'It is. But what you've just told me—I think you've scrambled my brain, because now I'm...' she spread her hands '...speechless.'

He reached across the table, took her hand, pressed a kiss into her palm and folded her fingers over where he'd kissed her. 'That's one of the things I value about you. What you see is what you get.'

She didn't reply, but her eyes sparkled again with unshed tears.

'I thought maybe I could show you some rough ideas for the butterfly house, later this afternoon.'

'I'd love that,' she said.

And he was looking forward to seeing her reaction. He'd spent half the night sketching, and it was the first time he'd felt really inspired since Emma's death—the first time his designs had flowed instead of feeling mechanical and as if he was simply ticking boxes. It was all because of Alice: without her, he wouldn't have remembered how much it made his heart sing to work with glass, or discovered how amazing a butterfly house was. It felt like coming back into the spring after a very long, dark winter. New shoots everywhere, green starting to soften the bare branches, birds singing madly in the morning. He was starting to get the joy back in his life, and he wanted more.

After lunch, Alice wanted to visit the shop. She emerged with a recyclable shopping bag slung over her shoulder; she didn't say what she'd bought, and Hugo didn't want to be pushy and ask.

'Do you want me to carry that for you?' he asked instead.

She smiled. 'Thank you, but I can manage.'

So instead he held her hand while they crossed the river and walked back through Battersea park, past the rose garden and under the pergola.

'I know it's pretty much past its best now, but the wisteria's still so pretty,' she said. 'I love walking through Kensington in wisteria season.'

He'd never really been bothered about wisteria before, but he couldn't resist kissing her under the pergola, with the lilac blooms hanging down. 'Works for me,' he said with a grin.

Back at his house, he opened the glass wall to the garden.

'Is it OK for me to potter round your garden?' she asked.

'Sure. Have a seat on the patio. I'll make coffee,' he said.

'I brought something to go with it.'

When he'd finished making the coffee, she was sitting down, looking at something on her phone. It took him another ten minutes to notice that the bag she'd had slung over her shoulder was missing—and there was something in his garden that definitely hadn't been there before. 'There's a pot of flowers in my garden.'

'A *small* pot,' she said.

'Flowers.' That must've been what she'd bought from the shop at the Chelsea Physic Gardens. 'I don't do flowers.'

'They're Leucanthemums—Shasta daisies,' she said.

Big white ones. Flowers he didn't have a clue what to do with.

'They're beginner flowers. You can neglect them and they'll still be fine,' she reassured him, clearly guessing at his concerns. 'They don't mind full sun or partial shade, they're hardy, and they're not fussy about soil type. The main thing is that they're great for pollinators.'

He still couldn't get his head round this. 'You bought me a plant.'

'Call it a garden-warming present.'

'I moved here two years ago.'

'Late garden-warming, then. Because I didn't know you two years ago.'

She'd just put flowers into his very plain outdoor area, showing him he didn't have to be surrounded by plain boxes. Although she'd only moved him a tiny fraction out of his rut, it was enough to make him slightly unnerved. He'd wanted to move on, but now it was happening he wasn't entirely sure he was quite ready for this.

As if he'd spoken aloud, she put her arms round him and kissed him. 'I'm sorry. I'll take it back with me if you really hate it.'

How could she take it with her, when she didn't have a garden? And he was being ungrateful. The gift had been motivated by kindness. 'It's not that I hate it. I'm just not a gardener.' He knew about buildings, about glass and staircases. Even though Rosemary had talked to him a lot about plants when he was young, and his mother was very fond of her outdoor space, Hugo didn't have a clue about how to maintain a garden. Alice had pushed him out of his comfort zone.

'Was Emma the gardener? Because I didn't mean to trample on a sore spot. I'm sorry.'

'We didn't have a garden at our flat,' he admitted. 'And, no, she wasn't really a gardener.'

She looked thoughtful. 'So technically you're a garden virgin.'

Just when he thought he'd worked her out, she said something that threw him. 'Did you just call me...?'

She kissed him again. 'I apologise. But just watch. I promise this will be worth it.'

Ten minutes later, there was a bee buzzing round the pot of daisies. And, ten minutes after that, there was a butterfly.

'See?' she asked softly. 'The difference one little pot can make. When was the last time you saw a bee or a butterfly out here?'

'Hmm,' he said, refusing to be drawn.

'So now can I see your sketches?' she asked.

'They're indoors.'

She followed him into the kitchen, and he brought out his files and spread the sketches on the table. He'd sketched a cylinder with a domed top, more or less what he'd suggested at Kew. 'The panels on the sides remind me of the Victorian glasshouses we saw at Kew. The ones from Viola's era. This is perfect,' she said. 'There's plenty of space for the plants and the butterflies, as well as the heating system and the puparium.' She looked at him. 'But what *I* think isn't important. What really matters is the planning committee's view.'

'I tweaked your application—*our* application,' he corrected. 'Hopefully we can get outline permission now, then work on the detail later. Have a look at what I've done. If it sounds right to you, I'll submit it tomorrow.'

'OK.' She took a small box from her handbag. 'By the way—parkin. I made some this morning. It'll go nicely with coffee.'

'From your gran's recipe?' he asked.

She nodded. 'Which isn't me trying to fill Emma's shoes by baking stuff. Just that you said you'd never tried it, and it's my turn to bring in departmental goodies tomorrow, so I saved you a bit from the batch I made.'

'Good plan,' he said. He opened the box and tasted the gingerbread. 'Now I know why Kit raves about this. Thank you. It's lovely.' He pulled up a file on his laptop and passed it across to her. 'Here's the revised application. Does this work for you or do you want me to change anything?'

She read through it. 'You've said everything I did, except it sounds slightly different.'

'Little tweaks in the wording, that's all.' He raised his mug of coffee. 'Here's to the butterfly house. And may the planners love it.'

'May the planners love it,' she echoed.

After dinner, Hugo drove Alice home. He kissed her lingeringly on her doorstep, enjoying the warmth of her mouth against his and the feel of her arms wrapped round him, holding him close. He'd been at such a low ebb; and Alice made him feel as if he were slowly coming towards the light at the end of a very long and lonely tunnel.

'I'll see you later in the week,' he said when he finally broke the kiss.

'Staircase or butterflies?' she asked.

'Both, if you've got time,' he said.

'Call me. Wednesdays are always good for me,' she said.

'I'll check my diary and move things around, if need be,' he promised, and kissed her again. 'Wednesday it is.'

He waited until she was safely indoors before going back to his car and driving home. Funny how she'd made such a difference to his life. Her butterflies and the way she encouraged him to talk about glass and staircases made him feel so much lighter of heart. He actually found himself looking forward to the day when he woke up, now, because he knew he'd talk to Alice at some point—even if it was only a brief text exchange of nerdy facts. And how much better that was than the last three years, when he'd been dragging himself from one dismal minute to the next and the struggle had exhausted him.

Back at his house, Hugo sat at the kitchen table with a mug of tea, looking out at the garden. That one bright pot of white daisies made the whole space feel different—as if the garden had a focus. Just the way that Alice herself had brought brightness and focus into his life again.

Could it be that his life was finally changing for the better?

On Wednesday, Hugo took Alice to see the helical staircase at City Hall. 'This is something I wish I'd built. And just imagine this as a butterfly house,' he said.

She looked thoughtful. 'Or the Sky Garden. Thousands and thousands of butterflies. It'd be amazing, like seeing a migration of Monarchs—did you know they sound like a waterfall when they fly on migration because there are so many of them?'

'No, but I can imagine it. I still haven't got over that Blue Morpho landing on me. Or seeing the Swallowtail in the fens.'

'I'd like a mix of butterflies in our house, based on Viola's journals,' she said. 'And I definitely want her drawings of those species on the website. Ruth's husband is a website designer, so I was hoping he might be able to help us out.'

'That'd be great,' he said. 'I was going to check with my father, in case he has any more family papers or photos that would be useful.'

'That would be brilliant,' she said. 'And maybe tonight I can show you where I've got to.'

'I'd like that,' he said. 'We could get a takeaway for dinner.'

'There's a really good Chinese near me,' she said. 'They do the best dim sum ever.'

'Sounds perfect,' Hugo said.'

He kissed her goodbye at the Tube station. 'See you tonight. I've got a late meeting, so would seven be OK?'

'It's fine.' She stole a last kiss. 'See you then.'

Over the next couple of weeks, Alice and Hugo were busy at work—Alice with marking and exams, and Hugo with a project—but they managed to see each other a couple of evenings a week and spent the weekends at Rosemary's house. Hugo made lists of what needed to be done in the house and which contractors to ask for quotes, while Alice worked out what needed to be done in the garden—which plants would go where, how the re-wilding would work, and which plants and species they needed for the butterfly house. In between, Alice continued to work on the journals and Viola's biography, and Hugo made more detailed plans for the butterfly house, checking sizes and volumes with Alice to make sure it was the right space for the number of butterflies she wanted to keep in the house.

'Some of this we can do ourselves,' Hugo said at the end of the second week. 'Maybe we can talk friends into coming here to wield a paintbrush or do some weeding and planting.'

'Not until we've got the outline planning permission,' Alice said. 'I don't want to jinx anything by starting things too early.'

'Superstitious?' He stole a kiss. 'OK. But maybe we can make a start on tidying the garden. Whatever happens with the planning, that needs to be done.'

'Says the man who doesn't garden,' she reminded him with a smile.

'Just tell me what's a weed and what isn't.'

'I don't necessarily want to get rid of the weeds. They're good host plants for caterpillars.'

'I can follow directions,' he said.

She frowned. 'You'd take directions from me?'

'Where you have more knowledge and experience than I do, of course.' He looked surprised. 'It would be very stupid not to.'

She really, *really* had to stop assuming he would behave like Barney and want to be in charge all the time. 'All right,' she said. 'Maybe I can ask Ruth and her husband to come and help us at the weekend.'

'And I could ask Kit and his wife,' he said.

Meaning they'd be meeting each other's best friends.

It was another step forward in their relationship, letting each other that tiny bit closer.

Would Kit like her? Would Ruth approve of him? What if they didn't like each other? If their closest friends didn't think they were right for each other, there was a good chance that their families wouldn't, either. And Alice didn't intend to repeat her mistake of not being accepted by her partner's friends.

In the end, Hugo arranged for them all to meet at Rosemary's house to spend the day working on the garden, following up with a barbecue at Hugo's house in the evening.

Alice was already busy working in the garden when Kit and Jenny arrived.

'Nice to meet you, my fellow countrywoman,' Kit said, greeting her with a hug. He reminded Alice of her uncles, with his broad Yorkshire accent and his ready smile, and she warmed to him immediately.

She was just making coffee when Ruth and Andy arrived. Once the introductions were done, Alice asked, 'So do you all want a tour of the house and the garden before we start work?'

At everyone's nod, she led them through into the house. 'We're moving Rosemary's study upstairs, and arranging it so it looks like it would've done in Viola's day,' she said. 'The other rooms on the upper floor will be teaching areas and a library. Downstairs, we'll keep the kitchen for making refreshments, though we'll need to tweak it a bit, and the dining room will be the cafe. Rosemary's study will be the shop, and the living room will be an exhibition area.'

'Is that a William Moorcroft tea set on the dresser?' Ruth asked when they were back down in the kitchen.

'It is,' Hugo confirmed. 'And I'll make you a cup of tea in it later.'

'Seriously? You do know it qualifies as artwork in its own right and it's—'

'—worth quite a lot of money,' Hugo finished with a smile. 'Yes. But my great-aunt believed in using things rather than saving them for best.'

Ruth picked up a cup. 'This is stunning. I love the colours. I've never actually touched any of his work before. This is such a privilege.' She smiled at Hugo. 'Thank you.'

In the garden, Alice showed them the areas they were going to tidy up and the bits they were planning to re-wild; Hugo explained where the butterfly house was going to be and showed them the plans.

'This is going to be amazing,' Andy said.

'*If* we get planning permission,' Alice said. 'If we don't...'

Hugo rested a hand on her shoulder. 'Then we'll keep submitting plans until we make it work. And we'll get public opinion on our side—like your crowdfunding thing. Emma's best friend is in PR, so maybe we can talk her into helping.'

Over the course of the day, Alice thoroughly enjoyed working with Kit and Jenny, chatting to them about what she was trying to achieve with the garden. 'I want it to help children to connect with nature, and maybe take some of the ideas back to their school or even their home. Although not everyone has access to the garden—I only have plants on the windowsill of my flat—even a plant in the window can help.'

'I'd like to see more butterflies and bees in our garden,' Jenny said. 'Maybe you and Hugo could come for dinner one night and you can give me some advice?'

'I'd love that,' Alice said.

'I'd love that, too. It might distract her from the guerrilla gardening at my house,' Hugo said.

'Guerrilla gardening?' Ruth asked.

'My neat, square garden seems to sprout a new plant every time Alice visits,' Hugo explained. 'She started with these big white daisies, and then...' He shook his head sorrowfully. 'They just seem to pop up from nowhere. Triffids, the lot of them.'

'He means lavender, salvia and white cosmos. But they're easy to look after,' Alice said. 'Think how many bees and butterflies you've seen in your garden since I sneaked the flowers in, Hugo.' She gave him a hopeful look. 'It would be even better if you had a tiny wild corner.'

'Which translates as unrestrained nettles,' Hugo grumbled.

'And thistles,' Alice added cheerfully. 'Which is why we've

got them here in Rosemary's garden. The emerging caterpillars can't travel far so they need good host plants.'

'You're actually making that horrible square of his into a proper garden?' Jenny asked. At Alice's nod, she beamed. 'Good.'

'You're all ganging up on me,' Hugo mock complained. 'I'm going to make tea. Even though none of you deserve any.'

'I'll help,' Ruth offered.

'Thank you, Alice,' Kit said when Hugo left the garden. 'It's good to have my best friend back. He's been struggling for a while and the only place he seemed to function was at the office, and even there he wasn't happy. Jen and I tried to support him, but nothing we've done seemed to help. We tried to fix him up with one of her friends, to stop him being quite so lonely, but that made things worse, and...' He shook his head sadly. 'We were idiots. Thank you. You've made a huge difference to him.' He paused. 'I assume you know about Emma?'

'I do, and we're going to call the cafe after her—Emma's Kitchen,' Alice confirmed.

Kit looked pleased. 'That's so nice.'

'It must've been so hard for him, losing her like that,' Alice said.

'It broke him,' Kit agreed. 'But I think you're showing him how to put the pieces back together.'

Just as Hugo was doing for her, Alice thought. He was giving her the confidence in herself that Barney and his cronies had taken away.

At the end of the afternoon, they all headed back to Hugo's house for the barbecue.

'That's another pot for my garden, isn't it?' Hugo accused on the train to Battersea, staring at Alice's recyclable bag.

'I can't hear you. It's too loud on the Tube,' Alice said with a grin.

'I can't see a pot,' Jenny said, looking around at everything except Alice's bag.

'Me, neither,' Kit said, putting his hands over his eyes.

'What pot would that be?' Ruth asked.

Andy looked out of the window. 'No pots here, my friend.'

'Oh, for pity's sake. I give in,' Hugo said, rolling his eyes.

Kit and Alice did a fist bump, and everyone laughed.

Back at Hugo's place, Alice added the pot of lavender to the collection she'd started at the sunny edge of the patio.

'That looks amazing—so much better than that boring square of lawn,' Jenny said. 'And look! There are butterflies.'

'Plus the lavender's from Rosemary's garden. It belongs with Hugo—a family legacy sort of thing,' Alice said.

'Agreed,' Kit said. 'Now let's get this barbecue started.'

Kit and Jenny had organised the wine, Ruth and Andy had brought bread and salads, Alice had sorted out puddings and Hugo had bought meat, fish and veggie options. And it was one of the nicest evenings Alice had spent in a while, getting to know Hugo's best friends while he got to know hers.

'I like him a lot,' Ruth said in the kitchen as they were clearing away and making coffee. 'He's one of the good guys. And I like the way he treats you.' She looked Alice straight in the eye. 'I never met Barney, but I know his type. Hugo isn't like that.'

'I know,' Alice said.

'Barney?' Jenny asked.

'Ally's ex from her undergraduate days. Posh, conceited, selfish, and he treated her badly,' Ruth explained.

Jenny rolled her eyes. 'I know the type, too. Hugo's posh, but not the rest of it. He's a sweetheart. He's had a rough time—but you've made a real difference to him, Alice.'

'It's very early days,' Alice said. 'There are no guarantees.' But she was really starting to hope that this would work out. She liked the man Hugo really was—not the uptight, closed-off man she'd met at the solicitor's, but the architect who loved light and glass and space. The man who understood exactly how she felt about butterflies and listened to her ideas.

They spent the rest of the evening sitting on the patio, drinking coffee and chatting. When the others had left, Hugo walked Alice to the Tube station. 'I liked Ruth and Andy,' he said.

'Good. They liked you, too—and I liked Kit and Jenny.'

He kissed her. 'I'm glad. You made a hit with them, too.'

She stroked his face. 'That's good. I mean, I know dating someone doesn't mean you're dating their friends, but it helps if you all get on.'

'It does indeed.' He kissed her as the train came in to the station. 'See you tomorrow.'

The following weekend, Alice was starting to get antsy. 'It's been three weeks now, and we still haven't heard a thing from the planning people.'

'It doesn't necessarily mean bad news,' Hugo reassured her. 'Holiday season can slow things down.'

'What if they don't give approval?' Alice asked.

'Then we look at the reasons why they rejected the plans and tweak our application to take them into account.' He stole a kiss. 'You can wait for hours to see a butterfly, right? This is the same sort of thing. Be patient.'

She sighed. 'Sorry. I'm behaving like a spoiled brat.'

'No, you just want to get on with things. And we've got everything lined up ready for when we finally get a yes. We've got local businesses whose apprentices need a project to work on, my friend James will do the survey, and Emma's best friend Pavani is a PR specialist and she's getting together a list of possible sponsors to add to the crowdfunding you've already done.' He smiled. 'Why don't we do something tomorrow instead of working on the house or the garden?'

'Such as?'

'Go to the sea,' he said. 'I thought maybe we could go and see a rare butterfly on the South Downs on the way to the beach—the Duke of Burgundy.'

She raised her eyebrows. 'Been researching on the Internet, have we?'

He looked pleased with himself. 'Apparently it's a real conservation success.'

'It is,' she agreed. 'But unfortunately you've just missed the season where the adults fly.'

'How? It's only the middle of July.'

'It's still too late.' She smiled. 'But there are other butterflies we could go and see in Sussex. Marbled Whites, Gatekeepers, maybe a Purple Emperor.'

'You're on. I'll drive,' he said. 'We can see the butterflies in the morning, paddle in the sea and eat chips for lunch, and have afternoon tea on the way back to London.'

'That sounds like the perfect day,' she said. 'I'd really like that.'

He stole a kiss. 'I'll pick you up at seven-thirty.'

'Are you sure you want to drive? Wouldn't you rather nap in the car?' Just to hammer the point home, she hooted softly at him.

'Sussex isn't as far as Norfolk so we don't have to leave quite so early. I can cope.'

'You're on,' she said. 'Remember sensible shoes and big socks.'

'Yeah, yeah.' His eyes crinkled at the corners. 'Are you this bossy with your students?'

'Absolutely,' she said. 'One of my colleagues was bitten by a tick, some years back. Because she didn't notice the rash, she didn't go to the doctor early enough. Even a month of antibiotics didn't cure Lyme's disease, and she was really ill for a couple of years. It's as debilitating as chronic fatigue syndrome. She still can't work full time, and it's so frustrating for her.'

'Point taken,' he said. 'Sensible shoes, big socks, and I'll see you at seven-thirty.'

CHAPTER EIGHT

HUGO PICKED ALICE up at seven-thirty, as arranged, and they drove to the South Downs. Alice thoroughly enjoyed wandering hand in hand across the footpaths with him, spotting butterflies, and the highlight of her morning was photographing a cluster of Purple Emperors.

'I thought you were teasing about them being purple,' Hugo said. 'They're stunning.'

'Aren't they just?'

From the Downs, they headed to the sea and strolled across the pebbly beach, eating hot, crispy chips.

'I hardly ever go to the sea,' Alice said. 'It's a long way for a day trip. Though when I was small we used to go and stay in Whitby every summer. I'd spend hours beachcombing with Grandad, finding fossils and bits of jet and amber, and we'd eat fish and chips on the cliffs, trying to avoid the seagulls.'

'Living in London, the quickest beach for us to go to was Brighton,' Hugh said. 'I was fascinated by the Pavilion and the pier, but I was always a bit disappointed that the beach was stony. My mother's parents lived in Suffolk, and I loved going to visit them because they lived near this enormous sandy beach and I could spend hours and hours searching for shells and building sandcastles.'

'So what kind of sandcastle does an architect build?' she asked.

'Traditional. Moat, four towers with a flag made of twigs and seaweed, a drawbridge lined with shells, and windows of sea-glass.'

She could just imagine Hugo as a small, intense child, searching for shells and sea-glass to fill his bucket, then making his sandcastle; it made her heart feel as if it had done a backflip.

'So what kind of sandcastle does a butterfly expert build?' he asked.

'Rather less elaborate than yours,' she said with a grin. 'But my gran always went to the beach with flags in her handbag, made from cocktail sticks and pictures she'd cut out of magazines. There were butterflies for me, ponies for my cousin who loved horses, and kittens for my cousin who loved cats.'

'It sounds brilliant,' he said. 'Are you all still close?'

She nodded. 'Grandad's no longer with us, but everyone else is. They all think I'm a bit weird, because I'm the only one in the family who went to uni. My Uncle Jack makes the same terrible joke every single time he sees me about Dr Alice diagnosing someone with butterflies in their tummies, but he doesn't mean any harm by it.'

'It must be nice having a big family,' Hugo said.

'It is. I had a "blink and you'll miss it" spot on a Sunday evening TV programme, last spring. Mum told everyone, and I guess it was a good excuse for a family gathering because she made me come home for the weekend, and everyone came over to ours to watch it and eat cake and drink bubbly.' And Alice had been moved to tears by the pride on their faces as they'd nudged each other and cheered when her face had flashed up on the TV screen.

'That's so nice,' he said.

'I love my family. And I need to make more effort to go up to Yorkshire, because my flat's too small for more than a couple of people to stay at a time.' And maybe, just maybe she could ask Hugo to join her.

Maybe.

Because it was still early days, and she didn't want to get her family all excited at the idea of her finally settling down, when she still didn't know exactly where this thing between herself and Hugo was going.

'So—afternoon tea,' he said when they were back at the car. 'My mother makes the best scones ever, and my father's got some photos and documents he thought you might be interested in.'

When it registered with her, Alice went cold. 'We're going to see your parents?'

'For afternoon tea.' He frowned. 'That's OK, isn't it?

Oh, help. They'd met each other's best friends and it had been fine, but she wasn't sure she was quite ready to meet his parents.

'Alice? What's wrong?'

'I, um…just wasn't expecting this.'

'They're not going to give you a hard time about Rosemary's house,' he said, taking her hand and squeezing it. 'I was always the one in guard dog mode, and I'm on your side. Pa's thrilled about Viola's biography and the journals, and I know he and Ma would love to hear about your plans for the garden.'

What would they think of the scruffy scientist with the messy hair and faded jeans? Hugo came from a posh family. Would they expect cashmere and pearls, the way Barney's family had? Alice remembered the whispers she hadn't been supposed to hear, the disapproval.

Really, Barney, couldn't you have found someone better?

And, although Alice didn't think that Hugo's parents would mock her behind her back, the way Barney's social set had, she was worried that they'd be disappointed in her.

'Uh-huh,' she said, but she was quiet all the way to the village where the Greys lived. And she was quieter still when she realised that they lived in an old rectory—an enormous place at the end of a really, really long driveway.

You don't belong here, oik.

The words echoed in her head, spinning round and round.

'Alice?' Hugo asked.

Belatedly, she realised he'd parked the car. She had no idea what he'd said to her or how long he'd been waiting for an answer.

'Sorry. Bit of a headache,' she fibbed. And then she had to support the lie by hunting in her handbag for paracetamol.

With every step across the gravel, she felt worse. An impostor. The girl from t'pit; the oik from the council estate. The Northern version of Eliza Doolittle.

The front door opened and Hugo's parents came out to greet them, a small black and white cocker spaniel with a madly waving tail following at their heels.

'Ma, Pa, this is Dr Alice Walters,' Hugo said.

Right now he sounded even posher than he did in London, and it worried Alice. Was this who Hugo really was?

'So nice to meet you, Dr Walters—or may we call you Alice?' Hugo's mother asked, holding out her hand in welcome to shake Alice's.

'Alice, please,' Alice said.

'I'm Serena, and this is Charles.'

'Pleased to meet you,' Alice said, shaking his hand too.

'And this is Soo.' Serena gestured to the little dog. 'Do you mind dogs, Alice?'

'No, I like them,' Alice said. At least that was one thing they had in common. She bent down to make a fuss of the dog, who immediately threw herself onto her back and waved an imperious paw to indicate that she wanted a tummy-rub.

'I've put the kettle on,' Serena said.

Just as Alice's own mother would have done; that forced the voice in Alice's head, which was yammering that she didn't belong here, to drop down a notch in volume.

'Hello, darling.' Serena wrapped her arms round Hugo, who hugged her back and greeted his father just as warmly.

'I'm so thrilled you're writing Viola's biography, Alice. I always loved those trays of butterflies in Rosemary's study,' Charles said. 'I've been digging through the family archives and I've found some things that might be useful for you.'

Alice noticed that Charles' breathing was a little ragged. Was this what Hugo had meant when he'd said his father was unwell?

'Come and sit down, Alice,' Serena urged. 'It's lovely in the garden right now. Would you prefer tea or coffee?'

'I like both, but please don't feel you have to wait on me. Let me help,' Alice said.

Serena patted her arm. 'Charles is dying to show you what he found. But I'll say yes to some help later.'

This wasn't a rejection, Alice reminded herself. 'OK. Thank you.'

Charles had a box sitting on the table on the patio. 'Viola's letters—that is, letters people wrote to her,' he said. 'I've sorted them into bundles from the writers in date order. I thought they might be useful for the biography, so you can borrow them for as long as you need.'

'Thank you—that's wonderful,' Alice said.

'And there are photographs, some of which might be dupli- cates of Rosemary's,' Charles added. 'Feel free to use anything that works for the book.'

'That's really kind,' Alice said. 'I didn't realise we were drop- ping in to see you today, or I would've brought my file of pho- tographs for you to look through, too. But I'll be happy to bring them down at any time over the summer.' She glanced quickly through the contents of the box. 'These are wonderful. Thank you so much. I'll credit you with anything I use.'

Charles looked pleased.

Soo was clearly Serena's shadow, and her reappearance her- alded Hugo's mother arriving with a tray of tea.

'I'm sorry we didn't meet before, Alice,' Serena said. 'Rose-

mary clearly thought a lot of you, as she entrusted Viola's biography and journals to you.'

'I thought a lot of her,' Alice said. 'My condolences on your
loss.'

'I saw you at the funeral,' Charles said. 'In the background.'

Alice nodded. 'I wanted to pay my respects—but, given what
was happening at the time, I didn't want to make things awkward for your family.'

'That's very thoughtful,' Serena said. 'But Hugo's reassured
us about what you're both planning to do with the house—turning it into an education centre and a museum.'

'Named after both Viola and Rosemary,' Alice said. 'Though
we're still waiting to hear from the planning people.'

'This is what the butterfly house will look like, if the plans
go through,' Hugo said, taking out his phone and showing his
parents photographs of his sketches.

'The doors remind me of the Palm House at Kew,' Charles
said. 'You fell in love with the place when Rosemary took you
there. So did I, when I was a boy.'

'So will you have butterflies there all year round?' Serena
asked.

'Yes—we'll have tropical butterflies, and we'll buy the pupae
from sustainable farmers,' Alice explained. 'The English ones
will be in the re-wilded garden during the spring and summer.'

Serena and Charles were interested in everything she had
to say about the re-wilding; finally, Serena asked, 'So can you
recommend things we can do here to attract more butterflies?'

Hugo groaned. 'Ma, I know where this is going. Don't let
Alice talk you into giving her pots of stuff for my garden.'

'If you mean that abomination of a square outside your patio,
I'd be more than happy to donate pots of stuff,' Serena retorted.

Alice grinned. 'You're out-womanned here, Hugo.'

'Indeed. Come and see the garden, Alice. We'll leave the
men to their tea and we can talk about plants.' Serena stood

up, tucked her arm through Alice's, and led her further into the garden.

'At least Charles will sit down and rest with Hugo there to talk to him. He has COPD,' Serena said, when they were out of earshot. 'When he overdoes things he struggles to breathe. And then he gets cross. But will he sit down and rest?'

'That's hard,' Alice said sympathetically. 'My grandfather—the one who was a miner—had emphysema, so I know what it's like.'

'Men never listen.' Serena rolled her eyes. 'I also wanted to thank you, without embarrassing Hugo. It's the happiest I've seen him look in nearly three years, and when he's talked to me about the butterfly house he's been designing for Rosemary's garden it's the first time he's sounded enthusiastic about a project since—' She stopped and bit her lip. 'I assume he's told you?'

'About Emma? Yes, he has,' Alice reassured her. 'It must've been so hard for all of you.'

'It was,' Serena confirmed, looking sad. 'And I've worried about Hugo every day ever since. He shuts himself away, and it's so hard to reach him. There's nothing I can do or say that will help. But you—since he's met you, he's sounded so much better. The light's back in his eyes. He doesn't look defeated all the time.' She grimaced. 'I apologise for being an interfering mother and making him bring you here. I just wanted to meet the woman who's brought my son back into the world again, so I could say thank you.'

'Hugo and I are very different,' Alice warned.

'That's a good thing. It means you'll broaden each other's horizons instead of living in an echo chamber.'

No censure. No discreetly rolled eyes about Alice having the wrong accent and the wrong background. Here, she was accepted for who she was. Whatever barriers she and Hugo might face in the future, his family wouldn't be one of them. She wouldn't have to pretend she was somebody she wasn't.

And it felt as if a huge weight had been rolled off her chest, letting her breathe normally again.

Alice thoroughly enjoyed wandering round the garden with Serena and Soo, making suggestions of dog-friendly plants for particular corners and tiny tweaks that would encourage butterflies and bees.

'I have to confess, I do have a gardener,' Serena said.

Hugo's parents were posh enough to have a gardener?

Maybe Alice's uneasiness showed in her expression, because Serena grimaced and waggled her fingers. 'Arthritis stops me doing as much as I'd like to do, and Charles has brown fingers, not green. And I couldn't bear to be without a garden. So this was the compromise. Jacob lives in the village. He does all the stuff that makes my hands hurt, but he's all about the vegetable patch and he's terribly sniffy about my flowers.' She smiled. 'I had to bully him into letting me have a herb garden. But even he admits that home-made pesto is the best.'

It sounded, Alice thought, as if Serena and her gardener were good friends and bantered together a lot. So it wasn't the same sort of thing as the way Barney's family had looked down on their domestic staff.

'How would Jacob feel about you having a wild corner in the garden?' she asked.

'He'll stomp about, muttering about slugs,' Serena said. 'And we'll have a huge fight about the damage caterpillars would do to the cabbages.'

Alice smiled. 'I'll send you all the figures so you can guilt him into it.'

'Done,' Serena said. 'Now, if you wouldn't mind doing the cuttings yourself, you can have whatever you like for Hugo's garden.'

'Some of your honeysuckle,' Alice said promptly. 'I'd like some for Rosemary's garden as well, please.'

'Of course. Come to the potting shed.' Serena grinned. 'I know where Jacob keeps the spare key. Third stone from the left.'

Alice retrieved the key, and between them they sorted out some pots and some cuttings.

'So Hugo's actually letting you redo his garden?' Serena asked.

'I'm not giving him any choice,' Alice said. 'I brought lavender from Rosemary's garden, and Kit and Jenny are giving me some plants from their garden next week. That horrible minimalist square is going to be a riot of colour by the time I've finished with it. Kit's going to keep him distracted while Jenny and I sneak in and plant some spring bulbs. He'll complain about it, but secretly he loves it. You can see it in his eyes.'

Serena's eyes filled with tears. 'Emma would have liked you so, so much.' She hugged Alice. 'I'm not going to say any more now. We'll go and make afternoon tea.'

But Alice felt *accepted*. And that made all the difference in the world. Instead of worrying that she was going to say or do the wrong thing, she could relax and just be herself. And it made her hope that she and Hugo really had the chance of a future together.

Serena insisted on both of them taking scones and cake back to London, and the goodbye hug that Hugo's parents gave Alice was very warm indeed.

'Sorry I sprang that visit on you,' Hugo said, once they were out of the village.

'That's the biggest "sorry, not sorry" I've ever heard,' she retorted.

'What, like the one you're about to say about being sorry you raided my mother's garden to put more pots into mine?' he asked archly.

'I'm not sorry about *that* in the slightest,' she said. 'Honeysuckle is one of life's pleasures. If I had a balcony, I'd have a pot of it for there, too.'

He laughed. 'At least you're honest about it.' He paused. 'My parents liked you very much.'

'I liked them, too,' Alice said. And she intended to suggest a field trip to Yorkshire later in the summer so Hugo could meet her family, too. Because now she was confident they'd like each other.

CHAPTER NINE

On Monday, Alice came home from the university to discover an official-looking envelope in the post. The last time she'd opened an envelope with that particular return address, it had been bad news. Would it be different, this time?

This was so ridiculous. She was far from being a coward, and she'd never been afraid of getting exam results. Then again, she'd always had a good idea how she'd performed in exams. This was all completely out of her control—and of Hugo's. She had absolutely no clue whether the planners were going to say yes or whether the letter would contain another rejection.

She rang Hugo. 'Are you super-busy?'

'Just wrestling with some figures,' he said. 'What's up?'

'I think I've got a letter from the planning people.'

'What does it say?'

'I haven't opened it, yet,' she admitted.

'Why?'

'Because I'm terrified they're going to turn us down.'

'Hang up and I'll video-call you,' he said, 'so then we can open it together. Sort of.'

She ended the call, and he video-called her back.

'Shall I hold the phone so you can see the letter?' she asked.

'For you to show me the whole letter on a phone screen I'd

need a magnifying glass to read it this end,' he said. 'Just open it and read it out loud.'

She undid the flap and took out the contents.

'OK. "Dear Dr Walters, Thank you for your revised planning application—"' She stopped, because she couldn't quite take in the next line.

'Alice? Is everything all right?'

'Yes.' Dazedly, she looked at him on the screen.

'Did they say yes or no?'

'They said—' and she still couldn't quite believe it '—yes.'

He whooped. 'Brilliant! We are so going out to celebrate tonight. If you call Ruth, I'll call Kit, and dinner's my shout. I'll call you in ten minutes.'

But when he called back, they both had bad news. 'Jenny's got a work thing tonight.'

'And Ruth's doing a lecture as part of the university's community project,' she said. 'Our celebratory dinner will have to be another night.'

'We'll have two celebrations, then—because I think this sort of news deserves champagne right now. You, me, a takeaway and my back garden tonight?' he suggested.

'OK. You organise the takeaway and I'll bring the champagne,' she said.

'Perfect. What sort of takeaway?'

'Anything. But just remember pizza only comes as thin crust.'

'Pizza and champagne works for me. See you at seven?'

'I'll be there.'

Although she didn't bother dressing up, Alice changed into clean jeans and a T-shirt. At seven precisely, she arrived at Hugo's house with a bottle of champagne she'd bought from the supermarket chiller cabinet and a pot. 'Celebratory scabious,' she informed him, handing him the pot of pink wildflowers.

'You made that up,' he accused.

'Your point is...?' She spread her hands, laughing.

He laughed back, and kissed her. 'It could've been worse, I suppose. Celebratory nettles.'

'Now that's an excellent idea.'

'We've had this conversation. You are *not* filling my garden with nettles.'

'A tiny pond?' she suggested.

'No.' But she noticed he was smiling when he added the pot to his growing collection. And she also noticed that he had a watering can. A posh metal one, painted green, with a gold-coloured watering rose. She coughed. 'Well, look at that. Been shopping, have we?'

'No. Ma had it delivered to the office this morning, with instructions about how to water the pots,' he said.

'Good, because virgin gardeners should absolutely not choose a watering can without help. Your mum knows what she's doing, so the rose will work.'

'You're putting roses in my garden now?'

'A rose is the thing on the end of the can that does the watering, as I'm sure you know perfectly well. Given that your mum loves her garden and so did Rosemary, I'm calling you on pretending to know a lot less than you really do.'

'Maybe,' he said. 'I like watching you be bossy.'

She had no answer to that, so she kissed him.

There were two glasses and a wine cooler waiting on the patio table; Hugo opened the champagne.

'I want to make a toast,' he said. 'To Viola, who studied butterflies; to Rosemary, who kept all her papers and loved butterflies enough to give us her garden; and to us, because we're going to make the butterfly house happen.'

'To Viola, Rosemary and us,' Alice echoed. 'And to the butterflies.'

After the pizza was delivered and they'd eaten it, followed by the posh salted caramel ice cream and raspberries Hugo supplied for pudding, they continued to sit in the garden, holding hands and talking while the light faded. Finally, Alice started yawning. 'Sorry. My lark tendencies are kicking in. I'd better head for the Tube.'

He met her gaze. 'Or you could stay here tonight.'

Her heart skipped a beat. 'In your spare room?' she checked.

His cobalt-blue eyes were intense. 'Or in my room. With me.'

Stay the night.

Take their relationship to the next level.

Alice wanted to; yet, at the same time, it scared her. This was a big step. They'd gone from hand-holding to dating, to meeting each other's best friends and in her case meeting his family; so far, they'd negotiated all the tricky moments. But this... This was something that could bring them closer together—or it could show just how big the gap was between them.

She didn't think Hugo would deliberately hurt her, the way her exes had, but was he really ready for this? Were they rushing things? Worry made her mouth feel as dry as if they'd been drinking vinegar instead of champagne. She knew she had to be brave and ask the difficult question. 'What about Emma?'

'Emma didn't live here. She never even saw this house,' he said. 'None of the furniture is stuff we chose together. Everything in this house was a fresh start for me.' His fingers tightened briefly round hers. 'You're the only woman I've dated since she died, and the only woman who's been here apart from my mother and a couple of close friends and colleagues.'

She stroked his face, knowing she'd put pressure on a soul-deep bruise. 'Thank you. I just didn't want you to think I'm trying to...' She paused, wanting to find a kind way to say it, except there wasn't one. 'Trying to take her place,' she said in the end.

'I know you're not.' He kissed her lightly. 'And there are no strings. I don't have any condoms, and I don't expect you to have sex with me. But, if you'd like to, tonight I want to go to sleep with you in my arms and wake up with you tomorrow.'

No pressure. No demands. No expectations.

An intimacy that, in some ways, was deeper than just the mechanics of sex.

He'd told her what he wanted. Now she could be brave enough to admit the same. 'I don't have any condoms, either, but I'd like to go to sleep in your arms and wake up with you.'

His kiss was so slow and so sweet that it brought tears to her eyes.

'I'll sort out the laundry overnight,' he said. 'There's a spare new toothbrush in the bathroom. Leave whatever you want washed outside the door, and I'll leave you a T-shirt to sleep in.'

'Thank you.' She loved the fact that he was so organised and so matter-of-fact about things. He'd made it easy.

When she peeked outside the bathroom door, clad only in a towel, there was a plain black T-shirt folded neatly on the floor, large enough to work as a makeshift nightshirt.

Shyness threatened to engulf her, but she put it on and walked into his bedroom.

It was very plain and minimalist, as she'd expected. The bed had a black wrought-iron headboard; the bedding was in tones of blue and grey, matching the curtains. The floor was of sanded boards with a rug next to the bed in the same tones of blue and grey. There was no artwork on the walls, and nothing on top of the chest of drawers except a phone charger.

He was sitting on the end of the bed, looking at something on his phone.

'Thank you for sorting everything out,' she said.

'You're very welcome.' He looked up at her with a smile. 'If you'll excuse me, I'll use the bathroom. Choose whichever side of the bed works best for you. Oh, and just in case you need a phone charger.' He gestured to the dressing table. 'There's a socket either side of the bed.'

She waited until he'd left the room before choosing the right side of the bed and plugging in her phone. Maybe this hadn't been a great idea. Maybe she should've gone home. This was a new level of intimacy, and she wasn't completely sure either of them was ready for it.

Her worries must've shown on her face, because when he came back into the room he sat on his side of the bed, drew her hand to his mouth, kissed her palm and folded her fingers over the kiss. 'No pressure,' he said softly. 'You can use the spare room if you're more comfortable. Or I can.'

'No, I want to. But it's been a while since either of us has done this,' she said.

'It feels weird,' he agreed. 'But I'm glad you're here.'

And that conviction melted some of her worries. 'Me, too.'

He climbed properly into the bed, switched off the light and drew her into his arms. 'No pressure,' he said again.

'No pressure,' she whispered. She brushed her mouth against his, and her lips tingled to the point where she couldn't resist doing it again. And again.

'Alice.' He drew her closer and kissed her back.

Kissing led to touching. Exploring. Discovering where a touch could elicit a sigh of pleasure or a murmur of desire. Her shyness melted away in the dark, and she matched him kiss for kiss, touch for touch.

'I can't do quite everything I want to do,' he whispered, 'but if you'll let me...'

'Yes,' she whispered back, and allowed him to strip the borrowed T-shirt from her, just as she allowed her to remove his pyjamas.

She discovered that Hugo was a generous lover, arousing her with his hands and his mouth until she was breathless, and then pushing her further until she climaxed and shattered in his arms.

Afterwards, he drew her close, so her head was resting on his shoulder and her arm was wrapped round him.

When she was finally able to collect her thoughts, she said, 'Thank you. But this isn't fair. You're...' Left on the edge, unfulfilled, while she was languorous and sated.

He kissed her lightly. 'It's fine. Next time. And in the meantime I'm going to do complicated equations in my head. Go to sleep, my lark.'

'This feels horribly selfish.'

'Tomorrow,' he said, 'you can make it up to me. Any way you please.'

Which put all sorts of pictures in her head. 'Tomorrow,' she promised.

The warmth of his skin against hers and the darkness of the room pushed her swiftly into sleep.

Hugo lay awake when Alice had turned onto her side, spooned against her. Part of him felt guilty; even though he'd made his peace with Emma, this was the first time he'd made love with someone since she'd gone. And it was weird to be sharing his space again instead of lying there, thinking how big and empty the bed felt. Weird, but comforting as well.

Even though he hadn't reached his own release, he was glad Alice had agreed to stay. He'd enjoyed touching her, the way she'd responded to him.

He liked Alice, full stop. More than liked her. If he was honest with himself, he was halfway to falling in love with her. Since she'd burst into his life, as brightly as one of her butterflies, he'd felt lighter of spirit than he had for years. Instead of just existing, he was connecting with the world again. And it felt really, really good.

He had a feeling that someone had hurt her badly in the past; she'd said her exes had wanted to change her. But maybe he could help her past that, the way she was helping him to move forward again. Maybe she'd trust him and open up enough to tell him what was holding her back, and he could help her feel differently about the situation—make her see just what an amazing woman she was.

The next morning, Alice woke, slightly disorientated; then she remembered the previous night.

She was in Hugo's bed.

And he was spooned against her, his arm wrapped round her waist.

She started to twist round and was about to wake him with a kiss, when he murmured, 'Go back to sleep, Emma.'

Emma.

He thought she was Emma.

She swallowed hard. Whatever Hugo had said about wanting to move on, subconsciously he clearly wasn't ready. He was still in love with his late wife; and Alice was making a huge mistake, letting herself fall for an unavailable man. Not one who wanted to change her, this time, but one who wished she were someone else.

And it hurt so much. She'd tried to resist him but over the last few days she'd let herself fall for him. She'd let herself believe that this time love would work out for her; but she'd been so very, very wrong. This wasn't like Barney and his callousness—Hugo wasn't the sort to ride roughshod over other people—but if anything it hurt more because she knew she could never be what Hugo really wanted. She wasn't the woman he'd loved for most of his adult life. She wasn't *enough*.

How was she going to deal with this?

The first thing she needed to do was to collect her clothes, get dressed, and leave Hugo's house before he woke. Give herself some space to think and work out what to say, so she didn't hurt him: but she knew she couldn't be with him until he was *really* ready to move on.

Given that he wasn't a morning person, she hoped that also meant he was a heavy sleeper.

Tentatively, she wriggled out of his arms, then climbed out of the bed. His discarded T-shirt—the one he'd peeled off her, the night before—was on the floor. She slipped it on, took her phone off charge, and managed to tiptoe downstairs without waking him. Once she'd retrieved her clothes from his washer-dryer,

she dressed swiftly and wrote him a note, which she propped
against his coffee machine.

Had an early meeting.
Will return your T-shirt later.
A

And then she quietly let herself out of his house.

Hugo woke when his alarm shrilled; and then he realised something was wrong.

Alice wasn't beside him.

Had he dreamed last night?

No, because the pillow was rumpled.

Tentatively, he slid his arm across her side of the bed. The
sheet was cold, so clearly she'd been gone for a while.

Maybe she was downstairs and had just let him sleep in?
After all, she was a lark.

But, when he went downstairs, he discovered that the house
was empty.

There was a note propped against his coffee machine. He
read it and frowned. It was very businesslike and left him feeling that something had gone very wrong between himself and
Alice, but he had no idea what or why.

He tried calling her, but her phone went to voicemail. Maybe
she really was in a meeting and it hadn't been a polite excuse.
But, when she didn't reply to his message by lunchtime he
texted her.

Busy tonight? Think Kit and Jenny are free for our celebratory
dinner, if Ruth and Andy are?

The reply came within five minutes.

Sorry, can't. Have a departmental thing tonight.

That definitely felt like an excuse. She hadn't mentioned anything to him about a departmental thing yesterday, when they'd talked about celebrating the planning decision.

He decided to ask her outright.

Is everything OK? Have I done something to upset you?

Instead of texting back, she called him. 'Hi.'

'Are you OK?' he asked.

'Yes. Are you?'

But she sounded distant. Polite. 'What's wrong?' he asked.

She sighed. 'You and me—I think we need to move things back a step.'

What? Last night—he'd felt a real connection with her. He was so sure she'd felt the same. 'Why?'

'Because I don't think you're ready to move on with anyone else, right now,' she said.

But he was. He'd *told* her he was. 'Why?' he asked, confused.

'Because you called me Emma,' she said.

'What?' For a moment, shock paralysed his vocal cords. He swallowed hard. 'I'm sorry. I really didn't mean to do that.' But he didn't remember doing it. 'When?'

'This morning.'

He frowned. 'I didn't speak to you this morning. You were gone before I woke.'

'First thing. When I woke. You were still pretty much asleep.'

'Then how did I...?'

'You told me to go back to sleep. And you called me Emma.'

Her voice was very calm, very even, and he didn't have a clue what was going through her head—though he was pretty sure he'd hurt her. 'I'm sorry,' he said again. 'I didn't mean to do that.'

'I know you didn't. But you called me by her name. That

tells me you still haven't fully come to terms with losing her. So I think for now it's better that we stick to being colleagues.'

'Alice, I... This...' She wasn't being fair. She'd said herself that he'd been half asleep. But getting angry about it wasn't going to solve the problem. He needed to prove to her that she'd got this wrong. That he did want her. Yet, right now, she was wary and skittish, and it was important that he didn't push her even further away. He raked a hand through his hair. 'That's not what I want.'

'You're still in love with Emma, which is completely under- standable, but it's also not fair to either of us. So it's better for us to be just colleagues.'

No, it wasn't. At all. But she'd really got the wrong end of the stick and he needed time to regroup and work out just how he could convince her of the truth. 'Are we still celebrating the planning decision with Kit and Ruth?'

'Of course.'

And he'd just bet that she'd make sure she was sitting as far away from him as possible at dinner and would make an excuse to leave before everyone else.

'Let me know dates and times,' he said, 'and I'll arrange something.' And work out how to persuade her to give him an- other chance.

It was Friday night when he finally got to see her again. Just as he'd predicted, she sat as far away from him as possible. And she was really, really quiet. So quiet that Ruth followed him when he went to the bar to order another bottle of wine.

'What's happened between you and Alice? If you've hurt—'

'Yes, I have hurt her,' he cut in, 'and I've apologised. It wasn't intentional. And, actually, it's hurt both of us.'

Ruth frowned. 'What happened?'

'She stayed with me on Monday night. I'm rubbish in the mornings. You don't get any sense out of me until after my sec- ond cup of coffee. I called her Emma's name when I was still half asleep and I didn't even realise I'd done it. She told me, later in the day, and called it off between us.' He blew out a breath. 'She says I'm not ready to move on. I *am*. But she doesn't believe me, and I don't know how to fix it.'

Ruth's eyes widened. 'I had no idea.'

'Is that something that's happened to her before? She said something about her exes wanting to change her. Was it someone who wanted to make her into a carbon copy of his ex or something?' He shook his head in frustration. 'Because I don't want to do that. I know she's not Emma. She's herself, and that's just the way I want her. I want my nerdy scientist with her mad hair and her amazing facts and the way she sees the world.'

'Then find a way to tell her,' Ruth said.

'That's the problem,' Hugo pointed out. 'She's avoiding me. She doesn't answer my calls—she just texts me to say she's busy with a departmental thing, and I know it's not true. What do I have to do to get her to talk to me? Dress up as a butterfly?'

Ruth's mouth twitched at the corners. 'That might be fun.'

'But it wouldn't get her to see that I lo—' He stopped mid-word as it hit him.

He loved Alice.

And it felt as if he'd just fallen off a cliff, because he didn't know how she felt about him. Only that she'd backed away, which made him think that maybe she didn't feel the same way as him.

'That you…?' Ruth prompted.

He shook his head. 'Sorry to be rude, but it's something I want to talk to her about before I talk to anyone else.' And that was the problem. Getting her to talk to him. 'But I need to find a way to persuade her to talk to me.'

'For what it's worth,' Ruth said, 'I think you're good for each other. She's blossomed since she's been with you.'

'Thank you. I think. But I need more practical help, Ruth. I need to find out what really worries her, so I can talk it through with her and find a solution that works.' He looked at her. 'I won't ask you to break her confidence, and to be honest I think she needs to tell me herself. Can you get her to talk to me?'

'I don't know,' Ruth admitted. 'You need the equivalent of nectar guides.'

Nectar guides. The thing that attracted butterflies.

Alice wasn't a butterfly, but there was something to do with butterflies that he knew—at least, *hoped*—would attract her and get her to talk to him. 'Of course. You're a genius.' He hugged her. 'Thank you.'

'What are you going to do?' Ruth asked.

'Arrange nectar guides,' he said. At her mystified expression, he added, 'I'll explain later.'

Alice was quietly polite for the rest of the evening, and Hugo excused himself early. As soon as he was out of earshot, he rang his mother.

'Ma, where can I buy nettle seeds?'

'Nettle seeds?' Serena sounded surprised. 'I have no idea. Who would want to buy nettle seeds?'

He did. Desperately. 'If I can't get seeds, where can I get the plants?'

'Why?'

He explained the situation and what he planned to do.

'That's *incredibly* romantic,' she said. 'Leave it with me and I'll talk to Jacob. Come down tomorrow for lunch and I'll have it sorted.'

'Thanks, Ma.' He paused. 'She's important to me.'

'I know. For what it's worth, I think this is your best shot. If your father did something like that for me...'

'Too much info, Ma,' he said, smiling. 'I love you. See you tomorrow.'

The next morning, he headed for Sussex. Last time he'd driven this way, he'd spent the day walking hand in hand with Alice on the Downs and on the beach. He'd kissed her. He'd introduced her to the people he loved most in the world, and they'd liked her. The sun had been shining, and life had felt so full of promise.

Today, it was raining. And that was oh, so appropriate.

Jacob was at the house when he arrived.

'You can buy nettle seeds,' he said. 'They take fourteen days to germinate.'

'I can't wait that long,' Hugo said.

'So your ma told me. And there are no nettles in *this* garden.'

Hugo dug his nails into his palm to contain his impatience. 'So where do I get them?'

'I've got friends at the allotments who can't stay on top of their weeds. If you want to come and take them, you're welcome.'

'We prepared seed trays for them this morning,' Serena said. 'So you'll need to put the back seat down for them.'

'Thanks, Ma.'

Hugo spent the day down at the allotments just outside the village, in the rain, weeding patches under Jacob's watchful eye and transferring small nettle plants into the seed trays. Jacob donated his second-best garden fork, spade and trowel and gave him precise instructions on how to make a flowerbed and transfer the nettles. 'I still think you're crazy, mind. Any normal person would do that with flowers. Bedding plants.'

'Trust me, she'd prefer these to bedding plants,' Hugo said.

Sunday was also pouring with rain. Hugo really didn't enjoy digging up a large corner of his lawn, or planting the tiny nettles. He was cold, wet and grumpy by the time he'd finished. And it really wasn't butterfly weather. And it didn't look quite as good as he'd hoped. In the end, he took a photograph from his bedroom window. At least from there you could see the message.

Maybe he'd miscalculated this. Big time.

Especially as now he had to talk Alice into coming here to see it. What if she said no? Then, he decided, he'd have to cheat massively and tell her it was a group thing—and swear Ruth,

Andy, Kit and Jenny to secrecy and ask them to turn up an hour later than her, to give him enough time to talk to her.

A hot bath and two mugs of tea did nothing to improve his mood.

What if this wasn't enough?

What if she didn't believe him?

He was about to text her to suggest meeting up when his doorbell rang. He shoved the phone in his pocket and quelled the hope that it might be Alice. Of course it wouldn't be Alice.

James, a friend from his university days who'd qualified as a surveyor and had promised to survey Rosemary's house for nothing as a donation towards the project, was standing there. 'Sorry, Hugo, I know it's a Sunday, but I thought you'd want to know the results of the survey.'

From the expression on his friend's face, it wasn't good news. 'Come in,' he said. 'Tea, coffee or a beer?'

'Coffee, please. Though you might need gin,' James warned, and proceeded to deliver the bad news.

When James had left, Hugo called Pavani. 'Sorry to be pushy, Pav, and I know it's Sunday, but we've got a problem with the house that means we need money. Have you heard back from any of the potential sponsors?' he asked.

'I'm glad you called—yes, I have,' Pavani said. 'Something came in on Friday, and I've only just had the chance to look at what they said. I'll send the details over now so you can take a look. I can set up a meeting for whenever works for you.'

'Thank you. You're wonderful,' he said.

And then he made the call he'd intended to make, except for very different reasons.

It went straight to voicemail; he sighed inwardly. 'Alice, it's Hugo. I need to talk to you about Rosemary's house. We have good news and bad news, but we definitely need to discuss it. Please call me when you're free.'

Half an hour later, she rang. 'Hi. Sorry I didn't pick up your call earlier. What's happened?'

'Good news or bad, first?'

'Bad,' she said.

'The house has subsidence. James did the survey this morning; he hasn't written it up yet, but he came to tell me what he'd found. It's going to take time—and extra money—to fix.'

'There isn't any spare money,' she said. 'We've already allocated everything I crowdfunded and some of the grants won't come through for months.'

'That's where the good news comes in. Pav said she's found us a sponsor and she's sending the details. Would you mind coming over so we can talk about how we move forward?'

She paused for so long that he thought she was going to say no. 'OK,' she said finally. 'I'll come over now.'

CHAPTER TEN

HUGO'S HOUSE. THE place where the dreams Alice had hardly dared admit to herself had popped, empty as a bubble.

But they needed each other to finalise the butterfly house project. And right now they needed to agree on a plan to move forward with Rosemary's house.

She took the Tube over to Battersea and knocked on his door.

There were dark shadows under his eyes when he opened the door, and she felt guilty; had she done this to him, shoved him back into the shadows where he'd been for the last three years? Then again, she'd been selfish in dragging him into the light when he wasn't really ready.

This was such a mess.

He looked as miserable as she felt. She wanted to put her arms round him and tell him everything was going to be all right; but right now she didn't know if everything would be all right.

'Thanks for coming,' he said.

'You're welcome.' And how horrible it was, being reduced to formality with him. Though this was her own doing. She'd been the one to walk away.

'Coffee?'

It would be rude to refuse; plus it might help distract her

from his nearness. Give her something to do with her hands. 'Thank you.'

Once she was sitting at the table with a mug of coffee, he showed her the file James had given him. 'It's quite bad. The house needs underpinning. Although the house insurance will cover repairing the damage, it won't cover preventing future subsidence.'

She looked at James's figures and winced. 'We don't have that sort of money.'

'Which is where Pav's sponsor comes in. Apparently it's a firm of stockbrokers who want to showcase their green credentials, and they think sponsoring us will help them do that. They get their name on our website and a "sponsored by" board in our reception area, and Pav's suggested holding a special event once a quarter for their clients. I think we should accept.'

'OK. So who are they?'

He opened the file Pav had sent over.

Alice looked at it, and her vision blurred.

Rutherford and Associates, Stockbrokers Managing partner: Barney Rutherford

No.

It couldn't be.

She took a deep breath to calm herself. When she thought about it rationally, Barney wasn't an uncommon first name and Rutherford wasn't an uncommon surname.

All the same...

'Can I just check something?' she asked, picking up her phone.

'Sure.'

She quickly flicked into the firm's website, and clicked on the 'about us' section.

And there he was. Barney Rutherford. Expensive suit, hand-made shirt, silk tie. Probably the same kind of shoes that Hugo wore. A little fatter, a little less hair, but still recognisable as the man who'd hurt her so much all those years ago.

'No,' she said.

Hugo frowned. 'Sorry?'

'No. We're not taking that man's money. We'll have to find another way.'

His frown deepened. 'I don't understand. Do you know him or something?'

'Yes, and he has no moral compass whatsoever. He's not having anything to do with the butterfly house.'

'He's offering us enough to fix the house. Otherwise we might be held up for months and months.'

'I don't care.' Anger she'd suppressed for all these years felt as if it was bursting through her. 'We're not taking his money.'

'OK,' Hugo said carefully. 'But, as I can't see the problem, would you mind telling me why?'

She stared into her coffee. 'He was at Oxford when I was there. I hated my first year. Maybe I picked the wrong college, but I didn't fit in. I was the granddaughter of a coal miner and I had a funny accent. I came from a council estate instead of a country estate. I didn't go to a posh school.' She grimaced and shook her head. 'So I just got on with my work, and showed my face where I had to, but social situations were horrible. There were all these invisible tests I kept failing.

'I told myself it would be better in the second year, but it wasn't. And then Barney came up to me one day in the library. He said he'd noticed me in the quad. He wanted to go out with me. I thought it was probably some sort of joke, so I said no. But he persisted, and eventually I agreed.' She looked up at Hugo. 'And it was amazing. He made me feel as if I was special. All these girls from his background were just queuing up to date him, but he'd chosen *me*. I didn't like the people he mixed with very much, but he kind of protected me from them, and he taught me all the little social things that never occurred to me. He got me to change the way I wore my hair, the way I dressed, so I fitted in.'

It was all horribly clear to Hugo, now. He understood why Alice had been twitchy about meeting his parents, about wearing the right things. Especially as it sounded as if his background was similar to Barney's. She must've been terrified that they'd find her lacking.

'You didn't need to change who you were,' he said softly. 'There's nothing wrong with you at all.'

'I changed,' she said. 'I fitted in. And it was wonderful. I'd never been happier. I adored Barney. I really thought he was the one, and he dropped so many hints that I thought he was going to ask me to marry him at the Commemoration Ball. I got this really special dress. I actually used my overdraft, because I wanted it to be special in case he really did propose—it was something I wanted to remember for ever. It started out as the perfect evening, and even the bitchier girls in his set were nice to me.'

Hugo had a feeling that there was a 'but' coming. A seriously nasty 'but'.

'And then I overhead them talking in the toilets. They didn't know I was there. They were saying how Barney was going to win his bet; he was going to win a lot of money from his pals, that night, because he'd managed to turn the oik into one of them. I couldn't believe it. I honestly thought he loved me—but it turned out that he was mocking me as much as the others did. He was only going out with me for a bet. It was a weird kind of Eliza Doolittle thing. Make the girl from t'pit into a toff.'

She dragged in a breath. 'When I walked out of the toilet and washed my hands, the other girls were still there and they looked horrified. I could see them mouthing frantically to each other, wondering if I'd overheard. I just ignored them and walked back into the ballroom. Barney was talking to his friends and he didn't see me come up behind him. But I heard what they said. It was all "tonight's the night". Earlier, I would've thought that they knew he was going to propose to me, but after what I'd just heard I knew it had a different meaning.'

Hugo was shocked by how unkind Barney and his friends had been, but he wasn't going to interrupt Alice now. She needed to get this out of her head, once and for all.

'I asked Barney to come outside with me—I wasn't going to have this conversation in front of his mates. Then I said I'd heard that he was dating me for a bet. He blustered, but I could see the truth in his eyes. I asked him if tonight was the deadline for his bet. And then he said yes. I asked how much he was going to win. He wouldn't tell me, and I said if he had a shred of decency he'd donate that money to a shelter for the homeless. That I never wanted to see him again. And then I walked out.' She bit her lip. 'I felt so stupid. So used. I thought he loved me. And all along I'd just been a joke to him. Free sex, because I was stupid enough to think he mattered and I gave him my virginity—and no doubt he boasted about *that* to all his mates, too.' She shrugged.

'The last week of term was awful. Everyone was laughing at me, at how stupid I'd been to think that someone like Barney Rutherford would ever be serious about someone like me. I thought about just leaving Oxford so I didn't have to face any of them again, but that would've meant they'd won. So instead I went to see my personal tutor and asked if I could move college. I said it was awkward because I'd split up with Barney, and I wanted to concentrate on my studies and not get distracted by anything else. My tutor was lovely and told me to stay at college, and he helped me find somewhere else to live for the third year. I didn't socialise much in my last year, just focused on my work.' She lifted her chin. 'I graduated top of my year and scooped a couple of awards. But best of all I got my place to do my MA and then my PhD in London. And it was a lot better—people actually liked me for myself, here. It didn't matter where I came from.' She dragged in a breath. 'And that is why I'm not taking *anything* from Barney Rutherford.'

He took her hand. 'First off, that was a really horrible thing to do to you. I don't understand the kind of man who'd behave like that, and you really didn't deserve to be treated like that. Secondly, I think you're amazing because you rose above it all and didn't let them drive you out.'

'But did I?' she asked. 'I seem to be completely useless at picking Mr Right. Every man I've dated since then—well, except you—has wanted to change me. It always starts off all right, but then he wants me to dress differently or do my hair differently or speak differently, or do something more girly and less scientific, or...' She shook her head. 'I think there's something wrong with me. I can't move on from being the oik who doesn't quite fit in.'

'You're not an oik,' he said.

'No? Barney and his lot were right. Appearances matter.'

'Only on a very superficial level,' he said.

'Come off it, Hugo. Look at your industry. It's about beautiful buildings.'

'But if they're beautiful and don't do their job, they're a failure,' he pointed out.

'Everyone dresses in posh suits.'

'It's a convention,' he said. 'Though, actually, if you're a really brilliant architect, you can wear odd socks and crumpled clothes and everyone will just think you're quirky.'

'Even if you've got the wrong accent and the wrong background?'

'There's no such thing as a wrong accent and a wrong background. It's what you do that matters,' he said. 'What's in your head and what's in your heart.'

Why couldn't she believe him? Why couldn't she move on?

'But even you,' she said. 'You wanted me to be something different.'

He shook his head. 'I've never asked you to change the way you dress. Actually, I happen to *like* the way you dress. You're incredibly cute. Especially with those sassy slogans on your T-shirts.'

'I don't mean that.' She looked away. 'That morning... I was so happy, when I woke in your arms. And then you called me Emma, and I knew it wasn't me you really wanted. You wanted her. And I can't be her. I just can't.'

His intake of breath was audible, and she winced. 'Sorry. I didn't mean that to sound as bad as it did.'

'It sounded bad,' he said, 'and it *is* bad, because it's not fair. Other than Emma, you're the first woman I've slept with in more than a decade. And you know I'm an owl, Alice. You can't even talk to me until I've had two cups of coffee in the morning, because I'm so not a morning person and what comes out of my mouth won't make any sense. Yes, I miss my wife. I loved her so much and we were happy together. But she *died*, Alice. She's not here any more and nobody can bring her back. She wouldn't want me to spend the rest of my life, alone and grieving—though that was exactly what I was doing until I met you. And then you started changing things. You changed the way I see things, showed me that there's still light in the world and I need to stop trudging along in my lonely little rut and reach for the sunlight. You showed me there are butterflies. That I can stop existing with boxes around me, that putting flowers everywhere makes life better.'

He stood up. 'Come with me. There's something I need to show you. And I don't care that it's raining and I don't care if you trudge mud all over my floor—or—' He waved one hand in seeming exasperation, clearly failing to find the right words. 'Oh, just come with me, Alice. Please.'

She followed him out into the garden. And then she saw what she hadn't noticed when she'd walked into his house: that the right-hand far corner of the garden wasn't a neat manicured lawn any more. He'd dug a flower bed.

'It's a flower bed,' she said.

'No. No, it isn't.' He shook his head and took her hand. 'Look closer.'

She walked across the lawn with him, and then she realised.

He'd planted *nettles*.

'You're making a wild corner.'

'It's a nectar guide. An Alice guide,' he said. 'And I got it wrong because you can't see it properly at this angle. You need to see it from my bedroom window—and I don't want to tell you to go upstairs and look at it because I don't want you to get the wrong idea.' He pulled his phone from his pocket, flicked into the photo app and selected a photo. 'Here.'

She stared at it.

The flower bed contained a heart shape. And written in nettles were the words *Hugo Loves Alice*.

'You love me,' she said in wonder.

'Yes. I love you enough to change my garden for you—and do you have any idea how hard it is to find baby nettles?'

'How did you do it?' she asked.

'I spent the whole of yesterday digging various people's allotments and taking out weeds—in the rain, and just so you know I refused to move the thistles on the ground that they're important butterfly food sources—in exchange for baby nettles,' he said. 'I brought them back from Sussex in seed trays donated by my mother. And I spent the whole of today using Jacob's second-best spade, fork and trowel to make a proper bed for them and planting them. In the rain. Because I didn't know how else to tell you how I feel.'

'You love me,' she said again, not quite taking it in.

'Yes. I love the real you. The scientist who sends me nerdy facts and teases me about my shoes and worries about ticks. The woman who has slogans on her T-shirt and mad hair. The woman who sees beauty and teaches other people how to see it, too. You're like those Morphos you showed me at the butterfly house—all quiet and hiding in the background, like they are when their wings are closed. And then you start talking about your subject, and you open up, and you're stunning—just like a Morpho flying. I can't take my eyes off you. And I'm not saying that because I've got any hidden agendas. I love you and I want to be with you. I know I messed it up and I hurt you, and I'm sorry. But I really do love you, Alice.'

'I'm sorry, too,' she said. 'I let my past get in the way. I didn't give you a chance to explain. I thought I knew best—and I don't.'

'I'm glad you realise that,' he said. 'Because I think we've got a future. Just we both need to compromise a bit.'

'Yes.' She looked at him. 'I love you, too, Hugo. Even though you're posh and you're a walking clothes horse, you're... You've shown me things, too. Beautiful structures, the way the light gets in. The way you feel about glass and staircases, that's like the way I feel about butterflies. You get me, and I get you. And I hurt you as much as you hurt me, by being proud and stubborn and too scared to take a chance on you. I'm sorry.'

'We're both going to have to work on communication, in the future,' he said. 'But, for now...' He cupped her face in his hand, dipped his head and kissed her. 'I love you,' he whispered. 'And now I think we'd better go back inside before we're both completely soaked.'

Once he'd closed the glass door behind them, he drew her back into his arms. 'If you don't want to take Barney's money, that's fine. We'll find another sponsor.'

She kissed him. 'Why do I feel there's a "but"?'

'Because there is one,' he said. 'He hurt you. He owes you a massive apology. And we could make something good happen out of something bad.'

'How?'

'Take the money. Except *you'll* be the one to take it and make very sure he knows who you are. And that you've won, because you're the one who's made a real difference to the world—to your students, to the butterflies, and to me.'

Could she?

Should she?

'Think about it,' he said. 'I'm here if you want to bounce ideas. Whatever you decide, that won't change how I feel about you. I love you; my family and my best friend think you're wonderful; and I maybe need to work a little harder until you think I'm good enough to meet your family.'

'You're good enough,' she said. 'I think they'll see you the same way Ruth does. And she thinks you're fabulous, by the way.'

'Good,' he said. 'So we get to start again?'

She shook her head. 'We don't need to start again. You were right the first time. We just need to communicate a bit better in future.'

'So was Jacob right and I should've written that message in proper flowers?'

She laughed. 'No. You were right to say it with nettles. Give my butterflies somewhere to lay their eggs and for their caterpillars to feed. It's the most romantic thing I've ever, ever seen.'

'You,' he said, 'are *weird*.'

She grinned. 'Takes one to know one...'

Two days later, Alice headed to Rutherford and Associates, walking hand in hand with Hugo, wearing her favourite T-shirt and jeans and hiking boots.

'That looks like battle gear,' Hugo said.

'It is,' she said. 'I don't need to dress up or have a posh accent; it's who I am and what I can do that's really important. I'm a butterfly specialist—so I'm going to look like one.'

'You've missed a few words out, Dr Walters,' he said. 'You're also brilliant, brave and generally fantastic.' He kissed her lightly. 'I'm going to loiter in the coffee shop across the road. Call me if you need me—but I don't think you will. You're more than good enough on your own, just as you are.'

Ten years ago, she wouldn't have believed him. Maybe even

earlier in the summer she wouldn't have been sure. But now, she knew he was right. She was good enough, just as she was.

She took a deep breath. 'I'll come and find you when I'm done.'

Five minutes later, she was in Barney's office.

'Thank you for coming to talk about the project, Dr Walters.' Then he peered at her. *'Alice?'*

She inclined her head. 'You remember me?'

His face suffused with colour. 'Yes.'

'The oik. Your Yorkshire version of Eliza Doolittle.' She made her accent that little bit broader. 'But it isn't what you look like or what you sound like that matters, Barney. It's who you are. How you treat other people. How you behave.'

He stared at her.

'It's all right. I'm not going to start a fight. I don't expect you to apologise.' She looked at him. 'I don't need your approval or your apologies, because I already have the respect of people who actually matter.'

'So why are you here?' he asked.

'Because,' she said, 'you offered sponsorship for the butterfly house. And I'm looking at this purely as a business transaction. Yes, I could take the moral high ground and refuse your money—but then we'd have to find another sponsor, and I'd rather spend my time on other things. So I'm here to accept your money. And I wanted to do it in person so you know I'm not intimidated by you or your family or your friends—not the way I was at Oxford.'

He looked at her. 'I wasn't very nice to you.'

'No, you weren't,' she agreed.

'I didn't know you were involved in this project.'

'Does that mean you're withdrawing your offer?'

He gave her a wry smile. 'No. It doesn't. Please, take a seat.'

She did so. 'So why did you offer us the sponsorship?'

'My clients want green investments, so it makes sense for us to sponsor something involving ecology,' he said.

'Why the butterfly house?'

'Because I have a daughter. Daisy's four years old and she loves butterflies,' he said. 'I wanted to do something for her, too, something she could be proud of when she grows up.'

So maybe Barney had changed.

He shifted in his seat. 'When she's older, if anyone treats her the way I treated you at Oxford, I'll want to tear him apart with my bare hands. I know you said you didn't want an apology, but you deserve one.' He took a deep breath. 'I'm sorry, Alice. I'm not who I was back then, either. I hope I've grown up, become a better person.'

She hoped so, too.

'I'll match my company's sponsorship personally. In the circumstances, that's the least I can do.'

She hadn't expected that. 'Thank you. Obviously you've had the information from our PR people, but I think you need to know exactly what we're doing.' And she talked him through the project, everything from Viola's work through to Rosemary's, to the design Hugo had made for the butterfly house and the kind of educational resources they were going to offer. As she talked, her confidence grew. And she wasn't The Oik any more. She was Dr Alice Walters. Professional. Good at what she did.

'That,' Barney said when she'd finished, 'sounds amazing. My clients are going to be thrilled.' He smiled. 'And so is my daughter.'

Alice knew she could walk away now, triumphant. Or she could do something better: she could build a bridge. 'We're rewilding the garden over the summer as well as building the butterfly house. Bring your daughter to see us, with her mum. She can help to plant something, and then she'll always know that she helped make a difference to that little corner of the garden.'

'I'd like that,' he said. 'Thank you, Alice.'

She stood up, and reached across the desk to shake his hand, knowing that finally she had closure on her past. 'You're welcome. And thank you for sponsoring our project. You're help-ing to make a difference.'

Then she walked over to the coffee shop to meet Hugo.

'Are you OK?' he asked when she sat down opposite him.

She nodded. 'I faced him. I wasn't sure if I was more angry or worried that he wouldn't take me seriously—but then I realised that you were right. I make a difference. It's not just what I do at work, it's who I am as well.' She smiled. 'And he apologised.'

'Good. That was long overdue.' He leaned over and took her hands. 'And I'm guessing he's going to give us the money Pav asked for and a bit more.'

She looked at him, shocked. 'How did you know?'

'Because you, my love, were going to talk to him about the project. And when you talk about butterflies, you sparkle and you light up the room. You're amazing and you're irresistible.'

Hugo valued her for who she was. Loved her for who she was. And that made her hold her head that little bit higher. Finally, she'd moved on from being the oik Barney's set had laughed at. She was herself. She was *enough*.

'We don't have to accept his money,' Hugo said, when she didn't say anything. 'This is your project. You make the call.'

'It's your project too. And Rosemary's, Viola's and Emma's. It's teamwork.'

'But you,' Hugo said, 'are my priority.'

And how amazing that made her feel. He was putting her first. 'We'll accept it,' she said. 'Because this gorgeous architect I happen to know taught me the value of building things with good foundations. His daughter likes butterflies. I told him to bring her to the house and she can help plant something.'

'Great idea.' He inclined his head. 'Congratulations on nail-ing the deal.'

'With your support.'

'I didn't do anything.' He shrugged. 'I just sat here, drink-ing coffee.'

'You were here as my backup if I needed you.' She stole a

kiss. 'You believed in me. More than that, you've taught me that I'm OK with who I am.'

'My brilliant, gorgeous butterfly specialist.' He kissed her back. 'I love you. And I can't wait for the future.'

'My brilliant, gorgeous architect. I love you, too. And we're going to build the butterfly house. Fulfil Rosemary's dream.'

'And,' he said softly, 'our own. You, me and the future.'

'You, me and the future,' she echoed.

EPILOGUE

A year later

'I WONDER WHY Philip Hemingford wants to see us in his office,' Hugo asked Alice as they walked through Chelsea together.

'Last time we had an appointment with him, he practically had to referee a fight,' Alice said. 'When you thought I was a gold-digger.'

'And you thought I was a vain clothes horse.'

She looked pointedly at his shoes. 'Says the man with hand-made Italian stuff on his feet.'

He laughed, and kissed her. 'And who was it who found me that suit on our honeymoon, Dr Grey?'

'You looked cute in it,' she said with a grin.

Hand in hand, they walked into the solicitor's office. He was already waiting for them.

'Lovely to see you both,' he said, shaking their hands in turn. 'Thank you for the invitation to the opening of the butterfly house next week. I'm looking forward to it.'

'Pleasure,' Alice said.

'So what can we do for you?' Hugo asked.

'I have a letter from Miss Grey. You've met the conditions for it to be given to you,' he said.

'A letter from Great-Aunt Rosemary? For both of us?' Hugo looked confused.

'Yes.'

'Do you have any idea what's in it?' she asked.

He shook his head. 'None at all. Miss Grey was a bit of a law unto herself.'

'Perhaps we should ask you to read it to us,' Hugo said. 'And we promise not to shout at each other.'

The solicitor gave a small smile. 'I'm glad to hear that.' He opened the letter and scanned it.

'What does she say?' Alice asked impatiently.

My dear Hugo and Alice,

If you're reading this, then I know my dearest wish has come true. I've been trying to get you to meet each other for months, but whenever one of you was at the house with me the other one wasn't.

The only way I could think of to get you to meet was to change my will. I knew you'd have to be at the solicitor's, and I hoped that if you worked together—with you in charge of the garden and the butterflies, Alice, and you in charge of the buildings, Hugo—you'd see the same that I do. That you're perfect for each other.

I know you've both suffered a lot in the past, and I think you'll make each other very happy.

Congratulations on your wedding, and I do hope you'll forgive an old woman for interfering.

With much love to you both,

Rosemary

Hugo and Alice looked at each other.

'Matchmaking from beyond the grave,' Hugo said.

'And she was right. We're perfect for each other,' Alice said. 'If she hadn't changed her will and put in those conditions, we probably wouldn't have met.'

'We wouldn't be married,' he said.

She rested her hand on the almost imperceptible bump of her stomach. 'I have a feeling that this little one's going to be a girl. And I also think her name should be Rosemary Viola Emma Grey.'

'Rosemary Viola Emma Grey,' Hugo echoed, and his eyes were full of love.

* * * * *

Firefighter's Unexpected Fling
Susan Carlisle

MEDICAL
Pulse-racing passion

Books by Susan Carlisle

Harlequin Medical

Pups that Make Miracles

Highland Doc's Christmas Rescue

Christmas in Manhattan

Christmas with the Best Man

Summer Brides

White Wedding for a Southern Belle

Midwives On-Call

His Best Friend's Baby

Heart of Mississippi

The Maverick Who Ruled Her Heart
The Doctor Who Made Her Love Again

The Doctor's Redemption
One Night Before Christmas
Married for the Boss's Baby
The Doctor's Sleigh Bell Proposal
The Surgeon's Cinderella
Stolen Kisses with Her Boss
Redeeming the Rebel Doc
The Brooding Surgeon's Baby Bombshell
A Daddy Sent by Santa
Nurse to Forever Mom
The Sheikh Doc's Marriage Bargain

Visit the Author Profile page
at millsandboon.com.au for more titles.

Dear Reader,

It was an extra pleasure to work with my fellow author Amy Ruttan on this duet. We had fun deciding the setting, the relationship between characters—the list goes on. I've not written about a fire department before and found it interesting. My brother was a fireman so I knew a little something about that life, but learned more.

Since not all fire departments are the same I asked Jason Burnside, an Austin, Texas, firefighter, for his help. He was kind enough to answer pages' worth of questions. I had to use a small amount of poetic license here and there, so don't hold that against him. Jason, thanks for all your help.

Sally and Ross's story was great fun to write and I loved both of these characters. I hope you enjoy their love story, the behind-the-scenes look into fire-station life and a trip to the Austin, Texas, area.

Happy reading,

Susan

To Brandon Ray.

Some family you love even though they married in!

CHAPTER ONE

SALLY DAVIS PULLED her bag and a portable bottle of oxygen out of the back of the ambulance. The heat from the burning abandoned warehouse was almost unbearable. Her work coveralls were sticking to her sweating body.

This structural fire was the worst she'd seen as a paramedic working with the Austin, Texas, Fire Department over the last year. Her heart had leaped as the adrenaline had started pumping when the call had woken her and the dispatcher had announced what was involved. These were the fires she feared the most. With a warehouse like this, there was no telling who or what was inside. There were just too many opportunities for injury, or worse.

She watched as the flames grew. The popping and cracking of the building burning was an ironic contrast to the peace of the sun rising on the horizon. She didn't have time to appreciate it though. She had a job to do.

Moments later a voice yelled, "There's someone in there!"

Sally's mouth dropped open in shock as she saw Captain Ross Lawson run into the flames. Even in full turnout gear with the faceplate of his helmet pulled down and oxygen tank on his back, she recognized his tall form and broad shoulders. Sally's breath caught in her chest. What was wrong with him?

Her heartbeat drummed in her ears as she searched the doorway, hoping…

Sally had seen firefighters enter a burning building before but never one as completely enveloped as this one. She gripped the handle of her supply box. Would Ross make it out? Would there be someone with him?

The firefighters manning the hoses focused the water on the door, pushing back the blaze.

Every muscle in her body tightened as the tension and anticipation grew. Ross was more of an acquaintance, as she'd only shared a few shifts with him since moving to Austin. However, he and her brother were good friends. More than once she'd heard Kody praise Ross. From what little she knew about him he deserved Kody's admiration.

Right now, in this moment, as she waited with fear starting to strangle her, she questioned Ross's decision-making. Since she had joined the volunteer fire department back in North Carolina, Sally had been taught that judgment calls were *always* based on the safety of the firefighter. She doubted Ross had even given his welfare any thought before rushing into the fire.

The loss of one life would be terrible enough but the loss of a second trying to save the first wasn't acceptable. In her opinion, Ross was taking too great a risk, the danger too high. He hadn't struck her as a daredevil or adrenaline junkie but, then again, she didn't know him that well. Was this particular characteristic of Captain Lawson's one of the reasons Kody thought so highly of him?

James, the emergency medical tech working with her, stepped next to her. "That takes guts."

A form appeared in the doorway, then burst out carrying a man across his shoulders. The sixty pounds of fire equipment he wore in addition to the man's weight meant Ross was carrying more than his own body weight. Sally had to respect his physical stamina, if not his reckless determination.

Two firefighters rushed to help him, but he fell to the ground before they could catch him. The man he carried rolled off his back to lie unmoving beside him, smoke smoldering from his clothes.

"You take Captain Lawson. I'll see to the man," Sally said to James as she ran to them.

Ross jerked off his helmet and came up on his hands and knees, coughing.

Placing the portable oxygen tank on the ground, she went to her knees beside the rescued man, clearly homeless and using the warehouse to sleep in, and leaned over, putting her cheek close to his mouth. As the senior paramedic at the scene, she needed to check the more seriously injured person. Ross had been using oxygen while the homeless man had not.

Her patient was breathing, barely. She quickly positioned the face mask over his mouth and nose, then turned the valve on the tank so that two liters of oxygen flowed. By rote she found and checked his pulse. Next, she searched for any injuries, especially burns. She located a couple on his hands and face. Using the radio, she called all the information in to the hospital.

"We need to get this man transported STAT," Sally called to her partner.

Another ambulance had arrived and took over the care of Ross, leaving James free to pull a gurney her way. With the efficiency of years of practice, they loaded the man and started toward the ambulance. She called to the EMT now taking care of Ross. "How's he doing?"

The EMT didn't take his eyes off Ross as he said, "He's taken in a lot of smoke but otherwise he's good."

"Get him in a box. I still want him seen," she ordered.

Ross shook his head. "I'm fine." He coughed several times.

"I'm the medic in charge. You're going to the hospital to be checked out, Captain."

He went into another coughing fit as she hurried away. She left the EMT to see that the stubborn captain was transported back to the hospital.

Minutes later she was in the back of the ambulance—the box, as it was affectionately known—with the homeless man. While they moved at a rapid speed, she kept busy checking his vitals and relaying to the hospital emergency room the latest stats. The staff would be prepared for the patient's arrival.

The ambulance pulled to a stop and moments later the back doors were opened. They had arrived at the hospital. A couple of the staff had been waiting outside for them. Sally and one of the techs removed the gurney with the man on it.

As other medical personnel began hooking him up to monitors, she reported quickly to the young staff nurse, "This is a John Doe for now. He was in a burning warehouse. Acute smoke inhalation is the place to start."

Just as she was finishing up her report, the gurney with Ross went by. She followed it into the examination room next to the John Doe. Ross's coat had been removed and his T-shirt pulled up. He still wore his yellow firefighter pants that were blackened in places. Square stickers with monitoring wires had been placed on his chest connecting him to machines nearby. Aware of how inappropriate it was for her to admire the contours of his well-defined chest and abdomen, she couldn't stop herself. The man kept himself in top physical shape. It was necessary with his field of work but his physique suggested he strove to surpass the norm. No wonder he'd been able to carry the man out of the burning building.

His gaze met hers. Heated embarrassment washed over her and she averted her eyes. Ogling a man, especially one that she worked with, wasn't what she should be doing.

Ross went into another round of heavy coughing that sent her attention to the amount of oxygen he was receiving. The bubble in the meter indicated one liter, which was good. Still, at this rate it would take him days to clear the smoke from his lungs.

Sally stepped closer to his side and spoke to no one in particular. "How's he doing?"

One of the nurses responded. "He seems to be recovering

well. We're going to continue to give him oxygen and get a chest X-ray just to be sure that he didn't inhale any more smoke than we anticipated."

"I'm right here, you know." Ross's voice was a rusty muffled sound beneath the mask. He glared at her. This time her look remained on him.

"You need to save your voice."

He grimaced as a doctor entered. What was that look about? Surely, he wasn't afraid of doctors.

Slipping out of the room as the woman started her examination, Sally stepped to the department desk and signed papers releasing Ross and the John Doe as her patients into the hospital's care. Done, she joined the EMTs at her ambulance.

She gave James a wry smile. "Good work out there this morning."

"You too," he replied as he pulled out of the drive.

In the passenger seat, she buckled up, glad to be out of the back of the box. She wasn't a big fan of riding there.

She shivered now at the memory of when she'd been locked in a trunk and forgotten while playing a childhood game. To this day she didn't like tight spaces or the dark. Being in the square box of the ambulance reminded her too much of that experience. It was one of those things she just dealt with because she loved her job.

Sally leaned her head back and closed her eyes. Ross's light blue gaze over the oxygen mask came to mind. She'd met Ross Lawson soon after she had moved to Austin and gone to work for the Austin Medical Emergency Service, the medical service arm that worked in conjunction with the fire department that shared the same stations and sometimes the same personnel when a fireman was also qualified to work the medical side. As an advanced paramedic, she was assigned Station Twelve, one of the busiest houses of Austin's forty-eight stations. It just happened that it was the same station where her brother and Ross worked. She hadn't missed that twinge of attraction when she and Ross had first met any more than she had this morning. But she had never acted on it and never would.

A relationship, of any kind, was no longer a priority for her. She'd had that. Her brief marriage had been both sad and disappointing. Now she was no longer married, all she wanted to do was focus on getting into medical school. It had been her dream before she'd married, and it was still her dream. At this point in her life a relationship would just be a distraction, even if she wanted one. She was done making concessions for a man. Going after what she wanted was what mattered.

The ambulance reversed with a beep, beep, beep. It alerted her to the fact that they had arrived at the firehouse. When they stopped, she hopped out onto the spotless floor.

She loved the look of the fire station. It was a modern version of the old traditional fire halls with its redbrick exterior and high arched glass doors. A ceramic dalmatian dog even sat next to the main entrance. The firefighters worked on one side of the building and the emergency crew on the other. They shared a kitchen, workout room and TV room on the firefighter side. They were a station family.

James had backed into the bay closest to the medical side of the building. The other two bays were for the engine, quint truck and rescue truck. They hadn't returned yet. The company would still be at the warehouse fire mopping up. When they did return, they would also pull in backward, ready for the next run.

Before she could even think about cleaning up and heading home, she would have to restock the ambulance and write a report. The ambulance must always be ready to roll out. More than once in the last year she'd returned from a call only to turn around and make another one.

"Hey, Sweet Pea."

She groaned and turned to see Kody loping toward her. "I told you not to call me that," she whispered. "Especially not here."

He gave her a contrite look. "Sorry, I forgot."

"What're you doing here anyway?"

"I left something in my locker and had to stop by and get it. My shift isn't until tomorrow."

Sally smiled. She couldn't help but be glad to see her older brother. Even if it was for a few minutes. He was a good one and she had no doubt he loved her. Sometimes too much. He tended toward being overprotective. But when she'd needed to reinvent her life, Kody had been there to help. She would always be grateful.

"I heard that Ross was the hero of the day this morning." He sounded excited.

"Yeah, you could say that." He'd scared the fool out of her.

"You don't think so?"

Sally started toward the supply room. "He could have been killed."

Kody's voice softened. "He knows what he's doing. I don't know of a better firefighter."

"He ran into a fully enveloped burning warehouse!" Sally was surprised how her voice rose and held so much emotion.

"I'm sure you've seen worse. Why're you so upset?"

"I'm not upset. It just seemed overly dangerous to me. Instead of one person being hurt there, for a moment I thought it was going to be two. He has a bad case of smoke inhalation as it is." She pulled a couple of oxygen masks off a shelf.

"How's he doing?" Kody had real concern in his voice.

She looked for another piece of plastic line. "He's at the hospital but he should be released soon. They were running a few more tests when I left."

"He's bucking for a promotion, so I guess this'll look good on his résumé. See you later."

"Bye." She headed back to the ambulance with her arms full. She had no interest in Ross's ambitions and yet, for some reason, his heroics had been particularly difficult for her to watch.

Ross returned to the station a week after the warehouse fire. He had missed two shifts. The doctor had insisted, despite his arguments. He liked having time to work on his ranch but the interviews for one of the eight Battalion Chief positions were coming up soon and he should be at the station in case there were important visitors. Now that he was back, he needed to concentrate on what was ahead, what he'd planned to do since he was a boy.

Thankfully the man he'd gone in after was doing okay. He would have a stay in the burn unit but would recover. Just as Ross and his grandfather had. Ross rolled his shoulder, remembering the years' old pain.

He'd hated to miss all that time at the station, but it had taken more time to clear his lungs than he had expected. Still, he had saved that man's life. He didn't advocate running into fully engulfed houses, but memories of that horrible night when he was young had compelled him into action before he'd known what he was doing.

Memories of that night washed over him. He'd been visiting his grandpa, who'd lived in a small clapboard house outside of town. He'd adored the old man, thought he could do no wrong. His grandfather had taught Ross how to work with his hands. Shown him how to mend a fence, handle a horse. Most of what he knew he'd learned at his grandfather's side. His parents had been too busy with their lives to care. So most weekends and holidays between the ages of ten and fourteen Ross could be found at his grandfather's small ranch.

The night of the fire, Ross had been shaken awake by his grandpa. Ross could still hear his gruff smoke-filled voice. "Boy, the place is on fire. Get down and crawl to the front door. I'll be behind you."

The smoke had burned Ross's throat and eyes, but he'd done as he was told. He'd remembered what the firefighter who had come to his school had said: "Stop, drop and roll." Ross had scrambled to the door but not before a piece of burning wood had fallen on his shoulder. But the pain hadn't overridden his horror. He'd wanted out of the house. Had been glad for the fresh air. He'd run across the lawn. It had been too hot close to the house. Ross had coughed and coughed, just as he had the other morning, seeming never to draw in a full deep breath. He'd looked back for his grandpa but hadn't seen him. The fear had threatened to swallow him. His eyes had watered more from tears than smoke.

Someone must've seen the flames because the volunteer fire department had been coming up the long drive. Ross had managed between coughs and gasps of air to point and say, "My grandpa's in there."

The man hadn't hesitated before he'd run toward the house. Ross had watched in shock as he'd entered the front door. Moments later he'd come out, pulling his grandpa onto the porch and down the steps and straight toward the waiting medics. It wasn't until then that Ross had noticed the full agony of his back.

Both he and his grandpa had spent some time in the hospital. They'd had burns and lung issues. His grandfather had been told by the arson investigator that he believed the fire had started from a spark from the woodstove. Ross only knew for sure he was glad his grandpa and he had survived. Regardless of what had started the fire, Ross still carried large puckered scars on his back and shoulder as a reminder of that fateful night.

Last week, the moment he'd learned there was someone in the house he'd reacted before thinking. His Battalion Chief hadn't been pleased. Only because the outcome had been positive had Ross managed to come out without it damaging his career. He had been told in no uncertain terms that it wasn't to happen again. The message had been loud and clear: don't have any marks against you or you won't make Battalion Chief.

It was midafternoon when he was out with the rest of the company doing their daily checkup and review of the equipment that he saw Sal walking to the ambulance. Her black hair was pulled up away from her face and she wore her usual jumpsuit. She glanced at him and nodded. Memories of the look of concern in her eyes and a flicker of something else, like maybe interest, as she'd watched him in the hospital drifted through his mind.

Ross had known she was Kody's sister before she'd joined the house. Over the past year they had shared shifts a few times. With him working twenty-four hours on and forty-eight off and her not being able to work the same days as her brother, they hadn't often been on the same schedule. Still, he'd heard talk. More than one firefighter had sung her praises. A few had even expressed interest in her. They had all reported back that they had been shot down. She wasn't interested. There was some speculation as to why, but Ross knew, through Kody, that she was a divorcée. Maybe she was still getting over her broken marriage.

Swinging up on the truck, Ross winced. He had hit something, a door facing or a piece of furniture, on his way out of the burning house. At the hospital they had been concerned with the smoke inhalation and he'd not said anything about his ribs hurting because he hadn't wanted to be admitted. The pain was better than it had been.

He checked a few gauges and climbed out again. This time he tried not to flinch.

Sal came up beside him and said in a low voice, "I saw your face a minute ago. Are you all right? Are you still having trouble breathing?"

"No, I'm fine. I'm good."

She gave him a skeptical look as her eyebrows drew together. "Are you sure?"

"Yeah." If he wasn't careful, she'd make him see a doctor. Did she have that God complex firefighters joked about? The one that went: What's the difference between a paramedic and God? God doesn't think he's a paramedic.

She scrutinized him for a moment. It reminded him of when his mother gave him that look when she knew he wasn't being truthful. "You were in pain a second ago."

He'd been caught. She wasn't going to let it go. Had she been watching him that closely? He'd have to give that more thought later. "I have a couple of ribs that were bruised when I came out of the house."

"Did you tell them at the hospital?"

Now he felt like he had when his mother had caught him. Ross gave her a sheepish look. "No."

"That figures." She shook her head. "You firefighters. All of you think you're superheroes."

He grinned. "Who dares to say we're not?"

She just glared at him. "Feeling like one of those a minute ago?"

He relaxed his shoulders. "I've been wrapping it. I just have trouble getting it tight enough without help."

"You shouldn't be doing that. You need to stop that and just take it easy. Ribs take a while to heal."

"It's hard to do that when you have chores to do at home."

"Don't you have a wife or girlfriend who could help with those?"

"I don't have either." He'd never had a wife. Had come close once but it hadn't worked out.

"Come in here—" Sal indicated the medical area "—and let me have a look. Get rid of that bandage." She didn't wait for him, instead she walked toward the door as if she fully expected him to follow her orders.

Ross hesitated a moment, then trailed after her. He looked back over his shoulder. He didn't need any surprise visits from the bosses just when he was being looked over for more injuries. He hated showing any signs of weakness.

He rarely came to this side of the building. Sal was in the spacious room with a couple of tables and chairs, and a wall of supply cabinets.

She pushed a stool on wheels toward him. "Take your shirt off, then have a seat."

He couldn't do that! She would see his scars. He didn't completely take his shirt off around people for any reason. How to get around doing so had become a perfected art for him. The other morning at the hospital it had been a fight, but he'd convinced first the EMT and then the hospital staff it wasn't necessary to take his shirt off.

She left him to go to a cabinet across the room. Ross took a moment to appreciate the swing of her hips before he pushed his T-shirt up under his arms.

When she returned, she had a pair of scissors in her hand.

"Hey, I don't think you'll need those."

She smirked. "They're to cut the bandage if I need to." She then gave him an odd look but said nothing about his shirt still being on.

He explained, "It hurts too much to lift my arms."

She nodded, seeming to accept his explanation. "Your bandage is around your waist, not your ribs. It wasn't doing you any good anyway."

He gave her a contrite look. "I told you I'd done a poor job of it."

"You're right about that. It doesn't matter. I'm taking it off. And you're leaving it off."

"Is that an example of the tender care I've heard so much about?" Ross watched her closely.

Her gaze met his. "I save that for people who shouldn't know better."

One of his palms went to the center of his chest. "That was a shot to my ego."

She huffed. "That might be so but I'm stating truth. Can you raise your arms out to your sides?"

He winced but he managed to do as she requested. Sal stepped closer. She smelled of something floral. Was it her shampoo or lotion? Whatever it was, he wanted to lean in and take a deeper breath. Her hands worked on the bandage, removing it; her fingers journeyed across his oversensitive stomach.

He looked down. Her dark hair veiled her face. It looked so silky. Would it feel that way if he touched it?

No! What was going on? He'd never acted this way around any of the other women he worked with. He hardly knew Sal. She was the sister of one of his best friends. Was he overreacting because he'd not had a date in so long? Whatever it was, it had to stop. His sister wanted to set him up on a blind date. Maybe he should agree.

Sal gathered the bandage in her hand, stepped away from him and dropped the wad into a garbage can.

Ross couldn't help but be relieved, but he was disappointed at the same time. He lowered his arms.

"Okay, arms up again. Show me where you hurt."

With his index finger, he pointed to the middle of his left side. Sal bent closer. Seconds later, her fingers ran over his skin. "Does it hurt here?"

"Yeah."

"I can see some yellowing of the skin. You should've said something at the hospital." She straightened.

Why did she sound so put out? "You've already said that. Besides, the chest X-ray was clear."

She stepped closer. "I'm going to check you out all the way around."

In another place and time, that would have sounded suggestive. And from another person. He and Sal had never had that kind of interaction.

She ducked under his arm and stepped around to his back and then returned to his front before moving away.

Ross missed her heat immediately. He didn't even know her, and he was having this reaction. Why her? Why now?

"If that isn't better in a few days, you need to have another X-ray. You also need to take some over-the-counter pain reliever for the next few days."

Even in a jumpsuit more suited for a male, Sal looked all female. He must have messed up his mind as well as his side in that fire. These thoughts had to stop here.

Her quipping "You can pull your shirt down now" brought him back to reality.

Ross walked toward the door, tucking his shirt in as he went. "Thanks, Sal."

"By the way, I think what you did at that house was both brave and stupid."

CHAPTER TWO

ROSS DIDN'T OFTEN get involved in the social side of the fire department but he was making an exception this time for two reasons. One, the annual picnic was a good place to take Olivia and Jared, his niece and nephew, while they were visiting. Two, it would be nice if he was seen by the bosses interacting positively with his fellow firefighters and the first responders at his station. He needed any edge he could get to gain the promotion.

The event was being held at one of the large parks in town. Not being a family man, Ross had only been to a few of them. There would be the usual fare of barbecue, baked beans, boiled corn and Texas-sized slices of bread. Desserts of every kind and drinks would also be provided. Along with the food were child-friendly games and crafts. Jared and Olivia were excited about the games. He was more interested in the menu; it was some of his favorite food groups.

Ross looked around the area for a parking space. The weather was clear. It would be a perfect day for the event. He scanned the vehicles to see if any belonged to the members of his station. Kody had said he would be there. Would Sal be with him? Why would he care about that? She'd been on his mind too much lately.

Ross enjoyed having the kids around. They came for a weekend now and then, but this time they were staying for a little more than a week while his sister and her husband were out of town. Normally, they would have stayed with his parents but they were off on a cruise. He had sort of volunteered and then been asked to take them for ten days. On the days he worked, a friend's wife had agreed to watch them.

He pulled his truck into a spot in the already half-full parking lot teeming with people. Seconds later, Jared and Olivia were climbing out, their eyes bright with excitement.

"Yay, there's face painting. I want to go over there." Olivia pointed to a tent not far away.

"I want to go ride the pony," Jared said over his sister.

Ross raised his voice above it all. "Circle up here. We need to have a couple of ground rules. Number one, we stay together, and number two, we stay together. If I lose you kids, your mother and father will be mad at me." He grinned at them. "Got it?"

"Got it!" they chimed in.

"Okay. Why don't we go have lunch first, then we can make the rounds and do anything you like afterward?"

He raised a hand for a high five. Jared and Olivia enthusiastically slapped his palm.

They made their way to the buffet-style line that had formed under a large shelter and joined it.

The kids each held their plates as he served pulled pork onto their sandwich buns. While he was filling his plate with ribs, he looked across the table to see Sal taking some as well. How long had she been there? "Hey, I didn't see you over there."

This was the first time he'd ever seen her in anything but a jumpsuit. Today she was wearing a simple sky blue T-shirt that was tucked into tight, well-worn jeans. A thin belt drew his attention to her hips. She looked fit but not skinny. Her hair flowed down around her shoulders. This version of Sal was very appealing.

Her eyelids flickered and she said shyly, "Hi, Ross. I think you're a little busy to notice much."

"You're right about that." He looked for the kids and found there was a gap between him and them. He saw Sal's grin and forgot what he was doing. He hurriedly returned to picking out his ribs and moved forward. The kids each added a small bag of chips to their plates. When they were all finished, they picked out canned drinks from large containers filled with ice.

When Ross turned around after getting his, he noticed Sal pulling her drink out of a bucket next to his. It didn't appear anyone was with her. Their eyes met and she gave him a soft unsure smile. She looked away over the sea of picnic tables and walked away. Would she have joined them if he'd asked? Did he want her to?

"Come on, kids, let's see about finding a place to sit." He nodded forward. "Jared, head out through the picnic tables that way."

The boy did as Ross said and he and Olivia followed. As they moved along, a number of people he knew spoke to him. He called "hi" and kept moving. Finally, he saw Jared doing a fast walk toward an empty table. Relieved they had found one, Ross settled in for his meal.

He spied Sal weaving through the tables, obviously searching for a place to sit.

She came close enough that he raised his hand and called, "Hey, Sal, come join us. We have room."

Her face brightened at her name, but when she turned his way she looked hesitant, as if trying to figure out a way to refuse, but she came their way.

As she set her lunch down next to Olivia's and across from him, she said, "Thanks. Kody and Lucy are coming but they're running late." She looked around her. "There sure are a lot of people here. I had no idea that it'd be like this." She slipped her legs under the table.

"Austin's isn't a tiny fire department. The families really

turn out for the picnic." What was happening to him? He didn't invite single women he worked with to join him for a meal. It was against departmental policy for firefighters and medical personnel at the same station to see each other. But this wasn't a date. He was just being nice.

He wasn't dating right now anyway. In college, he'd dated as much as any of his friends. During the early years of joining the department he'd done the bar scene with some of the other bachelors for a few years but that had got old fast. It was hard to see about the ranch and work his odd hours and keep that lifestyle.

Once he'd been serious about someone, but it hadn't worked out. She'd hated his schedule and had been afraid he might be hurt or killed. After a messy breakup, he'd decided to concentrate on his career and not worry about the aggravation of maintaining a relationship for a while. For now, he'd like to keep things casual, uncomplicated. Maybe after making Battalion Chief he would give serious thought to settling down. But that wouldn't or couldn't include seeing someone he worked with.

"I see." She glanced at Jared and Olivia. "I didn't know you had children."

Olivia giggled.

"This is my niece and nephew. They're spending a couple of weeks with me while my sister and her husband are out of town. Sal, this is Jared and Olivia."

Olivia gave her a curious look. "Your name is Sal? That's a boy's name."

"That's what your uncle calls me at work. My name is really Sally."

His niece wrinkled her nose. "I like Sally better."

Ross did too. It suited her. To think he had never really wondered what her full name was.

Sally looked down at Olivia and smiled. "You know, I do too."

That was interesting. Why didn't she ever correct anybody at the station?

Sally turned her attention to her food and the rest of them did as well. She handed over a napkin to Jared. Ross looked at him. He had barbecue sauce running down his chin.

The boy took it from her.

"Good sandwich?" Sally asked, smiling.

"Yes." Jared grinned.

"I can tell. Mine's good too."

"Uncle Ross's must be good too because it's all over his face." Olivia pointed to him.

They all laughed.

"He looks like a clown," Olivia blurted out.

They all broke into laughter again.

"What?" He wiped his mouth and looked at the napkin. There was a lot of sauce on it.

"It's still on there," Jared stated.

Ross tried again to clean his face.

"It's *still* on there," Olivia said with a giggle.

"You guys are starting to hurt my feelings." Ross liked the sound of Sally's laughter—sweet and full-bodied.

"Here, let me see if I can help you." Sally held up her napkin. "Lean toward me."

Ross did as she suggested as she shifted toward him. Their eyes met and held for a moment. There was a flicker of something there. Awareness, curiosity, interest?

Sally blinked and her focus moved on. A moment later she rubbed a spot on his cheek and sat back.

"She got it," Olivia announced.

However, she had left a warmth behind for him to think about.

"Jared," Sally said a little too brightly, as if she had been affected as well. "How old are you?"

"Nine."

"What do you like? Football? Baseball…?" Her attention remained on him as if she was truly interested.

"Soccer."

"Soccer. I've watched a few games but I don't know much about the rules."

Ross grinned as Jared lapsed into a full monologue about soccer playing. It hadn't taken long for Sal, uh, Sally to find the kid's sweet spot.

When he ran out of steam Sally was quick to ask, "Olivia, do you have something special you like to do?"

"I like to draw."

"Do you draw people, or animals or landscapes?" Sally took a bite of her sandwich while waiting for an answer.

Olivia wrinkled her forehead. "Landscapes? What's that?"

"Pictures of trees and grass," Jared offered.

"That's right." Sally gave him a smile of praise.

"No, I like to draw horses. I drew a picture of Uncle Ross's horses."

Sally's attention turned to him. She seemed surprised. "You have horses?"

"I do. I own a few acres out west of town."

"You need to come see Uncle Ross's horses sometime. They're beautiful." Olivia let the last word trail out. "Their names are Romeo and Juliet."

Sally smiled at her. "Are they, now?" She looked at him with a teasing grin on her lips. "Interesting names for horses."

"Hey, they were already named when I bought them."

She grinned. "So you say."

They returned to eating their meals.

As they finished, Olivia asked, "Uncle Ross, can I go have my face painted now?"

Jared turned to him. "And I want to ride the pony."

"We can't do both at the same time. Who's going first?"

Both their hands went up.

Sally covered her smile with a hand.

Ross looked at her and shook his head sadly. "I can handle a company of men at a fire with no problem but give me two kids."

Her look met his. "I think you're doing great."

She did? For some reason he rather liked that idea.

Sally pushed her plate to the center of the table. "Maybe I can help. I can take Olivia to have her face painted while you take Jared to ride the pony. We can meet somewhere afterward."

Ross looked at the children. "That sounds like a plan, doesn't it, kids?"

They both nodded.

He looked around. "Okay, we'll meet over there by the flag-pole."

Sally stood. "Then we'll see you in a little while. Olivia, bring your trash and we'll put it in the garbage on the way."

To his surprise Olivia made no argument about cleaning up. Instead she did as Sally asked. As they headed toward the face-painting booth, Olivia slipped her hand into Sally's. She swung it between them.

Sally strolled with Olivia across the grassy area toward the activities. Ross's niece and nephew were nice kids. They seemed to adore him and he them. Her ex-husband, Wade, had never really cared for children. He'd always said he wanted his own but he'd never liked others', thought they were always dirty. More than once he'd worried they would get his clothes nasty when they were around. Thinking back, she didn't understand what she'd seen in him. How she'd even thought herself in love.

Wade had been the local wonder boy. Everyone had loved him, thought he was great. She had too, which was why she'd given up almost everything she loved to make him happy. They hadn't been married long when she'd learned he was having an affair. She'd tried to work it out but Wade wasn't going to change his ways. How had she been so oblivious? What she had thought was real and special had all been a lie. Finally, she'd filed for divorce.

Her judgment where men were concerned was off. All her trust was gone. Never would she be taken in like that again. She mentally shook her head. She wasn't going to ruin a nice day thinking about her ex-husband.

Half an hour later, she and Olivia were on their way to the flagpole. Olivia had a large fuchsia star on one cheek and smaller ones trailing away from it up across her forehead, along with a smile on her lips. Sally couldn't help but smile as well at how proud the girl was.

As they approached the pole, Ross and Jared walked up. The grin on Ross's face when he saw Olivia made Sally's grow. He had such a nice smile. Wide, carefree and inviting. She'd really been missing out on something special by never having seen it before. Most of their interactions had been working ones where there had been no time for smiles.

Ross went down on one knee in front of Olivia. "I love your stars."

Sally watched the similar-colored heads so close together. Ross would make a good father someday. "How was your pony ride, Jared?"

"It was fun, but not as much fun as riding Uncle Ross's horses."

"Can we go play in the jumping games?" Olivia pointed toward the inflatable games set up across the field.

"Yeah, Uncle Ross, can we?" Jared joined in.

Sally looked back at the crowd in line for food. Were Kody and Lucy here yet? She didn't want Ross to think he had to entertain her as well.

"Sure we can." Ross started that way with Jared and Olivia on either side of him. He glanced over his shoulder. "Sally, you coming?"

"Sure." She hurried after them. If he didn't mind, it would be nicer than just standing around waiting on Kody and his daughter to show up.

As Jared and Olivia played in the inflatable game with the

net sides, she and Ross stood outside watching them dive and roll through the small multicolored balls.

After a few minutes of uncertain silence, she said, "Jared and Olivia are really sweet."

"Yeah, I think they're pretty great. Their mom and dad are raising them right."

"Is your sister older or younger than you?" She was more curious than she should be about Ross.

"I'm older, but sometimes she treats me like I'm the younger one. She worries about me being a fireman, or not being married. I know she cares but it does get old."

"I know the feeling. Kody likes to worry over me. My father encourages it as well. I don't know what I'd do without Kody though. He's the one who encouraged me to move out here. Best thing I've ever done."

Kody had told her that she needed to get away from the memories. More than once he had talked about how much he and Lucy liked living here. He'd even tried to get their parents to move out west as well.

"That's right, y'all aren't from around here. You moved out here from North Carolina, isn't that right?"

"Yeah, after my divorce Kody told me there was plenty of work for a paramedic out here. So I decided to come."

"Kody said something about you having been in a bad marriage. I'm sorry."

Sally was too. She didn't take marriage lightly.

"Hey, Aunt Sally."

She turned to see Lucy running toward her with Kody not far behind. Lucy reached her and wrapped her arms around her for a hug. Sally loved her niece. On Sally's days off she often helped Kody with Lucy. Occasionally he needed Lucy to stay over at Sally's while he worked his shift. Sally didn't mind. She enjoyed spending time with her niece. "Hey there. I was starting to wonder where you were."

Kody joined them. "Sorry, the birthday party Lucy was at

went longer than I expected." He reached out a hand and spoke to Ross. "Hey, man."

Ross gave Kody's hand a hardy shake. "Glad you made it. Have you tried the ribs yet? They're great."

"Yeah, we just ate, then saw y'all down here. Thanks for taking care of my sister."

Heat went through Sally. She didn't need taking care of. She gave her brother a quelling look. "Kody!"

He acted as if she hadn't said anything as Ross said, "We saw each other and I invited her to eat with us. No big deal." Ross made it sound as if he was trying to explain keeping her out too late to her father.

"Daddy, can I jump?" Lucy pulled on Kody's hand.

"Sure, honey."

Lucy kicked off her shoes and entered the box. Soon she was busy having fun with Jared and Olivia and the other children.

A few minutes later the man monitoring the game told the children inside that it was time to give others a chance. The kids climbed out, put their shoes on and joined them.

Sally put her hand on Lucy's shoulder. "Lucy, I'd like for you to meet Jared and Olivia. Jared and Olivia, this is Lucy. She's my niece."

"Like Uncle Ross is our uncle," Olivia chirped.

Sally smiled at her. "That's right."

A man announcing over a microphone the relay games were about to begin interrupted their conversation.

"Can we go watch, Uncle Ross?" Jared asked.

"Sure. You guys going?" He looked from her to Kody.

"Why not?" Kody responded for them both.

They walked toward the field that had been set up as a relay course. A crowd was already lining up along each side of the area marked with lanes.

"The first race is the egg carry. Children only. Get your spoon and egg and line up."

All three of the kids wanted to participate.

Jared and Olivia were in lanes next to each other. Ross stood behind them. Lucy, with Kody doing the same, was in the lane next to them. Sally stood on the sidelines to cheer them on. The children put the handle of a plastic spoon in their mouth and sat the boiled egg in the other end.

The man said, "You have to go down and around the barrel with the egg in the spoon. First one back wins. Go on three. One, two, three."

The children took off. Olivia only made it a short distance before her egg fell out. She hurried to pick it up and place it in the spoon again. Lucy and Jared were already at the barrel. Not getting far, Olivia lost hers again. She looked at Ross, her face twisted as if she was about to sob.

With what looked like no hesitation, Ross hurried to her. He went down on one knee and said something to Olivia. He offered her the spoon. She looked unsure but placed it in her mouth. Ross added the egg, then wrapped his arms around Olivia's waist and lifted her. He walked with a slow steady pace toward the barrel. Sally's heart expanded. Ross Lawson was a good uncle. They were way behind the others but the crowd cheered as Ross and Olivia rounded the barrel and headed for the finish line.

They were the last to cross the line but the people acted as if she was the first. Ross placed Olivia's feet on the ground and went down on a knee. The little girl dropped her spoon and egg, and turned around, beaming at Ross. She wrapped her arms around his neck and gave him a hug. What could have been a horrible memory for his niece, Ross had turned into one of joy.

Ross and Olivia joined their little group once more and they watched more of the races, cheering on people they knew.

A little while later the man with the microphone said, "Okay, it's time for the three-legged race. We're going to do something a little different this year to start out with. We need a male and female to represent each fire station. We're going to have a little friendly house-to-house competition. Pick your partner, and come to the line."

"Uncle Ross, you and Sally need to go," Jared said.

"Yeah, you need to," the girls agreed.

"I don't think so." Sally looked around for an excuse not to participate. She received no help from Kody, who just grinned at her.

"Someone does need to represent our station." Ross studied her.

"Go, Aunt Sally." Lucy gave her a little push.

She returned Ross's assessing look. Surely he wouldn't want to do it.

He said with far more enthusiasm than she felt, "Come on. Let's win this thing."

It figured Ross was competitive.

They hurried to a lane. Ross quickly tied the strip of cloth lying on the ground around their ankles. The entire time she tried not to touch him any more than necessary. She wasn't very successful. They met all the way up the length of their legs. Her nerves went into a frenzy when Ross's arm came around her waist. He felt so solid and secure. What was going on with her?

"Put your arm around me," Ross commanded.

With heart thumping harder than normal, Sally did as he requested. Her fingers clutched his shirt.

"Not my shirt, *me*." His words were teasing almost, but demanding, drawing her gaze to his face, which was fierce with concentration and determination. She bit back a laugh as her fingers gripped the well-founded muscle of his side.

"You really do want to win?" she murmured.

He glanced at her with disbelief. "Don't you? We start with our outside leg. You ready?"

"Uh, yeah?" She wanted to run for her car.

The man asked, "Runners ready?"

"Okay, here we go." Ross's voice was intense.

"Go!" the man said.

Ross called, "Outside, inside…"

They were on their way. He was matching the length of his stride to hers. Ross continued to keep the cadence as they hurried up the lane. She tried to concentrate on what they were doing but the physical contact kept slipping in to ruin it. When she tripped, his grip on her waist tightened.

"Outside, inside…" He helped her to get back in sync.

As they made the turn around the barrel, he lifted her against his body as if she weighed nothing. After they had swung around, he let her down and said, "Inside."

Her fingertips dug into his side. Ross grunted, but didn't slow down. His ribs must still be tender. She eased her grip and concentrated on their rhythm again.

The crowd yelled and Ross held her tighter, plastering her against him. They picked up speed.

Between breaths Ross said, "Come on, we're almost there."

Sally put all the effort she had into walking fast. They were near the line when Ross lifted her again and swung her forward with him. The crowd roared as they crossed the finish line. They stumbled hard and went down. Ross landed over her. They were a tangle of arms and legs and laughter.

Ross's breath was hot against her cheek. Her hands were fanned out across his chest. His arms were under her as if he had tried to protect her from the fall. As he looked at her, his eyes held a flicker of masculine awareness. Her stomach fluttered with a feminine response.

"Stay still. I'll untie us." His breath brushed over her lips.

"Well, folks, that was a close one," the man said.

"Aunt Sally, you won! You won!" Lucy's voice came from above her.

"We did?" she grunted as she and Ross worked to untangle themselves from each other.

Ross finally released their legs and stood. He had that beautiful smile on his face again as he offered her a hand. She put hers in his. He pulled her up into his arms and swung her around. "We sure did!"

"Oh." Her arms wrapped around his neck as she hung on. Just as quickly, he let her go. It took her a moment to regain her balance.

Lucy hugged her and Kody slapped Ross on the back. Jared and Olivia circled them, jumping up and down.

"You were great." Ross grinned at her with satisfaction.

She brushed herself off. "Thanks. You did most of the work."

"Okay, everyone," the man said. "There's ice cream for everyone before we have the stations' tug-of-war events."

"I don't know about you guys but I think Sal and I earned some ice cream," Ross said to their group.

"It's Sally, Uncle Ross," Olivia corrected him.

Ross looked at her. "Sally and I, then."

"I've always called her Sweet Pea," Kody quipped.

Sally groaned.

Ross glanced at her and beamed mischievously.

Sally started walking. The three kids joined her. She might never live this day down.

Ross spooned another bite of ice cream into his mouth. He, Kody and Sally were sitting at a table finishing their food while they watched the kids playing on the park playground equipment. The kids had become fast friends.

He looked at Sally. Her concentration remained on her bowl. She'd really been a trouper during their race. Yet by her expression he'd gathered she hadn't wanted anything to do with it. Was her silent objection to the race or running it with him?

His reaction to having her bound to him had been unexpected. That response had grown and hung like a cloud over them when they had been tangled in each other's arms. There had been a smoldering moment when she had looked at him with, what? Surprise? Interest? Desire? He was male enough to recognize her interest but smart enough to know that she was off-limits, for a number of reasons.

Sally was the sister of a friend. She worked with him. From what he understood she wasn't yet over her divorce and had no interest in dating. More to the point, she didn't strike him as someone who would settle for a fling. As for himself, he couldn't afford to have his mind or emotions anywhere but on his job right now. A real relationship would be a distraction, and something about Sally made him believe that she would be the definition of distraction.

Then there were his scars. More than once they had turned a woman off. A number of women he'd dated had expected a big, strong firefighter would be flawless, would look like a subject of a calendar. They had been disappointed by him.

Thankfully Kody asking him a question directed his mind to a safer topic. A few minutes later the announcer called the tug-of-war teams to the field.

Ross said to Kody, "Well, it's time for the fun to begin. We need to win this thing. I've heard about all I want to about how strong the Twos are." He raised his voice. "Come on, Jared and Olivia, it's time for the contest."

The kids stopped playing and started toward them.

Sally chuckled. "You're really looking forward to this, aren't you?"

"Oh, yeah. All I've heard from Station Two is how they won last year. I'm ready for payback. Do you mind watching Jared and Olivia while I'm pulling?"

"Not at all."

"Lucy too?" Kody added.

"Sure. I've got them all. You guys go on. I'll bring the kids."

He and Kody loped across the field to join the other members of the station. When they reached the part of the field where the tug-of-war would take place, Ross raised his hand. "House Twelve. Here."

Other station captains were doing the same. There was a great deal of commotion as everyone located their fellow companies.

The announcer came on again. "Firefighters and first responders may I have your attention?"

The crowd quieted.

"This is how the competition is going to work. We've set up brackets by pulling station numbers out of a hat. Those will pull against each other. The winner will continue on to the next bracket until we have a winner. Now each house needs to huddle up and decide which six people from your station will be pulling. There must be at least one woman on the team. If your house doesn't have enough people present, then you may recruit from your family members. If you have any questions you need to see Chief Curtis up here. As always, he's our final word."

Using his "at a fire" voice, Ross spoke to the people around him. "Okay, Erickson, Smith, Hart, Kody and me. Rogers, you'll be our designated woman. Does that work for everyone?"

"Ten-four, Captain!" they cheered.

"Great. Now, get into position and get ready to give it all you've got."

Those who weren't chosen went to join those lining the tug-of-war area. Ross and his team moved to the large-diameter rope lying on the ground. A piece of cloth was tied in the middle of it. A chalk line had been drawn across the pulling area.

He glanced over to see Sally and the kids standing near the line. There was excitement on their faces. They all hollered, "Go, Twelves!"

Each team member picked up a section of the rope. Ross anchored at the back where a knot was tied.

The announcer said, "We have our first two teams. The Twelves and the Thirty-Fives. On the word *go* I want you to start pulling. You must keep pulling until the last man is over the line. Is everyone ready?"

"Ten-four!" both teams shouted.

Ross called, "Dig in, firefighters. Let's win this thing." He grabbed the rope tighter.

When the announcer yelled, "Go!" Ross pulled as hard as he could. The grunts of the others ahead of him joined his as they slowly walked backward. The shouts of the crowd encouraging them grew louder. Suddenly there was slack in the rope and he staggered to keep himself upright. They had won. The crowd cheered as his team turned to each other, giving each other high fives.

He would be in pain before the day was done with that much exertion. His ribs had objected when Sally had gripped his side during the three-legged race. With the pulling, they had spoken up loudly again. Still, he was going to do his part to win the tug-of-war. His team needed him. The key was not to let on he was hurting.

Sally and the kids joined him and Kody, giving them their excited congratulations.

Sal said, "Hey, kids, how about helping me get some bottled water for our team?"

"Okay!" all three of the kids agreed.

Sally and the kids hurried away and soon returned with arms filled with bottles. Those standing around took one. Ross finished his in two large gulps. With the next competition about to begin, they moved to the side to watch as the next two teams took the field.

Soon it was time to compete again. They won the next three pulls and were now in the final facing Station Two.

Ross lined up again with his team.

"Go, Uncle Ross, go!" Olivia yelled.

"Go, Twelves! You can do this!" Sally called.

Ross's heart pounded in anticipation as the announcer said, "Go!" On that word he dug his heels into the ground and pulled with all of his might. His hands, arms and shoulders strained. The muscles in his legs trembled with the effort to move backward. Sweat ran into his eyes and still he pulled. His side burned. Clenching his teeth, he tried not to think about it. Concentrate was what he had to do.

The crowd shouted, voices mixing into a roar of encouragement.

Despite the pain he continued to tug. His legs quivered from the effort. Once, twice, three times the team was pulled forward. Only with strength of will did they remain steady and reverse the movement.

He dug deep within himself and called, "Let's take these guys."

With a burst of energy, Ross pulled harder. The others must have done so as well. They made steady steps backward.

Not soon enough for him the announcer said, "And the winner is Station Twelve."

A cheer went up. Ross put his hands on his knees and gulped deep breaths. The other members of the station surrounded them. A bottle of water appeared before his face. He looked up. Sally held it. She gave him a happy smile that made his already racing heart thump harder. All his efforts were worth it for that alone.

"You were great." Her voice was full of excitement.

Ross returned her smile. "Thanks. It wasn't just me. We did it as a team."

"Yeah, but you got them to give their all."

His ego expanded. He had to admit he liked her praise.

Others coming to congratulate him on the victory separated him and Sally.

As everything settled down, the announcer said, "Well, that's all for this year's picnic, folks. We look forward to seeing you next year. Be safe on your drive home."

Everyone slowly drifted off. Their party started toward the parking lot.

"Can I ride piggyback, Uncle Ross?" Olivia asked.

He didn't think his body could tolerate it, but didn't want to disappoint her.

Before he could say anything, Sally suggested, "How about holding my hand?" Lucy already had one of them. "I think your uncle Ross is tired after all that pulling." She gave him a knowing smile.

"Okay." Olivia took it.

Thank you, he mouthed to her.

She nodded.

"We're down this way." Kody nodded, indicating the other end of the parking lot. He gave Sally a quick hug. "See you soon."

Lucy did the same. "Bye, Aunt Sally."

"I better head to my car too." Looking unsure, Sally let go of Olivia's hand. "It was nice to meet you, Olivia and Jared. I enjoyed the day." She started off.

"Hey, wait up, we're going that way too," Ross called.

Sally paused. Olivia took her hand again.

"We'll walk you to your car." Why he'd decided that was a good idea, he didn't know. Sally was fully capable of getting to her car by herself.

"Uh, okay."

He grinned. "You thought you'd get rid of us easier than that, didn't you?"

"I'm not looking to get rid of you." She glanced at him. Her cheeks were pink. "You know what I mean."

He chuckled, then immediately winced.

Her face turned concerned. "Are your ribs still bothering you?"

"You're not going to get all up in my face if I tell you yes, are you?"

Her lips drew into a thin line. "I might."

"Yeah, today's activity didn't help much." He didn't like people seeing weakness in him and for some reason it really mattered that she didn't.

"Have you been taking it easy, until today, that is?" She studied him.

He couldn't meet her gaze. "Well, I've been trying. How's that for an answer?"

She quirked her mouth to one side in disappointment. "When you get home, run a hot bath and soak. It'll help. You do know someone else could have taken your place in the tug-of-war?" There was a bite to her words. She wasn't happy with him.

He grinned. "Yeah, but what fun would that have been?"

She shook her head. "Men. Here's my car. Bye, Olivia and Jared. See you later, Ross."

He and the kids called goodbye and continued on.

Why did he miss her already?

As he was about to start the truck, there was a knock on his window. He jumped. It was Sally. She motioned for him to roll down the glass.

"Hold out your hand."

He did. She deposited some capsules.

"These'll help with the pain. Bye, Ross." She said the last softly.

Something sweet lingered as she walked away. Something better left alone.

CHAPTER THREE

TWO DAYS LATER Ross was in his chair in the office doing paperwork when the ambulance backed into the bay. He watched out the window as Sally came around to the rear of the ambulance. She looked tired. They had already made twice as many runs as the fire side had during the shift.

His company had spent the last few hours washing the trucks, checking the supplies and making sure the station was in pristine order. Now some of the men were in the exercise room working out while others were watching a movie in the TV room.

One of his men stopped at the open door and looked in. "Hey, Ross, it's your turn to cook tonight. Do we need to make a run to the grocery store or do you have what you need?"

Each shift shared kitchen duty. Some stations had one person who liked to do the cooking, while others had a revolving schedule and the crew took turns. His station shared the duty. They assigned two people per shift to handle the meal. His turn had come up. He wasn't a great cook but he could produce simple meals. Mostly he hoped to have someone more skilled than him as his partner.

"I'll check. Who's on with me?"

"Sal."

He'd planned to stay out of her circle as much as possible, spooked as he was by his over-the-top reaction to their time together at the picnic. Cooking a meal with Sally wouldn't accomplish that, but how could he get out of it without causing a lot of questions or hurting her feelings? No solution occurred to him, so he resigned himself to spending time with her. Surely he was capable of that.

During the last few weeks it seemed as if they had seen more of each other than they had in months. In spite of their one day on and two off schedules, he was aware she often worked extra hours in order to have extended time off. What did she do during that time? Why that suddenly mattered to him, he had no idea. He huffed. It wasn't his business anyway.

Ross again glanced into the bay, then back to the man. "They're just rolling in. I'll give her time to clean up, then go see what she thinks. They've already made a couple of runs this afternoon. I don't know for how much I can depend on her."

"Ten-four."

A few minutes later Ross crossed the bay to the door of the medical area. Sally was going through a drawer. "Hey."

She turned. "Hey."

"Tough shift?"

"You could say that. Two big calls back-to-back." She shrugged. "But you know how that goes."

She was right, he'd had those days as well. "I hate to add to it but we have KP duty tonight. I'd say I'd handle it, but I'm not a great cook."

Sally grinned. "You're not one of those stereotypical firemen who has his own cookbook?"

Ross chuckled. "No, Trent who works over at Tens does. I bought his cookbook to be supportive but that doesn't mean I know how to use it. I could see if one of the other guys wants to help."

"What gives you the idea I'm not any good either?"

He wasn't used to people putting him on the spot and gave her a speculative look. "Are you?"

Her eyes twinkled. "Yeah, I'm a good cook."

Ross wiped the back of his hand across his forehead. "Woo, that's a relief. If we need something, my crew can make a run to the grocery store."

"I have a couple more things to do here, so I'll meet you in the kitchen in a few minutes and we'll see what we've got available. Surely you can open some cans if I'm called out."

"That I can do." He left and headed toward the kitchen.

This was the first time they'd been partnered in any real way. They had each done their jobs during runs but had never really interacted until the picnic. He rather liked Sally. She challenged him even at creating a meal. He wouldn't have thought he would appreciate that kind of confrontation but he did.

He was already in the kitchen area when she showed up. "Any ideas?"

"Let's see what's in the pantry." She opened the oversize door off to the side and propped it open with a crate, despite the fact the closet was large enough to hold both of them with ease. Was she fearful of being in a closed space with a man, with him in particular, or was there something else? It was just as well he wouldn't ever take a chance on being caught in a suggestive situation with a female at the station. Having that on his record would ruin any chance for advancement. This promotion was important to him, his opportunity to make a real difference.

It had been while he was in the hospital after the fire that he'd decided one day he would help people as that firefighter had helped his grandpa. As soon as Ross had graduated from high school, he'd joined the same volunteer fire department that had saved them. He'd continued to do so while he was in college. After that, he'd joined the Austin Fire Department. He loved everything about being a fireman.

In some odd way, he was determined to outdo fire. To be smarter than it. Learn to anticipate its next move. He wanted to control, conquer it so no one else would ever have to live through those moments of fear he'd had.

Sally ran her fingers down the canned goods stacked on a shelf. "Yeah, I think we have enough here for vegetable soup. Corn, beans, chopped potatoes and tomato juice. Two tins of each should do it and we can always make grilled cheese sandwiches."

He pursed his lips and nodded. "That sounds good."

Ross stepped to the doorway but didn't enter. Their meal would have to feed six firefighters and two medical support techs.

"Is there any ground beef left over, or roast beef in the freezer or the refrigerator?" she asked as if she'd been thinking along the same chain of thought.

"I'll check." As he walked across the kitchen, he could hear the clinking of cans being shifted.

After rummaging through the freezer for a moment, he announced, "Yeah, there's two or three pounds of ground beef."

"Pull it out to thaw. It can go into the soup," she called from the closet before she appeared with her arms full of cans. She dumped them on the counter as he placed the beef in the sink.

"There's a couple more cans in there. Do you mind getting them?"

He went to the closet and retrieved the cans sitting off by themselves. "Are these them?"

"Yeah."

With his foot, Ross pushed the crate back into the pantry and let the door automatically close before going to the counter. He put the cans beside the others. "What now?"

Sal looked at him with her hand on a hip. "This is a partnership, not a chef/sous chef situation."

"I prefer the chef/sous chef plan." Ross grinned.

"You act as if you don't do this often."

He leaned his hip against the counter. "I don't, if I can get out of it."

"Okay, since you've designated me to be the chef, I'm going to put you to work. Start by opening all the cans. You're qualified on a can opener, aren't you?"

"I can handle that. It's electric, isn't it?"

Sally laughed. "Yeah. It is." She turned her back to him. "And they let him be captain of a company."

Ross pulled the opener out from under the counter. "I heard that."

Pulling a large boiler out from under the cabinet near the stove, she put it on a large unit and turned it on. Ross opened cans and set them aside as he covertly watched Sal uncover the still-frozen meat and place it in the pot. She worked with the same efficacy that she used in her medical care.

"So you just have that recipe in your head? Carry it around all the time?"

Sally glanced over her shoulder. "I made it for my family all the time growing up." She tapped her forehead. "I keep it locked away right here."

"Well, I have to admit I'm impressed. I had no idea you had such skills."

"I'm not surprised. We really haven't worked together much."

Ross sort of hoped that would change even as he sternly told himself, yet again, he wanted no interferences in his life right now. Socializing with a female he worked with would definitely qualify as that.

"It's nothing but meat and a few cans of vegetables." She turned serious. "But the secret ingredient is Worcestershire sauce. Would you mind checking the refrigerator door and see if there's any there?"

He did as she requested. "There's half a bottle."

"That'll be enough." Her attention remained on what she was doing. "We'll make it work. Is there any ketchup, by chance?"

Ross opened the refrigerator door again. "Yeah, there's some of that."

"Then bring that too."

"Ketchup?" He'd never heard of such a thing.

"It'll add a little thickness to it and also a little sweetness."

"You really are a chef."

"It takes more than ketchup soup to make you a chef."

A loud buzz followed by a long alarm then three shorts indicating it was their station being called ended their conversation. Ross was already moving as Sally turned off the stove and put the pot into the refrigerator along with the open cans.

As they ran down the hall toward the bay, the dispatcher's voice came over the loudspeakers. "Two-car accident at the intersection of Taft and Houston. One car on fire."

Moments later Ross was sliding his feet into his boots next to his crewmates. He jerked up his pants and flipped the suspenders over his shoulders. It took seconds for him to pull on his turnout gear that had sat ready on the bay floor. Grabbing his coat, he swung up and into the passenger seat of the engine, while the other firefighters got into their seats behind him. He secured his helmet with the strap under his chin.

One of his men was assigned the job of pushing the buttons to open the huge overhead door. The driver hopped in and they wheeled out of the station with the siren blaring. His company worked like a well-oiled machine. They were out the door in less than a minute. They had four to get to the scene. This economy of effort was another of his leadership qualities that hopefully would get him an edge on that promotion.

Sally and her crewman were right behind them. The traffic pulled to the side and stopped, allowing them to go by. At the lights they slowed then continued on. The goal was not to create another accident in their speedy effort to get to the first emergency.

As they traveled, Ross was on the radio with dispatch, getting as much information about the accident as possible. His heart rate always rose as the adrenaline pumped and thoughts of what to expect ahead raced.

They pulled up to the accident but not too close. Sally and her partner did the same. Ross's stomach roiled. The driver's-side door of one car was smashed. It had been the center of impact. The passenger door behind it was a mangled mess but standing open. A child-size jacket hung halfway out the door and a doll lay on the road.

Smoke bellowed from the hood of the other car and oil covered the area. His job was to get the fire contained and put out. Thankfully there was no gas spreading.

"We need a fire extinguisher up here. Spread for the oil."

As his men worked with the fire, he could see that at least the car seat remained intact inside the first car and the child was gone. Looking about, he could see Sally's partner assessing the kid, who looked about four years old. The bigger issue now would be getting the woman who was still wedged in the front out.

Another ambulance arrived.

Ross continued to give orders and his men moved to follow them without questions. They knew their duties and went to work. He moved closer to the car to see Sally climbing into the back seat.

"What do you need?" he asked.

She didn't look at him. "We're going to need the Jaws of Life to get her out. The car is crushed so badly the front doors won't open. I suspect the driver has internal injuries. We need to get her out right away."

Using the radio, Ross said, "Rob, we need the Jaws of Life. Jim, you help him."

The men rushed to the supply truck. Ross looked at Sally again to see her securing a neck brace on the woman. All the time she was reassuring her patient she would be fine, and her child too. He walked away long enough to see that everything was under control with the other car. The driver was sitting on the curb, dazed but otherwise looking uninjured. One of the EMTs from the second ambulance was seeing to him.

A couple of his firefighters were rerouting traffic along with the police.

He rejoined Sal as his men with the heavy-duty machine returned to the car. They inserted the mouth of the instrument into the area where the doors met and the machine slowly pushed the two apart. It took precious minutes. The metal creaked as it bent and groaned as it shifted. Finally, the firefighters were able to separate the doors.

"We need the gurney over here," Sally called, then said over her shoulder to Ross, "We'll need some help getting her on it."

Ross and another firefighter moved into position, while she and another EMT stood across from them.

"I want us to slowly move her out, scooting her along the gurney." This was Sally's area of expertise and he would follow her lead.

Minutes later the patient was in the box with Sally in attendance and sirens blaring, headed toward the hospital. Ross and his company went to work seeing that the vehicles were loaded on wreckers and debris was cleared from the road.

By the time Sally finally made it back to the station kitchen, she found Ross stirring the soup, which bubbled gently on the stove. He was more talented than she had given him credit for.

"Hey, I'm glad you could join me. I thought I was going to have to take all the glory." He grinned at her. The kind that caused a flutter in her middle. Why him? Why now? He was a nice guy. The kind she might be able to trust. She shook her head. If it was another time in her life, she might be tempted.

She smirked. "Like I was going to let that happen."

"You were right. Looks like I can brown meat and dump cans of vegetables." He sounded pleased with himself.

"Turns out you have more talent than you let on."

"Some say that about other areas as well." His comment sounded offhand but she suspected there might be more to it. Was Ross flirting with her? No, that wasn't possible. What if it was? She had to stop thinking like that. There was nothing but trouble down that road.

Suddenly self-conscious, she cleared her throat. "So where were we before we were so rudely interrupted?" She pulled the loaf of bread that was sitting on the counter toward her. "I'll get the grilled cheeses ready. Everyone must be hungry." She started buttering bread.

"What're you doing there?"

"Making fast and easy grilled cheese sandwiches. Pull out one of those large sheet pans, please." Sally kept moving the knife over the bread as she spoke. "Then get the sliced cheese and start putting it on the bread. We'll slip it into the oven, put it on broil, and we should have grilled cheeses in no time."

Ross went to work without question. Soon they had the sandwiches browning. "I'll get the plates, bowls and things while you go tell everyone soup's on."

"Are you always so bossy?" Ross asked as he exited the kitchen.

Did he really think she was dictatorial? She never thought of herself as being that way. Yet Wade had complained she was always on his case. Toward the end of their marriage, she guessed she had been. Wade hadn't ever been at home. More often than not he'd been between jobs; either it wasn't the right one or he was too smart to work with the people around him, or some other excuse. His parents had raised him to believe he could do no wrong.

She'd dreamed of being a doctor all through high school but after she and Wade had married he'd not wanted his wife going to school. He'd said school took up too much of her time. Time she could be spending with him. He'd never been a fan of her working as a paramedic, but she'd refused to give up volunteering when she'd been needed so badly by their rural community. That was the only thing she had defied him on. She had wanted their marriage to work.

Looking back, she could see how selfish Wade really was.

That had certainly been brought home when she'd learned he was having an affair. But where she'd really messed up was not seeing through Wade before she'd married him. Her judgment had been off, so caught up in the fantasy rather than the reality. Next time, she'd be more careful about who she opened her heart to.

Ross returned with the other firefighters on his heels. Over the next hour the company shared a meal, told stories and laughed. When the meal was over, she and Ross cleaned up, each thankful that most of the dishes went into the dishwasher.

Ross was washing the last of the pots when his phone rang. He shook off his wet hands and pulled the phone out of his pocket. He moved away from the sink and Sally stepped into his spot. She was tired and still had paperwork to take care of. Hopefully they wouldn't be called out anytime soon.

As she rinsed off the pan, Ross said with a disappointed note in his voice, "I'll work something out." He paused. "No, you can't help it," he said, before saying his goodbyes and hanging up the phone.

Sally hesitated to say anything, afraid it might be wrong, but didn't want to appear unsympathetic. "Everything all right?"

"No, not really. The lady I have watching Olivia and Jared while I work? Her mother has had an accident and Marcy has to go help her. That leaves me having to find someone to help me out."

"Would swapping shifts help?"

He was scrolling through the numbers on his phone. "Naw, I've got a meeting with the Chief. One I can't afford to miss." Ross spoke more to himself than to her.

"What day are you talking about?" Sally dried her hands on a dishrag.

"This Friday." He still wasn't giving her his attention.

"I'm not on the rest of the week. I have too much overtime. I'll watch them. If you don't mind Lucy joining us."

"Hey, if you'd do that it would be great. Jared and Olivia would love to have someone to play with."

"There's only one problem." She paused until she had his attention. "I don't think three kids are going to be happy overnight at my place. It's too small. I guess I could ask Kody if we could go there."

"Y'all can come to my place. There's plenty of room there. A lot of space outside to play. Plus, Jared's and Olivia's stuff is already there."

"Are you sure?"

He took the pot from her and put it under the cabinet. "Of course I am. You're doing me a favor."

Sally wasn't sure that going to Ross's house was a good idea. It seemed as if they were getting too friendly. Yet her place was so small and Kody's would be a little tight for three active kids as well. She didn't see another good choice. "That would probably be best."

He studied her a moment. "I'll owe you big-time for this."

"Don't worry about it. It sounds fun. The kids and I'll have a good time together."

"If you could come out around eleven, that should give me time to show you around then get to town in time to start my shift. I'll text you my address." He headed out the door.

"Hey, don't you need my number?"

He looked bashful. Cute, in fact. "I guess that would be helpful."

"You don't arrange childcare often, do you?"

"Nope." Ross grinned. "It's a fine art I'm just now learning."

She gave him her number. He punched it into his phone, then he was gone.

CHAPTER FOUR

SALLY HAD MADE a serious mistake by agreeing to watch Ross's niece and nephew. Doing so was another step into further involvement in Ross's life. Being together at the picnic had revealed she was far too attracted to him. An attraction she neither wanted nor needed. She must stay focused. Still, she liked the guy. The last time she'd been this enamored with a man, she'd been devastated. That mustn't happen again. She wouldn't allow it. The upside to the day's arrangement was that Ross would be at work the entire time.

And she would be with the kids...

In his home. His personal space. She hadn't thought that through either. She would be where he lived. Touching, sitting and sleeping among his personal belongs. No, she hadn't considered that part of this agreement at all. She should have done so before she'd blurted out her willingness to help. Yet helping out a fellow firefighter went with being a member of that family. It was just what a team player did in an emergency situation.

Ross had texted her his address as promised. Sally had picked up Lucy from Kody's house on her way to Ross's. Lucy had been so excited about seeing Jared and Olivia again she couldn't get in the car fast enough. The idea of an overnight stay had heightened her anticipation. She'd chatted most of the way about all the fun they would have. Sally certainly hoped so. The closer she came to Ross's house, the tighter Sally's nerves knotted. She hadn't acted this way over seeing a man in a long time. Control—she needed to get some over her wild emotions.

The drive was ten miles out of town to where the land rolled gently, the trees were tall and the fields green. When she had moved to this part of the country, it hadn't taken long for her to fall in love with Texas. Even though she liked her apartment, she wished she could find a place with more outdoor space.

The day was beautiful with the sun shining in a blue sky as she turned the car off the two-lane highway onto a dirt lane. On either side were fenced pastures with a few trees here and there. The lane ended at a white clapboard house with a porch along the front. Large oaks shaded one side and the lawn surrounding the house was neatly mown. Behind it there was a small red barn with a couple of horses in the corral.

She sighed. When she got her medical degree, this was just the type of place she would look for. There was something restful, comforting about it. A place someone could find contentment. She loved everything about it, immediately.

When she'd taken Kody up on his suggestion to move to Texas, she'd realized how right he'd been. She'd had no trouble getting a job and there had been something cathartic, cleansing, about leaving all the ugliness of her marriage behind and starting over again. It had taken some time, but she'd finally settled in, had decided on a plan and was now focused on seeing it through.

Soon after arriving in Austin, she'd enrolled in college and finished her degree. Sally smiled. To think she was studying to take her MCAT now. If she did well enough, she hoped to enter medical school in the fall, while continuing to work part-time at the firehouse when she could. She wasn't going to let anyone or anything divert her this time.

As she climbed from the car, Ross stepped out of the beveled glass front door.

A warmth washed over her. Especially not a man with striking blue eyes and a hunky chest.

He came to stand beside a wooden post of the porch. He wore his usual fire station uniform of navy pants and T-shirt with the department logo on one breast. Practical work boots completed his attire. He appeared healthy and fit. His welcoming smile made him even more handsome than she remembered. Her stomach quivered. She had to get beyond this fascination with Ross. Still, couldn't a girl enjoy a moment of admiration for a man?

He drawled, "I see you found us."

Returning his smile, she gathered her purse. She'd bring in her MCAT study books after he'd left. Lucy had already hopped out of the car and gone to meet Jared and Olivia, who were in the side yard.

Ross came down the wide steps. His agile movements reminded her of a panther she'd once seen in a zoo. "Are you ready for this?"

"What if I said I wasn't?" She glanced at him as she gathered Lucy's and her overnight bags.

He grimaced. "I don't know what I'd do."

She grinned, looking at the kids. "I'm going to be fine. We'll all be fine."

"Here, let me get those for you." He reached for the bags.

"Thanks." His hands brushed hers and she quickly pulled away. The physical contact had intensified her growing nervous tension.

They walked side by side to the house. Happy laughter from the kids filled the air. Ross moved ahead of her and hurried up the steps. Tucking Lucy's bag under his arm as he reached the door, he opened it and held it. She strode by him, making sure they didn't touch. If they had, would he have felt the same electric reaction she had when their hands had met?

The room Sally entered was dim and it took a moment for her eyes to adjust. Only a few feet inside the door, she looked around the large open space. The high ceiling was supported by dark beams. The walls were a cream color complemented by a gleaming warm wooden floor. It was furnished with a brown leather sofa and two armchairs along with an old chest she assumed he used as a coffee table. A TV hung over the mantel of a stone fireplace.

In the back of the house was the kitchen. A large bar separated it from the living area. A table for four sat to one side. Windows filled the corner, giving a beautiful view of the barn, trees and the fields beyond. Everything was neat, but masculine.

This was a man's abode. Ross's. Sally shivered. She had truly entered the lion's den.

Ross set the bags down beside a door to a small hallway and walked farther into the house. "Come on in. Let me show you around. As you can see, this is the kitchen." He pointed toward the hallway. "Over there are two bedrooms. Jared and Olivia are in them. Olivia has the one with the twin beds so there's an extra bed for Lucy. On the other side of the house is my room. The sheets on the bed are clean. Ready for you."

Her breath caught. Her eyes widened. Finally she blinked. "I, uh, think I'll just sleep on the sofa. That way I'll be closer to the kids in case one calls out." Spending the night in Ross's bed would be far too...personal? Uncomfortable? Nerve shaking? Lonely? Whatever the word was, she wouldn't be doing it.

"I want you to be comfortable. I think you'd be happier in a bed. It's the only one I have that's available." He shrugged. "But all that's up to you." She made no comment and he continued, "You can find all kinds of movies and games in the cabinet beside the fireplace. The kids know where everything is."

She nodded.

"I've already ordered pizza for dinner tonight. It should be delivered at six. Right, here's the tip." He tapped some bills on top of the counter. "My number is on this pad if you have any questions, anytime."

Sally moved closer to look.

"There should be plenty of sandwich fixings in the refrigerator. I also have peanut butter and jelly. Chips. And drinks."

Her smile widened as she softly laughed.

His look turned serious. "What's so funny?"

"You are."

"How's that?" He watched her too close for comfort as if he didn't want to miss any change in her expression.

"Firehouse Captain turned Mr. Mom."

He chuckled. One that started low and rough then slowly rolled up his throat and bubbled out. "I do sound a bit that way, don't I?"

"You do, but it's nice to know there're supplies, I'll give you that. Thanks for taking the time and thought to make it as easy as possible for me."

"You're welcome." He picked keys up off the counter. "I'd better get going."

She followed him out onto the porch.

"Oh, I forgot. Could you see that the horses are fed tonight and in the morning? Jared knows what to do." He moved to the porch railing and called, "Jared and Olivia."

Both children stopped playing and looked at him. "I don't want you giving Sally any trouble. If she needs help, you do so. No argument about bedtime either."

"Yes, sir," they called in harmony.

He smiled and nodded. "Good. I'll see you tomorrow."

"Bye, Uncle Ross." Olivia waved.

"Yeah, bye," Jared said as an afterthought as he ran for a ball.

Ross turned to her. "I really appreciate this."

"You've already said that."

"I know, but I do." He walked to her, stopping just out of reach. His gaze met hers. A spot of heat flushed through her middle that had everything to do with his attention. "Well, I'll see you tomorrow around one." He went down the steps.

"Okay."

He hadn't made it to his truck before he said, "Call if you have any questions."

"I will." Sally wrapped her arm around the post he had stood beside earlier and leaned her cheek against it. She watched him leave. Ross put his hand out the window and waved. She stayed there until he was out of sight.

What would it be like to have someone who wasn't eager to leave her? That she could say bye to who would look forward to returning to her. At one time she'd believed she had that. Instead Wade had acted as if coming home to her was a chore. Why had he married her if he hadn't really wanted her? In less than a year he had been off with someone else.

She wanted a man who desired her. That she was enough for. Maybe one day she would try again, but that wasn't going to happen anytime soon. She had plans, dreams. That was what she should be thinking about. She was better off without the obstacle of a man in her life for the time being.

Yet here she was seeing to Ross's niece and nephew. At his house. When he'd driven away, it had seemed as if they were husband and wife and she were seeing him off to work. But that wasn't reality. She was the babysitter and nothing more. And she didn't want anything but that.

Lucy interrupted her troubling thoughts with, "Aunt Sally, we're hungry."

"Well, it's about lunchtime. Come on in."

The kids stomped up to the porch.

"Let's go see what we can find in the kitchen."

After lunch they returned to playing. The pizza Ross had promised arrived just as he'd said it would and they ate it picnic style under one of the oak trees.

The sun was low as they finished then went to feed the horses. Jared took the lead. First, he turned on the hose to add water to the trough. Sally grinned at his puff of importance as he went into the barn to get grain. He returned with a gallon tin can full and let each of the girls dump a part of the feed into two buckets for each of the horses.

As Lucy took her turn, she hit the rail with the end of the can. It went flying and landed in the water trough. She gasped and tears filled her eyes.

Sally placed a hand on her back. "It's okay, hon. We'll get it."

"I'll do it." Jared started pulling his shirt off.

Sally looked at him in dismay. "What're you doing?"

"It'll get wet if I don't take it off." He handed her his shirt, then leaned into the trough far enough that his head almost touched the water. When he straightened pulling the can out, the water inside spilled all down his front.

Sally laughed. "Obviously you knew what was going to happen."

Jared grinned, dropped the can on the ground and took his shirt from her. "Yeah, we drop it in almost every time we visit."

"How come a boy can take his shirt off and a girl can't?" Lucy asked.

This wasn't a discussion Sally wanted to get into, especially with other people's children. She just had to keep the answers simple. "Well, because boys and girls are different. Especially when they get older."

"Uncle Ross is a boy and he never takes his shirt off," Olivia announced. "Not even when he's swimming."

What was she to say to that? "Guys don't have to take their shirts off if they don't want to."

"When it's hot I like to take mine off." Jared picked the can up and headed for the barn.

Olivia's statement left Sally curious. She'd have thought a man with Ross's physique should be proud to show it off.

Lucy took Sally's hand. "Sometimes when I'm playing with the water hose, I take mine off."

It was time to change the subject. "Let's go get a bath and have a snack before bedtime."

By just after dark, Sally had all the kids in bed. She wasn't sure who was happier, them or her. She'd had less active days at work. Plopping on the couch, she stretched out her legs, letting her head rest on the pillowed leather behind her. Sally closed her eyes and sighed. She and the kids had had a nice day. They were a good tired and she was as well. While she was trying to convince herself to get up and do some studying, her phone rang.

Digging in the back pocket of her jeans, she fished it out.

"Hey, how's it going?" Ross's rich voice filled her ear.

Her heart did a little pitty-pat. "We're doing great. Have you been worried about us?"

"More about you. Two kids can be a handful so I can imagine three's more difficult."

He had been thinking about her? "Everybody's fine. They're all in bed now." She yawned.

"I bet you're thinking about going as well." The timbre of his tone suggested ideas better left locked away. She sat straighter. "I'll be up for a little while longer."

"I really thank you for this."

It was nice to feel useful to a man to whom she was attracted. For so long she'd felt unworthy. In the end duped and rejected. "You don't have to keep saying that. How did your meeting with the Chief go?"

"Really well."

He'd asked her some personal questions, so she felt entitled. "Do you mind if I ask what's going on?"

"No. It's just that I'm on the shortlist for Battalion Chief. I've been trying to make a good impression. Not being there when the Chief's making his rounds wouldn't have been good."

"You'll make a great Battalion Chief." Of that she had no doubt.

"I don't have the job yet."

"Maybe not yet, but you'll get it." He was good at his job and others noticed. She certainly had.

"The competition is pretty strong. I've worked with all of them at one time or another."

"I can't imagine anyone being more qualified than you."
And she couldn't.

"Thanks, Sal, for that vote of confidence. It means a lot."
Ross's voice held a note of gratitude.

She couldn't stem her curiosity about him. "Have you always
wanted to be a firefighter?"

There was a pause. "Yeah, ever since I was a little boy."

"That's a long time." Her amazement rang in her voice. They
shared something in common. They both had known what they
wanted to do since they were young.

"I'm not that old." He chuckled.

"You know what I mean. What made you want to be a firefighter?"

This time he didn't falter before answering her. "I saw firefighters at work when I was a kid and I decided then that I want
to help people like they did."

She almost said *aww* out loud. "That's very admirable. Was
it a bad fire?"

"The worst. My grandfather's house was a total loss." His
voice had grown rougher with each word.

She could tell that it had been a life-changing event for him
in more than one way. "Oh, Ross. I'm sorry. I hope he was all
right."

"He was. He rebuilt. You're sitting in his house now. He left
it to me when he died a few years ago. I've made some updates."

Sally looked around. "I like your house. I want something
like it one day."

"I'm happy there." There was a pause, then he said, "Tell me
something, are you going to sleep in my bed tonight?"

Heat flowed hot and fast throughout her body. Her mouth
went dry. Ross coming on to her. She liked it.

The buzz of the fire station alarm going off, then the dispatcher speaking, was all she could hear for the next few seconds.

"Gotta go," Ross said. "See you tomorrow." More softly, as
if a caress, he finished with, "Take care, Sweet Sally."

"Bye," she said into an empty line. Sweet Sally? She liked the sound of that coming from Ross.

Ross neared the end of the drive to his home with keen anticipation. He was coming home to someone. Was his life really that isolated? Not until this moment did he realize how much he liked the idea of having someone waiting on him at home. He'd looked forward to seeing Sally and the kids. Hearing how their time together had gone.

He grinned. Maybe now he'd get an answer about where she'd spent the night. It still shocked him that he'd dared to ask. Had called her Sweet Sally. After all, she was doing him a favor and he'd hit on her. He hoped things wouldn't be strained between them now. He should have kept that question to himself. In a twisted way he was relieved to have been out on a run most of the night. At least he hadn't had time to think about her in his bed—without him.

He'd put taking a real interest in a woman on the back burner for so long his reaction to Sally was unsettling. Did he dare take a chance on her? Gambling on how a woman would respond to his scars, he'd kept most of them at arm's length. He'd let Alice in but that hadn't ended well either.

Maybe it was time for him to think about more than his job. Still, the idea of living through major rejection again struck him with fear. Was it Sally in particular or just that it was time for him to try again that had him thinking this way?

He parked his truck next to Sally's car, then grabbed his duffel bag.

The kids were playing right where they had been when he'd left the day before. They called hello as he climbed the steps. A fireman's schedule with the staggered hours had always seemed like a difficult schedule for a family to live around but there was something nice about the idea of having children. What had caused that idea to pop into his head? He'd been satisfied with Jared and Olivia's visits and hadn't thought of having his own children in a long time.

These days he was having all sorts of odd thoughts.

As he entered the house, he was tempted to call, "Honey, I'm home," but he didn't think Sally would appreciate his humor. An amazing aroma filled the air. There was food cooking in the oven. Sally's back was to him as she chopped something.

Her hair was pulled up in a messy arrangement, yet it suited her. She wore a flowy top of some kind and jeans. There were sandals on her feet. There was nothing special about her clothes, yet the combination made her appearance fresh, simple and disturbingly sexy.

Music played softly from the radio. She swayed and hummed along. It was strangely erotic. His blood heated. He wanted to walk up behind her and pull her back against him. Leave her in no doubt of his need for her. How would she react to him kissing her neck?

Not a good idea. At all. Tamping down his desire, Ross cleared his throat. "Hey."

She turned and smiled. "Hey. I didn't hear you come in."

He walked toward her, sniffing. "I'm not surprised. What's that wonderful smell?"

"My father's favorite meat pie. I thought since we've had sandwiches, pizza and cereal that we should have a real meal. We voted to wait on you."

He could get used to this. "Are you saying what I left wasn't nutritious enough?"

She shrugged. "I'm not complaining. I like to cook and it's nice to do it for more than just myself."

"You're welcome to cook for me anytime." He met her look and held it.

Her gaze turned unsure as she said, "Will you call the kids in and tell them to wash their hands while I get this on the table."

"Sure thing. Let me put my bag up first." Yes, he liked coming home to Sally, the kids and a meal. He sure did.

Picking up his bag, Ross went to his bedroom. Sally hadn't slept there. Nothing had been moved and he had no doubt that her scent would have lingered. For some reason these days his body picked up on every detail of hers despite his best effort not to notice. The idea she had slept on the sofa bothered him. She should have been comfortable at his house.

Stepping to the bath, he saw that she hadn't been in there either. He didn't know much Shakespeare, but he did think maybe the woman did "protest too much." He grinned. Maybe she was more affected by him than she wanted to admit.

He went outside to call the kids. After a good deal of noise and shuffling around, including adding a chair to the table, he and the kids were seated. Sally placed a bowl of salad on the table and joined them.

He looked at Sally. Her face was rosy from being in a warm kitchen. Tendrils of her hair had come free and fallen across her cheek. She pushed at them with the back of her hand. She was lovely. "It looks wonderful, Sweet Sally."

Olivia giggled. "It's just Sally."

He waved his hand over the table. "Don't you think she's sweet? She did all this for us. I sure do."

The kids chorused their agreement.

Sally giggled and her color heightened. "Thank you."

This was a real family moment. The type of thing he'd not given a thought to having in a long time. He liked it. Found himself wanting it more often.

The kids spent the rest of the meal talking about all they had done while he was gone. Sally remained quiet, listening and smiling. Not once did she make eye contact with him, despite the fact he was sitting across from her. Was she afraid of what she might see or what he might find in her eyes? He'd have to give that more thought.

After their meal was over, she said, "Kids, please carry your plates to the sink, then you may go back out and play. Lucy, we'll need to be leaving soon."

They did as she asked without an argument, which Ross couldn't believe. When they were gone, he turned to her. "How do you do that?"

She stood and picked up her plate. "Do what?"

He gave her an incredulous look and pointed with his thumb over his shoulder. "Get them to do something without back-talking?"

She shrugged and carried the plate to the sink. "I'm a woman of many talents."

"I don't doubt that." Some of those he'd like to explore.

Sally began filling the dishwasher. Ross brought the rest of the dishes off the table to her. They finished straightening the place together.

"We make a pretty good team in the kitchen." Ross returned the dishrag after wiping the table off, trying to keep his mind off the other things they might be good at together.

Sally dried her hands and hung the dishcloth on a knob. "Seems that way."

Ross noticed a stack of books at the end of the bar and walked over to see what they were. He placed a hand on them. "Are these yours?"

"Yes." Sally picked them up and hugged them against her chest as if protecting them. "I don't want to forget them."

"This says MCAT on it. Are you studying to take the test to be a doctor?" He didn't even try to keep his surprise out of his voice.

"Yeah. I'm trying to get into medical school."

He leaned a hip against the counter. "I'm impressed. I had no idea." How had he not heard talk at the house? "Is it a secret?"

Sally shook her head. "No."

Apparently, he'd been so caught up in his wish of being Bat-talion Chief he'd not noticed that about her. What kind of boss would he be if he didn't see more outside of his own world? He needed to do better. "So, when's the test?"

"Two weeks from today."

"Good luck."

"I'm afraid I'm going to need it."

"I doubt that. I think you'll make an amazing doctor." And he did. The more he knew about Sally, the more captivated he was by her.

Her eyes were bright. "Thanks for that. I hope I do."

He gave her his best encouraging look. "I've no doubt you will."

"Thanks, that's nice to hear. I've always dreamed of being a doctor."

"Is this your first time taking the test?" Ross was far too interested in her life, but he couldn't stop himself from asking.

"Yes."

"Why haven't you done it before now?"

"My husband didn't want me to go to school. He wanted me to be there when he came home."

Something close to anger boiled within Ross. The dirtbag hadn't even supported his wife's dreams. Kody had said he was a jerk, but Ross had had no idea how big of one.

Ross heard the laughter of the kids. "I'm sorry. I'm sure you didn't get much study time here."

"I did some this morning while the kids were playing. When I get home, I'll go at it hard. Only thing is that they're replacing the siding on my apartment complex, so I'll have to work around that. Speaking of going, Lucy and I need to be doing that."

Ross was reluctant to see her leave. He found he really didn't like that idea.

"You're welcome here anytime. I mean, it's quiet here. You can come out anytime, whether or not I'm here."

"I don't know…" She looked uncertain.

He raised a hand. "Hey, just know the offer's there if you need it."

"Thanks. That's kind of you." She gathered her books and left them at the front door before she stepped outside and called, "Lucy. We have to go now."

"Do we have to?" Lucy whined.

"Yes. Your daddy's expecting you, and I have studying to do."

Ross joined her with her bags in hand.

She grinned at him. "So much for my talents."

He laughed. She reached for their belongings. "I'll carry them to the car."

The kids came up on the porch.

Olivia pointed her small finger toward the rustic star nailed over the door on the beam above his and Sally's heads. "Look, Uncle Ross, you and Sally are standing under the Texas star. You have to kiss her!"

Ross had forgotten about the star. It was a game he'd been playing with Olivia since she was a baby. Before she left from a visit, he gave her a kiss under the star.

"When you're standing under the star, you have to kiss the one you're with. Isn't that so, Uncle Ross?" Olivia gave him an expectant face.

Sally's eyes had grown wide. "What?"

Ross spoke to Olivia. "Yeah, but that's between you and me. It's not for everyone."

"But you kiss Mom and Grandma under it," Olivia insisted.

"I, uh, don't think that's necessary." Sally took a step away.

"That's not what you said, Uncle Ross," Jared said. "You said you must always tell the truth."

"I did say that." He was caught in a trap and he was afraid Sally was as well. He looked at her. "You wouldn't want me not to be a man of my word?"

"It seems I have no choice." She didn't sound convinced. In fact, she acted as if she'd like to run. Yet she put the bags down and placed her books on top of them.

He took her hand and led her back to where they had been standing under the star. She must have been in shock because she offered no resistance. He placed his hands on her waist. Their looks met. He said softly, "You do know it won't be a fate worse than death, don't you?"

"I'd like to think so."

He kissed her, stopping any further words with his mouth. Her lips were soft and warm. Everything he had imagined and more.

Sally's hands came to his waist and clutched his shirt as if she needed him as a stabilizer. After the first seconds of indecision, she returned the kiss. His body hummed as his hands tightened with the intention of pulling her closer. This kiss was too sweet, too revealing, too little. It had quickly gone from an intentioned friendly kiss under the star to one of passion.

"Ooh."

"Ick."

"Ugh..."

The sounds coming from the kids made him draw back. Ross looked into Sally's eyes. She appeared as shaken as he. He registered the shiver that ran through her. Sally broke from his hold and he didn't stop her.

"Lucy, we need to go." There was a quiver in Sally's voice as she grabbed her books.

He reached for the bags before she had time to pick them up and followed her to the car. She opened the door and without looking at him said, "You can just throw those in the back seat."

"Will do. Thanks again for helping me out."

"You're welcome. Lucy, buckle up." Seconds later she and Lucy were ready to go.

Ross stood out of the way as Sally turned the car around and headed down the drive. He watched her go with his body still not recovered from their kiss. By the way Sally had acted, she'd been as affected as he had been. One thing was for sure, he wanted to kiss her again. If he had anything to say about it, it would happen again—soon.

CHAPTER FIVE

FEWER THAN THREE days had passed but that wasn't enough time for Sally to erase the memory of Ross's lips against hers. In fact, she'd relived those moments over and over to the point where it had disrupted her study schedule. Yet another example of how letting a man into her life again could derail what she really wanted. She had to put an end to the daydreaming.

Doing well on the MCAT was too important. Instead of focusing on questions and the correct answers, she had been thinking of the tingling sensation having Ross's arms around her had generated and the throbbing in her center as he'd kissed her. She'd been aware of their attraction but had had no idea how electric it was until his lips had touched hers.

Would Ross try to kiss her again? She had to stop thinking about him.

She had to focus on her studies, work around her emotions as well as the construction being done on her apartment complex. With air hammers going off constantly and the banging of siding falling, she'd quickly learned she couldn't get any studying done at home.

She'd tried waiting until the workmen quit for the day but that had left her studying well into the night. Once, she'd gone to a coffee shop but even there she had become too distracted. The library had been her last resort, but the chairs weren't comfortable after an hour or two. She needed her own little nest, a place to spread out her books. What she wanted was for the work on her apartment complex to be completed, but that wasn't going to happen anytime soon.

Now she was dragging her books into the fire station, hoping it would be a slow shift so she could get some studying time in. Pulling her bag out of the car, she headed inside. She groaned long and deep. Ross's truck was in the parking lot. He was working today. She took a deep breath, trying to settle her heartbeat.

Unfortunately, he was the first person she saw. The living, breathing diversion in her life. To make matters worse, she ran straight into him as he circled the back of the engine while she walked between it and the rescue truck. He grabbed her shoulders, but quickly let go and stepped back. Even that brief touch was enough to set her blood racing.

"Are you okay?" His eyes searched her.

"I'm fine," she answered around a yawn.

He studied her closer. "You sure? You look tired."

"Thank you. That's what every woman wants to hear." Her voice was overly haughty.

"Hey, that wasn't a criticism, but concern."

She shifted her bag. "I'm sorry. I'm just a little on edge. And tired. It's not your fault. I shouldn't take it out on you." Though some of it *was* his fault.

His voice turned sympathetic. "What's the problem?"

"I've been trying to study and they're working at my apartment complex. It's so noisy during the day I've been staying up late at night. I've taken all next week off to study but I don't see things getting better. I've got to find someplace quiet to concentrate."

"I told you you're welcome out at my place."

Sally's breath caught. What was he suggesting?

Ross must have seen her look of astonishment because he hurriedly raised a hand. "Hey, it's not what you're thinking. I have to be at the training center all next week. So I'll be working eight to five. The kids are with my parents now. You'd have some peace and quiet to study. By the time I come home in the evenings, they should be done for the day at your place."

It did sound like a doable plan. An exceptional one. "That's really nice of you. But I can't put you out like that."

"You won't be putting me out. I won't even be there. How could you disturb me?"

Ross made it sound as if she would be stupid not to agree. It'd be better than skipping around from one place to the other trying to get some real studying done. Just the thought of sitting on Ross's porch swing as she worked had its appeal. Yet...

She shook her head. Things between them were already too... She couldn't put a word to it. Didn't want to. Going to his house again would only make them more involved. "I don't know. I'm sure I'll figure out something."

"This is what I'm going to do. I'll leave a key under the mat. If you want to go, go—if you don't, don't. Just know you're welcome."

One of the firefighters called out to him.

"See you later, Sally."

He didn't give her another look, as if they were two old friends and didn't have that kiss hanging between them. Maybe it hadn't been as big a deal to him as it had been to her.

After doing her usual shift routine, she managed to get in a few hours of study before the intercom buzzed and the station was called out on a run.

She and Ross shared no conversation outside of what was essential during the accident. She left at noon the next day and returned home to find the construction trucks parked in front of her building. She ground her teeth. This just wasn't the time in her life for this. She had to find some quiet. It would be another week of bangs and clangs but now they would be right outside her walls. Her test was only four days away. She'd taken time off work to cram all she could into her brain but how much of that could she get done here?

The idea of sitting on Ross's swing with a breeze blowing and the horses in the pasture popped into her mind. The image was too sweet. She might ace the test if she studied there.

When Ross had suggested she go to his house, she'd had no intentions of doing so, but with the men working on her building in particular it seemed silly not to. If she timed it right, she could arrive just after Ross left for the day and leave before he came home. The worst that could happen was that he'd come home early. Then she'd make an excuse and leave.

The next morning Sally loaded all her books and notes into the car and headed out of town. She needed quiet and Ross's place offered that. If it meant she had to push away her anxiety over using his place to get quality time in her books, then she'd manage it. The bigger picture was more important. Just turning up his drive eased her nerves.

His home looked just as inviting as it had before. She climbed out of the car. More than that, it sounded as serene as she had hoped. The only noises were from chirping birds and the occasional snort of a horse. Filling her arms with books, she climbed the steps to the porch. She placed her armload on a small table near the swing.

Going to the door, she glanced at the star hanging above and refused to give it any more thought. Doing so would waylay her plans for the day. She didn't have time for *what if*s and *maybe*s. All her plans, dreams and hopes were concentrated on what would happen on Saturday. She must be prepared.

Just as Ross had promised, the key was under the mat. Unlocking the door, she filled a large glass with water, returned outside and set the glass on the table. She picked up a book and settled on the swing. Using the big toe of one foot, she gradually started it to moving.

Time passed quickly and it was soon lunchtime. She'd brought her food and enjoyed it on the porch. Needing to do something to give her mind a rest, she decided to cook Ross dinner in appreciation for giving her this great place to study.

She found enough in the pantry to put together a small chicken casserole and a dessert. Leaving a note of thanks for Ross on the counter, she made a list of items to buy on the way home for tomorrow's meal and returned to studying.

The next days passed much as the first one. By Friday afternoon, Sally felt confident about the test ahead. She'd managed to get a great quantity of quality studying done. She'd be forever grateful to Ross.

His truck came down the drive as she was on her way to the car to leave. Her breath caught and her heart beat a little faster. He was early.

Ross pulled up beside her, his window down. "Hey, I was hoping I'd see you before you left. I wanted to wish you luck."

"Thanks. I could use all I can get. I really appreciate you letting me come out here. I don't know what I'd have done if I hadn't."

He put his arm on the window opening and leaned out. "Hey, I'm the one who should be thanking you. The meals have been a nice treat. I'll miss them."

"You're welcome. It's the least I could do." She opened her car door.

"How about sharing dinner with me tonight?" His words didn't sound as confident as she would have expected them to.

Sally considered it for a moment. She was tempted, but she needed to keep her focus. Get a good night's sleep. Be prepared for tomorrow. Not be distracted. And Ross was undoubtedly a distraction. "Thanks, but I'd better not. I need to get home. Get ready for tomorrow. I have an early morning and even longer day and I still have notes to check." Now she was overselling her decision.

"I understand. Maybe another time." There was a note of disappointment in his voice.

"Maybe." She couldn't afford to give him encouragement. Or herself any either. She moved to get into the car.

"Good luck tomorrow. I know you'll do great."

She gave him a tight-lipped nod as she climbed into her car. "I sure hope so."

He called, "Hey, Sweet Sally, I have faith in you."

She liked that idea. Wade had never encouraged her or made her feel confident. That Ross did bolstered her spirit. She felt special. Something she hadn't experienced where a man was concerned in a long time.

Ross had spent the day doing chores around the place and wondering how Sally was doing on her test. Why it mattered to him so much, he had no idea. Possibly because he knew it mattered to her. He was beginning to care too deeply for Sally. The last time he'd let someone in it had ended badly but for some reason he couldn't seem to resist Sally's pull.

He was glad that he could help her by giving her a place to study. The meals had been a pleasant surprise each evening. It had been fun to guess what would be waiting on him next. He feared he could get too accustomed to having a hot meal waiting on him. He'd probably gained five pounds over the week. Because of Sally his home seemed warmer and more inviting.

More than that, knowing Sally had been thinking about him had gotten to him on a level he didn't want to examine. Damn, he had it bad. He was starting to think like a sappy teenager.

What he should be doing was thinking about being Battalion Chief, planning what he wanted to say at his interview. He would tell the review committee that he wanted to use the position to help implement new and innovative firefighting techniques. He knew personally what fire could do to a person's life and he wanted to make positive changes where he could. For Austin to become a world-renowned department who used cutting-edge practices. As a member of the higher ranks, he could help make that happen. Maybe help keep a boy and his grandfather from ever being hurt in a fire. He hoped to help change the department for the better and, more important, save lives. That was what getting promotions had always been about for him since he'd started working at the fire department.

Finished with all he had planned to do for the day on the ranch, and thinking through his ideas for the interview, Ross still couldn't get Sally out of his mind. That afternoon he cleaned up and drove into town. He went by the farm supply store to pick up a few items. After making a couple more stops, he ended up at the fire station. Kody was working. Maybe he had heard from Sally. Just how long did one of those tests last?

He and Kody leaned against Ross's truck talking about nothing and everything. More than once Ross was tempted to ask him about Sally but stopped himself. He didn't want to be that obvious about how involved he was in her life.

"Lucy had a great time at your house the other day. Sally said she enjoyed it as well. I had no idea you were such a family man." Kody grinned.

He'd enjoyed their time together too but he wasn't going to let Kody know that. "I don't know about that. I'm pretty sure Sally got the short end of the stick. She did all the work. Three kids to watch is a handful."

"From everything she said, she had fun. She couldn't say enough about how much she liked your place." Kody sounded as if he were making casual conversation but for some reason Ross questioned that.

"Yeah, she came out this past week to study while I was at the training center."

Kody gave him a speculative look. "She didn't tell me that."

Ross shrugged. "She said she needed a quiet place to study, and I offered."

Kody's eyes narrowed. "She didn't say anything to me. Didn't ask to use my place."

It was Ross's turn to grin. "You don't expect her to tell you everything. You do know she's a grown woman?"

"Yeah, but I'm her big brother. It's my job to know what's going on. She's had a hard time of it."

"Little overprotective, are you?" Ross would be as well if Sally belonged to him. That wasn't going to happen. He couldn't let it. Still...

Kody huffed. "She says the same thing." He gave Ross a direct look. "I'm just concerned about her. She's been hurt badly in the past. I'd hate for her to go through that again."

Ross held up a hand. "Hey, you're jumping the gun here. We're just friends."

"I'm just sayin'—" Kody's phone rang and he pulled it out of his pocket, looking at the number. "Speak of the devil." Into the phone he said, "Sweet Pea." There was a pause, then, "Yeah." A pause. "Really? Call the auto club and have it towed in. Can you get a taxi home? I hate it but I'm at work."

"What's going on?" Ross asked. He sounded more concerned than he should have.

Kody studied him a second. "Sally's car won't start."

"I can go." He was already heading to the driver's door.

Kody looked a little surprised. "Okay." He said into the phone, "Ross is coming after you." There was quiet. "No, he offered. He's right here. He should be there in about twenty minutes. You get in the car and lock it. Don't open it for anyone except the tow driver or Ross."

"Tell her to stay put. I'm on my way. You text me the address." Ross hopped into his truck.

Ross shouldn't have been as happy as he was that Sally was having car trouble but it gave him an excuse to see her.

He made the drive in less than twenty minutes. Sally's car was parked near a walkway into a large glass-and-brick building on the Austin State University campus. There were only a few other cars in the lot. She was waiting in the car just as Kody had told her. When he pulled up, she got out. Wearing a light blue button-down shirt, jeans and ankle boots, Sally looked younger and more vulnerable than he knew she was.

She gave him a weak smile. "I appreciate you coming."

"Not a problem. I was at the house when you called. What seems to be wrong?" Sally looked exhausted, as if she had been through the mental mill.

"I don't know. It just wouldn't start. I've called the auto club and they're on their way but it'll be another forty minutes or so."

"Do you mind giving it a try?"

"Okay." She turned the key. The engine just made a grinding noise.

Ross opened the hood and moved the battery cables. He leaned around and called, "Try it again."

The car acted as if it wanted to come to life, then nothing.

Ross closed the hood as he shook his head. "You just got all my mechanical knowledge."

This time she grinned. "I guess it's a good thing the tow truck is on the way."

"Come on over to my truck and we'll wait there." He held the passenger door open for her.

Sally acted reluctant for a moment but gathered her purse and joined him in the truck.

Once inside he turned so he could see her face. "So how do you think you did on your test?"

She sighed deeply. "It was harder than I thought it would be. I don't know how I feel about it. I guess all that's left to do is cross my fingers."

He crossed his. "Mine'll be as well."

Sally rested her head back on the seat and closed her eyes. "I'm just glad it's over. I'm exhausted."

"When was the last time you had something to eat or drink?"

She opened her eyes to slits. "We had a lunch break, but I was too nervous to eat much."

"You stay put. I'm going to that convenience store across the road to get you a drink and something to eat. When we've taken care of your car, we'll stop and get you something more substantial." He opened his door and climbed out. "Lock the door while I'm gone. I'll be right back."

Sally murmured something but he suspected she was already half-asleep.

Ross made a quick walk across the parking lot to the store. When he returned, Sally was just as he'd assumed she would be—sound asleep. Her chin hung to her chest and she softly snored. Climbing in as quietly as possible, he gently put an arm around her shoulders and brought her head to his shoulder. She settled against him. Everything about the moment seemed right.

He pushed his disappointment away when all too soon the tow truck arrived. "Sally, wake up. The tow truck is here."

She moaned and burrowed closer to him, all warm and sweet.

"Sweet Sally, come on, wake up."

"What?" She blinked, looking perplexed.

"The tow truck is here."

She quickly sat up and shifted away. "Oh, yeah. Sorry."

"No problem."

She scooted out her door. He stepped out, joining her and the tow driver.

Half an hour later they were back in his truck and on their way.

Ross glanced at Sally. "I'm going to get you something to eat. Do you have a preference?"

"I want a big juicy burger." Just as she answered, thunder rumbled. The sky had been slowly darkening.

"Consider it done."

Ross pulled into the first fast-food place he came to and into the drive-thru line. While they were waiting for their food, the wind picked up. Thunder rolled and lightning flashed in the sky off to the west.

"Sally, I know you've had a tough day but would you mind if we run out to my place for just a moment before I take you home? The horses are out and in this weather they get nervous.

I hoped it would go north of us but it doesn't look like that's going to happen."

He handed her their bag of food as she answered, "I don't mind. With a nap and a burger, I'm ready to go. If I'm not, I need to learn to be, if I want to be a doctor."

She'd already finished her sandwich by the time they were on the outskirts of town. Ross glanced at her and grinned. "Good?"

There was no repentance in her smile. "I was starving."

He chuckled. "Would you like to have my other one?" Ross held up a second burger, still in its wrapper.

"No, that's not necessary," she said in a sassy tone. "But I'll have some of your fries if you aren't going to eat them."

"Well, that figures." He placed his container on the seat between them.

"What do you mean?" Her complete attention was on him. He liked it that way.

"They're the best thing you can order at that place. I like my fries super crispy."

"I do too." She plopped the last one of hers into her mouth and reached for his.

As they turned onto his drive, large raindrops hit the windshield. Angry lightning split the sky.

"Looks like it's going to be an ugly one," Sally said. "These are the kind of days that go by so fast at the house you don't know if you're coming or going. More traffic accidents than you can count."

Ross laughed and pulled the truck to a stop. "I've had more than my share of those days too. This shouldn't take long. The key is still under the mat. Make yourself at home. I'll be back in just a few minutes."

Sally watched Ross sprint off around the house toward the barn. The rain was coming down harder. Thunder and lightning were filling the sky in a regular rotation as she ran to the porch. She opened the door, going in and turning on a light. Stepping to the large picture window at the back of the house where the table was located, she searched for a glimpse of Ross at the barn.

She continued to look out the window as the storm grew. The rain fell hard enough to make it difficult to see. Minutes ticked by, enough she started to worry something had happened to Ross. Just as she was about to go out after him, he came through the back door in a burst of wind and water.

Grabbing a dish towel, she hurried to him and handed it over.

"Thanks." Ross took it and wiped his face.

"A tree came down on the fence. The horses are out. I've got to go after them and fix the fence. I'm sorry about this. You're welcome to stay here, or I can call you a taxi?" He pulled a kitchen closet door open. Rubber coats hung inside it. On the floor were mucking boots. Ross grabbed a jacket and boots, then went to a chair and started putting on the high-top rubber shoes.

Sally picked up a pair as well.

"What're you doing?" Ross gave her an incredulous look.

"I'm going with you." She sat at the table and started removing her shoes.

Ross returned to gearing up. "You don't need to do that. You've already had a long day."

"I'll survive. You don't even know where the horses are. You're gonna need help."

Ross opened his mouth.

"I wouldn't even bother arguing. I'm going." She pulled on a boot. It was too large but she would make do.

He grinned. "Figures."

As he shrugged into his coat, she picked out one and did as well.

"Ready?" Ross took two large flashlights off the shelf in the closet.

Sally pulled the cap up over her head. "Ready."

He nodded and opened the door.

She could hardly see with the storm blocking what little of the sun was still up. The angry sky made what light there was a spooky haze of yellow green. At least it wasn't completely dark. She didn't want to go crazy in front of Ross. Her silly childhood fear wouldn't impress him. At least having the flashlight would help her keep her sanity.

The rain blew sideways as she braced herself against the wind. It didn't take long for it to blow her cap back. She would just have to get wet. Ross headed toward the barn. She followed. As they went, she saw one of the giant limbs from the oak in the side yard had fallen on the fence.

"What're we doing in here?" Sally shook her coat as she entered the barn, relieved to get out of the wet for a moment. Her hair was drenched and the front of her jeans soaked.

"I wanted to get a couple of halters and leads." Ross went into a small tack room.

"Where do you think we'll find them?"

He called out to her as he moved around in the room. "I don't know. If the fence was up, I'd say in the trees out in the pasture. With the fence down, I'm not sure. I'm going to try out by the road first. I can't afford for them to cause an accident. In this weather cars can't see them."

Ross's concern was evident in his voice. He soon joined her again, carrying what he had come after. He handed her one of the halters. "This won't be a fun trip."

"I've done un-fun things before. Ready when you are." She wasn't going to let him stop her from helping, especially after he'd done so much for her.

"Hopefully they didn't go far." He had a resigned look on his face as he lowered his head and left the barn.

Sally joined him. He led the way down the drive. The wind let up some but the going was still difficult as they trudged along with their flashlights moving in a back-and-forth pattern in the hopes of seeing the animals. As they came to the paved road, there was still no sign of the horses. She could sense, by the hunch of his shoulders, Ross's frustration and concern. He moved the beam of light wider.

"I'm going to check those trees across the road," he shouted.

"Okay." She joined him and pointed her flashlight that way. There, standing under the trees, were the horses.

They sidestepped as if nervous as she and Ross approached.

Ross put his hand out, indicating she should hang back. He slowly approached them.

Sally could imagine him speaking softly to them. She'd bet he did the same when he made love. Ooh, she needed to concentrate. Thoughts like that did nothing to keep Ross in the friend slot where she had placed him.

Ross waved her forward. He handed her a lead attached to the halter on Juliet and took the halter she carried. She'd been right. He talked to Romeo the entire time he worked. It was solid and reassuring. Something she missed in her life.

"Ready?"

She nodded.

"Hold the halter and the lead." He demonstrated. "If there's more lightning, they may balk. They're pretty skittish."

Sally made sure to place her hands in the same position that Ross used. She'd been around horses some but never under these conditions. As Ross had suspected, the sky did light up again. Both Romeo and Juliet jumped and flinched but she managed to keep Juliet under control. Romeo reared but Ross soon calmed him.

"Let's get them in the barn." He started toward his place and she kept pace.

They made it to the barn without any more mishaps. Being in the dry again was like heaven. Slinging her wet hair out of her face, she looked at Ross. He was every bit as wet as she and it only made him look sexier.

He grinned. "Well, I'm glad that's over."

Sally couldn't agree more.

Ross led Romeo into a stall. She waited. He soon joined her and took Juliet to another stall.

When he returned this time he said, "I'll still have to go out and see about the fence. Do you mind giving them a couple of cups of oats? You'll find it in the tack room."

"I'll take care of them." Sally pushed at her hair but a strand stuck to her cheek.

Ross, using a finger, moved it away from her eyes. Their gazes met. "You were great out there, Sweet Sally." His hands went to her waist and he pulled her to him. "What would I do without you?"

For a second she thought he might kiss her. Thought how it would warm her from the inside out as a hot drink did on a cold night. This close, Ross smelled of rain, earth and healthy male. Alive.

But instead he let her go and left the barn, leaving a honeyed heat coursing through her veins.

Ross had expected Sally to go to the house when she'd finished with the horses but instead she stayed outside to help him. He had pulled the truck over so he could use the headlights to work by. Thankfully the rain had eased.

As he used the chain saw to cut limbs off the tree branch that had broken the fence, Sally pulled the debris out of the way. Wet and with the high pitch of the chain saw ringing in their ears, they worked side by side. They soon had the worst of it off the fence.

Ross cut off the saw. "Why don't you go on in the house and clean up? I have to get some tools and get this fence back into place. I'll finish the cleanup later. I'll be in soon."

"I can help you." She kept pulling limbs.

Was there anything that Sally couldn't do or wouldn't do? She was a special person. He put the saw in the shed and found the tools he needed to repair the fence. When he returned, she was still cleaning up the area.

Ross started removing the broken barbed wire.

Sally came to him. "What can I do to help?"

He picked up a tool. "Do you know how to handle a claw hammer?"

She lifted her chin. "I sure do."

He'd given up on encouraging her to get out of the weather. "Then go to the next post and start taking out the staples."

While he worked on replacing the wire on his post, Sally went to the next one. He joined her and she moved on to the next one. She was good help but he wasn't surprised by that, though he was thankful. Because of her he wouldn't be out all night repairing the fence.

An hour later she held the wire as he hammered the last staple into place.

"That'll do it until morning." Ross picked up his tools.

"Give me those. I'll put them away while you move the truck." Sally reached for the toolbox.

Ross let her have it and off she went to the shed. He found her again just inside the kitchen door, struggling to remove her boot. "Hey, let me help you with that. Hold on to the counter and I'll pull it off for you."

"It has been winning." She leaned her butt back against the counter, held on and lifted her foot.

Ross tugged and the boot slipped off. "Okay, the other one."

Sally lifted her other foot. He pulled that boot off as well and dropped it on top of the first one with a thump.

"You want help with yours?" she asked.

"No, I can get them." He started working his boot off. "What I'd really like is for you to head to the shower."

"I know you're used to giving orders—"

"All I want is for you not to get sick. I'll bring you some warm clothes to put on."

She put her hands on her hips and gave him an indignant look. "I'm made of stronger stuff than that."

He grinned. "I've no doubt of that, but just so I don't have to worry, humor me. Please? You're welcome to my shower or you know where the spare one is."

Sally glared at him for a second, then turned and walked toward the guest bathroom.

Disappointment jolted him. He wished she'd chosen his— with him in it.

Ross shucked off his clothes in his bathroom and pulled on a pair of shorts and a T-shirt. Going to his chest of drawers, he found a T-shirt and sweatpants for Sally.

He knocked on her bathroom door. The sound of running water reminded him that the only thing between him and a naked Sally was the door. He swallowed, then called, "There's some clothes on the floor for you."

"Okay, thanks."

Ross returned to his bathroom, turned on the shower to cold instead of hot.

When he came out to the living room again, he didn't expect to find Sally lying on his couch asleep. He shouldn't have been surprised. She'd had an emotionally hard day taking a life-changing test, then to have car trouble, wrangle horses and fix a fence in a storm. She'd withstood more than most and remained in a positive mood as she'd done them all. She had the right to fall asleep.

He quickly checked the station schedule on his phone to make sure she wasn't on duty the next day, then went to the spare bedroom to turn back the covers. Back in the living room, he lifted Sally into his arms, noting how slight she was for a woman with such a strong will. He carried her to the bed, covered her up and tucked her in. After a moment of hesitation, Ross placed a kiss on her forehead. "Thanks for all your help, Sweet Sally."

Ross had had hopes for a more satisfying kiss tonight. He had to admit he was disappointed. But Sally needed rest. He went to the kitchen looking for a snack. Opening the refrigerator, Ross searched it for some ideas. As usual, there was little there but he did have one more plateful of the last casserole Sally had made for him. He dished it out, warmed it in the microwave and sat down to watch a sports show.

Between shows he started their dirty clothes in the washing machine. He rarely had women's clothes joining his. There was something intimate about his and Sally's clothes comingling. Erotic and right at the same time.

Before going to bed, he went out to check on the horses. They were secure but thunder rolled in the distance. They were in for another round of bad weather. Inside again, he looked in on Sally. She was sleeping comfortably on her side, her hands in a prayerful manner under one cheek. Leaving the door ajar, Ross went to his room. He climbed into bed. Would he be able to sleep knowing Sally was just steps away?

Sometime later the sound of screaming jerked him awake. For a moment Ross was disoriented until he remembered that Sally was across the house. His eyes darted to the alarm clock on his bedside table. It was blank. The electricity was off. A scream ripped the air again. This time he had no doubt it came from Sally.

Rushing across the living room, he worked his memory not to stumble into the furniture. Too late he realized he hadn't paused long enough to pull on shorts or a shirt. He was only wearing his boxers. There was no time to turn back. Sally needed him.

Another shriek caused ripples down his spine. She sounded terrified.

Lightning flashed and he could see her huddled against the headboard. Her head was down in the pillow she clutched to her chest. She was sobbing and shaking in panic like a wounded animal.

He took a few steps into the room. "Sally, it's Ross." He kept his voice low so as not to scare her further. "I'm right here. Everything's okay. You're at my house. The electricity is off."

Lightning lit the sky once more.

Her eyes opened. There was a wild look there. They remained unfocused. She didn't recognize him. He moved to the bed. "It's Ross. It's going to be okay. I'll get some candles."

She gripped his forearm, her fingers digging in. "Don't go! Don't leave me."

The fear in her voice went straight to his heart. This was a side of Sally he'd never seen. He suspected few had. "Sweetie, I'm just going after candles. I'm coming right back."

"No." Her grip tightened. He'd have fingernail marks in the morning.

Ross sat on the bed and pulled her into his arms. Rocking softly, he said soothing nothings to her just as he had to the horses earlier. Sally seemed to ease. "I won't leave you."

Why was Sally so scared of the dark? She'd always acted so invincible.

He couldn't leave her, but they couldn't stay here all night. The bed was too small for both of them. If either one of them was going to get some rest, they had to go to his bed.

"Sally, I'm going to get up now. I'm going to carry you to my room. Hold on."

She made an unintelligible sound as he stood and lifted her into his arms. As she clung to him, he picked his way to his room without any missteps. He placed her on the side of the bed he'd been on and tucked the covers around her. Even in the darkness of the room he could see that her eyes were shifting from side to side with distress. "I'm going after candles. Just into the bath. I'll be right back."

In a weak voice she whined, "You won't leave me?"

"Sweetie, I'd never leave you. I'll be right back."

He hurried to the bathroom to gather the fat candle and matches he kept there for power outages. Placing the candle on the bedside table, he lit it. That little bit of light in the dark room removed most of the fear from Sally's eyes.

"Hold me." The words were low and sad.

She didn't have to ask him twice. He slid under the covers beside her and pulled her close. She shifted into him, sighed and her breath soon became warm and even against his neck.

CHAPTER SIX

SALLY WOKE TO the sun shining through the window of a room she didn't recognize. Her back was against a solid wall of heat. She moved her hand. Her palm brushed across coarse hair on the muscled arm around her waist.

A shiver of panic ran through her. Slowly glimpses of waking in the dark, terror absorbing her, Ross coming to her, then him carrying her to his bed settled in her mind.

Oh, heavens, she'd begged him to hold her.

Could she have embarrassed and humiliated herself more? She was a grown woman afraid of the dark. At her house she was prepared for events like the one last night. She always had a flashlight next to her bed and one in the kitchen and living room. In an unfamiliar place, she had come undone. How was she ever going to face him?

The mattress shifted beneath her. It was going to happen sooner rather than later. She moved to slip out from under Ross's arm.

"Sally, are you awake?" His voice was rusty from sleep, making him sound terribly sexy. Worse, he sounded worried about her.

How was she going to explain her bizarre behavior?

She continued to slide across the sheet until she was out of touching distance and as far away from him as the bed would allow. She was grateful it was king-size. She put her feet on the floor and turned from the waist to face him. At least she was still wearing the T-shirt and sweatpants he had loaned her. That gave her some armor in this uncomfortable state of affairs.

Ross quickly pulled on a T-shirt. The bedsheet covered his lower half. He was decent, yet she was too aware that moments earlier she had been in his arms, against his bare chest. He lay on his side with his head propped on his hand, waiting and watching her.

"Mornin'," he drawled, as if it were a regular occurrence to have her in his bed.

"Good morning." Sally paused. She must be the one to address the elephant in the room. Adjusting her position for comfort while searching his face, she reluctantly added, "Thanks for helping me last night. I guess you're wondering what happened."

"I'd like to hear the why, but right now I'd like to know if you're okay." He watched her too closely. As if he was gauging her emotional stability.

"Yes, yes, I'm fine, except for being extremely embarrassed." She glanced out the window to the side of the house. From here she could see the damaged part of the fence and the barn. The sky was clear. It all looked so peaceful now. A complete one-eighty from the upheaval in her.

"I'm sorry I had to bring you to my bed. I hope you haven't taken it the wrong way. We both wouldn't fit in that smaller bed and you wouldn't let me go. We needed someplace to sleep."

Heat washed through her. The best she could tell, the section of his bed they had been sleeping on was approximately the same size as the bed in the other room. Had she moved next to him? Or had he stayed close to her? It didn't matter now. What did matter was that it should not happen again. Even if it had been nice to wake up to.

"It's okay." She tried to make it sound far more insignificant than it was to her. "You don't owe me an explanation. I know I was acting crazy."

He lifted a corner of his mouth. "I'd go with 'out of character.'"

Sally winced. "You're being kind. I think *crazy* is accurate."

"I'd like to know what happened, but only if you want to tell me." Curiosity was written all over his face as he waited, his eyes not leaving her.

She crossed her legs and settled more comfortably on her side of the bed. Ross had a way of putting her at ease even when she didn't like the subject.

"When I was a kid, a group of us were playing hide-and-seek. I hid in a trunk. One of the kids thought it would be funny to lock me in. I was stuck there for hours before my mother found me. Now I'm terrified of the dark and small spaces. Silly, I know. My ex-husband used to make fun of me all the time."

A dark look covered his features. "I don't think it's silly. Everyone's scared of something. They may not show it, but it's there anyway."

"Yeah, right. Like you're afraid of anything. I've seen you run into a burning building."

His look was unwavering. "I assure you, I am."

"Like what?" It was suddenly important that she know. Ross seemed invincible to her.

He shifted, acted unsure, not meeting her eyes. It was as if he had said more than he'd intended. But sharing her own fear had made her realize how important it was for him too. "So tell me. What're you afraid of?"

"You aren't going to let this go, are you?" His words were flat.

"No. You know my secret. I promise not to share yours."

"Turn your head."

It was an order but she did as he requested. The mattress lifted, letting her know Ross had stood. What was he doing?

"You can look now." Ross was wearing a pair of shorts and

walking toward the window on his side of the room. He spoke to the windowpane. "I don't make a habit of telling this. In fact, I don't ever tell this."

Sally moved around the bed to sit where he had lain. It was still warm.

"Remember I told you about the fire that took my grand-daddy's house?"

"I do." She'd thought of that boy many times.

"There was more to the story."

She held her breath. This wouldn't be good.

"As I was coming out of the door of the house, part of the ceiling fell on me. My shoulder was burned."

Sally sucked in her breath.

"I have some ugly scars as reminders of that night." His shoulders tensed.

She wanted to reach out to him. "So that's why you always wear a shirt. I'm sorry, Ross, I had no idea."

"Few people do. Like I said, I don't share this with everyone." There was an emotion in his voice she couldn't put a name to. Disappointment? Fear? Uncertainty?

"Why're you telling me?"

"Because you wanted to know, and I didn't want you to think you were the only one with hang-ups."

Goodness, he was a nice guy. Sally had forgotten that there were men who had compassion for others. She arose and went to him, placing a hand on his shoulder. "Thank you for trusting me with your secret."

He flinched.

Sally took a step back. She shouldn't have touched him. Especially his back.

Ross said something under his breath and turned to meet her gaze. He reached for her. She stumbled against him. Seconds later his lips found hers. His kiss was hungry, igniting something long dormant in her. Her arms reached around his neck and pulled him tight. She would have crawled up him if she could. She couldn't get close enough.

They were two hurting souls who carried secrets that had found release by sharing with each other.

Ross teased the seam of her mouth and she opened to him. Her tongue greeted his like a long-lost friend. His danced and played with hers until her center throbbed with need.

"Sweet Sally," Ross whispered against her jaw as he kissed his way up to nibble at her ear. She shivered. "I always want you to touch me. Please touch me."

How could she resist such a tempting invitation? Her fingers found the hem of his shirt and she ran her hands upward over his chest. It was as firm with muscles as she remembered. The little brushing of hair was soft and springy. Her hands traveled to his waist then on to his back.

"It feels so good to be touched by you. I've dreamed of this too many nights." Ross kissed behind her ear.

He'd been dreaming of her? Her heart picked up a beat. She brought his mouth back to hers and kissed him with all the desire that had been building for days. He was the kindest, most caring and charming man she knew. A hero in every way.

While she kissed him, his hand pulled at her shirt. Lifting it, he drew it off and dropped it to the floor as his mouth floated over the top of one of her breasts. She shuddered from the pleasure. He stepped back and looked at her for a moment. "So perfect."

Ross lifted a breast as his head bent and his wet, warm mouth slipped over her nipple. The throbbing in her core pounded as her blood ran red hot. He slowly sucked and worshipped first one breast then the other. She closed her eyes, absorbing the pleasure of having Ross touch her as she ran her hands through his hair, savoring every tantalizing movement of his tongue. She'd found another of his talents.

When Ross broke the contact, she sighed in disappointment. He gave her an intense look, desire blisteringly strong in his eyes. Swinging her into his arms, he carried her to the bed and laid her gently on it. "I want you, Sweet Sally. I desire you with everything in me. What happens between us is up to you. You have the control."

She opened her arms to him.

"Say it, Sally. Say you want me. I need to hear it."

Her gaze met his. "How could I not want you, Ross? Of course I want you. Please."

He tugged his borrowed sweatpants off her, leaving her bare to him. She grabbed for the sheet but his hand stopped her.

"No, I want to see you in the morning light. You're so amazing."

He studied her with such intensity that she blushed all over. Sally looked away but not before she saw the length of Ross's manhood pushing against the front of his shorts. He desired her. After learning she wasn't enough for Wade, it was exhilarating to see visual evidence of Ross's need for *her*.

"This is unfair. You need to take your clothes off." She almost whined.

There was a swish of material and her eyes jerked back to him. His manhood was even more impressive without covering. Ross put a knee on the bed as if he were coming down to her.

She placed a hand on his chest. "Shirt too. I want to touch, see you."

"But…"

Her heart went out to him, but she wouldn't let him think he wasn't good enough in every way. "Ross, I trusted you and you need to trust me."

His face showed pain seconds before he murmured. "Others have been disgusted."

She rose so that she could cup his face. Turning it back to her, she gave him a long kiss. "I'm not those others. You're more than your scars to me."

His earnest eyes found hers. "I want you too badly. I can't take the chance."

"Sit down." She patted the bed beside her. He stepped back, looking hesitant. She sat up, trying to appear more assured than she felt, especially since she was naked in the daylight in front of Ross. She needed him to decide what the next move would be.

Slowly, Ross sat next to her. She kissed his arm at his shoulder. "I want to see. After this first time, it won't matter ever again between us. I want to admire all of you. I don't want just part of you."

Moments passed. Finally, he removed his shirt in one quick jerky motion. He put his elbows on his knees.

She didn't look at his back right away. Instead she ran her hand lightly across his shoulders. He flinched but settled. Her fingers gently touched each dip and pucker. "Such strong shoulders. You have to remember I've seen what they're capable of. Felt them hold me."

Some of the tension in him eased away.

Sally looked at his back. Covering one entire shoulder blade were wrinkled, reddish marks and twisted skin. She drew in a breath, not from the ugliness of the sight but from the horror of the pain Ross must have experienced. Moisture filled her eyes. Her heart broke for him.

Ross moved to stand. Her fingers wrapped his biceps, stopping him as she laid her head against his arm. "I'm so sorry you had to go through that. It must've hurt beyond words."

He eased back to the bed but there was still stiffness in his body.

Sally moved so she was on her knees behind him. She placed her lips on his damaged skin. Ross hissed. His skin rippled.

"You don't want to do that." His voice was gruff.

How had other women acted when they saw him? What had they said to this amazing man to make him feel so unworthy, ashamed of himself? Her tears fell. Didn't he know how special he was? She placed her hands on his shoulder, keeping him in place. She gently kissed the scarred area, then worked her way to the nape of his neck.

She wrapped her arms under his, pressing her breasts against his bare back. Her hands traveled over his chest as she continued to kiss him. First the back of his ear, then his cheek. Her hands dipped lower, to tease his belly button, then to brush his hard length.

With a growl that came from deep within his throat, Ross twisted and grabbed her, flipping her to the bed. His mouth found hers in a fiery kiss.

Ross's length throbbed to the beat of his racing heart. When had a woman made him feel so wanted, needed? Undamaged? Ross couldn't get enough of Sally. Of her tenderness, concern, her compassion. It had taken his breath away when she had kissed his scars. As if she had peeled away all the hurt associated with them. No one had ever understood what it had been like for him as a boy or a man to carry those scars. Until Sally. She had cried for him. He'd seen her eyes.

He would make it his mission to give her all the pleasure she deserved, in and out of bed. Her breasts had been silky against his back when she had pressed against him. It had been years since he'd allowed a woman to see his deformity, to remove his shirt. To know all of him, even the broken parts. The wonder of being so close heightened his desire for Sally.

He cupped her breast and swept his thumb across her nipple until it rose and stiffened. His mouth surrounded it, his tongue swirling. Sally moaned and lifted her hips against him.

"Easy, Sweet Sally, we've all day, if you wish."

He left her breast to place a kiss on her shoulder blade. Her hands flexed on his back in a begging motion. His lips took hers as his hand glided over her waist, along her hip to her thigh. It circled to the inside of it, then returned to her hip. He was rewarded by her legs parting in invitation.

Ross accepted it. His hand fluttered near her heat. Asking, then begging, before he ran a finger over her opening.

The purring sound that came from Sally increased his hunger to a consuming need.

He dipped his finger into her hot center. She squirmed. Slipping it in completely, he then pulled it out. Sally trembled. Her tongue, entwined with his, mimicked the movement of his finger. Lifting her hips, she pushed toward him. Holding her tight, he entered her again and increased the pace. She arched against him, her body tensing before she broke their kiss and eased to the bed. Her eyes drifted closed on a soft sigh.

Ross was gratified by her pleasure. But he wanted to give her more. She deserved it. He rose over her and kissed her deeply. Her arms circled his neck. She returned his kisses with her own. Her lips went to his cheek, his temple, to his neck, then down to his chest. Her hands ran over him with abandon. When they went to his shoulders, he faltered, but Sally didn't slow her movements. He forgot his apprehension and concentrated his thoughts on the feel of Sally's hands touching him, bringing him closer.

Ross captured her hands and gave her a gentle kiss before he rolled away from her. Fumbling with his bedside-table drawer, he located the package he was looking for. He looked down at Sally. She looked beautiful and bereft at the same time. Opening the package, he covered himself. His gaze met hers. "Are you sure?"

"Oh, yes, I'm sure." She drew him back to her.

Ross settled between her legs. His tip rested just outside her heat. Supporting himself on his forearms, he leaned down to give her a long slow kiss. Slowly he entered her. And with a final push he found home.

He almost pulled out completely before he drove into her again. His mouth continued to cover hers. Sally lifted her hips to his, meeting and matching his rhythm until they created their own special tempo. She quivered as her fingers dug into his back. He pushed harder, his pleasure growing.

On a cry of ecstasy, Sally stiffened and relaxed against the bed. He groaned and followed her into a joyous oblivion he'd never known before.

* * *

Ross woke to the sound of water running in the bathroom. Sally came into the room, wearing her own clothes. Apparently, she'd gone looking for them in the dryer. Her hair was pulled back and damp strands framed her face. His chest expanded with pride. She had the looked of a woman recently fulfilled.

"You're awake."

He frowned as she didn't meet his eyes. He didn't want any uncomfortable moments between them. He smiled. "I am, but I missed you when I woke."

She blinked. "You did?"

"I did." Ross sat up. "You could've woken me. I would've liked that."

Sally gave him a perplexed look. "Really?"

They watched each other for a moment. What was she thinking? Had he said something wrong? "Yeah. Who wouldn't want you beside them?"

The worried look across her features disappeared, then she smiled. "Thank you. That's not what I'm used to. My ex-husband didn't like for me to linger in bed. He always wanted me to get up and get a shower."

Ross wanted to hit something. "Look at me, Sally."

She did.

Hopefully she could see the sincerity in his eyes. "You're welcome to stay in bed with me as long as you want or you're free to leave whenever you want. It's up to you. I want you to understand this next part. It's very important that you do." He paused. "I promise I'm nothing like your ex-husband. I don't, nor will I ever, control your actions. You can always trust me, and I'll always be honest with you. Inside and outside of bed."

"Oh."

"Yes, oh. And by the way, right now, I'd like to have your sweet lips on mine but if that isn't what you want, then that's fine."

Her eyes opened and closed a couple of times before a smile

came to her lips. She came to him. Placing her hands on his shoulders, she leaned down. Her kiss was hot and suggestive, setting him on fire again. When he tugged her toward the mattress, she stepped away.

Looking down at him, she teased, "Hey, I need some food if I'm going to keep up with you."

"Okay, let me get a shower and I'll take you out to eat." Ross flipped the sheet back. He didn't miss the sparkle of interest in her eyes as she looked at him.

"Uh...you don't have to do that. I'll see what I can find in the kitchen." She stepped toward the door.

Ross headed toward the bathroom, chuckling. "Good luck with that."

It wasn't until the water was running over him that he realized that he'd been completely naked in front of another person without being self-conscious. And Sally's look had been an admiring one. What miracle had she performed on him?

Done with his shower, he found Sally busy in the kitchen. "I see you found something. It smells wonderful." He walked up behind her, giving her a kiss on the neck. "What're you fixing?"

"I found enough for an omelet and some toast. That work for you?"

"It does. As usual, I'm impressed. Your cooking is one of the many things I like about you." He turned her to give her a proper kiss. "What can I do to help?"

"How about getting a couple of plates for me and setting the table while I finish up these eggs?"

He did as she requested. She plated an omelet and started on another. He took the bread out of the toaster and added it to the plates. She carried those to the table while he filled her glass with water and poured himself a cup of coffee. At the table, Ross sat beside her instead of across from her. He wanted her within touching distance.

They ate for a few minutes, then Sally said, "I called about my car. It's going to be Monday or Tuesday before they can get to it. I know you've a lot of things to do around here so I hate to ask you to take me home." She looked away from him. "But I'd really rather not have Kody come get me. He'd ask a bunch of questions I don't want to answer."

Ross understood that. Kody was protective, even making his position clear to Ross. He didn't want the third degree from him either. "Do you have any plans for today?"

Sally shook her head. "No, other than I'd planned to sleep and not open a book."

"You could do that here, if you want. I'll be glad to run you home, but I first need to check on a few things around here after the storm."

"Do you mind if I help?" She leaned forward as if eager to do so.

The women he knew were generally more interested in their fingernails than doing manual labor. He couldn't keep his surprise out of his voice. "Sure, if you want."

"If you don't want me to…"

He reached across the table and took her hand. "I'll take any help I can get, anytime, especially if it's yours."

That put a smile on her face.

"I need to see about Romeo and Juliet. They need to be let out into the pasture. Then we need to check the fence—since I did the work in the dark there may be more repairs. Next is the tree. You sure you're in for all that?"

"I'm sure." Sally smiled as she cut off a bite of omelet and forked it into her mouth.

After eating, they cleaned up the table and kitchen together. With that done they once again pulled on the high boots and headed outside.

"Horses first." Sally walked beside him toward the barn.

"Yep." They took a few more steps before Ross asked, "Do you mind telling me about your ex-husband?"

She was quiet for a moment. Ross feared he might be ruining things between them, but he needed to know about the man who had clearly done Sally so much hurt.

"There's not much to tell. We were only married for a little over a year. He was the Mr. It in our part of the world. The football quarterback from a prominent family, the good-looking guy, the one with the best car. Why he looked at me, I have no idea."

"I know why. Because you're great," Ross assured her. She was an amazing person. Why wouldn't she recognize that?

"Thanks. That's always nice to hear but harder to believe after being married to Wade."

"Based on what you said earlier I'm guessing your ex was pretty controlling." Ross glanced at her, measuring her reaction to his statement.

"It turns out he was. I didn't realize it at first. Maybe it was there all along and I just didn't want to see it. I was already working as an EMT when we married. I have always dreamed of being a doctor. Wade knew that, but he didn't want me to go to school. I gave it up for him. It turns out that he didn't give up anything for me. Including his girlfriends."

Ross stopped short and looked at her. "What're you talking about?"

"Kody didn't tell you?"

"Tell me what?" For those who knew him well, they'd have recognized his ominous tone.

"Wade ran around on me. He started about six months into our marriage. I tried to make it work. Crying, begging, counseling—nothing worked."

Ross blurted a harsh word before bringing her into a hug. "You deserved better than that. It's a good thing he doesn't live in town or I'd beat him to a pulp with my bare hands."

She gave him a watery grin and started walking again. "That's close to what Kody said. I guess I just wasn't enough for Wade."

"Enough?" Ross followed her. He couldn't believe what he was hearing.

"Of course you were, and still are. You're *more* than he deserved." He gave her a look he hoped showed her just how sexy and desirable she was. "I should know."

They entered the barn.

Her smile was appreciative, but her eyes still said she didn't totally believe him. "Kody encouraged me to move out here because he didn't want me facing people every day who knew the truth. At first, I wasn't brave enough to make the move, then I decided I had to."

Ross cupped her face. "You're brave in every way I can think of."

"That's nice of you to say."

Ross lifted her chin with a finger. "Hey, I'm not being nice. I'm telling you the truth."

Putting her hands flat on his chest, she backed him against the wooden stall gate and kissed him with a passion he'd only dreamed of. His hand slipped under her shirt and found the warm skin there. Her finger curled into his jean loops and brought his hips tightly against her. His body became rocket hot. He was going to have her right here on the barn floor.

Only the whinny and nuzzle of a horse's nose against his head brought Ross back to reality. He and Sally chuckled and patted Juliet.

"She must be jealous." Sally grinned.

"Or just hungry," Ross quipped as he opened the stall door and brought the horse out. He ran his hand over her coat and looked at her legs.

"Is anything wrong?" Sally asked, standing nearby.

"Nope. Just making sure she didn't get hurt in the storm." He then let the horse wander out of the barn into the pasture. He gave Romeo the same care before letting him go. "Now to the fun stuff."

They went to the shed, collected his tools and headed for the fence.

"You want to do fence work again? Worse, stack wood?" Ross still couldn't believe Sally was choosing to do that type of work.

"Sure. You could use the help, couldn't you?"

"It would be nice to have." And it would.

She shrugged. "I'm a captive audience."

"I can take you home first." Ross was really hoping she would stay. He enjoyed her company. Sally looked unsure for a moment. Did she think he wanted her to leave? "Hey, you're welcome here for as long as you want. I'm glad to have you anytime."

Her expression eased. "I like it here. I just don't want to overstay my welcome."

He stepped to her and took the tips of her fingers in his, not daring to bring her any closer for fear he'd never get the work done. "That could never happen. Stay all day..." his voice lowered "...all night too."

She looked at him and gave him a soft smile. "I'd like that."

His heart soared. "Then it's settled. Now, let's get to work. When we get the fence and tree taken care of, I'll cook you the best steak you've ever eaten and show you the stars."

That put a teasing smile on her face. "You're cooking?"

He tapped the end of her nose. "You just wait and see."

Over the next few hours they worked together making the fence stronger and cleaning up the limb that had fallen. Ross couldn't have asked for better help. Sally seemed to know what he needed done before he had to ask.

"You've done this kind of work before," Ross stated as he stacked firewood from the truck at the back of the house.

"More than once. My father believes that every woman needs to be prepared for what comes along. Kody and I were expected to help out the same."

"Smart father."

She smiled. "I think so. For me to do things like this used to drive my ex-husband crazy. His idea of work was to call someone on the phone."

Ross had heard enough about her lousy husband. He didn't want to hear any more. "You're welcome to do as much or as little as you want. I'm happy for the company."

She looked off toward the grazing horses in the pasture. "This is such a great place. How could you not like working on it?"

"I feel the same way." Ross threw the last log on the pile. "Let's clean up and go pick out our steaks."

"I was thinking, since I have limited clothes and these are dirty again, I'd stay here and take a nap and let you pick mine out."

He walked into her personal space and looked into her face, flushed from vigorous activity. "You trust me that much?"

"And more."

Ross raised a brow. "More?"

"Sure. Let's see, I've seen you run into a burning building and save a man's life, watched you care for your niece and nephew, and you saved me when my car broke down. You're a hero. All you're missing is a cape. I think I can trust you with a steak."

He swaggered his shoulders. "Put that way, I do sound pretty impressive. But you forgot one thing."

Her brows grew together in thought. "What's that?"

"How good I am in bed."

Sally's cheeks turned pink. "That goes without saying."

Male satisfaction swirled through him and he leaned into the heat of her. "It does, does it?"

She slapped at his arm. "Don't get too full of yourself. Now you're fishing for compliments."

Ross wrapped an arm around her waist and pulled her tight against him, kissing her soundly. He wiggled his eyebrows wickedly. "I'm even better in the shower. Want to find out?"

Hours later Sally stretched like a cat in the summer sun. The sound of Ross's truck returning had woken her from a nap on the swing. She smiled. He was right, he did have talents under running water. They'd made love in the shower and then on the bed before he'd dressed and left for the store. Made love? Was she falling in love?

She sat up. What was she doing playing house with Ross? She had plans that didn't include him. She'd temporarily lost her mind. But she couldn't deny that she liked being around him. He was fun, interesting, exciting. All the things she'd been missing in her life for too long. Just seeing his smile made her happy.

No, she wouldn't go down that road anytime soon. She had her life planned out and she wasn't going to deviate, not even for someone as wonderful as Ross. But why couldn't they be friends? Enjoy each other's company for a while? After all, it had only been a couple of days. What she had to do was see that things between them stayed fun and easy. Nothing messy. She'd had messy and wasn't going there again.

Sally stood to meet Ross. He stepped out of the truck with both hands full of grocery bags. He was so handsome that it almost took her breath. What made him even more appealing was that he had no idea of how incredible he was.

His smile was bright and sincere. He appeared as glad to see her as she was him. She liked that. Now she could see that her husband had never looked that way when he'd returned to her.

"Hey, sleepyhead, I can see you've been hard at it."

She leaned against the porch rail. "You told me to take it easy."

He started up the steps. "I didn't say that."

"That's what I heard."

Ross chuckled. The sound was rough but flowed like satin over her nerves. That was him. Metal on the outside and cotton on the inside.

"You need help?" She reached for the bags.

"Not with these but there's a couple more bags in the truck." He gave her a quick kiss.

Sally held the door open for him, then went to the truck. She returned with two more bags and a bundle of flowers.

Ross was unwrapping a steak from white butcher paper when she joined him. "The flowers are beautiful."

"I thought you might like them."

She narrowed her eyes at him but grinned. "Are you romancing me, Ross Lawson?"

He gave her a kiss. "Would it be all right if I were?"

Her heart skipped a beat. She loved the concept but she had to make sure things didn't get too serious. "You do know that for both of our sakes we have to keep this uncomplicated?"

"I do, but that doesn't mean I can't give a friend flowers, does it?" He pulled out a couple of baking potatoes then a loaf of bread from one of the bags.

When he put it that way it was hard to argue with him. "Can I help you do anything?"

He continued to sort items. "Nope. Tonight's your night off. I'm gonna cook for you, if you don't mind?"

"I don't mind at all." In fact, it was sweet of him. She wasn't used to people doing things for her.

Ross turned on the oven and put the potatoes in. "It'll be about an hour before it's ready. You're welcome to keep me company or go back out to the swing."

"Do you mind if I pick out some music?"

"No, as long as it's country and western." He gathered some spices.

"That figures." She went to his stereo beneath the TV and found a radio station. "I'm going to at least set the table."

"Okay. And do you mind seeing to the flowers? They're *not* my thing."

Ross prepared them a lovely meal that included flowers in the center of the table. While they ate, they talked about music, movies and TV shows they liked.

It was just what Sally needed, relaxed and enjoyable. Ross was good company. Why didn't he already have a special someone? "Have you ever been married?"

His head jerked up from where he'd been cutting his steak. "That came out of the blue."

She lifted a shoulder and let it drop. "You're such a good guy I was just wondering why you aren't taken."

"I think there was a compliment in there somewhere but, to answer your question, I was engaged once."

Somehow it hurt her that he'd had someone he'd cared enough about to ask to marry him. "You were?"

He nodded. "Alice. She's a local Realtor."

Sally knew who she was. "She's the one with her picture on the billboard."

"Yep, that's the one."

Sally stopped eating and rested her chin on her palm, watching him. "So what happened?"

He put down his fork and knife. "It turns out she hated my job. And my scars were a constant reminder of the danger. After a while she just said she couldn't do it anymore. To make her happy I was going to have to give up being a fireman, and that I couldn't do. She couldn't get past her fear, so we broke it off."

"I'm sorry, Ross." She understood the pain of knowing you weren't what the person you loved wanted.

"I have to admit it took me a while to get over her, but we would've been miserable. I could've never made her happy. I know that now."

Sally reached across the table and squeezed his hand.

They finished their meal and cleaned up.

When the last dish was put away, Ross said, "Dessert will be under the stars. It'll be dark soon. I have a few things to get together. While I do that, would you look in my closet and find something to keep you warm and bring me that sweatshirt hanging on the chair in my room? I'll meet you at the truck."

She did as he asked and was waiting beside the truck when he came out of the house with a basket in hand. Under his other arm was a large bundle. He put both in the back of the truck.

He held the door open for her. "Hop in."

Ross turned the truck around and started down the drive. He drove about halfway and stopped, turned off the truck and got out, leaving the door open. "Stay put. I'll be right back."

She leaned out the door. "Is something wrong?"

"Nope. This is where we were going."

She laughed as she watched him through the rear window. He climbed into the truck bed and unrolled the bundle. With it flat, he returned to the cab and plugged a cord into the electrical outlet. Seconds later an air mattress started to fill.

The pump was so loud she couldn't question him until the mattress was full. She called out the door once more, "Hey, Captain Lawson, this is starting to get a little kinky."

He came to the door and gave her a suggestive grin while he removed the cord. "Normally, I would've driven out into the pasture but with the storm last night it's too wet. So I'm improvising. Give me a few more minutes and I'll have everything ready. Don't look."

It was hard but she did as he asked.

Moments later he returned and offered her his hand. "Okay, come with me." He guided her around to the end of the truck. The tailgate was down. There was a sleeping bag spread out over the air mattress and another lay along the tailgate, making a cushion. Off to the side was the basket.

"What's all this?"

"Dessert under the stars like I promised." Ross looked proud of himself.

"Looks nice." She was impressed with the thought he'd put into doing something nice for her. Sally smiled at him. "I'm not sure about your plans for that mattress."

"Have you ever lain on a metal bed of a truck?"

"No."

He grinned. "Trust me, you'll like the mattress better."

His hands went to her waist and he lifted her to sit on the tailgate. He joined her, then reached for the basket. "Would you like a beer?"

"Sure."

He opened the basket and gave her a long-necked bottle with a Texas Star on the label.

Sally took a swallow. "It's good."

"I have a friend who microbrews this." Ross took a long draw on his before he reached into the basket again and pulled out a prepackaged chocolate cake with a filling. He offered it to her. "Dessert?"

A laugh bubbled out of her. She took it. "My favorite. Thanks."

He pulled his own out. "I aim to please."

They ate while swinging their legs, occasionally intertwining them as they watched the sun set. When the stars started to pop out, Ross put their empty bottles in the basket along with their trash.

"It's time to climb on the mattress. You go first, otherwise we might bounce the other one over the side."

Sally giggled and scrambled onto the mattress. When Ross joined her, she floated up, then down as if she were on a trampoline as he settled beside her. He pulled the sleeping bag they had been sitting on over them.

"Come here." Ross reached for her. She settled her head on his shoulder.

Over the next hour they lay there huddled in their own cocoon of warmth and silence watching the black sky fill with sparkling stars that looked like diamonds thrown across velvet. It was the most perfect hour of her life. One that she didn't dare hope to repeat.

Ross rolled toward her. His hand slipped under her shirt and traveled over her stomach as his mouth found hers. They made love beneath the stars.

She was wrong. It was the most perfect night of her life. So perfect Sally was sorry it couldn't last forever.

CHAPTER SEVEN

ROSS GLANCED AT Sally as he pulled into the auto-repair place Monday afternoon. The last couple of days together had been wonderful, but it had to stop. What was going on between them was surely nothing more than hot sex between two ambitious workaholics. She would be going back to work tomorrow. Him the next day. One day soon they'd be sharing the same shift. What then? He wasn't that good of an actor.

For them to date, or whatever they were doing, was against department policy even if they did somehow find time for it. Sally was bent on becoming a doctor. He had the promotion to think about and nothing could get in the way of that. If the word got out...

They hadn't said much on the ride in. It was as if Sally was working through what the last few days had meant just as he was. Could she be as uncertain of what was developing between them as he?

After pulling into a parking spot, he turned off the truck and took a moment to gather his thoughts, then looked at Sally. Her attention seemed focused on something out the front windshield.

"Sally—"

"Ross—"

They both gave each other weak smiles.

"You go first," Ross said.

"I'm not sure how this is supposed to go. I've not been in this position before." Her words were slow and measured.

This didn't sound like something he wanted to hear. But he couldn't disagree with her.

"Ross, I had a wonderful weekend."

Now he was sure it wasn't something he wanted to hear. "Why do I think there's a 'but' coming?"

She shrugged. "Because there is. I think we need to chalk this up to just that, a nice weekend. We need to just be friends."

"Ugh, that's the worst thing a woman can say to a man." Still, he couldn't argue with the wisdom of what she was saying.

Sally touched his hand for a moment, then withdrew it. "I really like you. But I can't be distracted from what I'm working toward."

"I'm a distraction?" He rather liked that idea.

She offered him a real grin then. "Yeah, you're a big distraction. I just think we need to stop this before it gets out at the house, or we get too involved. I don't have time in my life for this...whatever it is. It was a great weekend. Let's leave it at that."

Now she was starting to talk in circles. Yet those were the same thoughts spinning in his head.

She continued. "I think all we'd be doing is complicating each other's lives."

That was an understatement. She'd already gotten further under his skin than any woman since Alice. Yet being in a relationship with a person he worked with could only mean disaster.

"Besides that, I promised myself after my divorce I wouldn't be sidetracked from what I want ever again."

That statement didn't sit well with him. He didn't want her to change her dreams for him. "You think I want you to give up what you want?"

"No, I just think I'd eventually do it for you. I have before."

Ross didn't like that statement any better, but he could understand it. "I want to be Chief one day. Us seeing each other could be a problem. A big one."

She waved her hand. "See, that's just what I'm talking about. It makes sense that we just remain friends, no more. It would make life too complicated for us to date."

"I think you're right." So why did it seem so wrong? He reached and took her hand. "Good friends."

She squeezed his hand. "Very good friends."

"May this friend give his best friend one more kiss before she goes?" Could he survive if she said no?

She gave him a sad smile. "I'd like that. You're a fine man, Ross."

"You're really sweet, Sally."

He brought her to him and gave her a kiss that quickly turned from friendly to hot.

Sally broke away. "See you around, Ross." She opened the door and was gone.

Why did he feel as if he'd just agreed to something he might regret?

The next few days were long. He missed Sally. Wanted to see her, talk to her, touch her. Even being at his place didn't feel the same. He went into work for the first time with little enthusiasm simply because she wouldn't be there. He didn't like this arrangement and he was going to tell her so. There must be another way.

As soon as his shift was over, he would go to her place and talk to her. See if she felt the same.

Ross was walking in the direction of his truck the next day at the end of his shift, just after noon, when Kody called his name. He turned.

"Hey, man, you want to play some hoops for an hour or so? I don't have to pick up Lucy until three."

"No, not today. I've got something I need to take care of."

Like convincing your sister to come back to my bed.

"Well, okay. Talk to you later."

"Yeah." Ross climbed into his truck. Kody was a hurdle he'd have to face one day soon. Maybe he and Sally could keep their relationship from him and the department until it fizzled out, which it surely would. In the meantime, he wasn't ready to give up on Sally. Hopefully, she was of the same mind-set.

Ross pulled up in front of her apartment building ten minutes later. The work crew had moved on to the next building but they still made it difficult to find a parking place. Sitting with his hands on the steering wheel, Ross studied Sally's front door. What was he going to do if she wasn't home? Worse, if she didn't want to talk to him? He hated to appear desperate to see her, but he was. What if she rejected him? He'd been dodging that emotion for years. It didn't matter. He needed to see her, talk to her. Tell her how he felt.

Climbing out of the truck, he walked to the door with determination. He raised his hand to knock and lost his nerve for a moment. Then he knocked.

Sally had done most of the talking last time. Now he was going to do it. Maybe he could change her mind. He wasn't going to know until he tried.

He didn't hear any movement. Fear she wasn't home swamped him. He thought of returning to his truck, but then the latch moved. Moments later the door opened. Sally's questioning expression quickly turned to one of pure joy.

It filled him too. He smiled and opened his arms.

She squealed and jumped into them. Hers circled his neck. He chuckled, stepped inside and kicked the door closed with the heel of his shoe. She rained kisses over his face as he backed her against the wall.

"I know we shouldn't be doing this but I missed you." Desperation filled her voice.

He chortled with pleasure. "I guessed that." His mouth took hers in a hot, hungry kiss. She could have missed him only half as much as he'd missed her. It was heaven to have her body against his again.

"What're you doing here?" Sally asked between breathless kisses.

"I wanted to talk to you."

She pulled at his shirt. "Is that all you wanted?"

"Hell, no," he growled, returning his mouth to hers as he worked at the snap of her pants.

Sally had been longing for Ross, but hadn't known how much until she'd seen him in her doorway. Her heart had almost flown out of her chest with excitement. Her neighbors would have thought she had lost her mind if they had seen her acting like a kid at Christmas.

As she and Ross lay in bed, she scattered kisses on top of his chest as her hand roamed his middle.

She was in trouble. Once again she'd gone over the line into the land where her heart was becoming involved. The problem was she didn't know how to step back to safe ground. What she had to guard against now was making the mistake of changing what she wanted for Ross.

He groaned. "You keep that up and you'll get more than you bargained for."

She shifted so she could see his face. "Who said I didn't want more?"

Ross smiled indulgently down at her. "Mmm… That's the kind of thing I like to hear." He leaned in to kiss her.

"Ross, what're we going to do?"

The look in his eyes turned devious. "You don't know by now?"

She gave him a little pinch. "You know what I mean. We agreed to be friends."

"You don't think I'm being friendly?" His hand traveled over her bare butt.

"You're just not going to listen, are you?" Her voice held a teasing note.

Ross kissed her neck. "Who said I wasn't listening? I heard every word you've said."

"Ross, we can't do this."

"I think we did 'this' just fine. Great, in fact." His lips traveled lower.

"We have to stick to the plan." Her voice had turned sharper than she had intended.

He captured her gaze. "Look, why can't we just enjoy each other while it lasts? We don't have to make a big deal of it. We can keep it between us. We can be friends and still see each other when our schedules allow."

"I guess that'll work." She wasn't convinced. The more she saw Ross, the harder it became to give him up. Hopefully, one day soon she would have medical school to think about. There wouldn't be any time for a relationship. But she'd miss him desperately if she gave him up right now. Maybe if they just saw each other until she started school...

Over the next few weeks she and Ross fell into a routine. If they both had extended days off, then Sally would go to his place. They would work around the ranch, go out for dinner in a small town nearby. They couldn't afford being seen together by someone in the fire department, so they made sure to stay out of Austin. When their schedules had them working back-to-back days, then Ross would come to her apartment. She'd never been happier. Or more worried about her heart being broken.

It was exciting to know Ross would be waiting on her when she came home or be coming to her after his shift. Against her better judgment, she was caring for him a little more each time they were together. Still, one day soon it would all have to end, but that wasn't today.

Sally was leaving his place to go to work when Ross said, "I promised Jared and Olivia when they got out of school, I'd take them tubing on the Guadalupe River. We're going Saturday. Wanna come?"

"I wish I could, but I told Kody I'd watch Lucy. He's scheduled to work. He's started asking me what I'm doing with my time. I haven't seen much of either of them since you've been keeping me busy." Her look was pointed, yet she grinned.

"And I like keeping you busy." His smile grew. "Lucy's welcome to go. I know Jared and Olivia would have a better time with her along."

Sally's heart lightened. She would've missed seeing Ross. Her feelings for him were like trying to stop a runaway train. She was doing everything she'd promised herself she wouldn't do. "I'll talk to Kody and ask Lucy and let you know."

"That sounds like a plan. I'll get the tubes together."

"Can I do something?"

"No. I think I can take care of the sandwiches for lunch. All you have to do is get you and Lucy here in your bathing suits." He came in close, moving to stand between her legs where she sat on his kitchen counter. "I especially like that idea."

She grinned. "I thought you might." Then she kissed him.

Kody gave his okay that also included a suspicious look when she told him Jared and Olivia had requested that she and Lucy came tubing with them and Ross.

"You've lived here for over a year and had nothing to do with Ross Lawson. Yet in the last month or so you've spent the day with him at the picnic, watched his niece and nephew, studied at his house and now you're going tubing with him. Is something going on I should know about?"

"There's nothing going on. We're just friends. Aren't I allowed to have friends?"

"Yeah," he said, but gave her a narrow-eyed look implying he was unconvinced.

Early Saturday morning Sally picked up Lucy. This time Sally was the one the most excited about going to Ross's. She hadn't seen him in a couple of days because he had worked a double shift. He'd worked his regular shift, then gone to the Fire Department Office for a meeting the next day. There was something off in her day when she didn't get to see him.

She didn't know how much longer they would be able to keep their relationship a secret. It was getting more difficult every day. Sometime soon they'd have to work together. In fact, she was going to get to find out sooner rather than later how good of an actor and actress they were because the new schedule had come out the day before and they were to share a couple of shifts next week.

What then? Would someone notice the looks between them? Or that one knew more than they should about something the other did on their days off? It would be so easy to slip up. It could damage Ross's career and she didn't want that.

He deserved the Battalion Chief position. As a dedicated firefighter, a great leader and someone who had a vision for the future of the department, he was a perfect fit. More than that, he had a passion for fighting fire. It wasn't just a job to him. Ross completely believed in what he was doing.

As she and Lucy traveled closer to Ross's house, Sally's heart beat faster in anticipation. She smiled to herself. This was what happy felt like. It had been a long time since she'd been that. She'd counted on medical school to give her that feeling again. Then along had come Ross.

He and the kids were waiting on them beside his truck. He wore a T-shirt and swim-trunks along with a pair of tennis shoes. There was a ball cap on his head and his eyes were covered by aviator sunglasses. He had never looked better. She banked the urge to run into his arms, reminding herself to remain cool in front of the kids.

Lucy started waving before Sally stopped the car. The kids returned it, and Ross offered one as well.

He was at her door before she opened it. Was he as happy to see her as she was him? As she climbed out, he stepped toward her. Sally had no doubt he planned to kiss her. His intent was obvious. She stopped his movement with a hand to his chest and a dip of her head toward Lucy. Ross looked past her shoulder. With the sag of his shoulders and dimming of his smile, he nodded and backed away. Lucy would no doubt enjoy telling her father the moment she saw him again that Ross had been kissing her aunt Sally. She certainly wasn't prepared to field Kody's questions about that.

In an odd way, sharing a clandestine relationship with Ross was exciting. Fun like she hadn't had in a long time. She didn't have to share him with anyone. Yet some part of her wanted people to know this amazing man belonged to her. But did he?

"Come into the house. I've got to put our lunch into a dry bag, then we'll be ready to go." Ross started up the porch steps.

"Dry bag?" Sally followed him.

"It'll keep things dry. I'll tie it to my tube." He held the door for her.

"Great idea." She went inside.

"I'm full of those." He called over his shoulder, "Kids, we'll be right out. Make sure you've got your towels and anything else you need in the truck."

As soon as they were inside out of sight of the kids, he hauled her to him and kissed her. There was hunger there, yet tenderness as well. He'd missed her too. "I'm not sure how I'm gonna make it all day without touching you. With you just being an arm's length away."

Sally giggled. She seemed to do that often lately. It was empowering to her bruised self-image to be considered so desirable by such a remarkable male. Ross made her feel as if she was enough. That was something Wade hadn't done, ever.

Ross pursed his lip in thought. "Maybe it was a bad idea to invite you along."

She pulled away, pouting. "I could always get Lucy and leave."

"Over my dead body." Ross pulled her back to him. She liked

being against him. "I'll take my chances on having you around. I'll just have to work on my self-control today."

"That's more like it. You're just gonna have to restrain yourself, because I can promise you that Lucy will catch on pretty quick. I don't think either one of us wants to face Kody quite yet."

"I can handle Kody. You and I are adults. Now, how about one more quick kiss for the road?" Ross's lips found hers.

Too soon for Sally they went to the kitchen. Ross already had the sandwiches in individual plastic bags. He placed them in a heavy rubberized bag. "Do you have anything you want to put in here?"

"My phone?"

He carefully put the food in the bag. "I'll take mine, so why don't you leave yours in the truck?"

"Okay. I don't guess we need two of them."

"Roger that."

Ross locked up, and they joined the kids at the truck. The tubes were already loaded and secured by straps.

"Climb in, kids. Buckle up," Ross called.

They scrambled onto the back seat. Sally climbed into the passenger's seat and Ross got behind the wheel. The kids chattered for the hour it took to drive to the river. Ross pulled into the makeshift dirt parking lot.

When the kids climbed out, Ross put his hand over hers. "I'm sorry we didn't have a chance to talk, catch up."

She smiled at him. "I don't mind. I'm just happy to be with you."

He gave her a bright smile. "That was certainly the right answer."

"Come on, Uncle Ross. Let's get on the river," Jared called with impatience.

Ross unloaded the tubes, handing one to each of the kids then her. After passing out the life vests, he took a moment to secure the bag to his tube. "Okay, kids, huddle up."

The three of them circled in front of him. Sally joined them.

"What're the rules on the river?" Ross gave them an earnest look. He was such a good leader. He would one day make an excellent head of the fire department.

"Stay together," Olivia said.

"Wear your life jacket at all times," Jared added.

"Then we'll have fun," Ross finished. "Got it?"

In unison, they all said, "Yeah!"

He led the way to the riverbank. She helped the kids put on their life vests and get into their tubes and soon they were all floating down the river. The day was warm and the water cool. They leisurely rode the current, letting it take them at its speed. The kids laughed and splashed each other, then turned on her and Ross. A few times other people or groups passed them.

Once the kids were ahead of them enough that Ross came up close to her. His look remained passive and focused on the kids while the hand closest to her went beneath the water.

She jumped as his hand ran over her bottom. "Oomph."

"Easy," he said in an innocent voice. "You don't want to make a scene in front of the kids." As he said this, one of his fingers dipped under the leg opening of her bathing suit and worked its way around to the crease of her leg before it was gone. That was all it took for her center to start throbbing. With a teasing smile on his lips, he floated away.

"Not fair, Lawson."

He gave her a wicked grin over his shoulder.

Not much farther along, Ross called a halt, telling the kids to pull over to the sandbar where the water was placid. It was time for lunch. They brought their tubes out of the water and found a log to sit on. Sally pulled the sandwiches, health bars and bottled water out of the bag along with napkins and a small package of wet wipes. Ross had thought of everything.

It didn't take the kids long to eat. Soon they were asking to go swimming.

"You can go but stay close to the shore," Ross told them.

She and Ross watched as they headed for the water.

"This tube floating is fun. I've never done it before. I'm really glad I came. Obviously, this isn't the first time you've gone." Sally looked at Ross and bit into her sandwich.

"It was a regular pastime when I was growing up. Jared and Olivia have been a few times before."

"This won't be my last time either." With or without Ross, she intended to do this again. The only thing was that when she did, she'd always think of Ross. It would take some of the joy out of it.

"I'm glad you're having a good time." His attention remained on the kids.

Again, the thought he'd make a good father entered her head. And the fact that such a thing would never involve her left her a little sad. Shaking it off, she sighed. "There's nothing more refreshing than a day on the river when it's hot."

"I can think of at least one other thing." Ross's suggestive remark was accompanied by a heated look. Placing his palms on the log, he leaned back.

Sally took a swallow of water, set the bottle down in front of the log, then leaned back in the same manner as him. She placed her hand over Ross's, intertwining their fingers. Ross looked at her and smiled before his attention returned to watching the kids.

"I'm going to miss you tonight," Ross said in a mock whisper.

Sally tried to act unaffected, but her heart was already picking up speed. "You think so?"

His eyes flickered with burning need as he looked at her. "I know so. Lean over here. I want to kiss you."

"The kids—"

He glanced at them. "Aren't looking."

Her lips met him for a quick kiss.

With a sigh, Ross called, "Let's go, kids. Come clean up your trash and put it in the bag. We have to carry everything out we bring on the river. Then get your tubes."

Within minutes they were back on the water.

They had been floating for about an hour when they reached a bend in the river and heard, "Help, help, help."

In seconds Ross was off his tube. He shoved it toward her and started swimming. As he passed the kids, he ordered, "Stay with Sally."

He disappeared around the bend as she and the kids picked up their pace. As they rounded the curve, she could see Ross stepping out of the water at a calmer area up ahead. She directed the kids that way.

When they reached the spot where Ross had exited, she told the kids in a stern voice, "We're getting out here. I want you to pile your tubes here beside the river and go over there to that spot and sit." She pointed at a log. "Do not take your life preservers off. Stay put while I see if your uncle Ross needs my help. I'm trusting you to do as I say."

Ross was kneeling over by a woman lying on the ground in a small grassy area. There was another woman sitting on the ground beside her. Sally hurried to them.

"What's wrong?" she asked, coming up beside Ross.

Ross shifted and she could see that the woman had a compound fracture just above her knee.

"How did this happen?" Sally asked.

Ross said to the women, "This is Sally. She's a paramedic. She'll help you."

"We got out of the river to look at a flower and stupid me got my foot caught in a hole and fell," the injured woman said between tight white lips.

Ross could handle burning buildings or automobile wrecks, but he wasn't good at physical emergencies. He had EMT skills, which he rarely used. The woman had severely broken her leg and he was more than happy to turn her care over to Sally's excellent knowledge.

He went to where the kids sat. As he reassured them, Ross

searched the dry bag for his phone. Finding it, he punched in 911 then returned to Sally, who was talking to the injured woman.

"I've got 911 on the phone. What do I need to tell them?"

"Thirty-four-year-old female," Sally stated in a firm voice. She was clearly in paramedic mode. He relayed the message. "Compound fracture of the right femur. Treating for shock."

Sally already had the woman lying down with her uninjured leg up.

"Heart rate steady. Pulse one-twenty. Moderate pain. Splinting now."

Ross repeated everything to the dispatcher. He said to Sally, "A medivac can't get in here. The tree canopy is too heavy. We'll need to get her downriver to the takeout spot. It's about a mile away."

Sally spoke to the injured woman's friend. "Please see if you can find at least three pieces of wood or straight sticks that can be used as splints. They must be sturdy." As the woman moved away, Sally asked him with worry in her voice, "What's the plan?"

"I'm going to lash the tubes together and float her down. We're too far from the road for the ambulance, and the helicopter can't get in here."

Sally nodded. "Okay, I'll have her ready. Have one of the kids bring me the towels. I've got to manage shock if we're going to do this."

"I'll get started on the raft now." He hoped it went as smoothly as he had it planned. Ross went to the kids and issued orders for them to hunt for long sticks but to stay within eyesight of him. He sent the towels by Jared to Sally.

Pulling four of the tubes close to the river, Ross put them side by side. Without thinking twice, he jerked his T-shirt over his head. He then pulled a knife out of the dry bag and cut and tore the shirt into strips. He glanced at Sally to find her struggling to do the same with her shirt. Ross went to her. Taking the shirt out of her hands, he began tearing it as well.

"Thanks," Sally said.

He pointed. "I'm going to need one of those towels."

"Okay. I'll put my life jacket over her."

"You can have mine as well." He took it off. "I'll need any of your leftover strips."

The woman's friend came back with some sticks. Sally's attention returned to splinting the woman's leg.

The kids had found some sticks. Some he could use, others not. He sent Jared back out to look for more and had the girls hold things in place as he tied the tubes together with the strips of his shirt. He then tied the sticks on to give the woman a platform to ride on.

The whop-whop of the helicopter flying in could be heard in the distance.

"You ready, Sally?"

"Ten-four."

"Okay, kids, we're going to get this lady on the raft. Then I want you to each get in your tube. I'm going to tie you to the raft. Sally and I'll be swimming. Understand?"

The kids spoke their agreement.

"Stay here until we get the woman settled," he told the kids and then joined Sally.

She had the woman's leg secured in a splint of branches and strips of T-shirt. The leg was evenly supported on the bottom and the top. Sally had made sure it wouldn't move.

He spoke to her. "I've been thinking about the best way to move her. I could pick her up while you support her leg."

"I can help," the woman's friend said.

Sally looked down at the woman. "I don't see that we have a choice." She then said to the injured woman, "What happens next isn't going to be fun. Hang in there and we'll have you at the hospital in no time." She smiled. "And on pain medicine."

The woman nodded, her mouth tight. "That sounds good."

Sally turned her attention to the friend. "Take the towels

and life jackets to the raft. Lay one towel over the sticks. We'll cover her with the others again."

The woman did as Sally instructed and removed a towel and the life jacket lying over the injured woman and hurried off.

She soon returned, and she and Sally helped Ross get the injured woman into his arms by supporting her hips and legs. His thigh muscles burned as he strained to lift her. She cried out in pain but there wasn't anything they could do for her except be as gentle as possible. That he was already trying to do. It was a slow process walking over the rough ground, but they finally made it to the raft. Ross placed her on it. Sally quickly checked to make sure the woman's life jacket was still secure. She then covered the patient with the towels and her and Ross's jackets.

"Let's get the raft in the water," he said to the woman, then, "Kids, get your tubes."

It took the three adults to lift and scoot the raft out until it floated not to jostle the woman.

"Sally, will you take one of the front corners? You." He spoke to the friend. "Will you take the other? I'll take the back. Kids, get on your tubes. I'll tie you on."

Everyone did as he instructed. "Okay, let's get this show on the river."

Slowly they moved out into the current.

"I'm looking for slow and steady," Ross called. "No sudden moves."

It took them almost an hour to get to where the helicopter was waiting on the slow winding section of the river. As they came into sight, the medivac crew went into action. They had a gurney and supplies waiting at the river edge when they arrived. Sally gave a report while he saw to the kids.

As they watched the helicopter lift off, Sally said, "I'm glad you were there with me on this one."

His fingers tangled with hers for a moment. "I was just thinking the same thing about you."

She smiled up at him. "You do know you aren't wearing a shirt, don't you?"

"Yeah."

"You okay with that?" Sally gave him a concerned look.

"I'm a little antsy, but handling it."

Her fingers found his again. "I'm proud of you."

Ross squeezed her hand, then let it go. "Couldn't have done it without you."

"Oh, yeah, you could. I've no doubt you would've done whatever was necessary to get that woman to safety whether or not I had come along. That's just the kind of guy you are, Ross Lawson. You're made of hero material. Scars and all."

When Sally thought he was a hero, he felt like one.

"Thanks, you were pretty heroic back there too."

She laughed. "Now that we've told ourselves we're wonderful, how about let's go home?"

Ross laughed. "Let's go."

They gathered the kids and caught the next shuttle back to the truck. The other floaters riding with them asked questions about the incident and offered their appreciation for a job well done.

At the truck Ross turned to the kids and said, "I think we've all earned pizza and ice cream. Who would agree?"

The kids cheered. Sally smiled.

"Okay, I'll order in and stop and buy the ice cream. Since we don't have enough clothes on to get out anywhere."

It wasn't until then that he registered he'd not given a thought to riding the shuttle or being around the kids without a shirt on. They hadn't even noticed. Maybe he made more of a deal of his scars than they were. There was something freeing about that knowledge.

The kids climbed in the back seat of the truck. Ross hadn't driven far when he looked in the rearview mirror to find them all asleep.

"Hey," he whispered to Sally.

She looked at him. He nodded toward the back seat. "Don't you think you're too far away?"

Sally glanced behind her and grinned before she slid over against him. He put his arm around her shoulders and pulled her close. She kissed his cheek. "You were my hero again today. The raft was brilliant."

Ross kissed the top of her head. "No more than you."

He glanced at Sally. What had happened to him in the last few weeks? He'd changed. Sally had made all the difference.

CHAPTER EIGHT

SALLY PULLED INTO the fire station parking lot two days later with a grin on her face. She was going to see Ross. Her smile grew as she remembered how unhappy she'd been at the idea of seeing him just weeks before. It had been four days since she'd truly been in his arms and she missed him terribly. She could understand where his ex-girlfriend had been coming from about odd schedules. Working around them was difficult but she would never give Ross up just because of that.

The day was coming soon when she would have to. But even as she thought it, she wondered if she did have to give him up. Couldn't they work something out? Did she want to? It was already happening. She wanted to make changes in her life to accommodate Ross. But if she did, could she trust he would always be there for her? His job was important to him. If it came down to her or his job, he'd take his job every time, wouldn't he?

When she entered med school—make that *if* she entered med school, as she still hadn't heard back from her test—she could only imagine how difficult it would be to make time for a relationship. Would they be together that long? No, she wouldn't let things get that far. At the beginning, she wouldn't have thought she and Ross would have lasted this long but now she couldn't imagine not having him in her life. For now, she'd just have to enjoy the time they did have while it lasted.

There had been a particularly sad look in Ross's eyes when she and Lucy had left his house after they had gone tubing. It was nice to have a man so disappointed to see her go. To show it so honestly. After her husband's betrayal, her self-esteem had suffered greatly. Ross's attention had gone a long way in restoring it.

The day they'd tubed the plan had been for Lucy to stay the night with her, so Ross couldn't come over that evening. Kody had asked her to join him and Lucy for supper the next evening. All of this made it seem like an eternity since she'd had personal time with Ross.

She was beginning to believe they might have something special. She'd never felt this way before. That low-level hum of need for Ross was always there. That jump of excitement when she saw him always thrilled her. The anticipation of his touch made the prospect of seeing him more rousing.

Now she was thinking in circles. Not making sense. One minute she was thinking of when their time together would end and the next she was dreaming of a future with Ross. She had to stop thinking with her heart and focus on what her mind was telling her or she was going to get hurt, badly.

It had become tedious, even nerve-racking to keep their relationship to themselves. She was tired of it. Two grown people had every right to see one another. She wasn't ashamed of Ross and she didn't think he was ashamed of her. At least letting Kody and Lucy in on her and Ross's secret would help.

She pulled her bag out of the back seat of her car and headed into the station. Inside the engine bay, she turned toward the paramedic side of the building. She saw Ross on the other side with his hands in his pants pockets talking to one of the firefighters. He glanced her way. Even from that distance she could see the glimmer of awareness in his eyes. His body language changed, as if he wanted to drop what he was doing to come to her. Her heart did a skip and a jump.

Sally entered the paramedic supply room and walked on into the locker room to put her bag away. She sensed more than saw someone enter behind her. Glancing behind her, she found Ross. He stood with his back to the door, blocking it. If anyone tried to enter, they couldn't unless they pushed him out of the way.

"Ross, what're you doing?"

"Come here." The words were low and forceful.

She narrowed her eyes. This wasn't like him. "What?"

"Please come here, Sally." His voice was solemn but had a pleading note, as if he physically hurt.

That warm spot in the center of her chest that grew when she was around him heated. Now she understood. She walked into his arms. Ross's hands cupped her butt and he pulled her up against him as his mouth found hers. His searing kiss was sensual and stimulating, leaving her in no doubt where his mind was.

Ross soon set her at arm's length. "I keep that up and everybody'll see what being around you does to me."

She giggled.

He grinned. "You like that idea, don't you?"

"It does have its appeal." She gave him a nudge. "Now, Casanova, move out of the way and let me see if the coast is clear." He stepped to the side. She opened the door and looked out. "You're good to go, Captain Lawson."

As he went by her, she brushed his cheek with her lips.

The shift was a busy one. There were no fires but a number of auto accidents. One of them required the Hazmat team. Ross was especially trained for Hazmat so his crew was out cleaning up past the end of the shift. Sally didn't see him before she left. They hadn't discussed their plans, so she decided to go home. Disappointment washed over her as she drove out of the parking lot.

It was early evening when she settled down to read her mail. She still hadn't heard from Ross. She suspected he'd had a large amount of paperwork to do but she would've thought he'd have called or texted by now.

There was a knock at the door. Her heart started racing with hope.

Ross stood on her stoop. He didn't say a word. Just scooped her into a hug and kissed her. Her soul went wild with joy. She clung to him, wrapping her legs around his hips.

"Happy to see me?" He sounded pleased.

He pushed the door closed with his foot, held her with one arm and locked the door. Starting down the hall, he continued to kiss her as he found her bedroom. There he rolled them onto the bed with a bounce.

Sometime later, still in bed, they snacked on popcorn and watched a comedy show.

Ross fed her some corn. "After our shift I know the definition of hell. It's having you so close yet being unable to touch you."

Sally giggled. "I kind of like the idea. It's flattering."

"That may be so, but it's not much fun for me." He kissed the corner of her mouth.

"You can touch me all you want to right now." She gave him a suggestive smile.

His hand skimmed the inside of her thigh. "Now, that sounds like an excellent idea."

Ross started his shift two days later feeling rather good about himself. He looked out of his office window to see Sally standing beside the ambulance talking to her crew member. She glanced over her shoulder and made eye contact with him.

Heat washed through him. He was acting like a lovesick male horse that hung its head over the fence hoping the female horse in the next pasture would notice him.

Focus, Lawson. You have that promotion on the line.

He attempted to turn his attention to his paperwork. Instead his mind went to memories of his last few days off. A short while after the comedy show had ended, Sally had accompanied him home and they'd spent the time at his place. She seemed to thrive there. Which gave him a warm feeling deep inside that he didn't wish to analyze. She was becoming ingrained in his life, as necessary as the air he breathed.

He not only appreciated her body, he enjoyed being with Sally. She had a sharp wit that kept him on his toes. She thought nothing of working right next to him, even when the job included mucking out the barn. She was game for anything. More than that, she made him feel like the hero she said he was. Not once had he seen her flinch when he removed his shirt, which he'd started doing regularly when he worked on the farm. She treated him as if he were whole and flawless. With her, he was.

They didn't talk about the future. Ross worried if they did it would change things between them. He didn't want that. Giving up Sally would already be far harder than he had originally thought. He'd ride this wave of happiness for as long as it lasted. It was too wonderful to let go of.

Sally was a partner both outside of work and at work as well. Today, she'd be sharing the shift with him, then they would have another few days together. For him life was good. The only thing that could make it perfect would be to earn the Battalion Chief position. Hopefully he'd know about that any day now, after his interview a week ago.

The company made a few runs during the early evening but managed to have dinner in peace. He and Sally sat next to each other around the large table with the rest of the people at the station. They made an effort to appear as normal as possible, yet under the table he slid his foot next to hers and Sally pressed her lower leg against his.

The alarm beeped and the dispatcher came on over the intercom just after sunrise the next day. Rush hour almost always meant an accident and this one was no different. Ross hurried to the bay and suited up with his crew. He climbed into the truck and the driver flipped on the lights and siren.

Ross swung into emergency mode, already thinking through the possibilities of what was ahead for him and his firefighters. Dispatch told him it was a four-car accident. His team had to work their way through and around the traffic. The ambulance was right behind them.

As they arrived, Ross assessed the situation. Apparently, a car turning left in the intersection ran into the side of an oncoming car. The other two cars had hit their rears. The car that had been going straight took the worse of the crash. Gas covered the ground. A few people sat on the curb off to the left.

Ross was on the radio issuing orders before he climbed out of the truck.

"We need fire extinguishers out just in case. Make sure that gas doesn't spread. Don't let the medics in there until we know how many we have involved and the area is secure." He wouldn't put anyone in danger, especially Sally.

The ambulance pulled up next to his truck with the help of the police directing other cars out of the way. One of his firefighters led a woman to the ambulance. Sally took care of her while the other EMT checked on those on the curb.

"Are all the people in the cars accounted for?" he asked into the radio.

"Ten-four," one of his firefighters came back.

Ross's attention returned to the scene. His firefighters had the situation in hand. He glanced at the box to see Sally taking care of a man who looked as if he was in his thirties.

Into his radio he said, "Let's get traffic moving and clean up this mess."

"Ten-four," came back from his men.

Ross directed the wrecker into place, then started toward Sally, who had a different patient sitting on the back bumper of the box now. She stood in front of the man, tending his head wound.

The man started to stand, but Sally put a hand on his shoulder and eased him back down. In a flash her patient slung his hands high, one of his fists hitting Sally in the face. Her feet came off the ground and she landed on her butt.

Ross roared her name. Something inside him that he didn't recognize roiled to life. Bile rose in his throat. Raw heat flashed over him.

He ran toward Sally. Reaching the man, Ross curled his hands into his shirt. He didn't think—just reacted. Jerking him around and away from Sally, he lifted the scumbag to his toes and shook him. How dared he touch Sally?

Ross growled with fury. "You sure as hell better not have hurt her."

"Stop, Ross! Stop!" Sally's voice penetrated his anger. Her hands pulled at one of his arms.

The policeman took the moment to capture an arm of the man and Ross let go. Seconds later, the policeman had the man's hands secured behind his back.

"What're you doing?" Sally demanded in a loud voice despite the fact she stood in his personal space.

"Helping you!" Ross's heart pounded as if he'd been in a race for his life. The man had knocked Sally to the ground. She could have been seriously hurt.

Sally glared at him. "I could've handled him."

Ross studied her, making sure she had no major injuries, then ground out, "Yeah, I can see that by the shiner you're going to have."

Sally's partner joined them. "He's right. You took a hard shot. You're going to need to be seen at the hospital."

Sally shook her head. "I'll be fine."

"Do as you're told, Sally," Ross snapped and stalked off. Didn't she understand she could have really been hurt? His heart had constricted when she'd gone down.

Ross had been shocked at how quickly he'd reacted to Sally being hit. He was known for his calm demeanor and even thinking during an emergency. Emotions didn't enter into his decisions—ever. But where Sally was concerned, he stepped out of his norm.

His heart still slammed against his chest as he walked back to his post. Slowly he calmed down. Started thinking straight, but the damage was already done.

Sally had only been doing her job. Surely she'd been pushed and hit before by a crazy patient. The difference was it hadn't happened in front of him. Something primal had fueled him. He was going to protect his woman. In seconds, he'd shifted into defensive mode.

One of the firefighters handed him his radio. Ross hadn't even realized he'd dropped it. His lieutenant gave him an odd look when Ross joined him. Ross didn't acknowledge it. Instead he started issuing orders.

Who had seen his over-the-top reaction? Would they put two and two together and figure out he and Sally were seeing each other? Worse, would his loss of professionalism get back to the bosses?

Sally went to the hospital emergency room against her will even though she knew it was necessary. It was company and fire department protocol that it be done. Thankfully, X-rays indicated there were no broken bones, but she had to admit her face throbbed. It had already started turning dreadful colors just as Ross had said.

She'd been told not to return to the station. Someone had been called in to replace her. A policeman had given her a ride home.

Ross had broken their professional relationship. In two. She could've handled the situation. He had overstepped his bounds. His reaction had been way over the top. She'd never seen him act that way. Part of her appreciated him caring enough that he was that concerned about her, but it wasn't good for either one of their careers for him to go ballistic, particularly where she was concerned. It was just an example of why they should not be seeing each other. What if the higher-ups got wind of what happened? It might hurt Ross's record.

Yet she kind of liked the idea he'd ridden to her rescue. Chivalry wasn't dead. Once again, he was her knight in shining armor.

There was a knock at the front door. That would be Kody. She'd called him and asked if he and Lucy could come over for the night. She had to have someone with her. With a bag of frozen peas over her eye, she opened the door. Instead of Kody and Lucy, Ross walked in without invitation, carrying a white bag. She watched, bewildered, as he made his way toward the kitchen.

"Hey, you do know I'm mad at you?" she called to his back.

He glanced at her with concern on his face. "Are you all right?"

She followed him to the kitchen. "You know I am. You called twice while I was in the ER. All I have is a black eye. I'm under a concussion watch for the next twelve hours because of the bump on the back of my head, but I'm fine. About your behavior..."

In one swift move he put the bag on the table, turned to her and grabbed her shoulders, looking deeply into her eyes. "Let me make this clear right now. For the rest of my life whenever I see somebody hit you, I'll react the same way. No apologies." He pulled her to him and held her as if she were a new duckling. Tender, but reassuringly safe.

Had he been that scared for her?

Finally, he released a deep breath and let her go. "Have you eaten?"

"No."

"Great. I brought us Chinese takeout." He started removing small white cartons out of a bag.

Just like that they were moving on.

"You need to put those peas on that eye. It looks painful. By the way, why doesn't a paramedic have a disposable ice pack in her own apartment?"

"I'm not a paramedic *all* the time," she said in a huff.

He took her hand and kissed the palm. "I know that. I even like it. A lot." He kissed her and she returned it. "It hurts me to know you were hurt."

This type of attention she could learn to love. In fact, Ross would be easy to love. She was halfway there anyway. Her chest felt heavy. This was just what she'd been afraid would happen. Could she go back? Pretend those feelings didn't exist? Ross coming along wasn't part of her grand plan. "I'm all right, Ross. The guy was on drugs. Those people are always unpredictable. Next time I'll have a policeman secure their hands before I see about them."

"Next time? There better not be another one where you get hurt." He hugged her again. "For somebody who has dedicated their life to caring for people like you have, then have somebody do you that way..."

She cupped his face. "You do know it comes with the territory sometimes."

"Yeah, but that doesn't mean I have to like it." He suddenly looked tired. As if his emotions had gotten the best of him.

"Says the man who runs into burning buildings." She could well remember how she had felt when he had run into the burning house.

"Let's eat before it gets cold."

It was as if Ross couldn't stand to talk about what had happened anymore. As if his emotions were too open, fresh. She'd focused on her feelings and not enough on his. Ross was being so sweet she couldn't be mad at him anymore. He really had been scared.

They had just finished their meal when there was a knock at the door.

"That'll be Kody."

Before she could get up, Ross rose and went to the door. "I'll get it."

How was Kody going to react when he saw Ross at her place? He'd already started asking questions.

"Come on in. She's in here," she heard Ross say.

Lucy came down the hall. Ross and Kody were still at the door. What were they saying to each other?

"Aunt Sally, are you okay?" Lucy asked, making it impossible to hear the men.

"I'll be fine. You don't need to worry about me." Sally patted the cushion beside her.

Lucy plopped down.

A minute later Kody, flanked by Ross, came into the living room.

"So how're you doing, Sweet Pea?" Kody stood above her, studying her.

"A black eye and a bump on the head, but I'm fine. I should be good by tomorrow."

Kody dropped his bag with a thump. "So…" he glanced at Ross, then focused on Sally "…we're here to watch over you."

"That won't be necessary," Ross said from where he leaned against the wall. "I'll be here." His wooden tone implied his mind wouldn't be changed.

Sally's heart tapped as she looked between the two men.

Kody's head whipped around in Ross's direction. "Really?"

"Yes." Ross didn't miss a beat as he gave Kody a steady look. These were two bulls marking their territory of protection.

Abruptly Kody looked at her. "So it's like that?"

Sally nodded.

Kody looked at Ross, who flatly said, "It is."

Sally watched her brother's face harden. "I'm sorry to have bothered you. I didn't know Ross was coming when I called you."

"Lucy, honey, there's been a change in plans. We won't be staying tonight." Kody waved her toward him.

"But I wanted to stay," Lucy whined.

Sally put her arm around Lucy's shoulders. "When I'm feeling better you can come back."

Ross walked Kody and Lucy to the front door. Sally listened from where she was.

"Lucy, go wait in the truck. I'll be right out," Kody told her. The child obediently went. Sally held her breath.

"You break her heart and I'll break you."

Ross returned with a firm "Ten-four."

CHAPTER NINE

ROSS STOOD NEXT to the fire engine two days later, working on his monthly equipment inspection, when he noticed the Battalion Chief's truck pulling into the station parking lot. It was Battalion Chief Marks.

He and Chief Marks had been friends for some time. Ross had been in his company when he'd first joined the fire department. Chief Marks had been a mentor to him, even encouraged Ross to put in for the Battalion Chief position. What made this particular visit interesting was that he wasn't Battalion Chief over Ross's station. Was this good news or bad news?

Anxiety filled Ross. Did Chief Marks have news about the selection?

"Hey, it's nice to see you." Ross walked toward him with a hand extended as his friend entered the station.

"Ross." Chief Marks shook Ross's hand.

"How's Jenna and the kids?" Ross asked.

"Doing great."

"Good. What brings you over to my side of town?"

Chief Marks's expression turned serious. "I wanted to talk to you about something that has come up."

"That sounds ominous," Ross said a little more casually than he felt.

"Why don't we go into your office to talk?"

"Okay." Ross led the way. In his office, he dropped his clipboard on the desk and sat in the seat behind it. Chief Marks took the chair across from him. "So what's up?"

"I'm not going to beat around the bush on this, Ross. I heard something happened the other day during a run that had to do with a female paramedic."

Ross didn't try acting as if he didn't know what Chief Marks was talking about. "I was just taking care of my company."

Chief Marks's look held steady. "You sure there wasn't more to it?"

Ross knew there was more to it. However, what he was having trouble determining was just what "more to it" meant. He wasn't going to lie. That would come back to haunt him. This man was his friend. Had his best interests at heart. "Yeah, we're seeing each other."

Chief Marks leaned back in his chair, crossed his fingers over his belly and pursed his lips.

Ross returned his direct look. Sally had been upset with him. Apparently, she'd been right, if the Battalion Chief's question was any indication. It might have been unprofessional for him to have grabbed the man, but Ross was a human first and he had been scared for Sally. Seeing her hit had made him roaring mad. He'd be that way again where she was concerned. That was the problem. He couldn't ignore his feelings for her. Now he had to deal with the fallout of his actions.

"I'm going to shoot you straight here. This isn't good for your promotion. I don't think the Chief has heard about it, which is in your favor. Only time will tell on that. If he does, it very well may be the end of your chances for Battalion Chief. I'd hate to see that. You're a good firefighter. Are you in love with her?"

Was he? Ross wasn't sure. He did care—a lot. His performance the other day proved how much he cared. But love? That meant forever for him. He'd been concentrating so hard on not examining his feelings that he wasn't sure. "I think I am."

"Then I suggest you think things through carefully. What you decide may mean your career." Chief Marks stood.

Ross did as well.

"I hope I get to see you in the Battalion Chiefs' meeting soon." With that, Chief Marks left.

In his own way, he had told Ross what he should do. But could he?

He and Sally had started as a fling, a weekend together. Then it had stretched to a few weeks. Yet as the days went by he wanted more. She seemed to as well. They'd not spoken of ending things in weeks. Now that the time had come he didn't want to. What he felt for Sally was real. Something special. He couldn't just throw it away. They needed to find a way to make this work. Wasn't there some design where he could have both? He couldn't just walk away from her.

He desperately wanted that Battalion Chief job. He'd worked all his professional life to earn this promotion. He'd done the schooling, taken the additional classes and been the best captain he could be. The only hiccup had been this period with Sally. Why should the Battalion Chief position hang on his personal life? If he got the job and didn't have Sally, what would he really have? When had she become the most important? It didn't matter, just that she was.

The problem would niggle at him until Ross spoke to her. Surely together they could work something out where they could both have what they wanted. She would return to work the next day, but he had to talk to her before then. They couldn't share another shift until they'd had the conversation. He called her and she agreed to meet him at his place instead of him going to hers.

Ross didn't remember the drive home. All he could think about was the upcoming discussion. He needed a solution. Sally would be going to medical school soon, of that he had no doubt, and that would improve the situation greatly. If she'd moved, then they wouldn't be working together even between semesters.

His chest tightened. What if she didn't care as much as he

did? They'd never spoken of their feelings. He had to jerk the truck back to his side of the road before he was hit. Was he planning for something that didn't even exist? A fling was their agreement. Now he was wanting to change that. There had been no promises between them. What if she didn't want any? He and Alice had made promises and nothing had come from them—what if that happened again with Sally? Panic started to build. Suddenly the promotion seemed a small concern.

When Ross arrived home, Sally was waiting on the porch swing. He would always think of her that way. She loved the swing. It was her favorite place. His heart quickened. Sally was nice to come home to.

She came to the top of the steps and waited. He took her into his arms, kissing her with all the care he felt. She returned his kiss with equal enthusiasm.

Afterward she giggled. "I see that Texas star is still working for you."

"Yeah, and I'm going to use it every chance I can get." He kissed her again.

She reached for his bag. "Let me have that and I'll put it up while you go see to the horses."

He let her take the bag. Their talk would come soon enough.

Sally found Ross under the large oak tree a few minutes later. He stood beside the fence looking off into the horizon.

"Hey." She placed her hand between his shoulder blades and rubbed his back. "Something bothering you? How were things at the house today? Anything exciting happen?"

He didn't answer immediately while his attention remained on something out in the pasture. "Chief Marks came to see me."

She grabbed his arm. What did that mean? Had Ross gotten the Battalion Chief position? She wanted it for him so badly. She knew it meant as much to him as her doing well on the MCAT did to her. Excitement bubbled in her. "He did? Is it good news?"

Ross gave her a sad shake of his head. "Sweet Sally, I hate to disappoint you. No, what he came to tell me was that he'd heard about what happened at the accident the other day."

The colorful balloon of delight at the chance he might have the job deflated with a whoosh. Her stomach tightened.

"He wanted to know if I was seeing you. What the situation was."

She moved away just far enough she could see his face. "And...you said?"

He turned to look at her. "I told him the truth." Ross didn't say anything more for a few moments, then, "He thinks what happened at the accident site could affect my chances for Battalion Chief. The committee looks for any little thing to make a difference between candidates."

Sally bit her top lip. The day had come. "I see."

Ross turned to her. "Sally, help me find some way around this. Together we can come up with a plan. Maybe you could transfer? You're going to school sometime soon anyway. It could be temporary, then you could move back if I make Battalion Chief. I'd be over stations that didn't include Twelves."

She couldn't, wouldn't, be the reason Ross didn't get his dream. That had been done to her by Wade and she wouldn't be the one to do it to Ross. He deserved better. But to transfer? She'd told him once that she wouldn't do that. But what if she did and he didn't get the job? Or she didn't get into med school? She helped Kody with Lucy. If they were in the same station, they could work out the schedule easier. She lived nearby the station house. More than all that, she'd promised herself she'd never rearrange her life again for a man.

Ross had said nothing about his feelings. What if she up-ended her life for him? What if Ross never made a real commitment? What if all he wanted was what they had now? She couldn't take chances with her life like that. Too much damage had been done to her dreams and herself by her relationship with Wade and she refused to let that happen between her and Ross.

Sally shook her head. "Ross, I won't be the reason you don't get the job of your dreams. I've been in your spot before. I know what it's like to push your dreams away to make room for someone else's. Please don't ask me to."

He searched her eyes for something she couldn't identify before saying, "We knew all along that this day was coming. One way or another." His voice had become firm, taken on his captain-in-charge tone.

"Yeah, if it wasn't you, it would be me. Hopefully I'll know something about med school soon. It's been a nice ride while it lasted."

Ross sighed heavily. "It's just that I've worked toward moving up the ranks my entire career. This is my chance. Higher-ranking jobs don't come along often. I believe I can make a difference in Austin's fire department. That I'm the kind of leader they need."

Sally put a hand on his arm. "Hey, you don't have to sell me on the idea. I believe that about you as well. We agreed to keep it between ourselves for just that reason."

Ross was still focused on his job, she could understand that, even hoped the promotion was his, but still it hurt that he wanted it more than he needed her. That even after what she had told him about her marriage, he still had the nerve to ask her to transfer without any mention of his feelings.

But Ross hadn't led her to believe anything different about what he wanted in life. Had never mentioned the future, or wanting more. She shouldn't be upset. If the table was turned, wouldn't she give him up if it meant missing out on med school? She'd let Ross get too close. "This wasn't supposed to be this hard."

He faced her. "No, it wasn't. But we can remain friends."

Sally shook her head. "No, we've tried that before. Coworkers, yes—friends, no. It would never work."

"I guess you're right." His voice was flat.

She looked out at the green pasture with the sun shining across it. Ross's ranch had felt more like home than any place she'd been in a long time. But it had never really been hers. It was a part of that pretend world she'd let herself be drawn into once again.

"I better be going." She went up on her toes and kissed his cheek. His hands came to her waist and he brought her to him. Sally gently pushed him away. "Please don't. It only makes it harder. Please don't come in the house until I'm gone. Have a happy life, Ross."

She held her tears until she reached the front door. In a blurry haze, she gathered her belongings. Stuffing them haphazardly into a bag, she headed out of the house. Ross had honored her request, but he now waited at the bottom of the porch steps.

His lips formed a thin line on his handsome face. Maybe one day he would find the right woman for him, and the timing would be right. The thought made her heart feel as if it were being squeezed to death. If only they were different people.

"Can I help you?"

She shook her head and kept going. He didn't move as she threw her bag into the car, got in and drove away. Yet she was aware that his eyes didn't leave her.

Hours later Ross hit the fence staple another time despite it already being secure in the post. After Sally had left, he'd gathered his fence-repair bag, saddled Romeo and ridden as if the devil were after him to the remotest point of his property. There he'd started checking the fence that was already in good repair.

He was doing anything he could to drown out the voice that poked and prodded that she hadn't been willing to help him find a way around the situation. Hadn't wanted to fight for them.

He didn't like her decision at all, but he really couldn't give a good argument against it. Maybe she was right. Their relationship had been a diversion. If he got the Battalion Chief position, then he would start working on the Assistant Chief position. Yes, this was for the best. If they had waited till later on to break up, it would have just been harder.

So why did he feel as if his heart had been ripped out? Worse, something about the situation made him think he'd treated her far more badly than her husband had.

Maybe when this Battalion Chief stuff was over they could try again.

He shook his head.

No, as long as she was working in the same station as he it would never work. If she didn't get into medical school, she'd have to keep her job. And even if she did, she still wanted to stay on at the station for part-time work. One of them would have to give up something they greatly wanted in order for them to have a relationship.

Ross hit the post even harder.

What they'd had was all there would be.

He jerked his shirt off and used it to mop the sweat off his face. Afterward, he looked at it and groaned. Just a few weeks ago, he wouldn't have even done that. Even when he was alone. Sally had changed his world in more ways than one.

Ross didn't return to the house until just after dark. He wasn't looking forward to going inside where he'd shared such wonderful moments with Sally. She had permeated every aspect of his life. The thought of climbing in his bed without her drove him to sleep on the sofa.

The next few days weren't much better. Everything in his world had been turned upside down and not for the better. If he'd been miserable before, it came nowhere near the pain he experienced now. What he had to do was learn to live with it.

He hadn't even gotten to the hard part. Working with Sally and knowing he couldn't touch her.

Sally had gone home and flung herself on her bed to sob until there were no more tears.

With Wade it had all been make-believe, and now with Ross... The only difference was that she'd known this was how it would end from the beginning. Still, she couldn't stop her heart from being involved. It was breaking.

Ross hadn't demanded she make changes. He'd suggested it as an idea. She'd known how important the promotion was to him from day one. Ross didn't deserve any comparison to Wade. Had she been putting that on every man she met? Ross had proven trustworthy over and over.

Still, what if she'd been the only one to make concessions and their time together had run its course or Ross had become so caught up in his job their relationship had died? What would she have then? She just couldn't take that chance.

Done with her crying, she climbed into the shower, ordered her thoughts and put her emotions on autopilot before she dressed for work. At least there she would be distracted until she and Ross had to share a shift. That she wasn't looking forward to.

She returned to the station to great fanfare, but her heart was heavy. She put on a brave face, with the intention of not letting on how broken she was. Thankfully everyone was focused on her bright purple eye. It looked worse than it felt. Her heart was far more battered.

Her fellow shift members made fun of her, along with shadowboxing when they walked past her. A couple of them made jokes about Ross's over-the-top reaction to one of his company getting hit. None of them asked any deeper questions about why Ross had acted the way he did. She was glad. Not being honest with them would have bothered her. Talking about him would have made her cry. It would all be out if she let that happen.

She dreaded the day she and Ross shared the same shift. When she'd first become involved with him, she'd known that when they stopped seeing each other their working relationship would be strained. Now they were going to have to deal with just that. It wouldn't be fun, but she would keep moving. She couldn't give up her job just because it was difficult being around Ross.

Her fear came true a week later. The new schedule was posted and there along with Ross's name was hers on the same day. She came to work determined to keep her thoughts on her job and not let the fact she was just feet from Ross for a full twenty-four hours affect her work. She'd have to learn to deal with the reality that she couldn't talk to him on a personal level or touch him on an intimate one. Those thoughts almost caused physical pain. She understood in her head that their being apart was necessary, but her heart wasn't convinced.

Managing to make it to the locker room without running into Ross, she put away her bag. When she returned to the bay, she saw him standing beside one of the trucks talking to the captain of the outgoing shift. She stopped dead still. Her heart drummed against her ribs.

This situation was more excruciating than she'd anticipated. With a fortitude she didn't know she had, she picked up her clipboard and headed for the ambulance to do her routine shift check of the supplies. Ross looked in her direction. She nodded and kept moving. The rest of the shift she stayed on her side of the building. Despite that she was well aware of where he was at all times.

The only time her brain shut him out was when they were on a call. Thankfully it was a relatively busy shift. By the next day and shift-change time, she was more mentally than physically exhausted.

Ross had spoken to her a couple of times to give her directions during a run. There was never anything but professional interaction between them, which was as it should be, yet she longed for more. She'd put a bag of his things that he had kept at her place in the back of his truck before she'd left the station. That was the last of anything personal between them.

The next time they shared a shift, only a few days later, it was better. She kept to herself and had as little interaction with the firefighters as possible. What she feared would happen when she became involved with Ross had. Now she was reaping what she'd sown.

She'd been hurt when she'd found out Wade was cheating on her but none of those feelings compared to what she was experiencing now. It was like walking around as a shell of a person. Ross had become essential to her living and breathing, and not having him was slowly killing her.

She had to get out of this funk. Her grade on the MCAT should arrive any day. When she found out how she'd done, then she could really move forward, make plans. Her focus would be on school and what was happening at the hospital. Still, she would need to do part-time paramedic work to pay the bills and keep her certificate up to date. That would mean working with the fire department and possibly Ross, if he didn't get the Battalion Chief's position.

Somehow she'd get beyond this. Or would she?

It had been a couple weeks since she'd stopped seeing Ross when Kody started asking questions. She was at one of Lucy's school functions when he pulled her off to the side.

"What's going on with you, Sweet Pea?"

She wasn't going to tell him that she was heartsick. "I told you not to call me that."

"Don't evade the question. I know something's going on. You didn't look this bad when you divorced that jerk you married."

"I'm fine. I'm just anxious about my MCAT grades." Or she could tell him she hadn't slept a full night since the last time she was in bed with Ross.

Kody huffed loud enough that a couple of people looked at them. "I was on Ross's shift today."

"What does that have to do with me?" She didn't meet his look.

"It's just interesting that he has the same look."

She said softly, "We're not seeing each other anymore."

Kody bared his teeth. "I told him he'd have to deal with me if he broke your heart."

Sally placed a hand on Kody's arm, giving him a pleading look. "Please don't say anything to Ross. We both agreed it was for the best. His actions when I got my black eye were noticed by the bosses. I don't want him to lose his chances for advancement because of me. I'd never want to be responsible for that. I'm going to medical school, I hope, and I won't have time for a relationship. It's for the best. It's not Ross's fault."

"I just hate to see you hurting."

"I'll get over it."

Kody studied her. "Will you?"

Lucy's program was starting so Sally didn't have a chance to answer. If she said yes, she was afraid she would be lying to him as well as to herself.

CHAPTER TEN

Ross turned in his chair so that he could look out the window into the bay for a chance glimpse of Sally. He did that too often on the days she worked. His time was spent figuring out a way to get through those days in particular and life in general without her. He missed having her as part of his real world. Just seeing her at work wasn't enough. Then again, if he never saw Sally, maybe he'd get over her. Either way, he wasn't sure how to survive. What he was currently doing wasn't working.

Right now, she stood beside the ambulance grinning at her crew member. She hadn't smiled at him in days. Not having her happiness directed at him was a physical hurt in his chest.

Sally kept a low profile, staying on her side of the building as much as possible. The first couple of weeks, that had been fine with him, easier in fact, but now it made him angry, sad. This wasn't a way for either one of them to live. His days had turned tedious and challenging, in not a good way.

The last time they'd worked together he'd scheduled a station meeting that included the medical side before an inspection. He and Sally hadn't been in a room together in weeks. She'd sat in the back keeping as much distance between them as possible. As he'd spoken, a couple of times his glance had met hers. There had been a gloomy aura in her eyes. He'd stammered over his words. It was his fault it was there.

But wasn't it Sally who had agreed they'd just have a good time together? That she wanted no attachment because she didn't want a relationship to interfere with her plans? She'd known what they were doing wouldn't last. So why did she act as if she were taking it so hard? Did she care for him more than she'd let on? More than he'd realized?

At dinner that evening they made sure to sit on opposite ends of the long table where it wasn't easy to interact, yet he was aware of every move she made. Her laugh skated down his spine. It should be him sharing that with her. Something had to give soon. He couldn't continue to live like this.

They were just finishing eating when the alarm sounded. Relief washed over him. Was it wrong of him to be grateful for a call? At least on those he would focus on something other than Sally.

Everyone jumped into action, leaving their plates on the table.

The dispatcher called out: "Three-year-old. Stuck in storm drain. Fifth and Park."

Despite his desire to be elsewhere, this was a call Ross didn't want to hear. A sick feeling filled his stomach. He'd trained for this eventuality, but it was one he'd never been involved in and had never wanted to have to oversee either. He'd heard more than once at seminars that it was the most difficult, emotionally and physically.

To make matters worse, a storm was on the way. And it was getting dark. The clock was ticking on two levels. Could the situation be grimmer?

Ross was out of the truck the second it stopped at the scene and striding toward the policeman standing beside a sobbing woman.

"What's the situation?" he asked the policeman.

"This woman's child climbed in the drain after a ball and

fell in. He's been in there for about ten minutes now. We've heard him crying."

"Ma'am…" Ross placed his hand on her arm briefly, to get her attention "…I need you to talk to him. Tell him someone's coming to get him. Reassure him. Can you do that?"

She nodded.

Ross said into the radio, "I need a blanket over here."

Seconds later one of his firefighters brought it to him.

"Put the blanket down in front of the drain and have the mother talk to the child."

"Yes, sir," the policeman said.

Ross assured the woman, "We'll get him out." As he walked away, he said into the radio, "I need a plan of the drainage lines along here, asap."

"Copy that," his lieutenant replied.

"Have the policeman in charge meet me at the truck," he said into the radio.

"Ten-four. He's right here and on his way," the engineer came back.

Ross talked as he walked, surveying the area. "We're going to need rope, the tripod, and have medical on standby."

"Medical here." Sally's voice came across the air.

At the truck, he told the policeman to see that people stayed back and to reroute traffic. This rescue wasn't going to happen fast.

Ross spoke into the radio. "Remove your turnout gear. Put vests on. We're going to be here for a while. I need three men to meet me at the drain. We've got to get that cement cover off so we can see what's going on." Ross removed his gear. He was wearing a T-shirt, pants and his regular shoes, and added his reflective light coat. He put on a yellow hard hat.

When he joined his firefighters at the drain, the policeman guided the mother away so Ross and the other three men could flip the cover over and out of the way.

"These things are supposed to have a grate," one of the men said.

The policeman offered, "Yeah, but they get missed or rust out. This one doesn't have one for whatever reason and now there's a kid to save."

"Flashlight," Ross said.

Sally handed him hers. He shined it into the hole. It was about twenty feet deep and three feet wide. At the bottom he could just make out the top of a child's head where the drain fed into the larger cross drain. The boy wasn't saying anything now. However, there was an occasional whimper so they knew he was alive.

The problems were mounting. Rain was coming. The sun was setting. The boy was going into shock. Now the narrow drain.

One of the men stated the obvious. "Captain, none of us are small enough to go down."

Could the situation get any more challenging?

"I'll do it." Sally's voice came from behind him.

It could!

She was the slightest on the shift. To punctuate the need to hurry, thunder rolled. Rain would be here soon. The child could drown if they didn't get moving.

Ross's first instinct was to say no, knowing Sally's history. Plus, it was against regulations because Sally wasn't a firefighter, and she hadn't been trained for this situation. But there was no choice. If they didn't move now, the child would certainly die. Ross had to think about the bigger picture. Now that included putting Sally's life in danger.

"Get us some light here. Secure the tripod over the hole. Triple-check the rope and pulley. I'll get Sally into the harness," he told the men. "Sally, come with me."

He led her to the rescue truck. After making sure no one could hear him, he said in a low voice, "Are you sure about this?"

Sally gave him a firm nod. "I'm sure."

"It's everything you hate."

She gave him a determined look. "If I don't go, the child will die."

"We could look for another way." Yet he knew of no other way. He wanted to take this burden away from both of them.

"You and I know there isn't one, so help me with the harness." Her voice indicated she wouldn't discuss it further.

Resigned, Ross pulled the harness out of the storage box on the side of the truck. He helped her step into it, pulled it into position over her jumpsuit and around her leg before buckling it at her waist. "If I could have it any other way, I would."

She gave him a thin-lipped nod. "I know that."

He took out a helmet with a light on the front, placed it on her head. His gaze met hers as he buckled it under her chin. There was a flicker of fear in her eyes that pulled at his heart. Sally was the bravest woman he'd ever known. She was facing her fears head-on. Could he say that about himself?

"You know, to make this even worse, we're going to have to send you in upside down. The space isn't wide enough for you to turn around to put a harness on the kid. You'll have to go down headfirst, secure him in the basket, come up and we'll pull the kid out. You'll have a headset. I'll be right there with you the whole way."

After what had passed between them over the last few weeks, did that reassure her? Ross hoped it did. He wanted her to trust he was there for her.

"I understand. I can do this."

He grabbed a pair of leather gloves and handed them to her. "These may be a little too large, but they'll be better than nothing."

"Thanks." She pulled them on.

"Okay. Let's go," Ross said.

She called to her crew member to bring the child-size basket. "What's the boy's name?"

Ross asked into his radio, "What's the boy's name?"

"Mikey."

"Ten-four."

When they arrived at the hole, Ross said to Sally, "Don't take any chances. If you think something isn't right, come up."

"Ten-four."

Ross asked one of the firefighters for his radio head unit. He positioned it around Sally's neck. "You don't have to push anything, just talk. I can hear you and you can hear me." He set the channel so that it would only be the two of them on it. Flipping on the light and securing the basket to her chest, he said, "You ready?"

Their eyes held for a moment as the rain started to fall. Sally nodded and he clipped the rope onto the harness. She went down on her hands and knees. As she put her head into the hole, Ross and one of the other firefighters each took hold of one of her legs and guided her in. Another two firefighters manned the rope, slowly letting it out.

Ross's chest tightened to the point he couldn't take a full breath as he watched Sally's feet disappear into the blackness.

Fear clutched her heart as Sally slid into the tight space. The only thing that kept her going was the knowledge that if she didn't do this a child would die. It could have been Lucy, or Jared or Olivia.

By inches, she was lowered. Her head hurt from the blood rushing to it but soon eased as it adjusted. Either way she had to just not think about it. Using her hands, she guided her way down. She was thankful for the helmet light. Without it she wasn't sure she could remain sane.

"Sally, talk to me." It was Ross's deep, calming voice, yet there was still an edge to it. He was afraid for her. Ross knew her fear too well.

"I'm about halfway down. I see the child. He isn't moving."

She continued downward as her clothes began to get wet.

"It's really raining now, isn't it?"

"Ten-four." Ross hadn't even tried to keep his concern out of his voice that time.

"Okay, I've reached him. Hold me here." She hung just above the boy. He was sitting on the mush made of old leaves, grass clippings and garbage with his head leaning against the wall. "Mikey? I'm here to help you."

There was no reply from the child. A chill went through her. She pulled off a glove and used her mouth to hold it. Reaching down, she checked the boy's neck for a pulse. She blew out a sigh of relief. "He's alive, but in shock."

"Ten-four. Now get him in that basket and we'll get you up here."

Water poured in a steady stream around her and over her as she released the basket. It was growing higher in the shaft because the child plugged part of the cross-drain hole. She needed to get the boy out of the way to let water flow into the larger drain before it came above his head. If she could get the basket flat enough to get the child into it, she could move him out into the larger drain long enough for her to go completely down. The water was rising by the minute.

"Sally, talk to me!"

She spat out the glove and took off the other one. They were just in the way now.

"I'm thinking down here!" At least her frustration with Ross's demands was taking her mind off how dangerous all of this was. "Water is getting higher down here."

"We're diverting all we can."

"Lower me another foot." She went down. "Right there."

She needed to lay the basket down beside the boy, but she couldn't have him float away on the water rushing down the larger drain.

"Send the other line down."

Seconds later another rope came down beside her.

"What're you doing?" Ross demanded.

"I'm having to do some repositioning."

"Repositioning?" Ross's voice wasn't as steady as it usually was.

She clipped the line onto the basket, then laid it next to the boy.

Placing her hands under the child's arms, she used all her strength to lift him into the basket. She pulled the blanket in the basket over him the best she could and clipped him in. Water was beginning to wash over him.

"Give me some slack in the second rope."

"Ten-four," Ross came back.

"Now in mine." She went down. "That's good. That's good."

Sally pushed the basket out into the larger cross drain, making sure the boy's head stayed well above the water, then angled the basket against the wall.

"Let me down some more."

"What?" Ross all but screamed in her ear.

"Do it, Ross."

Seconds later she had her head in the larger drain. She was glad to see that it was about five feet wide. Her knees hit the bottom of the small drain. A moment of panic washed through her when she feared her feet wouldn't quite make it but they soon slid down the slick wall. Cold water poured around her. It was rising. Her teeth chattered. She was soon lying on her stomach, with her head raised in the cross drain as water flowed down her sides. Rolling over, she grabbed the boy and pushed the basket back through the opening.

The increasing pressure of the water current made it difficult to maneuver. She braced her feet against the wall to hold her position and held her head up to the point she strained her neck to keep it out of the water.

"Pull him up. Slowly. I can't see him or guide him. I'm having to do it all by feel."

Ross gave the order. The basket started moving. Soon it left her fingertips.

"What've you done? You're supposed to be coming up." Panic filled Ross's voice.

"There was a change in plan. It's a swimming pool down here."

She hoped with everything in her that she could get back into the other drain without any trouble.

"Uh, Ross, it's going to be a little tricky down here for the next few minutes. You mind talking to me and keeping my mind off it while I figure things out?"

"Aw, Sweet Sally, you're killing me. We have the kid. The EMT is checking him right now. He'll be on the way to the hospital soon."

Sally tucked her head back through the hole into the smaller down drain. So far so good. "How're Romeo and Juliet doing?"

"They're great." His voice lowered. "I think they miss you. I know I do."

If she hadn't been concentrating so hard on what she was doing, she would've reveled in that statement. Sally continued to snake her way upward into the drain.

"Tighten the rope."

Ross gave the order.

"Now pull me slowly. I'm not sure I'm going to make it through this way."

Ross's groan sounded as if he was in agony, then he gave the order.

With the help of the tension on the rope to support her and performing an extreme back bend, she slid through until she was on her knees. She'd have scrapes on her back from that maneuver. Her jumpsuit had been torn. "Stop."

The rope didn't move. She came to her feet. The water came to her calves. She needed to get out of here.

"Is everything all right?" Ross's voice held a note of panic.

"Ten-four. I just needed to stand up." Seconds later she said, "Hey, Ross, would you mind pulling me out of here?"

He snapped. "Let's get her out, guys."

She was halfway up when she said, "I've missed you too."

"You're going to be the death of me." The words were almost a caress.

Her head had hardly popped out of the hole before Ross's hands were under her arms and she was hoisted against him. "I don't know what I'd do if I lost you."

"Stop, Ross," she whispered, pushing against his shoulders. She looked behind him to see the Battalion Chief watching them. "Don't do this. How do you think it looks?"

Thankfully others grabbed her, so that it looked as if everyone was taking their turn in congratulating her, making Ross's embrace look as if it weren't anything special.

She wiped the dirt on her face as she stood in the heavy rain. To her great amazement Ross dropped his coat, pulled his shirt over his head and started cleaning her face. Embarrassed at his attention, she took it from him and used it to finish the job.

The shirt was soaked yet still warm from Ross's body. The musky smell of him clung to the fibers. Sally inhaled. It had been so long since she'd been close enough to enjoy his scent. She clung to his shirt.

Someone handed her a blanket. Ross pulled his coat back on. She winced when someone touched her back.

"Are you hurt?" Ross asked with concern as he pushed people away.

"My back."

He spoke into the radio. "I need a medic over here."

"I've just scraped my back. I'll be fine."

"Maybe so, but you'll be checked out." He handed her off to the paramedic. "Now go."

Ross didn't want to live through anything like the last eight hours ever again in his life. Sally going into the drain had been bad enough but those moments when he'd feared she couldn't get out had almost been more than his heart could take. He'd actually thought he was going to lose her.

He'd been such a self-serving piece of human debris. He'd never once considered Sally's feelings. He'd acted as if it had all been about him, his job. Not once had he questioned if what he was doing was right for them both. He'd encouraged her to have a fling with him when she'd not wanted to out of fear he would act the way he had. Sally had known herself too, known how invested she would become in their relationship.

It hadn't taken him long to learn that she didn't give by half measures, yet he'd pushed her into seeing him when she'd known full well what would happen. The worst part was that he knew her history and had done it anyway. As much as he would like to think that he was better than her ex-husband, he wasn't. He'd treated her the same way. As if her needs and dreams weren't as important as his.

He'd even asked her to make concessions for him. He'd not once considered doing that for her. What kind of person was he? Was he even good enough for Sally? With every fiber in his being he wanted her, loved her. If she would take him back, he'd do everything in his power to be worthy of her.

After they had cleaned up and returned to the house, he'd requested that all the company be allowed to go to the hospital and check on Sally. They went in as a group. Sally had been asleep most of the time. He was sure that she was exhausted from coming off an adrenaline rush, the cold of the water, the physical exertion she'd endured and the fear she'd had to control. The doctor said she would be fine. She only had bumps, bruises and some major scrapes on her back. They were going to keep her for observation until morning.

"Okay, guys, we need to get back to the house," Ross reluctantly announced. He'd have stayed if he had a choice. Instead he lingered behind the others. Reaching for Sally's hand that lay on the hospital bed, he found it warm, which was reassuring. He kissed her lips before whispering, "I love you."

"Captain…" His lieutenant stopped short at the door.

Ross looked at him as he straightened.

The man grinned. "It's about time you admitted it."

"You knew?"

His lieutenant shrugged. "Heck, we all do."

Ross was shocked. "How?"

The man chuckled. "By the way you look at her, or don't lately. But the real clue was when you called out her name during the night."

Ross rolled his eyes. "I'm not going to live it down, am I?"

The man squished up his nose and mouth and shook his head. "I doubt it."

With one last look at Sally, Ross left. Tomorrow he'd start eating humble pie and begging her to take him back. Promotion or not, he wasn't giving her up. If she'd have him. He was afraid that would be a huge *if.*

Kody would be caring for her. Ross had called him to tell him what had happened and asked him to take care of Sally until he could get off his shift.

"I thought you weren't seeing each other anymore," Kody said.

"That's going to change."

"It is, is it?" Kody asked with humor in his voice.

"Yes."

"Then I suggest you bring flowers and chocolate because she's going to need convincing. She'll never agree to play second best to anyone or anything else again." Kody's voice held a firm note.

"I know that. I already feel guilty enough without you piling it on. I don't plan for her to ever be second best again. She'll always be the most important to me. She'll come first."

"Then I'd make that clear and keep that promise."

"That's what I plan to do. Now, will you pick her up at the hospital and get her home until I can get there?"

Kody huffed. "Come on, Ross, I've been watching over her all her life. I can handle this."

"After this time, it'll be my job." Ross hung up.

The station had made the morning TV news and the newspapers. A picture of him embracing Sally was on the front page. Everything he felt for her was there for the world to see. Everything he hadn't wanted the fire department's higher-ups to know. Sally was being hailed as a hero, as she should be. His leadership hadn't gone unnoticed either, or the abilities of the other firefighters.

By the time shift change came around, Ross was anxious to get out of the station. He wanted to see Sally, hold her and reassure himself that she was really okay. He'd called the hospital a couple of times to check on her after they had arrived back at the house. On the last call he'd been told she'd gone home. She would be with Kody.

Ross drove straight to Sally's house from the station. He all but ran to her door. Once again he hesitated there. Would she want to see him? What would he do if she didn't? Beg. Yes, beg was the plan. Somehow, he had to get through to her. He took his courage in hand and knocked. She didn't answer. He tried again. Nothing. He tried calling her on the phone and there was no answer. Slowly he walked back to his truck. Where was she?

Maybe she was at Kody's. He tried phoning him. There was no answer. He went by Kody's house. He wasn't home either. Where were they? Could they be at the station picking up Sally's car? Ross made a circle back by there. Sally's car was gone. He tried her phone. Still no answer.

He'd just have to go home and keep calling. After he saw to the horses, he'd put on his best shirt and pants, buy some flowers and chocolate, and try again. Fear gripped him. Was she nowhere to be found because she didn't want to see him?

* * *

Sally hoped what she thought she'd heard Ross say at the hospital was true. That he loved her. Maybe she'd just imagined it because she wanted his love so desperately. She loved him with all her heart. She was admitting it by coming out to his place unannounced.

He had acted as if he'd been relieved, as if she was his world and he'd gotten it back when she'd come up out of the drain. She was afraid that he was going to lose it again with the Battalion Chief standing right there. Ross hadn't seemed to care. It had been wonderful being in Ross's arms again. Having him hold her always made things better.

She glanced at the letter that lay on the swing next to her. It might not solve all their problems, but it might help.

Her heart picked up its pace when she saw Ross's truck coming down the drive. She went down the steps to meet him. Would he be mad or happy to see her?

He pulled the truck to a jerking stop, hopped out and ran to her. "I've been looking everywhere for you." He stopped just short of pulling her into his arms.

"I told Kody to let you know I was coming out here."

"He didn't, but then, he was probably punishing me for being such a jerk," he all but growled.

She shrugged. "You could be right."

Ross studied her for a few moments. "Are you okay? Really okay?"

The concern in his voice touched her heart. Why didn't he touch her? "I'm fine. Really. I just don't want to have to do anything like that again."

"I don't want you to have to either. It almost killed us both." His gaze held hers. "I would've died if you had. I love you."

"You do?"

"I do with all my heart." The intensity of his voice filled her with joy. "You might not have seen much evidence of it lately, but I do."

"I had hoped what I'd heard at the hospital was true."

Ross stepped closer, almost touching her chest with his. "Does that mean I have a chance? To straighten up, strive to be worthy of you? I don't care about promotions anymore, if I can't have you. I can go to a smaller fire department and work. But I won't live without you. I can't."

She placed her hand on his chest. "You're my hero. You've always been worthy enough. I've never doubted that I could trust you, or that you would protect me or be there if I needed someone. Even if we were just friends. But to have your love is so much more."

Ross scooped her into his arms and kissed her as if he would never let her go. She wrapped her arms around his neck and returned his kisses with equal devotion.

When he set her on her feet again, he looked into her eyes. "I love you, Sweet Sally. I will always."

Sally cupped his face with her hand. "And I love you with all my heart."

He kissed her so tenderly that she was afraid she would cry.

"May I show you just how much I love you?" Ross took her hands.

"I thought you'd never ask."

He led her up the steps and into the house.

Ross lay with Sally snuggled beside him. There had been days he'd thought he would never have this again. And never again would he take moments like this for granted. They were too precious. Life was too precious. What mattered was he and Sally being together.

"Hey, handsome. What're you thinking up there?" Sally looked at him from where her head rested on his chest.

"I was thinking what a lucky man I am."

"That was a nice answer." Her fingers trailed over his skin. "I consider myself pretty lucky too. Oh, that reminds me." She hopped out of bed and pulled on his firehouse T-shirt.

Ross watched as her beautiful body with its back marred by

long scratches left the room. He winced. They were a reminder of what could have been. He heard the front door open. "Hey, where're you going?"

"I'll be right back. I have something to show you."

Seconds later the door opened again. Sally came into the room with an envelope in her hand.

"What do you have?"

She sat beside him. "This came in the mail yesterday. I didn't get it until I got home today. You were the first person I thought of sharing it with."

"What is it?"

"My MCAT score."

He sat straighter. "How did you do?"

She grinned at him. "Well enough to get into any medical school I want."

Ross gave a whoop and hugged her to him. "That's my Sweet Sally." He gave her a kiss.

"So, where're you thinking of going?" Could he stand it if she went far off? No, anywhere she went there would be a fire department. He'd just have to follow.

"I was thinking of staying here and going to Austin Medical. Kody has a doctor friend who could probably help me get a job afterward."

"Now, that sounds like a good plan. I'm so proud of you." He hugged her.

She met his gaze. "You know, it means a lot to me to have you in my corner."

Ross took her hand and kissed her palm. "You can always count on that."

"I've been thinking that now I know I'm going to medical school soon that maybe I should transfer to another station or maybe go to a private company."

He shook his head. "You don't have to do that. I won't ask you to."

She cupped his cheek. "You're not asking. Or demanding. If

that's what it takes to help you, then I'm willing to do it. What matters most to me will always be you."

His heart swelled with love. "And you'll always come first with me."

"I love you, Ross."

His lips brushed hers. "And I love you."

EPILOGUE

THREE DAYS LATER Ross was about to walk out the door of the station when he got a call from Chief Marks. He wanted Ross to come by his office and see him that afternoon. Ross hesitated. He and Sally had plans to celebrate her medical school acceptance with Kody and Lucy that evening. She was cooking dinner for them at his place.

He grinned. It was his and Sally's place now. He loved knowing she would be there when he came home.

"Can we do it right now? I've plans this evening."

"Sure, come on over," said Chief Marks.

A short drive later, as Ross entered the office Chief Marks stood. "I hear you had an exciting shift the other night?"

"Yeah, the house did."

"You know, most firefighters go an entire career and are never involved in a child rescue like that."

"I know." Where was he going with this? It could have all been said over the phone.

Chief Marks's look turned serious. "I also heard the paramedic did an outstanding job as well."

"Yes, Sally was amazing."

"She's the one, isn't she?" The Chief watched him closely.

Ross sat straighter in his chair. "Yes, sir, she is. She's also the one for me. I plan to marry her if she'll have me. I appreciate all you've done for me but if I have to choose between the promotion or her I'm always going to pick her."

Battalion Chief Marks smiled. "I don't think you'll have to do that. The Chief was very impressed with the reports he received about the rescue. Some of it wasn't by the regulations but the end result was excellent. The boy will make a complete recovery. The decision on the new Battalion Chief had pretty much been made, but your leadership during the rescue sealed the deal. The Chief gave me the honor of telling you myself. You'll be our newest and youngest ever Battalion Chief." He stood and offered his hand. "Congratulations. You earned it."

With a huge grin, Ross took his hand. "Thank you, sir."

"The Chief plans to announce it when you, your house and the paramedic, uh, Sally, are awarded a citation in a couple of weeks. But he wanted you to know about it now."

Ross left the Chief's office feeling on top of the world. He wouldn't ruin Sally's celebration of her success tonight. It should be all about her. Instead he would tell her his news while they were alone later in bed so they could have their own special celebration.

He touched his injured shoulder. Life was good. Especially now that he had Sally in it.

Sally was at her apartment with Lucy, packing up the last of the small things to take to Ross's. It hadn't required much persuasion on his part to get her to agree to move to the ranch. She loved it there. Almost as much as she loved him. The last few weeks had been a whirlwind. Between her acceptance to medical school, Ross getting his promotion to Battalion Chief and them both receiving citations from the mayor for their work saving the boy, her life and heart were full.

Tomorrow, after Ross and Kody's shift ended they and a few of the other station members would load up the furniture she wanted to keep and move it out to the ranch. One of the firefighters at the station was moving into her apartment and taking over the lease.

"Here, Aunt Sally." Lucy handed her an empty box she'd sent her after.

"Thanks. I think this should almost get it." Sally pulled a stack of books off a shelf in her living room.

The flash of red lights through the window and the sound of a large engine that she knew well drew her attention. What was going on? Was an apartment burning? Someone hurt? She hadn't heard a siren. But they usually turned them off when they entered a neighborhood.

"What's happening?" Lucy asked.

"I don't know but whatever it is the firefighters will take care of it, I'm sure."

The roar of the heavy truck sounded near as if it had pulled to a stop in front of her building. The emergency lights coming in from the windows reflected around the blank walls of the apartment. Sally hurried to the door. Lucy was at her heels. She opened the door to find the large red engine parked in front of her building. In the near darkness, the lights flashing made a real show.

Ross climbed out of the front passenger seat. He was wearing his usual firehouse uniform. This was his last shift before he started his new job, which would require a white shirt and black pants.

Sally walked toward him. "What's wrong? What're y'all doing here?"

Lucy ran past her. "Daddy!"

She looked beyond Ross to see Kody's truck parked behind the engine. The other firefighters on the shift stood by the engine with smiles on their faces.

"Ross, what's going on?" Sally asked.

He came to stand in front of her. "As my last official act as Captain at Station Twelve, I ordered this crew of firefighters to bring me here to ask you something."

She looked at the men at the truck, including her brother, whose smile had broadened, and his daughter, then around at her neighbors, who had come out of their apartments to see what was going on. "You couldn't have done it over the phone?"

He shook his head. "This isn't the kind of question you should ask over the phone."

Sally started to tremble. Her gaze met his.

Ross took her hand and went down on one knee.

Her heart beat wildly.

"Sally Davis, will you marry me?"

Her eyes filled with moisture, making Ross's handsome face blurry. She blinked. Nodding, she said, "Yes."

With a whoop, Ross came onto both feet and grabbed her, twirling her around.

There was clapping and cheers from those around them.

Ross set her feet on the ground before he gave her a kiss so tender she almost started tearing up again.

She looked at him with all the love she felt. "You know, Battalion Chief Lawson, I think Dr. Sally Lawson will sound perfect."

Ross smiled. "As long as we're together, life will be perfect for me."

Sally came up on her toes and kissed him. "For me too."

* * * * *

A Kiss To Remember

Naima Simone

DESIRE

Scandalous world of the elite.

CHAPTER ONE

"EXCUSE ME. Can I kiss you?"

Remi Donovan blinked at the tall, ridiculously gorgeous man standing at the library's circulation desk.

Impossible. He couldn't have just said what she thought he said. It was Declan Howard in front of her, after all.

"I'm sorry?"

His eyes briefly slid away before landing back on her in their lilac—yes, lilac—glory. "I know this is...unorthodox. And I wouldn't ask if it wasn't an emergency. But can I kiss you? Please?"

An emergency kiss?

Well, *okay.* She'd heard a lot of bullshit in her years—one couldn't have a high school teacher as a best friend, who regularly regaled her with students' excuses about homework and not be well versed in bullshit—but this? It definitely landed in the top ten.

But again. Declan Howard. Recent transplant to Rose Bend, Massachusetts, Declan Howard. Successful businessman Declan Howard.

Secret crush Declan Howard.

She blinked again.

Nope, the face of sharp angles, dramatic slants and mas-culine beauty didn't still disappear. A proud, clear brow that could rock a Mr. Rochester–worthy scowl. An arrogant blade of a nose that somehow appeared haughty *and* like it'd taken a punch and come out the winner. The slopes of his cheekbones and jaw could've received awards for their melodrama, and that mouth… Well, the less said about that sinful creation the better.

As a matter of fact…

She glanced over her shoulder just to make sure he wasn't talking to someone behind her.

When no one appeared, she turned back to him. Swallowed and forced a nonchalant shrug. He was still standing there want-ing to kiss her?

"Um. Sure."

Relief flashed in his eyes. Then they grew hooded, lashes lowering, but not fast enough to hide another flicker of emo-tion. Something darker, more intense. Something that had her belly clenching in a hard, heavy tug…

His arm stretched across the circulation desk and a big hand curled around the nape of her neck, drawing her forward.

Oh God…

That mouth. She would be a liar if she claimed not to have stared at the wide, sensual curves that were somehow both firm and soft. Both inviting and intimidating. She'd often wondered how the contrast of that slightly thinner top lip would compare to the fuller bottom one.

Now she knew.

In complete, exacting detail.

Perfection.

Giving and demanding. Indulgent and hard. Sharp as the drop in temperature on an October night in the southern Berk-shires. And as sweet as the candied apples the middle school PTA sold for their annual fall fundraiser.

His lips molded to hers, sliding, pressing… Parting. First his breath, carrying his earthy cloves-and-cinnamon scent, invaded her. Then his tongue followed, gliding over hers, greeting her before engaging in a sensual dance that teetered on the edge of erotic. And as he sucked on her tongue, then licked the sensitive roof of her mouth, she tipped closer to that edge.

A whimper escaped her, one that she would no doubt be completely mortified over later, and holy hell, he licked that up, too. And gave her a groan in return as if her pleasure tasted good to him.

She released another whimper, this one of disappointment as he withdrew from her. That whimper, too, she'd cringe over later. But now, as the library's recycled air brushed her damp, swollen lips and her lashes lifted, all she cared about was that beautiful mouth making its way back to her and—

Oh God.

She stiffened.

The library. She was in the middle of the library. During lunch hour. Right before the kindergartners from the grade school arrived for Friday Story Circle.

"Um..."

Say something.

You've got your kiss and rocked my proverbial world, now move along unless you'd like to check out a book. Can I suggest Crave *by Tracy Wolff?*

Because of course she'd noticed his preference for YA paranormal fiction. Jesus be a fence, one lip-lock with Declan Howard had rendered her befuddled. She—logical, reasonable, sometimes too plainspoken for her own good Remi—didn't do *befuddled.*

Until now.

"Thank you for that," Declan murmured. His eyes dipped to her mouth, and her breath caught in her throat.

If he tried to kiss her again, she would have to...to...*stop him.* Yes, yes. That's what she was thinking. Stop him.

Didn't matter that heat, smoky and thick, flickered inside her. She pressed her fingertips into the top of the desk, the solidity of the wood grounding her. And if she touched it, she wouldn't lift her hand to her tingling mouth.

"You're welcome. I—" She hadn't been sure what she'd been about to say, but the rest of it evaporated as Tara Merrick appeared behind Declan.

Remi knew the beautiful blonde who worked at The Bath Barn, the shop Tara's mother owned that sold bath products, lotions, perfumes and candles. This was Rose Bend, so of course everyone knew everyone. But Remi had never given the other woman cause to glare at her as she was doing now.

"Declan, I've been looking for you." Tara wrapped a proprietary hand around Declan's forearm, the sugary sweet tone belying the dark fire in her eyes.

"There was no need," Declan said, gently but firmly extricating himself from her grasp.

His purple gaze returned to Remi and, though she resented herself for it, electricity crackled over her skin. She resented it because the pleasure that had fizzed inside her chest like a shaken soda can over *Declan Howard* kissing *her* had fallen flat.

She might've sucked at calculus in college, but she didn't need to know infinitesimals to add one plus one: Declan had only kissed her for Tara's benefit. To make her jealous? To play hard to get? Remi didn't know. What she knew for certain?

It hadn't been because he so desperately needed to get his mouth on her.

It hadn't been because he wanted *her*, Remi Donovan.

And damn if that didn't just slice through her like a fierce winter wind?

"Remi, if you have a moment, I'd—"

She shook her head, cutting off Declan, not allowing her poor heart to flutter over him knowing her name. "I'm sorry but I don't. I really need to get back to work. Do either of you need to check out or return books?"

Her voice didn't waver, and thank God for the smallest of

favors. Declan studied her for a long, tense moment. She forced herself to meet his gaze and not back down.

For years, she'd fought the good fight—learning to love herself and to deep-six her people-pleasing tendencies. Right now, she waged an epic inner war against the whisper-soft voice pleading with her to just *Listen to what he has to say.*

Gifting him with an opportunity to apologize for using her? No thanks. She'd had her share of Pride Smackdown XII. The pay-per-view event would air next week.

"No, all good here. Thank you, again." With a nod, he pivoted on his heel and strode toward the exit.

With one last narrow-eyed stare, Tara hurried after him.

Only after the door closed behind both of them, did Remi heave a sigh.

And as a hushed smattering of whispers broke out behind her, she closed her eyes, pinching the bridge of her nose.

Weirdest. Friday. Ever.

CHAPTER TWO

It was official.

Declan had hit rock bottom.

How else could he describe the desperation that had him sitting in his car with an anxious stomach and a numb ass?

Damn, this was humiliating.

Yet, he didn't drive away from his parking space outside the Rose Bend Public Library, where he waited for Remi Donovan to emerge after locking up for the day. Maybe he'd missed his calling. He should've become a private investigator instead of a wealth manager. Uncovering Remi's work schedule had been ridiculously easy. All he'd had to do was sit in one of the library's reading nooks on one of the Thursday and Friday afternoons he visited Rose Bend. Soon enough, he'd overheard Remi, a coworker—a tall, lanky Black man who seemed to own an amazing number of DC shirts and Converse—and their supervisor discuss work schedules.

He shifted in the driver's seat of his Mercedes-Benz S-Class, fingers drumming restlessly on his thigh. If his colleagues in Boston could see him now, their laughter would threaten the buttons on their three-hundred-dollar shirts. After the humor passed, they'd just stare at him, bemused, and offer to escort him to the nearest high-end gentleman's club.

As if staring at another woman's body could possibly substitute for a certain five-foot-nine frame with gorgeous, natural breasts that would fill his big hands. And a wide flare of hips that never failed to draw his gaze when she strode around the library. And an ass that, by all rights, deserved its own religion.

Fine. He might be a little preoccupied with Rose Bend's beloved librarian.

The librarian whose mouth he claimed for all to see in the middle of the day for his own selfish reasons.

And try as he might—and he did try because he wasn't a prick—he could only rummage up the barest threads of remorse.

Because even though desperation had driven him to that circulation desk with the request of a kiss, desire had chosen her. The need to finally discover if that lush, ripe mouth would taste as good as it promised had won out. And at that first press of lips to lips...

His fingers fisted on his thigh, and he slowly exhaled. Lust tightened inside him... One move and he would snap. As if even now, he dined on that sweet, butterscotch-flavored breath. Licked into the giving depths of her mouth. Twined around that eager tongue. Swallowed that little, needy sound.

"Shit." He shook his head.

Reminiscing about this afternoon wasn't what he'd come here for. Wasn't why he'd set up a stakeout in front of the library. That kiss had been *cataclysmic*, but, in the end, it'd only been the impetus for a plan he needed one Remi Donovan to agree to.

That's all she could be to him—a coconspirator.

He'd learned his lesson the hard way with Tara. If he wanted to do casual friends-with-benefits relationships, he'd have to keep that in Boston, not here in Rose Bend, where the town was too small and everyone knew everyone's business.

Especially when the woman was the daughter of his mother's neighbor and friend.

Yeah, not his brightest moment.

The door to the library opened, spilling a golden slice of light onto the steps before it winked out. He opened his car door, stepping out to watch as Remi appeared, closing the large oak door and locking it.

He stared. Openly. Even though she wore a cream-colored wool coat against the night air, he could easily envision the dark green dress beneath that caressed every wicked curve. Another thing he liked about her. She didn't try to conceal or downplay the gorgeous body God had blessed her with—she worked it. And damn if that confidence wasn't sexy as hell.

Not here for her sexiness, he sternly reminded himself. *Get on with it.*

Firmly closing his car door, he rounded the hood.

Remi's head jerked up, her eyes widening as she spotted him on the curb, near the bottom of the library steps.

She didn't move down the stairs. A tight, almost-tangible tension sprang between them. It vibrated with the memory of that conflagration of a kiss. Of the need for *more* that sang in his veins.

A more he had to deny.

Christ. He tunneled his fingers through his hair. She'd been a beautiful distraction before he'd touched her, before he'd learned the butterscotch-and-sunshine taste of her. But now? Now that he knew? He was finding it difficult to focus on anything else.

He'd graduated from Boston University with a bachelor's degree in business administration and he'd gone on to acquire his dual degree, an Executive MBA in Asset Management. But at this moment, he'd become a student of Remi Donovan. And he wouldn't be satisfied until he earned a PhD.

"I'm sorry for just showing up like this," he said. "But I didn't have your phone number. And showing up during your work-day again didn't seem like a good idea."

"No." She finally spoke in a husky tone more appropriate for a sultry siren in an old black-and-white film noir than a small-town librarian. "That definitely wouldn't have been a good idea. As it is, my supervisor is contemplating tacking your picture to the bulletin board with Not Allowed scrawled across the top. I'm not sure if I've successfully convinced her you didn't accost me."

He winced, only half exaggerating. "God, I hope she doesn't resort to that. The library is one of the few places I can actually find some privacy and quiet." He frowned, thinking of Tara hunting him down earlier. "Well, it used to be."

She arched a delicate eyebrow, descending a step. A spiral of gratification whistled through him at that small movement toward him.

"Last I heard, you have a very nice home at the edge of town with plenty of space and, I would imagine, privacy."

The corner of his mouth curled. "Yes, I do have a nice home with a lot of space. But I also have a mother with boundary issues and a key to said nice house, which impedes my privacy." He shook his head, holding out an arm toward his car. "Can I give you a ride home?"

She studied his hand for a moment before lifting her gaze to him. "No, thank you. I drove to work this morning. Besides, I intended to walk down to Sunnyside Grille for dinner."

"In the dark?"

Declan glanced down the street. It was a little after six and the sun had just settled beyond the horizon in a spectacular display of purple, dark blue and tangerine. If he were a sentimental man, he would remove his cell and capture the beauty of it over the small Berkshires town.

But he wasn't sentimental; he was logical, factual. A man who dealt with numbers, figures and statistics—and data that assured him a woman walking by herself after dark wasn't a good idea.

A rueful smile flirted with her pretty mouth. "This is Rose Bend, not Boston. And the diner is just a few blocks away, not a long walk at all."

"So you're telling me crime doesn't happen in this town?"

"Of course it does. We wouldn't need a police department if it didn't. And if it eases your mind…" She held up her key ring. Showing him the small canister of pepper spray dangling from it. "I'm not an idiot."

"Never thought you were," he murmured, though that coil of concern for her loosened. Silly, when he barely knew her. When today had been the first time he'd really talked to her other than a murmured greeting or nod of acknowledgment. "Would you mind if I joined you?"

She hesitated, and he caught shadows flickering in her hazel gaze. "Why?"

He blinked. "I'm sorry?"

Remi crossed her arms over her chest, but a second later lowered them to her sides. The aborted gesture struck him as curiously vulnerable—and from the trace of irritation that flashed across her face, she obviously regretted that he witnessed it.

Curiosity and protectiveness surged within him. He wanted no part of either. Both were dangerous to him. Curiosity about this woman was a slippery slope into fascination. And from there, captivation, affection. Then… *No.* Been there. Had three years of hell and the divorce papers to prove it.

And this protectiveness. It hinted at a deeper connection, a possession that wasn't possible. A connection he'd avoided in his brief attachments since his ill-fated marriage six years ago. As stunning as Remi was, he wasn't looking for a relationship, a commitment.

At least, not a *real* one.

"Why do you want to join me? And let me help you out. I appreciate the chivalrous offer, but I'm a big girl—" a humorless twist of her lips had an unconscious growl rumbling at the base of his throat "—and I can take care of myself. So what's this really about?"

He parted his lips to… What? Take her to task for that subtle self-directed dig? For cutting him off at the knees by snatching away his excuse for escorting her to the diner? Admiration danced in his chest like a flame, mating with annoyance.

"I do have something to talk about with you. Can I walk you to the diner?"

After another almost-imperceptible hesitation, she nodded. "Okay."

She turned, and he fell into step beside her. Silence reigned between them, and he used the moment to survey the picturesque town that had so completely charmed his mother three years ago that she'd moved here. Elegant, quaint shops, trees heavy with gold, red and orange leaves, lampposts and cute benches lined Main Street. A well-manicured town square, with a colonial-style building housing the Town Hall, and a white, clapboard church with a long steeple soaring toward the sky completed a picture that wouldn't have been out of place on a glossy postcard.

Walking down this sidewalk with people strolling hand in hand or as families, their chatter and laughter floating in the night air, it was easy to forget that heavily populated, traffic-choked Boston lay three hours away.

He tucked his hands in the front pockets of his pants, pushing his coat open. The night air, though cool, felt good on his skin. Inhaling, he held the breath for several seconds, then released it, slowly, deliberately.

"Remi, I apologize if my kissing you earlier today caused you any problems. Sometimes I forget how small towns can be. Especially since I'm only here every other weekend, which isn't the case for you. I'm sorry I didn't take that into account." He paused. "Has anyone…said anything to you?"

"You mean besides my supervisor, who wanted to quarter and draw you, then lectured me on professional decorum? Or do you mean Mrs. Harrison, my hair stylist's grandmother, who'd been standing in the reference section and offered me her advice on how to handle a beast like you? Her words, not mine. Or do you mean Rhonda Hammond, the kindergarten teacher there for Friday Story Circle, who gave me a thumbs-up because she'd heard about it from a friend?"

He grimaced, nodding at a person passing by. "The grapevine is alive and well, I see."

"Thriving."

"Are you in trouble at work?" he gently asked. He'd never forgive himself if his impulsive—and yes, selfish—actions cost her job. "I know you already spoke to your supervisor, but I can, as well. I'll call first thing Monday—"

"That's not necessary." She stopped next to a bench across from the shadowed windows of a closed clothing boutique. "Declan, could you get to the reason why you showed up at the library?"

He stared down into her upturned face. Dark auburn waves framed her hazel eyes, the graceful slope of her cheekbones, the upturned nose and the wicked sinner's mouth. And that shallow, tempting dent in the center of her chin. It never failed that, whenever his gaze dropped to it, he had to resist the compulsion to dip his finger there. Or his tongue.

Madonna and Delilah. That's what she was. Saint and temptress. An irresistible lure that he had to resist.

"I need your help, Remi," he said, resenting like hell the roughened quality to his voice. Clearing his throat, he continued, "This is going to sound...odd, but... Will you be my woman?"

Her face went blank. "Excuse me?" she whispered.

His words played through his head, and he slashed a hand through the air between them. "Hold on, let me rephrase. Will you *pretend* to be my woman? *Pretend.*"

Relief and another, more complicated, murkier emotion wavered in her expression. He peered at her. The need to delve deeper prickled at his scalp.

But that damn curiosity. That protectiveness.

He backpedaled away from her secrets like they had detonators and a steadily ticking clock attached to them.

"Maybe you should start at the beginning." She leveled an inscrutable glance on him, then turned and continued walking down the sidewalk.

Resuming his pace next to her, he huffed out a dry chuckle. "I don't know how to relay this without looking like a dick." Stuffing his hands into the pockets of his coat, he continued, "I don't think it's a secret around here that I...took Tara Merrick out a few times."

"I believe the word you're struggling to find is *date*," she drawled.

He arched an eyebrow. "And I believe *date* is too strong a word," he shot back. "I took her to the movies, dinners—a few of those were at my mom's house so they really don't count, since she and her mother are my mom's neighbors—coffee. Nothing serious."

Remi stopped in the middle of the sidewalk and whipped out her phone. Seconds later, she started tapping on the screen.

"What are you doing?" Frowning, he nudged her to the side, out of the flow of pedestrian traffic.

"I'm pulling up my online dictionary. I mean, I'm just a librarian with a whole reference desk at my disposal, but I'm pretty sure you gave me the very definition of a *date*. But I want to double-check before I call you out. I so hate being wrong."

"Smart-ass," he growled, snatching the cell from her hand and tucking it back in her coat pocket.

His cock perked up at the mere mention of her fantastic ass even as he hungered to press his thumb to the plush bottom curve of her mouth and come away smeared with her deep red lipstick.

"And for your information," he said, voice lower, heavier, unable to scrub that image of her smeared lips from his mind. "It isn't a date when I'm up-front from the beginning that I'm not looking for any kind of attachment, and I warn her not to expect anything to come out of it. We were just two people enjoying each other's company while I was in town for the weekend. Nothing more. I was very clear about that."

I always am. I always will be.

She tilted her head to the side, her long dark red waves spilling over her shoulder. "Then why bother?"

"Because…" Declan turned, strode off, and the sweet scent of butterscotch and the aroma of almonds assured him she followed. "It made my mother happy. And after years of rarely seeing her smile after my father died, giving her a reason to didn't seem like much of a sacrifice on my part."

Silence beat between them, filled by the chatter of passersby and the low hum of Rose Bend's version of Friday-night traffic.

"That kind of detracts from your dick status," she finally murmured.

He glanced at her, a smile tugging at his mouth. "Thank you… I think."

"That's why you bought a house here, too, isn't it?" She slid him a look, and the too-knowing gleam trickled down his spine like an ice cube. "Mrs. Howard moved to Rose Bend three years ago, but you didn't buy a house here until last year. You're only in town every other weekend—really you could stay with her. There was no need for you to buy a house. But you did it so she would feel like she had family here. So she had her son here."

He shrugged, not liking this feeling of… Vulnerability. Of being so easily read like one of the books at her library.

"It was nothing. Like I said earlier, I need my space. And what little privacy she allows me." He smiled, even if it was wry. "Which brings me back to why I need you." Lust struck a match against the kindling of need in his gut, flaring into flames at his choice of words. He deliberately doused them. "After our… display at the library, Tara seemed to finally back off."

"Not how I saw it," Remi muttered under her breath, but he caught it.

"True, she chased me out of there, but when I told her we were involved, and what she saw was me being dead serious about what I'd been telling her for the past two weeks—which is that there would be no more movies, no more dinners—the truth seemed to sink in. But I'm not fooling myself into believing it will stick. Not if I don't follow it up with reinforced behavior. Otherwise, she'll convince herself kissing you was a fluke, and I didn't mean it when I said she and I were over." He rubbed his hand over his jaw, his five-o'clock scruff scratching his palm. "That we were never a 'we' to begin with."

"So you want me as your beard to run her off?"

He frowned. Her bland tone didn't hint that he'd offended her. Neither did her perfunctory summation. Yet, he still got the sense he had.

"My beard?" he repeated. "No, I wouldn't put it that way—"

"What other way is there to put it?" She waved a hand, dismissing the question. "And what do I get out of this little...bargain? Well, other than the title of the latest woman you dumped when we end the charade."

Oh yes, definitely offense there. And maybe a trace of bitterness.

"Remi." He gently grasped her elbow, drawing her to a halt. "I didn't mean to insult you."

"You didn't," she argued, stepping back and removing herself from his hold. Chin hiked up, she offered him a polite smile that halted just short of her hazel eyes. "I'm sorry, but I have to turn down your proposal."

Fuck the fake girlfriend arrangement. Fuck wanting her agreement. He'd inadvertently hurt her; she didn't need to say it. The evidence drenched those eyes, drowning out the green and gold so only the brown remained, dark and shadowed.

He reached for her.

"Remi—"

"If it's okay with you, I'm going to head back to the library. I'm not hungry anymore."

She sharply pivoted on her ankle boot, but just as she started to head in the opposite direction, the door to the establishment behind them opened and two older couples and a younger one spilled out into the night.

Remi skidded to an abrupt stop, her entire body going as rigid as one of the statues that littered the Boston Public Garden. Concerned, he dragged his gaze from the small group of people to her and shifted closer. Close enough to hear her mutter...

"Shit."

CHAPTER THREE

DECLAN'S CURIOUS STARE damn near burned a hole in the side of Remi's face, but she avoided meeting that sharp lilac scrutiny. Afraid that while she stood there in the middle of the sidewalk in her own version of an O.K. Corral showdown with her parents, her younger sister, Briana, her sister's new fiancé, Darnell Maitland, and his parents, Declan might spy entirely too much.

Too much of what she didn't want him to see.

Like the hated, grimy envy that had no place alongside her happiness for her sister.

Like the uneasy mixture of love and dread for her mother.

Like the anxiety-pocked need to run, run and never stop until her lungs threatened to burst from her chest.

"Remi, honey." Her mother, voice pitched slightly higher, switched rounded eyes from her to Declan and back to her. "What a surprise."

Translation: *What's going on and what're you doing with Declan Howard?*

No. *Nononono.*

Remi smothered a groan. Why was this happening to her? Today must be cursed. First, the hottest, make-her-lady-parts-weep kiss she'd ever experienced. Then the whispers, not-so-subtle high fives and unsolicited comments and advice. Then Declan's surprising appearance after work and his, uh, unconventional proposal.

And now this.

Twenty-six years as her mother's daughter had earned Remi a W-2 and pension in all things Rochelle Donovan. And Remi recognized that particular shrewd gleam in her mother's eyes.

No way in hell could Remi have Rochelle start thinking Remi and Declan were a *thing*.

"Hi, Mom, Dad." She forced herself to move forward and brushed a kiss over her mother's cheek, then gave her big, lovable bear of a father a hug. "Hey, sis. And future in-laws." Her smile for Briana, Darnell and the Maitlands came more naturally to her lips.

After all, it wasn't Briana's fault that she was three years younger than Remi, had fallen in love and was getting married, much to the delight of their mother.

"Hi, sweetie," Sean Donovan greeted. "How's my best girl doing?"

"Hey!" Briana playfully jabbed their father in the side with an elbow. "I'm standing right here."

"Sorry, you weren't supposed to hear that. You know you're my best girl," he teased.

Remi shook her head, grinning at their father and the joke that had been running around their house as long as she'd been alive. All the Donovan girls—her, Briana and Sherri, their oldest sister—knew with 100 percent certainty that Sean loved them equally and completely.

"I was hoping you could join us for dinner tonight," Briana said, then shot her a sly smile. "But now I see why you turned down the invite. You had a better offer. I ain't mad at you," she stage-whispered.

"What?" Remi blinked, heat blasting a path up her chest and into her face. Thank God for the dark. "No, this isn't—" She waved a hand between her and Declan, silently ordering herself not to look at him. "No," she repeated. Firmly. Because that glint hadn't disappeared from either her mother's or sister's gazes. But wait. Hold up a second. "And what invitation? I didn't get..." She glanced at Rochelle.

So did Briana.

"Mom?" Briana frowned. "I asked you to tell Remi about dinner tonight. You didn't call her?"

"I'm sorry, honey. I must've forgot." She winced, lifting a shoulder in an apologetic half shrug. "You were at work anyway, Remi. And besides, you probably would've been uncomfortable as a third wheel."

Anger and hurt coalesced inside her, shimmering bright and hot.

Her mother hadn't forgotten. More like she hadn't wanted to be embarrassed by her middle daughter's perennially single status. And as Briana's gaze narrowed on Rochelle, Remi could tell her sister knew it, as well.

"But," Rochelle continued, smiling at Declan, who'd remained silent since bumping into her family, "since you're here, why don't you join us? We were heading to Mimi's Café for coffee. You, too, Declan. We'd love to have you."

Panic ripped through Remi, and she glanced at Declan. As if he'd been waiting for that moment, his eyes connected with hers, and the clash reverberated like a collision of metal against screeching metal. She *felt* him. In her chest, belly... Lower.

"Declan?" her mother asked again, breaking their visual connection like cracked glass sprinkling to the ground.

He looked at her mother. Smiled.

"I would be delighted to join you. Thank you for inviting me."

Shit.

Again.

"What the *hell*, Remi? I heard Declan Howard kissed you in the middle of the library today, but I thought that was just gossip! But apparently not! You've been holding out on me." Briana hip-checked Remi, her mock scowl promising retribution. "How long has this been going on?"

Remi sighed, sneaking a peek in Declan's direction. He stood with her father and Darnell near the bakery case, talking. Part of her battled the urge to save him from a possible pumping of information by her father. But the other, admittedly petty, half thrilled in leaving him served up to that grilling since he agreed to this craziness.

"Bri, we're just friends," Remi hedged. Were they even that? In the years since his mother had moved to Rose Bend, she'd barely said a handful of words to him.

"Friends who tongue wrestle?" Briana nodded. "Yes, Darnell and I are the best of friends, too."

Remi snickered, then sipped her caramel macchiato. "I have no idea how he puts up with you."

"Right?" Briana beamed. She turned, scanning the café until her gaze landed on her fiancé. And her pretty face softened with such adoration that Remi cleared her throat. As if sensing her attention on him, the handsome IT analyst with dark brown eyes and beautiful almond skin, looked up and sent his fiancée the sweetest smile.

"I'd say, 'Get a room,' but you might take that literally," Remi drawled, those conflicting emotions of envy and happiness warring in her chest again.

Briana chuckled, and Remi rolled her eyes at the lasciviousness of it. *Yech.*

"Bri, I need to borrow your sister for a minute." Rochelle appeared beside Remi, slipping an arm through hers. "You should go entertain your future mother-in-law instead of flirting with your fiancé and making the rest of us blush."

Remi bit back a groan even as she allowed herself to be led away to a corner of the café. She'd been trying to avoid her mother since arriving at Mimi's. Even a cup of her favorite hot beverage couldn't make her forget that her mother had an agenda by inviting her and Declan to join a gathering she'd intentionally excluded Remi from in the first place.

And yeah, best not dwell too long on that.

"Honey, what is that you're drinking?" Rochelle scrunched up her nose.

Dread swished in her stomach like day-old swill. "Caramel macchiato."

"That's nothing but dessert in a cup. Tea is so much better for you." She shook her head, and her disappointment dented the hard-won, forged-in-fire armor of confidence Remi had built around herself—her heart. "Now, tell me about what's going on between you and Declan."

God, if she held in all these sighs, she would end up with gastric issues.

"Mom, don't get ahead of yourself," she warned.

"You know I'm not one to listen to gossip." Remi coughed, earning a narrow-eyed look from her mother. "But I heard about the kiss at the library. Really, Remi, a little more propriety would've been appreciated, but if the story is true…"

Remi didn't confirm or deny, just sipped her drink. But her mother obviously took her silence as confirmation, and a smile that could only be described as cat-ate-the-whole-flock-of-canaries spread across her face.

"If the story is true, then why haven't you brought him by the house for dinner? Do you know how embarrassing it is to hear that my daughter is dating one of the most eligible men in town from someone else? And here I've been so worried about—"

"Mom, please, stop. Declan and I— We're just friends," she interrupted, holding up her free hand, palm out.

Her mother's excited flow of words snapped off like the cracking of a brittle tree limb. She stared at Remi, the delight in her eyes dimming to frustration and… Sadness. It was that sadness that tore through Remi. As if her *mediocrity* actually pained her mother.

Rochelle's gaze dropped down to Remi's body, skimming

her dress. Before her mother's scrutiny even lifted back to Remi's face, anxiety and unease churned in her belly. Tension invaded her body, drawing her shoulders back, pouring ice water into her veins.

She knew what was coming.

Braced herself for it.

"Maybe... Maybe if you would try to dress just a bit more appropriately for a woman of your—stature, you could possibly be more than friends. If you wore clothes that...concealed rather than drew attention to problematic areas, perhaps Declan would focus more on your lovely face and ignore everything else."

The gentle tone didn't soften the dagger-sharp thrust or make the wound bleed any less.

That it was her mother who twisted the knife and sought to slice her self-esteem to shreds only worsened the pain.

"I'm only telling you this because I love you, and I want you to be happy like your sisters. You know that, don't you, honey?" Rochelle covered Remi's cold hand, squeezed it, the hazel eyes that Remi had inherited, soft and pleading.

I don't know that! If you cared, if you really loved me like you do Briana and Sherri, then you would see how you're tearing me apart.

The words howled inside her head, shoved at her throat with angry fists. Only the genuine affection in her mother's gaze chained them inside. That and her unwillingness to hurt her mother, even though Rochelle didn't possess the same reluctance.

"If you'll excuse me," Remi murmured, setting her drink down on a nearby table. She couldn't stomach it anymore.

Couldn't stomach... A lot of things anymore.

Without waiting for her mother's reply, she strode over to the small group where Declan stood. He glanced down at her, and that violet gaze sharpened, seeming to bore past the smile she fixed on her face.

Several minutes later, before she had time to fully register being maneuvered, she found herself bundled in her coat on the sidewalk outside the café, Declan at her side.

She didn't speak as they strolled back in the direction of the library, and he didn't try to force her into conversation. The events of the entire day whirled through her mind like a movie reel, pausing on the kiss before speeding on fast-forward to him showing up at the library only to pause on her discussion with her mother.

I want you to be happy like your sisters.

Remi could pinpoint the last time her mother had been proud of her. Because it'd been the time of her last heartbreak, her last failure.

And the whole town had been there to bear witness.

For Rochelle Donovan, happiness meant a husband, marriage, children. And Remi desired that—she did. But if she didn't have them, she wasn't less of a woman, less worthy. Not having the whole fairy-tale wedding and family thing wouldn't be due to the size of her breasts, hips or ass. And she refused to decrease in size—whether in weight, personality or spirit—for someone else to love her.

She'd been willing to do that once. Never again.

And yet... Yet, for a moment, Remi had glimpsed that flicker of pride in her mother's eyes again, and her heart had swelled. It'd been so long.

She was tired of being a failure in her mother's eyes. Of being a disappointment. Was it so wrong to yearn for that light in Rochelle's gaze directed toward her, the one Briana and Sherri took for granted?

Remi knew who she was. Knew her own worth. Owned herself.

But just once...

She slammed to an abrupt halt. And turned to Declan.

To his credit, he didn't appear surprised or alarmed. He just slid his hands into his pants pockets, his coat pushed back to expose that wide chest, flat abdomen and those strong thighs.

A swimmer's body—tall, long and lean. And powerful. Staring at him, she combatted the need to step close and closer still, curl against the length of him and just... Rest. She'd come to rely on herself a long time ago, but in the café, she'd uncharacteristically allowed him to take charge. And it'd been a relief. To let someone else carry the burden for a few moments—yes, it'd been a relief.

But that had been an aberration.

She just needed him for one thing.

"I've changed my mind. I'll pretend to be your girlfriend."

Declan cocked his head to the side, studied her for a long moment. "Why have you changed your mind?"

"Does it matter?"

"Yes," he murmured. "I think it does."

A flutter in her belly at his too-soft, too-damn-understanding voice. "No, it doesn't," she said. "Are *you* changing *your* mind?"

Again, he didn't immediately reply. "No, Remi, I'm not. I still need you."

Dammit, he should choose his words more carefully. A greedier woman could read more into that statement.

"Well then, I accept. But I have my own counterproposal." When he dipped his chin, indicating she continue, she inhaled a breath, held it, then exhaled, attempting to quell the riot of nerves rebelling behind her navel. "You have to agree to attend Briana's engagement party with me in a month. Four weeks should be more than enough time to convince Tara that we're a legitimate couple." She stuck out her hand. "Deal?"

Declan stared at her palm as if he read all her secrets in the lines and creases. Slowly, he lifted his intense gaze to hers and, without breaking that connection, engulfed her hand in his bigger, warmer one.

Then drew her closer.

And closer.

Until his woodsy cloves-and-cinnamon scent surrounded her, warmed her. Seduced her. She sank her teeth into her bottom lip. Trapping the moan that nudged at her throat and ached to slip free.

The hand not holding her hand cupped her neck, his thumb swept the skin under her jaw. She shivered.

And held her breath.

Those beautiful, carnal lips brushed over her forehead.

"Deal."

She exhaled.

These next four weeks were going to be... Killer.

CHAPTER FOUR

Declan: Hey, are you up?

Remi: It's 9:30. I'm not 80.

Declan: Is that a yes?

Remi: *sigh* Yes.

Declan: Is it ok for me to call?

Remi: Sure.

Remi stared at her phone screen, heart thudding in her chest, waiting on the black to light up with his name as if she were a teen and the captain of the football team had promised to call. And when the screen lit up with his name, she had to slap her traitorous heart back down with a reality check.

Fake relationship. Get it together. This isn't some chick flick starring Zendaya.

"Hello."

"Why don't I remember you being this snarky before?" he asked in lieu of greeting.

Because we've never had a real conversation past "Hi" and "Excuse me, I need to get to the creamer" at Mimi's Café. Since saying that would reveal more than she was willing to expose, she went with, "I'm not sure I can answer that. And tell me that's not what you called to ask me."

He snorted. "No. It hit me that we didn't come up with a cover story for how we got together. If our...relationship is going to be believable, we'll have to be of one accord with that."

"Wow." Remi shook her head even though he couldn't see the gesture. "Is even saying the word *relationship* painful?"

"Oh, sweetheart, if you only knew," he drawled.

No, Remi ordered her damn heart again. You will not turn over at that endearment. *Cut the shit!*

She cleared her throat, absently picking at the thread on the couch cushion beneath her. "So do you have any ideas for how we became completely enamored of one another?"

"I'm guessing me trying to stop you from bringing disease and destruction to the earth, but we ended up falling for one another is out?"

A loud bark of laughter escaped her, and she clapped a hand over her mouth even though no one lived with her to hear it. "And what's this disease that I'm so intent on bringing to the earth? Love?"

His mock gasp echoed in her ear. "How did you know?"

She snickered. "Okay, I've read *Pestilence*, too, and Laura Thalassa is brilliant. Oh, which reminds me." She snapped her fingers. "I've been meaning to recommend *Crave* by Tracy Wolff, if you haven't read it already. I think you'll love it."

"Thank you. I'll definitely pick it up." A pause. "How do you know what books I'll love?" he murmured.

Heat surged into her face, and she closed her eyes, lightly banging her head against the back of the couch. Dammit.

"I'm a librarian. It's my job to notice what people are reading." *Nice save*, she assured herself. She hoped. *Please God, let it be a nice save.* "Besides, when a man comes into the library and I catch him unashamedly reading YA paranormal romance, my nerd heart rejoices. And I want to feed his literary addiction."

When he chuckled, she silently breathed a deep sigh of relief. And sent up another prayer of thanksgiving. And maybe a promise to attend service on Sunday. It'd been a while.

"There's our story," Declan said. "We met at the library when you noticed what I was reading and suggested a book you thought I'd like. We struck up a conversation, I asked you out, the rest is history."

"It's like our own book nerd fairy tale."

"Book nerds are the shit."

"Hell yeah we are." Remi grinned, and once more had to order her heart to stop doing dumb things. Like swooning.

"'Night, Remi. And thank you again."

"Good night, Declan."

Remi: I've arranged our first date for Friday night after you get to Rose Bend. Hayride.

Declan: Pass.

Remi: Sorry. Bought the tickets. You wanted to be visible. What's more visible than a hayride?

Declan: Dinner. Coffee. A stroll. Standing in the damn street. All don't involve hay. Or hay.

Remi: We're doing it. Suck it up, city boy.

Declan: Why am I doing this again?

Remi: Hey! You kissed me!

Declan: Oh believe me. I can't forget.

Remi: ...

Declan: Too soon?

Remi: Bundle up. It's going to be cold.

Declan: So the hayride was fun.

Remi: ...

Declan: I can hear you saying I told you so.

Remi: Me? Nooooo.

Remi: But I did.

Declan: No one likes a know-it-all. Even beautiful ones.

Remi: You don't need to do that.

Declan: Do what?

Remi: Do the compliment thing when no one's around to hear it.

Declan: I can be truthful whether I have an audience or not, Remi.

Declan: If it makes you uncomfortable, I won't say or rather type it.

Remi: No it doesn't. Just... It's not necessary.

Declan: Are we having our first argument as a couple?

Remi: I think we are... And just for the record, I win.

Declan: Of course, dear. Yes, dear.

Remi: Such a good fake boyfriend.

Remi: Heads-up. If Tara asks, my nickname for you is baby-cakes.

Declan: WTF??

Remi: She was pushing it. Had to come up with something.

Remi: Ok, kidding. Sorta. But she did corner me today and was her usual petty self.

Remi: Why didn't you tell me you used to be married?

The phone rang seconds later, and Remi sighed before swiping her thumb across the screen. She should've expected this call, but her stomach still dropped toward her bare feet. All afternoon, since Tara had approached Remi outside Sunnyside Grille after lunch, she'd gone back and forth about whether or not she would ask Declan about his previous marriage.

Over the two weeks they'd been "together," the texts and phone calls had been constant, and when he came to Rose Bend, they'd spent every day together. As couples did. But they weren't real—no matter how her pulse tripped over itself at just the sound of his voice in her ear or the sight of his name in her messages. Or how thick, hot desire twisted inside her when his hand rested on her hip or cupped the back of her neck. A shiver rippled down her spine at just the memory of the possessive touch.

No. Not possessive. She had to remember and remind herself what this was. Fake. A sham. For the benefit of another woman who'd done what Remi could not allow herself to do.

Fall for him.

She could not be that naive or stupid.

Raising the phone to her ear, she said, "Hey."

"Remi," he replied. "What did she say to you?"

"She didn't go into details," she gently reassured him. Because from the tautness of his voice, it seemed as if he needed to be reassured. "It seemed more like she wanted me to know she had information about you that I didn't have." She hesitated but couldn't hold back the question that had been plaguing her for hours. "Why didn't you mention it, Declan?"

"It's not important."

The abrupt, almost-harsh reply echoed in the silence that fell between them, mocking his adamance.

"Your mom might not have moved to town yet during my last relationship, so you may not have heard about it. But it was the topic of conversation three years ago, for months." She inhaled a deep breath, bile pitching in her stomach at the thought of talking about Patrick and the disastrous, public ending of their relationship. But if she wanted Declan to trust her with his story, maybe she had to take that first step.

"Patrick Grey was a resident at the hospital in the next town over but lived here. We met at the annual motorcycle rally, and I fell hard, fast. Handsome, smart, and yeah, he was going to be a doctor. Not bad, right?"

She gave a soft, self-deprecating laugh. Because, yes, bad. If only she hadn't allowed those things to blind her to his other, not-so-favorable traits.

"We were together for a year and a half. And him being a resident, we didn't have a ton of time together. But I loved and enjoyed every minute when we were. So much that when he started criticizing my dinner or breakfast choices, or offering his opinion on what I wore, I didn't see his comments as negative. Just that he was concerned with my health or wanted me to look my very best. But when he started using what he called 'reward systems'—lose five pounds and he would agree to take me to the bar around his work friends—then I couldn't deny what I'd been ignoring."

"Remi," Declan breathed. "You don't have to tell me this."

"I'd like to say that I broke up with him," she continued as if he hadn't spoken, because *yes*, she did need to get this out. She hadn't spoken about it since it happened. It was time to purge herself of this festering wound. "But I can't. One Saturday morning, I walked into Sunnyside Grille to meet my sisters for breakfast since Patrick had to work a double shift. Or so he'd texted me. But that wasn't true. Because when I entered, there he was. Sitting in one of the booths near the door, sharing the Sunnyside Up Special with a slender, gorgeous brunette. Well, that's not true. They weren't sharing it because they were too busy kissing."

She swallowed hard, still seeing Patrick, the man she'd imagined building a life with, giving another woman what he should've only offered her. Three years had dulled that pain to a twinge.

"When he saw me, he didn't even apologize. Instead, he blamed me for sending him to another woman. He wasn't original. The usual. If I'd only taken care of myself, lost the weight, hadn't been so fat and lazy. In front of everyone in that diner. He didn't give a damn about humiliating me in front of my family, the people I'd grown up with. And I was so stunned, so hurt, I stood there and took it. Grace, the owner, came over and ordered him out. Told him to never bring his ass in there. And Cole and Wolf Dennison *escorted* him to the sidewalk." A faint smile curved her lips, and it went to show how she'd healed, because there was a time she'd never believed she could feel any humor with the memory. "But the damage had already been done. People get dumped all the time. But mine had been devastating, humiliating *and* public."

"What happened to the asshole?" he snapped.

She blinked. "Um, I don't know. I don't care. Last I heard, he found a position in a hospital out of state."

"That just means it's going to take me more time to track him down."

"What?" She laughed. "Declan, stop playing."

"Who's playing?" he growled. "And next time I'm in town, I'm treating Cole and Wolf to beers."

"That's...sweet." She smiled, and warmth radiated in her chest. "Thank you."

"You're perfect, Remi. I hope you know that. And fuck him if he was too much of a narcissistic, insecure bastard to realize it. Or I bet he did realize it. But to make himself feel better about himself, he tried to make you smaller. And I'm not talking about the size of your gorgeous ass or hips—which you fucking better not touch. I hope you know any real man would see the beautiful, sexy, brilliant woman you are and not ask you to change a damn thing. Hell, he would have to up his game to be worthy of you."

Her lips popped open. Thank God they were on the phone because she would've hated for him to glimpse the tears stinging her eyes or the heat streaming into her face. If he looked at her now, he would see her feelings for him. She didn't have to cross her bedroom to the mirror over the dresser and know that the need, the hunger, the... No, she backed away from labeling *that* emotion. But she knew those emotions would greet her in her reflection.

"Remi?" he murmured. "Sweetheart?"

Her fingers fluttered to the base of her throat, and she closed her eyes.

"I'm here. And thank you. I... Thank you."

"You're welcome, sweetheart. But I'm only speaking the truth." He sighed. "I get why you shared that with me. Thank you for trusting me. I know it wasn't easy." He paused, and several moments passed where his breath echoed in her ear. "Ava and I started dating in college. People said we were a 'golden couple,' whatever that means. I guess I can see it now. Similar goals—both financial majors, wanted to be entrepreneurs, desired a certain lifestyle, had the same ideals about the family we desired. She was beautiful, driven, ambitious, and I admired all of that about her. So after we graduated, we married."

A hard silence ricocheted down the line, deafening in its heaviness.

"I love my parents, especially my mother. But their marriage... It wasn't healthy. My father wasn't physically abusive, but emotionally, verbally? He cut her down with words, by withholding affection if she didn't have his dinner on the table on time or if she disappointed him in any small way. And my mother's identity was so entangled with his that when he died, she crumbled, didn't know who she was, how to carry on from one day to the next. That's why when she sold the house and moved here, I dropped everything and made it happen. She needed to escape anything that had to do with my father so she could *finally* discover herself apart from him. I think that was one of the things that attracted me to Ava. She had her own identity, her own goals. But I didn't count on that tearing us apart."

Questions pinged against her skull, but she remained quiet, letting him tell his story at his own pace. Yet her whole body ached with the need to wrap around him, hold him.

Protect him.

She shook her head, as if the motion could dislodge the silly idea. Declan didn't need her protection. Didn't need *her*.

"We both entered graduate school and took jobs in our fields. While my career seemed to rise fast, hers didn't go as smoothly. And listen, I'm a white man in a field that is set up for me to succeed. So I understood her frustration. I knew there were certain advantages for me that weren't there for her. But she turned bitter, and she took that bitterness out on the one person who unconditionally loved and supported her—me."

Remi almost asked him to stop because what was coming...

It had turned him off relationships all these years later. So it must've scarred him.

"It started with complaining about me not having enough time for her. So no matter how tired I was from work and school, I tried to give her more attention. Then she accused me of being too needy, so I pulled back. I'd arrive at work and discover that my files were missing information, or the numbers had been transposed. Or I had to make a presentation, and the Power-Point had disappeared from my computer. When we attended my office parties, she either flirted with my colleagues or deliberately insulted them. Or as I later found out, slept with them."

"Shit," she whispered.

"Yes, shit." He chuckled, but it didn't carry any humor. "She tried to sabotage my career before it could really begin. The betrayal..." He cleared his throat. Paused. "The betrayal when you've done nothing but love a person... It destroys something in you. Your trust. In other people. In yourself. It's not something you forget—or want to repeat."

She got it. God, did she get it.

"She didn't break you, though," she whispered.

"No," he whispered back. "She didn't."

"Declan?"

"Yes."

"I'm glad."

CHAPTER FIVE

LAST HALLOWEEN, DECLAN attended a friend's party, dressed as a pirate, and ended up going home with a sexy as hell cat—or maybe she'd been a mouse.

The Halloween before that, he'd spent the evening at a business dinner. And had his dining partner for dessert.

This Halloween, he stuffed goody bags with candy, toys and small books for the fifty or so excited children that crowded into the Rose Bend Public Library for the Spooks 'n' Books Bash.

Being the town librarian's "boyfriend" definitely had its perks.

He smirked as he tossed a mini pack of M&M's into a plastic bag decorated with goofy ghosts, cats and witches. In the three weeks since he'd started dating Remi, he'd gone to a high school–sponsored haunted house, judged a pumpkin pie contest that she'd volunteered him for when the scheduled judge came down with food poisoning, and gone on his first ever hayride. He'd eaten his first s'more in nineteen years, tasted his first cup of homemade spiced cider ever and snacked on honest-to-God grapenut custard, hauling out and dusting off childhood memories he'd long forgotten.

Yes, these last three weeks had definitely been an experience. As different from his outings with Tara as the Patriots from the Lions. He'd had fun.

Damn.

When had his life stopped being fun?

Not that his life was bad. God, no. It would be the height of white privilege to cry about a challenging career he enjoyed, the luxurious lifestyle it afforded him, the doors to the elite business and social worlds it opened to him. And he indulged in it all.

But did he feel that pure excitement like a child on Christmas morning or a kid soaring down a steep hill on his bike at full speed? Like a teen discovering the bloom of his first crush?

No. That had been missing.

Until now.

Until Remi.

His pulse an uncomfortable throb at his neck, his wrists, he scanned the library, and like a lodestone, his gaze found her. Maybe it was the dark fire of her hair—or the brighter flame of her very essence—but she seemed to gleam like a ruby among the crowd of parents who stood in the outer ring surrounding the children who gathered for story time.

A smile flashed across her face at something, brief but so lovely, and the air in his chest snagged.

Jesus, the power of it.

Like a hard knee to the gut and a gentle brush of fingers across his jaw at the same time.

He blinked, dragging his much-too-fascinated scrutiny away from her and back to the task at hand. Goody bags. Candy. Toys.

"Is this my son over here in the back doing manual labor?" His mother appeared in front of the table, a wide smile stretched across her pretty face. Tiny lines fanned out from the corners of Janet Howard's blue eyes as she nabbed a small box of crayons and swung it back and forth in front of him. "If I didn't see it with my own eyes..."

He snorted, holding his hand out and curling his fingers, signaling for her to hand over the box. When she did, with an even-wider grin, he drawled, "Laugh it up now, woman. But just because I work behind a desk doesn't mean I don't know the meaning of labor." He arched an eyebrow. "I mean, who do you think mows that big yard I have?"

She mimicked the eyebrow gesture. "That reminds me. James Holland lost your number. But he wanted me to pass along the message that he would be glad to take care of your lawn like he does mine."

"Freaking blabbermouth," Declan muttered, dropping the crayons into the goody bag. No sense of male solidarity at all.

"Hi, Declan." Tara strolled up to them, smiling widely. "This is so cute." She turned, waving a hand in the direction of the larger area set up with game stations, the story circle and tables of books. "When Janet told me she was stopping by, I had to tag along. All this time I've lived here, and I can't believe I've never made it to this charming little event."

"It's only the second time the library has held it. Remi started it last year," he said, pride for Remi and the staff's hard work evident in his voice. He didn't even try to conceal it.

He'd only witnessed the tail end of their labor, helping set up and put up decorations, but more than one person had regaled him about all the time and effort she put into the event. And when his mother's gaze narrowed on him, he met it. There was nothing wrong with being proud of a friend's achievements.

Fuck, he was a terrible liar. Even to himself.

His mother and Tara glanced at one another, then Janet hooked an arm through Tara's, clearly telegraphing where her allegiance lay. "Well, that's nice. I just remembered you mentioning you were spending Halloween here, so I thought we'd come over and see if we can convince you to join us for coffee afterward."

We.

He didn't bother looking at Tara, but kept his attention focused on his mother. "I'm sorry. Remi and I already have plans after this wraps up." Technically, they didn't, and he hated fibbing to his mother, but if he had to take Remi to Sunnyside Grille for a late dinner to make the lie true, he would. "But thanks for supporting the event."

His mother's smile tightened around the edges, and she turned to Tara. "Honey, would you mind giving me a moment with Declan?"

"Not at all," Tara said. He ignored her and the smug note in her voice.

If she expected him to bow to his mother's coercion on her behalf, then neither woman really knew him.

"Son—"

"Mom, I love you, and I would never intentionally disrespect you." He interrupted her before she could get on a roll. He flattened his palms on the table and leaned forward, lowering his voice, not desiring an audience for this long-overdue conversation that he would've preferred to have in private. "But that—" he dipped his head in the direction Tara had disappeared "—is not going to happen. There has never *been* any chance of it happening. Something I made very clear to Tara even if she decided not to hear me. I only took her out those few times because it made you happy to see me with her. Or with someone."

He stretched an arm out, clasped his mother's hand in his, squeezed. "I love you, Mom. You're the most important person in the world to me. And I would hate to see our relationship damaged in any way by you choosing this hill to die on. Tara's not for me."

"And this new woman is? A woman you haven't brought around and introduced to me, I might add?"

True. And he'd purposefully avoided doing so. His and Remi's relationship was fake; having her meet his mother smacked too much of "real." It crossed a boundary into territory he hadn't been prepared to enter. But Janet arriving here tonight might snatch that choice out of his hands.

Especially since Remi was headed their way.

He straightened, his gaze shifting from his mother and over her shoulder to the sexy, stunning woman walking toward them. How could she make a simple long-sleeved, V-necked shirt, a dark pair of high-waisted skinny jeans and ankle boots so hot?

Lust rippled through him, and he clenched his teeth against the primal pounding of it in his veins... In his cock.

Goddamn.

Kittens batting balls of yarn. Dad's old baseball mitt that smelled like Bengay and sweat. Grandma Eileen's dentures in a glass on the bathroom sink.

Thinking of anything that would prevent him from springing an erection in front of his mother and all these kids. But most of all his mother.

"Oh." His mother hummed. "That's the way of it."

Declan didn't tear his gaze from Remi. Couldn't. But if by some small miracle he could, yeah, he still wouldn't. Disquiet scurried beneath the throb of need. And he didn't want to glimpse the acknowledgment of that disquiet in his mother's eyes.

"Hey." Remi smiled, glancing down at the table packed with goody bags. "Thank you, Declan. So much. First you saved me with the pie contest and now with this. When my volunteer called out, I thought I was going to have a bunch of screaming kids on my hands." She laughed and turned to his mother. "We've met before, Mrs. Howard, but it's nice to see you again. Thank you for coming tonight."

"Nice to see you, too, Ms. Donovan. Or is it okay to call you Remi, since rumor has it you're dating my son?"

The pointed and faintly accusatory tone wasn't lost on Declan, and apparently not on Remi either, since pink tinged the elegant slant of her cheekbones. But to her credit, she didn't back down.

"Rumors in a small town?" Her lips curled into a rueful

twist. "If only we could monetize it, we could single-handedly support our economy. And yes—" she nodded "—I would be honored if you would call me Remi."

Declan smothered a bark of laughter. *Nice side step.* "Remi, my mother's not new to a library. When I was a kid, she used to take me there often and let me pick out any book I wanted, then let me participate in the scavenger hunts or watch afternoon movies. And she even volunteered at our school library sometimes. Or maybe she just wanted to keep an eye on me," he teased.

His mother snorted. "Both."

"Mrs. Howard, I don't know if you'd consider it, but the library can always use volunteers," Remi said.

"Volunteer? Me?" She scoffed, but Declan glimpsed the interest flicker in her eyes, even though her features remained guarded. "What could I possibly do?"

"Whatever you enjoy." Remi half turned, sweeping a hand toward the room. "If you like clerical duties such as helping us entering patron info into our computer system or returning books to the shelves or manning the help desk, that would be wonderful. Or since we are an interactive library, if you love working with the children, you can read to them, help with tutoring, assist us with our events or even man one of those scavenger hunts Declan mentioned."

Declan stared at her. Excitement shone in her hazel eyes, the gold like chips of sunlight, and enthusiasm lit her face so brightly, he blinked at its gleam.

She was beautiful. No—such a paltry, lazy word to describe the purity and loveliness of a spirit enhanced by a stunning face and body.

He'd met gorgeous women, dated them—fucked them.

But they all faded into an obscure corner of his past the longer he looked at Remi. His heart thudded against his sternum, a rhythm that drowned out the chatter of adults, the happy squeals of children. His world narrowed to her, to the fine angle of her cheekbones, the sweet sin of her mouth, the alluring dent in her chin. To the lush, sensual curves of her body.

Panic ripped through him, and out of pure survival, his mind scrambled back from a treacherous edge his damn heart should've known better than to go anywhere near.

"Declan?" Fingers touched the back of his hand, and just from the delicious burn, he didn't need to glance down and identify its owner. But he did anyway, because *not* looking at Remi Donovan wasn't even an option for him. A small frown creased her brow. "Everything okay?"

"Yes, fine." He flipped her hand over, rubbing his thumb over her palm, catching the small shiver that trembled up her arm. And because that vulnerability still sat on him, he repeated the caress. "I was just thinking how lucky this place is to have someone as loyal, hardworking and beautiful as you."

Her eyes widened, an emotion so tangled, so convoluted flashing in them that he couldn't begin to decipher it. He'd surprised her. Good. Though they were engaged in this arrangement, there was something freeing about being able to touch her, to murmur compliments and neatly, *safely* categorize them under "for the charade."

Like now.

"Thank you," she murmured, giving him one last lingering look before shifting her attention back to his mother. "Do you want to get a cup of hot chocolate, and we can talk more about volunteering?"

"Yes." His mother nodded, and warmth slipped into her expression and voice. "I would like that very much."

"Wonderful. Let's go before the kids beat us to it." She laughed, leading Janet away.

"Is that her plan, then?"

Declan clenched his jaw. Hard. Until the muscles along his jaw ached in protest. Instead of replying to Tara, he walked away from the table, knowing she would follow. Pausing next to a volunteer, he asked her if she would mind watching the goody bags for a moment, and then he continued to a quieter side of the room.

Before he could speak, Tara crossed her arms over her chest, her lips forming a sulky pout that he hoped to God she didn't think was attractive.

"Is that her new plan? To ingratiate herself with your mother?"

"No," Declan said, arching an eyebrow. "That's your strategy. Hers is simply being her. Interested in other people and their needs. Being *nice*. That's who Remi is."

"Please." Tara sneered. "It's an act. No one is that nice. Not without a motive."

"You don't say," he drawled.

Red stained her cheeks, and she huffed out a breath, her chin hiking up.

"That's not what I meant," she said through gritted teeth. "And you know it."

Declan sighed, pinching the bridge of his nose. Briefly closing his eyes, he dropped his arm and met Tara's dark brown eyes, glinting with tears.

"Don't." He didn't bother blunting the sharp edge of his tone.

Maybe if he suspected the tears were authentic, he would've. But he'd witnessed this ploy before; she'd tried to use it on him with no luck, and she regularly employed those tears with his mother with much more success.

"I'm going to say this once again. And this will be the last time, Tara. I've been patient and have tried not to hurt your feelings, but you don't seem to understand kindness. Or you see it as something to take advantage of. There. Is. No. Us. There never was. There never will be. Hear me. Accept it. Move on. And if you genuinely like my mother and enjoy spending time with her, then fine. But if you're doing it only to get to me, then leave her alone, too. I won't allow you to use her, and more importantly, I won't let you hurt her."

"Where was this concern for a woman's feelings when you led me on?" she scoffed. Tears no longer moistened her eyes, but anger glittered there, and it pulled her mouth taut, turning her beauty as sharp and hard as a diamond. "You shouldn't have slept with me if you *claim* we didn't have anything."

He nodded. "You're right. I shouldn't have allowed my dick to do my thinking. But I've never lied to you, Tara. I was always up-front that we wouldn't have a relationship—that I didn't want that with you. With anyone. I convinced myself that you accepted that, when obviously you had other intentions the entire time. That's on you, not me."

Tara shook her head. "That's not true," she said, quietly, sounding a little lost.

And for a moment, he softened. Thrusting his fingers through his hair, he said, "Tara, I didn't want to hurt you. It's the one thing I actively tried to avoid. And I'm sorry if I did."

"It's just..." Tara turned from him, tightening her arms around herself, her lips rolling in on each other, thinning. When she faced him again, her shoulders lifted, and she fluttered a hand between them. "I know there is affection between us."

"Tara."

"Y'know, whatever you're doing with Remi Donovan isn't fooling me or anyone in this town."

And that quickly, any sympathy for her evaporated. He stiffened, studying her, the frustration pinching her skin tight and adding a jerkiness to her usually fluid movements.

"I don't really give a damn what other people think, including you."

He ignored the voice that pointed out that he'd proposed the bargain with Remi in the first place because of Tara.

"Obviously. Because the thought of you wanting *her*, being with *her*, of all people, is laughable. She's boring, fa—"

"Shut the hell up," he growled. "Say one more word, Tara, and I'll forget that I was raised not to disrespect women."

"Excuse me."

Declan jerked his head up and to the side just as Tara whipped around.

Fuck.

Remi stood there, perfectly composed and calm. And if not for her eyes... His gut twisted, and he fisted his fingers, the blunt tips biting into his palms. The brown nearly swallowed the bright green and gold. If not for that darkness, he would assume she hadn't overheard Tara's ugly words.

Would assume those words hadn't landed direct, agonizing blows.

"Remi." He moved forward, Tara forgotten, his one goal to get to her. To somehow ease that hurt, make it disappear.

But she shifted backward. Away from him. And damn if a spike of pain didn't jab into his chest.

"We're about to give out the goody bags. When you're free, we could use your help passing them out." Dipping her chin, she pivoted and left, shoulders straight and without a glance back at them.

"Tara." His mother stepped forward, and for the first time, Declan noticed her. "I'm going to catch a ride home with a friend. I've known you for three years now, and you've never been anything but kind to me. But hearing you speak so horribly about someone a couple of minutes ago?" Janet shook her head. "It makes me wonder who you are when I'm not around. And if that is a person I want to know."

Janet reached for Declan, squeezed his hand and glanced in the direction Remi had disappeared.

"She's special, and you'd be a fool to let her get away." Brushing a kiss over his cheek, she left.

"She didn't mean..." Tara whispered, her voice catching.

Declan glanced over his shoulder at the other woman, spotting the moisture in her eyes, and for the first time, he believed her tears were real. But they failed to move him.

"She did. You just looked the consequences of your spite and pettiness in the face. I hope you remember them."

He walked away, leaving her alone. Like she deserved.

CHAPTER SIX

WHO KNEW A person could be completely numb inside and still smile, laugh and behave as if humiliation and pain hadn't pummeled her with meaty, bruising fists until she'd become a block of ice?

Seemed every day Remi discovered something new.

Returning to the Halloween event after overhearing Tara and Declan's conversation, then pretending nothing had occurred, had been one of the most difficult things she'd ever done. She'd been grateful for the coldness that had seeped into her veins, her chest.

But the library had emptied of parents, children, staff and volunteers forty-five minutes earlier, and now she sat in the passenger seat of Declan's car as he drove through the quiet streets. She couldn't escape the slow thawing around her heart. Couldn't escape her relentless thoughts. Couldn't escape *her*.

You wanting her, being with her, of all people, is laughable. She's boring, fa—

Remi squeezed her eyes shut, blocking out the scenery passing by her passenger window. Too bad she couldn't block out the memory of Tara's words. The other woman hadn't needed to finish the sentence for Remi to discern how it ended.

Fat.

Boring and fat.

Oh God how that hurt.

The mental door to that vault she tried so hard to keep shut creaked open and more memories crept out. Memories of her mother's and Patrick's voices.

A minute on the lips, a lifetime on the hips, Remi.

I just want you to be healthy, Remi.

Are you sure that choice of dress is wise? It's not very forgiving, is it?

The judgments, backhanded compliments and criticisms framed as concern poured into her mind. It'd taken Remi years, but she'd come to love and accept herself. But there were moments like tonight—like the other night with her mother in the café—when her hard-won confidence took enough of a hit that she wavered.

When she had to remind herself she wasn't lovable *despite* her weight or size.

She was lovable *because* of them.

Smothering a sigh, she silently urged the car to go faster. She longed to get home, drag on her favorite Wonder Woman pajamas, pop open a bottle of wine, put on *Pride and Prejudice*—the version with Keira Knightley and Matthew Macfadyen otherwise known as *the best version*—and lick her wounds.

Tomorrow. Tomorrow she would be okay, but God, she needed tonight.

"Remi, we need to talk about tonight."

The thaw inside her sped up, the red-tinged hurt throbbing. *Home. Just get me home.* It'd been years since she'd last cried in front of someone, and she didn't intend to break that record tonight. Not with him.

"I didn't get a chance to thank you for helping out with setting up and then stepping in when my volunteer didn't show. I really appreciate it. We all did," she said, switching the subject from what she suspected he really wanted to talk about.

"You're welcome. And the deflection isn't going to work," he murmured, voice gentle but firm. Too firm. "Since she would probably never apologize, I'm going to say 'I'm sorry' for Tara. What she sa—"

"Forget it. I have."

"Remi," he tried again.

"Let. It. Go."

Silence permeated the car, weighing down her shoulders, pressing on her chest. She desperately counted the minutes until she arrived home. Rose Bend wasn't that large a town, but right now it felt like the size of Boston.

Finally, he pulled up outside her house. Any other time, she would've taken a moment to admire the cute, quaint cottage that she'd saved for and bought on her own not far from the beautiful Kinsale Inn. But now, the sight of the yellow-and-white home only inspired relief. She reached for the door handle.

"Remi." Declan's hand clasped her wrist. "Wait."

She paused but didn't glance over her shoulder to look at him, instead perched on the passenger seat ready to flee.

"Please don't leave like this. Talk to me, sweetheart."

She trembled at the "sweetheart," her eyes briefly closing.

Whatever you're doing with Remi Donovan isn't fooling me or anyone in this town.

She wasn't his sweetheart, and everyone knew it. Hell, even her own mother found it hard to believe. Because a man like him couldn't desire, couldn't... *Love* a woman like her. A beautiful, charismatic, brilliant, sexy as hell man couldn't want a success-ful, independent, educated woman just because she happened to wear a size sixteen.

At least, that's what they believed.

Her? Well, before tonight, the last three weeks had offered her hope that Declan was attracted to her. Her mind had warned her that the heated glances, the fleeting caresses to her cheek, the holding of her hand, the jokes and laughter they shared, the phone calls and texts they exchanged—they were all part of the charade. But her heart failed to get the message. Her stupid heart took each gesture as proof that he felt *something* for her.

And she understood now why she grasped that hope so desperately.

Because in these three weeks, each caress, each glance, each compliment had worked toward transforming her long-time crush for him into love.

Yes, she so, so foolishly had fallen in love with Declan Howard.

Her head bowed, forehead pressing against the cold window.

She'd fallen for the most emotionally unavailable man in Rose Bend.

"Talk to you?" she said, leaning back in the seat and turning to him. "What is there to *talk* about? I told you I'm *fine*."

"Actually, you didn't. You just ordered me to let it go. But too many people in your life have done that, and I refuse to be another one who ignores your pain."

She stared at him, forcing her fingers to remain flat on her thighs and not to ball into fists. "Do you want me to admit that what Tara said hurt? Okay, yes. It hurt like hell. Do I want your apology on her behalf? No. I don't want it or need it. It's insulting to both of us. That should sum it up, right? Are we done here? Good."

"Hell no, we're not done. We're friends, dammit."

Oh God, didn't *that* just punch a hole in her chest?

"There. Satisfied? Now, good night."

She reached for the door handle again.

"If you get out of this car, I will follow you to that front door, Remi," he rumbled.

She threw her hands up in the air, loosing a harsh laugh that abraded her throat. "What more do you want from me? A pound of flesh? According to your ex-girlfriend, I can afford to sacrifice a few—"

His arm shot out, and his hand hooked behind her neck, hauling her forward. His mouth crushed down on hers, swallowing the words from her lips. Her moan surged up her throat, offering itself like a sacrifice to him. She was helpless at the erotic onslaught, opening herself wider and wider to this wild thing that masqueraded as a kiss. He took from her over and over, slanting his mouth, diving deep, sucking harder as if starved, as if desperate.

As if afraid she would disappear if he didn't gorge himself in this moment.

Or maybe she was projecting.

Declan lifted his other hand to her chin, swept his hand over the shallow cleft there. Once and twice. Such a simple, small caress, but it echoed in a soft flutter between her legs, and she clenched her thighs against the sweet, erotic sensation.

God, touch me there... Kiss me there.

The plea bounced inside her head, words she longed to utter aloud. She'd never believed that opportunity would be hers.

Did you want it to be?

The low, insidious whisper slid through her lust-hazed mind. And no matter how hard she pressed her lips to Declan's, how hard she thrust her tongue against his, she couldn't evict the question from her thoughts. Did she? If she took this step with him, there was no coming back. And for her, it wouldn't be just sex. Not with him. Her heart was already involved. Giving him her body, too, would cement an epic fall that would make Icarus's look like a mere stumble.

"Invite me inside."

Declan issued the hoarse plea-wrapped-in-a-demand, and it reverberated loudly in the confines of his car. She stared at him, emotionally on a precipice. One step off could mean joy for her... Or utter heartbreak.

Was she brave enough to find out which?

He brushed his thumb under the curve of her bottom lip, the

hand at her nape a gentle weight. But he waited, allowing her to make this decision, even though desire darkened his eyes to indigo and his mouth bore the damp, swollen mark of their raw kiss.

"Come inside."

Inside my house. Inside my body. My heart. My soul.

She issued the invitation, knowing he would only take her up on two of those. And even as he exited the car, rounded the hood and opened her door, she accepted it.

Moments later, she led him into her home, and as soon as they crossed the threshold, Declan closed the door behind them, twisting the lock. All without removing his hooded gaze from her.

Need dug its dark claws into her, and her thighs trembled with the force of it. How was it possible to *want* this much? To feel like if he didn't put his hands on her, his mouth on her, his cock *inside* her, she would crawl out of her skin? Lose her mind?

"Touch me."

Two words. They were all she could push past her constricted throat. They were all that were necessary.

He stalked forward, shrugging out of his coat, peeling his sweater and dark T-shirt over his head, dropping all the clothing to the floor. Her breath expelled from her lungs on a hard, long *whoosh*.

Jesus Christ.

Clothed, he was beautiful.

Bared, with golden skin stretched across taut, flexing muscle, he was magnificent.

She couldn't move, her gaze greedily bingeing on the wide breadth of his shoulders, the wall of his chest, the corded strength of his arms. That ridged ladder of abs with the dark silky line of hair that disappeared beneath the waistband of his pants.

A waistband his hands had dropped to.

"Wait." She popped her palms up in the universal sign of Stop.

"Let me," she whispered. "I want it." She clasped her hands together as if holding her passion for him between them. "I want you."

"I'm yours." He beckoned her closer, and as imperious as it seemed... Damn, it was hot, too. "Come get me."

Oh God, if only that were true, she mused, crossing the few steps toward him. If only he was really hers. To keep. She shook her head. No place for those thoughts here. Stay in the now.

"What're you telling yourself no about?" he murmured, tugging her closer, tunneling his fingers through her hair, his nails scraping over her scalp. Her lashes fluttered closed, and she turned into his big palm, sinking her teeth into the heel, giving him back a little of the pleasure/pain he'd doled out to her. A hiss escaped him, and when he fisted the strands of her hair, pulling, she nipped harder. "This is going to be over before it begins, sweetheart," he warned, dipping his head to take her mouth in a brief but thorough conquering. "Now what're you telling yourself no about?"

No way in hell could she answer that loaded question.

So she didn't.

Instead, she tackled his belt and the closure on his pants. Desperation climbed high inside her, neck and neck with lust. She wanted to drown herself in pleasure. In need. In him. Forget about what awaited her tomorrow. Forget the uncertainty.

For the first time, she was taking for herself and damn the consequences.

But he covered her hands with one of his, halting her frantic actions. The other cupped her cheek, tilting her head back.

"So many times I've wondered what goes on behind these lovely hazel eyes. What secrets you're keeping. And it's those moments, I consider switching careers and becoming an archeologist whose main job is unearthing those treasures." He danced his fingertips over her cheekbone, the arch of her nose, the top bow of her lip. "You wouldn't give up those secrets easily, but they would be worth the work. *You* are worth the work."

Her chest squeezed so tight, she locked her teeth around a cry. No one had ever spoken to her like that. She closed her eyes and bowed her head on the pretense of pressing a kiss to the base of his throat. Anything to avoid having him see the love she knew was in her gaze.

Declan gripped the sides of her shirt, balling it in his fists until it untucked from her jeans and bared her stomach. She lifted her arms, stamping down the nerves in her stomach. That dark hot need in his eyes couldn't be faked. He wanted her; he liked her body just as she did. Still... When the top cleared her head and the heat in that indigo gaze flared, the lingering remnants of doubt dissolved like mist.

"Fuck, sweetheart." Lust stamped his features, pulling his skin taut over his cheekbones, his lips appearing fuller, more carnal. "Let me..."

"Please," she damn near whined.

He lifted his hands toward her, but at the last minute, lowered his arms.

"Bedroom," he ground out.

Wordlessly, she turned and led him down the hall and into her shadowed bedroom. Moonlight streamed through the large windows, providing more than enough illumination. But Declan must not have thought so because he crossed to the lamp on her bedside table and switched it on, bathing the room in a warm, golden glow. Then he crossed back to her in that sensual, almost-feline glide of his, and lust wrenched low in her belly, high in her sex. She couldn't contain her whimper. Didn't even try.

When he reached her, Declan slowly lowered to his knees, his pose worshipful, reverent. As were the hands that removed her boots and jeans. As were the lips that pressed a kiss to her hip just above the line of her black panties.

As were the words that ordered her back on the bed, heels to the edge of the mattress.

She shuddered, excitement and vulnerability dueling inside her as she lay exposed to him, evidence of her overwhelming desire for him evident in her soaked flesh, in the damp panel of her underwear.

Teeth nipped at her sensitive inner thigh, and she jerked at the sensation and the taut anticipation of his mouth giving her what she so desperately hungered for.

"Shh," he soothed, brushing a caress over the tender area. "Tell me I can have you, Remi." He grazed his fingertips over her folds, and she gasped at the featherlight touch, arching into it. Her hands fisted the covers at her hips, needing something to anchor her.

"Have me, Declan." She bit her lip, trapping anything else that would've spilled forth without her permission. "Please have me."

Without further prodding, he stripped her panties off and dived into her.

He tongued a path up her folds, swirling and licking. Sucking. No part of her remained a mystery to him. She dived her hands into his hair, clutching the strands and holding on as he lapped at her, his ravenous growl vibrating over her flesh and through her sex.

Two thick fingers pressed against her entrance then inside her, stretching her, filling her. She cried out, grinding against his hand, his mouth. Pleasure struck her, bolt after bolt streaking through her. And as his lips latched on to her clit, and his tongue flicked and circled the pulsing nub, she curled into him, breathless, *aching*.

Declan rubbed a place high inside her, and she exploded, came so hard black crept into the edges of her vision. She tumbled back to the bed, her breath a harsh rasp in her lungs, her bones liquefied. Dimly, she was aware of Declan standing at the foot of the bed and the whisper of clothes sliding over skin.

The mattress dipped, and she focused on the gorgeous sexual beast crouched above her. While she silently watched, he tore open a silver packet, removed a condom and sheathed himself. And *oh God...*

Renewed lust fluttered, then flowed inside her in a molten rush. A cock shouldn't be lovely, but then again, this was Declan. It didn't seem possible that anything about him could be less than perfect. Including his dick. And long, thick, with a flared, plum-shaped head, he was indeed *perfect*. And mouth-watering. Before her mind could send the message to her body, she was reaching for him...

"No, sweetheart." He caught her wrist, bending down to crush an openmouthed kiss to the palm. "I want to make it inside you. Sit up."

He didn't wait for her to comply but tugged on the hand he held. Quickly, he divested her of her bra and dipped his head, sucking a beaded nipple into his mouth. Cradling her, he lifted her breasts, his thumbs circling the tip he hadn't treated himself to yet. Yet.

She clawed at his shoulders, tipping her head back, those pulls of his mouth echoing in her sex. Where she needed him. Now.

"Declan," she whispered. Pleaded.

"Take me in, Remi." He took her hand, wrapped it around him. "You take me."

She did.

Raising her hips, she guided him to her, notched him at her entrance. And cupping his firm ass, welcomed him inside her.

Their twin groans saturated the air.

She'd thought his fingers had filled her. No, they'd just prepared her for this... Possession. This branding.

Never had she felt so *whole*.

Slipping his arms under her shoulders, he gathered her close, and she did the same to him. Clinging to him. He held himself still, allowing her to become accustomed to the size and width of him. And yes, she needed those few moments. But as a fine shiver rippled through his body, she nuzzled the strong line of his jaw, nipping it.

"Move," she urged, flexing her hips against him. "Your turn to take me."

Tangling his fingers in her hair, he tilted her head back and claimed her mouth just as he claimed her body.

Over and over, he tunneled deep, burying his cock inside her, marking her as his. She undulated and arched beneath him, giving even as she accepted. The slap of skin on skin, the musk of sex, the damp release of sex greeting sex punctuated the room, creating music for their bodies' erotic dance. Each thrust, each grind, each growled word of praise shoved her closer to the edge, and she flitted close, then scampered back, not wanting this to end. Needing to be in this moment, in this space with him forever, but the pleasure—the mind-bending, body-aching pleasure—wouldn't permit that.

He reached between them, rubbed a thumb over the rigid bundle of nerves cresting the top of her sex. The scream building inside her was more than a voice; it was physical. And when he pistoned into her once, twice, three times, her body gave it sound.

She flew apart.

Her body. Her mind. Her soul.

Pieces of her scattered, and she doubted she could possibly be whole again.

As he stiffened above her, his hoarse growl of pleasure rumbling against her chest and in her ear, she gave in to the darkness closing in on her.

I love you. I love you.

And as she let go, she whispered the words in her head that she could never permit herself to say aloud.

I love you.

Remi's whisper echoed in Declan's mind, crashing against his skull like waves against the shore.

I love you.

She probably hadn't meant to let the admission slip out; she'd been halfway asleep as she uttered those three words that carved fear into his chest.

Maybe she didn't mean them. People said things like that in the heat of passion all the time, and they regretted it later. Let sex—especially such cataclysmic, hot as hell sex—get mixed up and muddled with emotion, and they were temporarily confused. Yes, that was it. Remi didn't—

That wasn't Remi. She might not have meant to say she loved him—might not have intended to let him know—but she'd meant it.

Or else Remi believed she did.

He propped his elbows on his thighs and dropped his head into his hands.

I love you.

A howl churned in his gut, surging up his throat, but at the last second, he trapped it behind clenched teeth. Pain, fear and anger—yes, anger—eddied inside him in a grimy cesspool. He wanted to lash out. To yell that he didn't ask for her love. That love wasn't part of their deal.

He wanted to curl his body behind hers and beg her to take it back, to please take it back. Before *love* crushed them both and he lost the woman he'd come to depend on, to admire, to desire, to need... God, he'd come to need her. Her texts, her calls, her smiles, her...

Everything.

Love would ruin who they were to each other.

Just as it'd diminished his mother, so she'd had to rediscover who she was as a person.

Just as it'd morphed into something ugly and destroyed his marriage.

People used that particular affection as a reason to hurt and damage one another every day, and he wanted no part of it.

Not even from Remi. Especially not from Remi. Because to witness how it would extinguish the light from those beautiful hazel eyes... How it would steal the radiance that shone from her like a beacon piercing darkness...

"I'm surprised you're still here."

Declan slowly straightened, glancing over his shoulder. Remi, with the cover tucked under her arms, sat up, her expression shuttered. Grief careened through him. It'd been weeks since he'd seen that look on her face. Since she'd closed him out.

"Remi..." he murmured, turning to her.

She shook her head. "At first, I thought it was a bad dream, but when I woke up and saw you fully dressed and sitting on the side of the bed as if you couldn't wait to bolt out of here, I knew it wasn't a dream. More of a nightmare."

"Remi, I don't want to hurt you."

She huffed out a low, dry chuckle. "This isn't about hurting me, but just the opposite—you're the one who doesn't want to be hurt."

He couldn't deny that. Hell, if he were brutally honest, he'd been running scared since he'd signed his divorce papers. But he'd been doing it so long, he didn't know how to stop. Didn't know if he had the courage to stop.

Even for her. And if anyone deserved someone to be brave on her behalf, it was Remi.

"You don't want to take the risk of falling in love and being hurt again, of being betrayed. And your greatest fear, Declan? You're afraid of loving someone so much, so deeply, that you lose yourself. That you become your mother. And there's nothing I could say... Not that I would never betray you, never do anything that would demean you rather than support you. Not that I might very well hurt you, but I would hope my love would pave the way for forgiveness, that you would see it wouldn't be intentional. True love only makes you stronger, better. You could never lose yourself in it. Because it would never allow you to become lost."

She spread her hands wide on her crossed legs, staring down at them before lifting her gaze to him. Tears didn't glisten in her eyes, but he almost wished they did. He'd rather have the tears than the bottomless, hard resolve he saw.

"But there wouldn't be any point in trying to make you believe that, because your heart is closed by fear. I'm scared, too, Declan. Scared to trust, to take a leap of faith on love when it's only disappointed me in the past. But I'm willing to take a risk on you. On us." She shook her head. "What I'm not willing to do is fake it any longer or settle."

Her shoulders straightened, and the deep breath she drew in resounded in the room. That, too, held the ring of finality.

"I love you, Declan. And you need to leave."

"Remi, I'm sorry."

"I know you are. And that makes you refusing to fight for yourself, for who we could be, sadder. Now, if you have any feelings for me, any respect at all, please go."

Stay, dammit. Don't you fucking go.

But he stood, exited the bedroom and her house as she requested.

Like the coward he was.

He drove through the dark quiet streets of Rose Bend, images of the evening bombarding him. Of them laughing and working together at the library. Of their kiss in the car. Making love in her bedroom. Of her eyes, dark with pain and pride, ordering him out.

A while later, he pulled his car to a stop and switched it off. But he didn't sit, parked outside his home.

Opening his car door, he numbly climbed out, rounded the

vehicle and climbed the steps to the blue-and-white Victorian with the dark blue shutters. Even before he knocked, the front door swung open and his mother stood in the doorway.

"Declan? What on earth? What's wrong?" she asked, tying her robe belt.

"Mom," he rasped. "I messed up."

CHAPTER SEVEN

"I LOVE YOUR MOTHER," Briana growled, sailing up to Remi with a smile that appeared more like a feral baring of teeth, "but she is seriously working my last living nerve."

Remi hid her grin behind her glass of wine, sending up a prayer, not for the first time, that she'd found a safe corner out of the path of Hurricane Rochelle. The whole week before the engagement party, their mother had been driving all of them nuts with the preparations. And today, with guests crowded into their home, enjoying the hors d'oeuvres and sipping a variety of beverages and celebrating the happy couple, Rochelle hadn't calmed down yet. After being ordered twice to circle the room with the appetizers, then told she wasn't doing it right, then being barred from the kitchen, Remi had been trying to fly under the radar.

"You know she's in her element. Even if she's acting a little batty. She just wants everything to be perfect for you." Remi slipped an arm around Briana's shoulders, hugging her close. "Besides, you have to give it to her. The place looks ah-mazing. The food is great. The guests are enjoying themselves. And you're engaged to a truly great guy."

"Yeah, you're right," Briana grumbled, then chuckled. As if

she couldn't help herself, her sister sought out her fiancé, locating him next to the living room fireplace, surrounded by several of his friends. "He's wonderful. And I can't wait to marry him."

"There you go. Just keep that in mind. And avoid Mom, like I'm doing."

Briana laughed, wrapping an arm around Remi's waist and squeezing. But then she sobered, wincing. "God, Remi, I'm so sorry. I wasn't thinking. Are you okay being here with all—" she twirled her hand in the direction of the party "—this? You know I wouldn't have minded if you begged off. I would've understood."

"*I* would've minded, though. And I'm fine. No way I would've missed my sister's engagement party. But thank you."

God, she loved her sister. Both of them. After Declan left her house a week ago, she'd called her sisters. Sherri and Briana had come right over and stayed with her for most of the weekend, holding her while she cried, bingeing Netflix and snacks with her when she didn't. And they'd been running interference with their mother, whose disappointment at her and Declan breaking up had seared her.

But it didn't make her change her mind or call him. She'd made the right decision for herself.

"What are we doing over here in the corner?" Sherri shoved a sun-dried tomato and basil roll-up in her mouth, following it with a healthy sip of champagne. Her older sister, barely five feet and willow thin, could eat her weight in hors d'oeuvres, run roughshod over her adorable three-year-old twins and rule her husband, who worshipped the ground she walked on. "Talking about people? Ditching Doug so he can't leave me with the kids? Avoiding Mom?"

"C," Remi said, taking her sister's glass and sipping.

"Oh, me, too." Sherri scrunched her nose. "And you know I was just kidding about the kids, right?" When Remi and Briana gave her the blandest of bland looks, she sighed. *"Fine.* Sue me. Doug so owes me for…for sticking his penis in me."

"Wow." Briana slipped the champagne away from their sister with a snicker. "We're going to lay off these until the toast, 'kay?"

"What? No, I—" The doorbell rang, and she clapped her hands, nearly bouncing on the balls of her feet. "That should be the babysitter. She was running late so she offered to pick the twins up from here. Sooo…" She snatched her glass back and took a healthy sip.

"You'd think she didn't get out much," Remi drawled, laughing, but as her mother led the newest guest into the living room, the humor died on her lips. *"Oh God."*

Declan.

Her breath stalled in her lungs, increasing the deafening thud of her heart in her ears, her head. Adrenaline rushed through her, temporarily making her dizzy, and she pressed her palm against the wall, steadying herself.

What was he doing here?

"What is he doing here?" Sherri whispered, echoing the question in Remi's head. "I thought you said he wasn't coming."

Remi had confessed everything to her sisters—the true reason behind The Kiss, the fake relationship, Declan's agreement to be her beard at the engagement party.

"I didn't think he was, either." She couldn't remove her eyes from him. No matter how much her pride begged her to stop making a fool of herself in front of all these people.

She'd been here before, except this scene had taken place in a diner, not at an engagement party. But her romance woes being center stage for the townspeople of Rose Bend again? No. Thank. You.

She straightened, pushing off the wall, and maybe he sensed her movement, because his gaze scanned the room before unerringly landing on her. It was like crashing into a star—hot, consuming and so close to flaming out.

She froze.

Inside, she longed to flee. Away.

Or straight to him.

"Sweet baby Jesus, Remi, that man is in love with you," Briana breathed.

Remi tore her gaze from Declan and frowned at her younger sister.

"What? What're you talking about, Bri?"

"C'mon, Remi—the man showed up at an engagement party. No man shows up at an engagement party all alone, voluntarily, unless, A, he's the groom or one of the parties involved is family, B, he's being blackmailed, or C, he has an agenda. You, big sis, are his agenda. That man is so in love with you." She leaned forward, jabbing a fingertip in her arm. "But I swear to God, if he proposes to you at my engagement party, I'm tackling him to the ground like J. J. Watt. And then I'll show up at your wedding and announce I'm pregnant. And expecting quadruplets."

Remi stared at her sister, caught between laughing hysterically and being horrified. Because she suspected Briana meant it.

"Remi, can you help me in the kitchen for a moment?" Their mother appeared in front of their trio, smiling brightly, but Remi spied the taut edges.

"Sure."

She followed her mom, pausing to smile at a few guests, putting on a good front, but her belly twisted into knots. Strain rode her shoulders, so by the time they entered the spotless kitchen, where more food platters covered the butcher-block island, her body was rigid with the strain.

"Declan showing up is certainly a surprise," her mother said, leaning back against the edge of the island.

Jumping right into it, are we?

Remi smothered a sigh, wishing she'd stolen Sherri's champagne.

"It is."

Rochelle threw her hands up, huffing out a breath. "Remi, he's here. That means something."

"It could mean a lot of things. The main thing being not wanting to be rude by not showing up." Although, she wondered, too. As of the night she'd kicked him out of her bed, her house, he didn't have an obligation to her anymore. "Mom, don't get your hopes up." She was preaching to the choir. "He's a nice guy, and that's all there is to it. We're done."

"Honey." She shook her head. "Why can't you just put in a little effort? You had a man who actually took an interest in you, and what happened? What did you do?"

Hurt slapped at her, and her head jerked back. "What did *I* do?" she whispered. "Why do you assume it's my fault?"

"Oh stop," Rochelle snapped, slicing a hand through the air. "I'm not assigning blame. I'm just saying I wish you would try harder—"

"And do what?" A calm settled over her. Almost as if she stepped out of her body and gave herself permission to speak, to no longer hold back on every hurt, every wound that she'd paved over with excuses, disregard or laughter. "Talk less, laugh softer. Wear baggier clothes. Lose fifteen pounds. Try harder for Declan or any other man? Or try harder for you, Mom?"

"Remi?" She frowned. "Whatever are you talking about?"

"Maybe at this point you've become so used to criticizing me that you don't notice. And I don't know which is worse—doing it on purpose or being so accustomed to taking my inventory that it has become habit. The problem is, with you, I always come up short. I've never been enough."

"Remi, honey," she whispered, tears glistening in her eyes. "That's not true."

"It is. I don't doubt you love me, Mom. But you have a lousy way of showing it. And if you don't change it, I won't be coming around as much. I can't accept that toxicity in my life anymore. I won't."

She crossed the space separating them, cupped her mother's arms and kissed her cheek.

"I love you, and I love myself. I need you to accept that."

Tears pricked her own eyes and her pulse pounded like a snare drum. She turned and exited the kitchen, moisture blinding her.

"Hey, I got you."

She didn't hesitate. Didn't question. She wrapped her arms around Declan, burying her face against his hard, welcoming chest. And when his arms closed around her, she sighed, relaxed into him. Feeling home.

"Come on, sweetheart," he murmured.

She didn't really pay attention to where he led her, but then the cold air brushed over her face. The backyard. Inhaling a deep breath, she pulled her hand free of his and paced several feet away. His earthy cloves-and-cinnamon scent clung to her nose, and she longed to roll in it, bathe in it. She had to move away, because yes, in a moment of weakness, she'd leaned on him, but she couldn't depend on that. Couldn't depend on him.

"What are you doing here, Declan?"

He studied her for several long moments, his lilac gaze piercing. "You did good, Remi. And I'm damn humbled by you."

She blinked. And blinked again. Stupid tears. Not now. Not in front of him.

"What?"

"I overheard what you said to your mom. That was incredibly brave, and I want to live up to you. Be worthy of that courage." He paused. "I should've never left your house last week. I should've told you no, I wasn't leaving, that I would fight for me, for you. For us."

If she could move, she would've stumbled backward.

Or run to him.

But fear, doubt—hope—kept her frozen.

"You called me out, and I was afraid. *Was*, Remi. I knew as soon as I drove away that I made the hugest mistake of my life. Over the last month you have become my friend, my confidante, my lover, my delight, my…freedom. You've helped me free myself from my past simply by being you. By showing me bravery, hope and faith. I want to take that leap with you, Remi. And I'm sorry that I hurt you, that I might've been one more person to make you doubt how beautiful, special and precious you are. If you can trust me with your heart again, I promise never to break it."

He reached into the inside pocket of his suit jacket and withdrew a folded sheet of paper and extended it to her.

As if her arm moved through water, she reached for that paper, accepted it. Her breath whistled in and out of her parted lips, and she tried to tamp down the hope that seemed determined to rise within her, but it welled too big, too huge.

She unfolded the sheet and scanned it. Once. Twice. After the third time she lifted her gaze to him. That hope she'd tried to stifle soared, and she didn't try to control it. Not when love surged with it.

"You're moving here full-time?" she rasped, the paper trembling in her hand.

"Yes." He moved closer to her, paused, but then eliminated the space between them. His hand rose, hovering next to her cheek, but he didn't touch her. "I'm leasing the building next to Cole Dennison's law firm. Of course, I'll still need to go back to Boston for some meetings, but I can run my business from anywhere. And I choose for it to be here. With you. Because I love you."

She cupped her hand over his, turned her face into it and pressed a kiss to the palm. Then rose on her toes and pressed another to his lips. On a groan, he took her mouth like a man deprived of water, of breath. And she was his oxygen.

God, she knew the feeling.

"Does this mean you're giving me your love again?" he asked, resting his forehead against hers.

She cradled his face between her palms, brushing her thumbs over his cheekbones. Smiling, she brushed a soft kiss to his mouth.

"You never lost it."

* * * * *

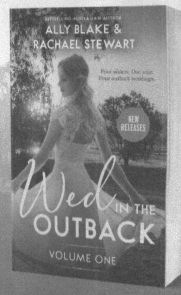
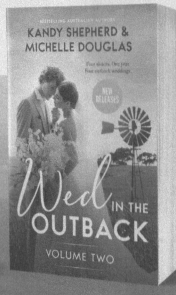